The Light Barrier

FROM THE SAME AUTHOR

The Green Gods (translated by C.J. Cherryh & Damon Knight)
The Birth of the Gods + *The Astronauts' Song* (translated by William Oarlock)

The Light Barrier
Bellatrix Gamma

by
Nathalie Charles Henneberg

Translated from the French by
William Oarlock

A Black Coat Press Book

ISBN 978-1-64932-438-2. First Printing. December 2025. Published by Black Coat Press, an imprint of Hollywood Comics.com, LLC, 18321 Ventura Blvd., Suite 915, Tarzana, CA 91356, USA: All rights reserved. Except for review purposes, no part of this book may be reproduced or transmitted in any form or by any means, electronic or mechanical, including photocopying, recording, or by any information storage and retrieval system, without permission in writing from the publisher. The stories and characters depicted in this novel are entirely fictional. Printed in the United States of America.

TABLE OF CONTENTS

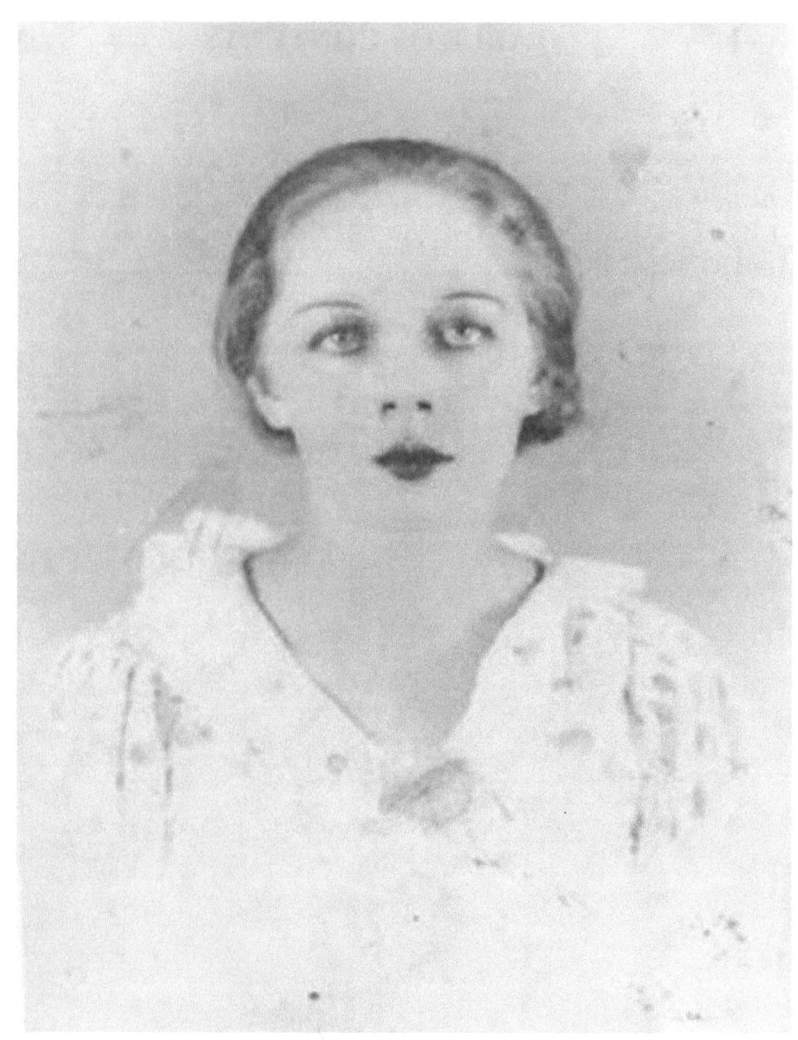

Nathalie Henneberg

Introduction

This is the third volume of a multi-volume collection of the works of Nathalie Charles Henneberg. The contents of these volumes are:

Volume 1: *The Green Gods* (*Les Dieux Verts*) (1961), translated by C. J. Cherryh, first published under the name of "Charles Henneberg". This volume also includes four short stories translated by Damon Knight.

Volume 2: *The Birth of the Gods* (*La Naissance des Dieux*) (1954), Henneberg's award-winning debut novel in the SF genre, and *The Astronauts' Song* (*Le Chant des Astronautes*) (1958), both also published under the name of "Charles Henneberg" and both translated by William Oarlock.

This volume, Volume 3: *The Light Barrier*, includes the novel *An Premier, Ère Spatiale* (*Year One of the Space Age*), the story of the first faster-than-light starship, originally serialized under that title in 1959 in the magazine *Fiction* (the French edition of *F&SF*) Nos. 71-73 under the name of "Charles Henneberg," but revised in 1972 and published under the title *Le Mur de la lumière* (*The Light Barrier*) and the name "Nathalie Henneberg" as No. 2 of the "Science-Fiction" imprint of publisher Albin Michel. It is this version that we have translated here.

This volume also includes *Bellatrix Gamma* (*La Rosée de Soleil*, lit. *The Sundew*), a tale of castaways on an alien world becoming entangled in the power struggle of its elemental inhabitants, also published in 1959 under the name of "Charles Henneberg" as No. 65 of Hachette's "*Rayon Fantastique*" science fiction imprint. Both novels are translated by William Oarlock.

Volume 4, *Starblood*, will include *Le Sang des Astres* (1963) and *The Lost Fortress* (*La Forteresse Perdue*) (1962) while Volumes 5 and 6 will be comprised of Henneberg's magnum opus, *The Plague* (*La Plaie*), first published in 1964, and its sequel, *The Fallen God* (*Le Dieu Foudroyé*), published a year before Henneberg's death in 1976. Finally, one or two more volumes—to be determined—will collect further genre short stories by Henneberg.

Our first volume includes a long introduction about Henneberg's life and works by French scholar Charles Moreau, which there is no need to repeat here. However, for those readers who may not have purchased any of our previous volumes, the basic facts are these:

Natalia Novokovski was born in Batum, Georgia, on October 23. 1910. Her family fled the Russian Civil War in 1920, taking refuge in Turkey, Syria and then Lebanon. There, she met and married Charles Henneberg zu Irmelshausen Wasungen (1899-1959), an adjutant in the French Foreign Legion, in 1937. They later settled in Paris in 1946. In 1952, Nathalie, using the gender-neutral nom-de-plume of "Dominique Hennemont", sold her first two novels, accounts of the French Foreign Legion, Then, after discovering science fiction, she submitted *The Birth of the Gods*, this time under the nom-de-plume of her husband. The novel was quickly accepted and won the prestigious Rosny Award in 1954. Astonishingly, none of her editors realized that Nathalie, not Charles, was the real author of these works. "Charles Henneberg" now being a household name, her career soon took off.

After Charles died of a heart attack on March 20, 1959, all the publishing agreements were signed by Nathalie, who, at first, claimed to be merely completing unfinished manuscripts left by her husband (hence the intermediate twin credits on the middle books in the series), until she finally claimed full credit for her work. Many critics continued to credit her earlier works to her husband, until much later when incontrovertible evidence was produced that definitively set the issue at rest: Nathalie Henneberg was always the sole author of all the works published under her late husband's name.

Nathalie Henneberg died in Paris June 24 1977.

She remains a unique voice in French imaginative literature. Combining classic French and Golden Age American SF with "Old World" literature, sagas and epics, her writing precedes the "New Wave" of the 1960s and later mythopoetic space operas of Ursula K. LeGuin, Roger Zelazny, C.J. Cherryh, Philip Jose Farmer and Joan D. Vinge.

William Oarlock

THE LIGHT BARRIER
(Year One of the Space Age)

*"There'd be monsters by the billions to plant on those other planets.
And these monsters would be human..."*

Clifford D. Simak, *Shadow World*

CHAPTER I
Destination Andromeda

"Take off for Andromeda at 8.17 p.m. Specialists and volunteers are requested to join Pier 12."

Nan stopped, as if struck by a ball. The emitter's black mouth howled. Yes, she remembered: it must have started like this, in the terrestrial twilight – crimson and flame.

In front of the central star station, an excited crowd stomped, drunk with events – the crowd of the year 2500, or, as it was commonly called, of Year One of the Space Age. The artificial suns of the Megalopolis bathed upturned, pale faces in gold; the snow was melting on the roses – all the greenhouses had been plundered. People kissed, swore with joy, mothers held out their young towards a new dawn and, as in a dark lake, the three-dimensional screens reflected in the air the same delirium, the same triumph. Millions of voices, so many loudspeakers, carried a single name to the clouds, like a single wave: a man had conquered hyperspace! A man had given Earth the entire Cosmos!

To celebrate this unknown that the continuum was giving back to her, thought Nan, the old planet had cooled off like a courtesan! There was enough to satisfy a fearful pride! The Metropolis was nothing but an ocean of neon lights, processions chanted the Name in the avenues, mind-blown children stared at a now accessible black sky.

Even the first navigator who, in his wretched twentieth-century rocket, had reached the Moon, even the one who, before dying, had bogged down in the Mare Chronium on Mars, gaspingly broadcasting his victory bulletin, had not been deified thus. It wasn't just a battle won. Humanity secretly understood that, having taken this step, there remained no obstacle before human genius. Earth now had the universe, the galaxies and their billions of quivering stars, within reach!

"They went there!" shouted someone in the crowd (the phrase conveyed the general emotion). "They've come back! Hyperspace is ours!"

A shrill voice corrected:

"You mean *he* comes back. He, the Hero. Arno Heller..."

And the thunder burst – the Name rolled, carried, cradled, caressed by the waves: "Arno Heller... ARNO HELLER! LONG LIVE ARNO HELLER!"

Nan covered her ears and began to run.

On the landing platforms, the crowd was a little less dense; she was finally able to stop, breathe, and suddenly felt very cold. You mustn't listen, she told herself, yes, you mustn't hear... Around her, the usual life of the great spaceport continued; every ten minutes, a vibration shook the cosmodrome; rockets and saucers took off and the night stirred up its flood of travelers in spacesuits.

The crews were bustling about, under their space helmets; a few travelers passed carrying their portable oxygen tanks. A sentence stood out. The first of this evening pronounced on a normal timber – without pathos and without shouting:

"That Heller! They only talk about him. And they forget the preface to his adventure: the Andromeda Disaster and all those unfortunate people who perished – orbital shocks or whatever!"

"After all, it was only an artificial satellite," protested a woman's voice, indifferent. "We have seen so much! They always end up disintegrating, I believe."

"Yes. But this was an outpost of the solar system."

"Interplanetary defenses held!"

"The Space Distortion Committee is still watching..."

The travelers moved away. Nan heard again:

"It doesn't matter. That rocket at Pier 12 shouldn't take off. I was told – I forget by whom – that there was nothing left of Andromeda..."

Nothing left.

But, opposite Nan, an advertising window irradiated its neon light, a golden planet blazed at the limit of the Milky Way, Earth was emerald and Mars, the color of ruby. A silver and rose-colored rocket soared towards the satellite. A tourist slogan lit up, saying:

VISIT ANDROMEDA – THE SPACE PARADISE – The world that defies the laws of gravity – where stars shine at noon – where stellar roses bloom! VISIT THE FUTURE!

"Why not?" thought Nan. "After all, it's true." It was a slogan from before the disaster, of course...

She was shivering a little. But yes, she was being stupid. She had to flee. This Earth, with its stories of weight, borders and segregations, was only a point in space: her own homeland was the universe...

To run away.

The plexiglass window gave her the image of a slender young girl – gylon coat and Florentine beret on ashen hair. Nineteen, maybe. She judged without indulgence the oval of her pale face, sensitive mouth, the "incredible" eyelashes, the perfect legs. I could have chosen better, she scolded herself. What idea do you have of loving these Primitives so much! This Bernardino, this Filippo Lippi! All in all, here's a girl any earthling boy could sleep with. But not if he sees my eyes...

She smiled at them – with only her lips. They were fearsome indeed. Huge and changing, in a teenage face, they were millions of years-old. They had plunged into immemorial abysses, peered into things horrible or beautiful – and the clearest thing was that they were in the way looked like a normal Earthwoman's eyes.

The crowd flowed around her, with indifference. People were going home, to an atmosphere saturated with ozone, sterilized, pink with neon suns; they were going to relive the prodigious day and the big city offered them the prestige of its stereos, its sensory parks and its parascopic phantasmagoria. They felt at home: masters of the solar system and soon of the cosmos! A crowd, all in all, much less human than Nan and stuffed full of fungoid Plutonians and blue Neptunians. Some Earthlings still wore their interplanetary body armor and moved uncomfortably. The locker rooms and testing rooms were always full: after three months of "external stay", rehabilitation was slow and painful. Yes: they called it rehabilitation! Nan laughed bitterly: not one of those defiant travelers had gone as far in space as she!

Shut up! she said to herself (her voice struck her as shrill). Maybe there are telepaths there...

Her fingernails dug into her smooth palms. A drop of blood beaded. Green blood.

At the same moment, a moderate voice uttered behind her:

"May I help you, free citizen?"

Nan turned quickly. A tall boy in an astronaut suit, dressed in turquoise plastic, looked at her with his head thrown back, like a pilot blinking before infinity. The sentence was banal, and he was certainly not the first walker to accost her, so she took pleasure in playing with the power of her eyes: she slowly raised the mesh of her eyelashes and darted her abyssal gaze in the face of the stranger.

Contrary to her expectation, the man didn't back down; he didn't even turn pale and only passed a beautiful uncertain hand over his eyelids, before apologizing:

"Sorry. I thought you were a stranger to the Metropolis."

He was going to walk away. But already, Nan's invisible, supra-sensitive antennae, which made her organism a formidable machine of perception, had already grasped her chance. She recognized, with a little throbbing pain, what time or death had not been able to erase from her brain cells: the sharp, golden face, a rust-colored curl and that seafaring gaze...

It's him. I can't be wrong. But what is he now? An engineer, perhaps, a cybernetician – not a pilot. Too sensitive, too refined, not audacious enough. But no (She ducked under the smooth forehead, collided with the mental defenses and smiled.) *It's all just a camouflage, a mask. Audacious, he is, even recklessly – but cold. A vision in diagrams: meticulous and rigid. A specialist in microbes or filtering viruses...? Worse than that...? Too bad!*

"Too bad," echoed the voice that had just the right rhythm, "that life is made up of arrivals and departures..."

Nan tried to laugh, obligingly:

"Are you saying that to me?"

"For both of us. It's rare, in this crowd, to meet a real human face. But, what about if we went in one of these hospitable dens where terrestrials distort their metabolism with the help of ethyl alcohol?"

She just took just enough moral time for reflection before answering:

"Don't believe that your personal charm..."

"Is it ever useful for something? No. I never overestimate my charm. You see, on the space docks, I'm a little alone..."

They found themselves a moment later (and Nan knew it was a necessary interlude) on the selenium stools of the first "den" they came across, converted into a rocket bar. There were upbeat stereos and Venusian cocktails. An elderly woman wearing make-up was consoling a very young Martian at a table.

Nan had slipped her fur coat off her shoulders and her legs shimmered under the neon lights. What should I tell him now? she wondered, having no experience of such encounters. She read her companion's superficial thought – he liked her very much, but he hesitated: Am I mistaken? Would she just...? Here a shameful and complicated notion, specific to Earthlings, which she managed to translate: around spaceports and in public places like these, there were girls who were selling – like meat on the butcher's stall. (Viola also had these ideas). Nan breathed with relief: if that was all that worried her! Seizing the last terms employed by her thought, she said:

"I'm not used to astronauts. To accept your invitation, I had two compelling reasons. You see, I'm a reporter... and, with the arrival of the Hyperspace Heroes, I haven't had time for dinner yet!"

"Oh!" he said. And triggering an automatic bartender, he ordered everything pell-mell: sausages, scrambled eggs, fruit from the canals of Mars.

Nan laughed:

"Don't do that," she protested. "Please, I have a capricious appetite. Here, I'll take this pretzel, with lots of salt..." (She had chosen the most harmless food, the closest to her ordinary diet, and thought, with boredom, that she would then have to go out to spit it all out. That would waste precious time.) "My other reason," she continued, "is more important. You're part of the crew taking off for Andromeda, aren't you?"

He looked at her and replied:

"How do you know?"

"You came from platform 12 and you were talking about arrivals and departures."

He laughed with good grace:

"What a gift of observation! Yes and no. I'm not part of the ordinary K-2 crew, I'm assigned there as an observer. We kind of do the same job, I think."

"Listen," Nan whispered, putting an insinuating wave of sweet music into her voice. (*Warning: the siren song is what I imitate the worst.*) "I too would like to leave... Oh! It's not a question of writing a sensational paper about the stars! Going anywhere, anyhow. Leaving Earth, its prejudices, its complications, its old family feuds – all this narrow horizon..."

"It's easy," he said. "You take a lunar freighter..."

Lord, he was hesitating! Of two precious hours, they had eighty minutes left. Nan did a little work under her domed, stubborn forehead, copied from a Pre-Raphaelite Virgin, then, straightening her white neck, she exhibited a row of purplish marks.

"I don't have enough money to buy a ticket," she explained. "The woman who does this to herself. It's a drug. I am starting to be afraid."

"And your father?"

"He perished in a stellar shipwreck."

Now she was no longer advancing in the darkness, she knew what could touch this tall, taciturn boy, with his green, prying eyes. (*No hip effects, my girl. No ecstatic smiles. He demands sincerity, however silly, and a weakness that allows him to launch himself, to protect. There were once knights... and there are always such men. Or is it always the only one – and you come across this one?*)

However, he must not have thought too long: Nan isolated, among discordant waves of music that the stereos poured out, a pure note – the very image of Andromeda – speaking of starry darkness, gardens of roses and pandanus. And she caused, according to her most beautiful memories, an unreal city to emerge on this grid, made of atomic horns and insane greenhouses, on the edge of nothingness. A plexiglass globe incrusted itself on a black sky where the stars shone in the middle of noon. It was the last milestone of the terrestrial universe – beyond could be heard infinity, hypervortices and nebulae twisting their spirals...

"Come on," said the astronaut as if he was struggling against a force too great to resist, "you know Andromeda, I can feel it. But I... I don't even know who you are!"

She said in a clear voice:

"My name is Anne Nangis. They call me Nan,"

"The former governor of the Asteroid Belt was your father?"

"My ancestor. He was a pioneer. I think that without him, you wouldn't have Andromeda or the other space stations."

"I think so too." He looked at her for a long time: a green light trickled under those eyelashes. "Admit all the same," he continued, "that the situation is strange. My name is Earl Stanley. That means nothing to you, no doubt; I occupy the position of an expert to the Andromeda mission. If, by any chance, you weren't what you say, you could be a Martian super-spy."

"I have no antennas!" Nan smiled awkwardly, and to cut short the explanations, she emptied the case containing her papers onto the bar. "Here's my journalist card," she said. "You can verify, it's a diseased duck that preaches bigotry and racial segregation, but it's the only one who agreed to hire a young colonial girl with no connections. Here's my identity card: I have stellar majority. My medical tests – three months ago, I was hoping to get a report to Neptune – my lungs are in good condition

14

and my skeleton is not lacking in calcium. I have my bachelor's and letters, mechanic and first-aid diplomas. Plus, I was born on Andromeda and my metabolism matches it, as you can see. I left the satellite when my grand-parents died, I didn't yet know that my father had just disappeared in a shipwreck off Venus. He was somewhat responsible for it, I'm afraid. Be-sides, I don't see why I'm making this confession to you!"

"So it's so essential for you," Earl Stanley asked slowly, "to leave Earth today?"

So essential, God! She united her forces in a beam, projected towards him the image of what she was fleeing: a cosmic terror, fabulous cata-clysms, a hell of fire and ice where one falls alive...

She didn't want to, but she couldn't go through that again!

She found only one word to answer:

"Essential...? Yes."

A silence followed. When he spoke, his face shone with an intolerable brilliance. Nan shivered: she had forgotten that he was so handsome!

"You know that an unnamed disaster has reached Andromeda. It may be that the asteroid has exploded, that it has a crumbled surface, that it is, finally, only a cluster of incandescent gases. We know nothing, I tell you. We're a commando of desperate people."

(She only thought: *I am too...*)

"We don't know how long we'll be in space. Also regulations allow only married couples."

"I know."

"Do you absolutely want to go there?"

"I have to go. Tonight."

"Something forces you to?"

"Yes. But don't think... This is not a criminal case."

"No. I do not think so. Did this happen today?"

"This evening."

Her hands were getting cold and she closed her eyes; she had to give imperative orders to her whole body, to her very viscera, to fulfil their functions.

However, she admitted to herself that the idea of flight had been rip-ening in her for many days. In fact, since that night at the editorial office...

She was on night shift at the *Little Solar Stereo*, a tabloid newspaper that occupied the smoky rooms of a residential building, among mirrors and dishonored mosaics. The switchboard, where she stayed more often than usual, was an important place, the low-level commercial box living mainly on blackmail. One of the editors who passed like shadows had made her understand that "a young colonial and a girl who didn't sleep around" could not hope for better treatment. Some evenings, Nan wondered what she was doing in this mess. (But on Earth a behavior was essential: caution. To blend in with the crowd. To be only an atom. Even when one had had enough. *Ad nauseam*.)

So she was operating the interplanetary videophone that night when a dreadful series of stereos announced the disaster. The Astral Belt, that defensive line that surrounded the solar system, was collapsing. The first news reported that orbital shocks had reached the main relays: the interplanetary defense was disorganized, it seemed that minor globes had disappeared. The thing seemed so unbelievable that Nan changed stations to verify. But the confirmations came from all points of the system, they crushed the Metropolis and, motionless, frozen in her cabin, the slender young girl understood...

Snippets of information sprang from the outskirts: it was said that on the first category (that is to say, inhabited) artificial satellites, the observatories, domes and launching pads had burst, that the linking installations no longer existed, that thousands of Earthlings had died horribly. The epicenter of the cataclysm was located on Andromeda, an essential relay. However, this tiny globe had struggled: a few S.O.S. signals came from the secondary domes which were collapsing – "were folding up like paper planes", a videogram had oddly noted. Clinging to her camera, Nan saw quite clearly this last operator, this last settler on a lost rock, a man clad in plastic and metal, lead shoes, who was trying desperately to reach beyond the abysses of darkness and light years away, an indifferent Earth to cry out to it: "We are dying!"

These people were not expecting any help...

Afterwards, all was silence.

Nan saw the plexiglobe, split. A world dying in flames – her homeland. All that remained of her childhood... Losing her trainee reserve, she rang, called, ended up reaching a vague editor who rebuffed her severely:

"Talk to whom? But you're mad, Nangis! What do you want us to report? A small space quake? Villainous crime or ultrasonic rape alone count in the eyes of the public! Spotlight on the victim's black underwear! We know our listeners, I think!"

As Nan had insisted, he gave her the order to go at once to a remote village where a drug case was developing. Furious, she had left. On the way, in her patched helicopter, she received information from competing sheets. For the first time since her father's death, she wept. It did her the greatest good, to cry normally, like any young girl, a world and a lost love. Fortunately, the fashion for grandiose slogans was no longer in vogue, Earth simply lowered her flags before airless space, the debris of rock – masses of charred and frozen of corpses – which tirelessly circled beyond Pluto.

For two weeks, forbidding herself to pronounce a certain name, establishing deep within herself the silence of a death watch, she worked like a brute. Until the moment when...

All the stereos in the world had burst at once. No one had wanted to believe it at first, and Nan less than anyone else. She was on her way back when the news came through. A Neptune station broadcast the incredible news: a line spacecraft, an ordinary ship which had taken off from Andromeda just when the cataclysm had occurred, had been caught in an hypervortex. Thrown very far, beyond the confines of the galaxy, then thrown back as if pulled by a tidal wave; it was the first ship that had come back from the void... And, in its hull, there were men!

From then on, the universal ether was only a delirious hymn: they were returning to Earth! They were on their way! They had conquered the void! The obstacle that had held back human expansion for three centuries no longer existed, since they had reached other nebulae! The road to the cosmos was open – and every navigator knew he would take it one day.

How, why did they go there? No one asked the unnecessary question. A phenomenon of spontaneous projection, declared mathematicians and philosophers (it was not an explanation, but they liked to use these hollow formulas). Spontaneous, damn it! Nan had thought. I seem to recognize something... The spatial tensors were in working order, of course.

Around her, the sprawling city howled its joy. She had to drop her helicopter in the suburbs and let herself be carried away by a delirious crowd on the moving sidewalks. The avenue that would tomorrow be called Hyperspatial Way cut through the metropolis with a river of versicolored lights; the dome of the Terran Senate was iridescent; and the Tower of the Interplanetary Admiralty was an archangel's sword.

At the first crossroads Nan reached, a belino, with a list of the survivors flashed like a victory slip. She only read one name, the first, and almost fainted.

It was only a brief weakness. Against her shoulder, in the human magma, pressed like a school of eels, a naked young woman in a silver lowlon made up like a clown – a "dragonfly girl" – modulated:

"So, his name's Arno Heller! He's commander of the freighter, isn't he?"

"Dear girl," protested a pleasant male voice, "he's only an auxiliary mechanic. He took over when the others were pulverized."

"Almost all of them are dead..." murmured a sad voice. "It seems that the living are unrecognizable or mad, of course. The shock, you understand? It's as if they had crossed nothingness."

(Nan shuddered: she knew something about it.)

"The scientists claim," resumed the sad voice, "that they've changed into 'ripples.' Inconceivable, isn't it?"

The young clown girl whispered:

"Me, I want to see him first, this Arno Heller. He hasn't changed. And he's very handsome, they say!"

Arno Heller – Arno Heller... The name already sounds like a brass band. Nan seized the violent waves of this amorous crowd which demanded a hero like a toy. Then she looked up and saw: a colonial newspaper had unearthed a sketch showing the pilot at age 16, when he had distinguished himself at a rugby match by punching the referee in the face. She knew this photo. The black and white image blazed in projection on the clouds, walls, screens...

It was like a nightmare.

The human current was sending her toward the starport: the whole town wanted to watch the landing, but not Nan. Tired of the struggle, she began to make her way with her elbows; the women swore at her and the wags hissed. The young girl ended up clinging to the access ramp to *Solar Stereo*. Disheveled, her cardigan lacerated, she went up the stairs.

For once, she walked back into her old office with the feeling of security of a castaway. Here, you see, people didn't pay much attention to destroyed asteroids, to speculations about hyperspace: they were good reptiles, swollen only with Earth blood!

However, after her first steps in the hall, she realized her mistake: even at *Solar*, everything was disorder and enthusiasm, salvoes of jet guns blew up the plexiglass walls and animated figures moved on the screens.

On the ground floor, the operators were dying of fatigue. The young star of the soap opera was sweating desperately under an astronaut's breastplate and the girls from the Revigo show were parading around, dressed summarily in cellophane spacesuits. It was called *Pleasures of the Cosmos*.

The political editor, a bilious man, swallowed his dinner: three vitamin pills. He called Nan:

"Nangis! Where are you with the drug story? Or the two dead lovers found in a glass bed?"

"Nowhere," Nan replied, curbing a murderous rage.

"How come?"

"News of your suicide appeared in the evening strip. It was reported that you had swallowed your venom sac."

The man stood up, all green, but the doors were already opening. The editor-in-chief – nicknamed the Monk – descended from the holy of holies. Paunchy and superb, he opened his arms to Nan:

"Baby moon! My sugar casserole! There, on my heart! Didn't you tell me you grew up with this hero? I mean, Heller! He comes from Andromeda, like you!"

It took the girl incredible mental discipline to reply nonchalantly, taking off her gloves:

"All the same, there were, 30,000 settlers on that satellite. And I didn't live in the same quarter."

They knew that all too well, dammit! But if at the *Solar Stereo*, they sometimes asked about Nick the Wrecker, Nan's father, who had lost a lunar freighter, they never mentioned the name of her great ancestor – North the Pioneer, master of the Astral Belt. (This didn't stop the word from slipping to influential people that the Monk "out of pity" kept the little talentless Nangis employed...)

Now everyone was talking loudly, trying to locate this Heller. He was the son of a mechanic – no, of an astral policeman. And who drank like a hole. And his mother was a taxi-girl... He himself was, of course, destined for the inglorious profession of crawling – these children born on steroids never go far...

"A pariah, in short?" whispered the fat literary critic.

"You know," Nan threw, "fifty years of Earth drooling doesn't give you an idea of the vibe of an artificial satellite."

"But still?"

She spoke – and immediately repented (as if they could understand!):

"It's... well, it's a moment-to-moment effort. Adaptation, first. Control – that, you can't let go, even if your veins burst. Strict discipline and thousands of prohibitions. We live in continual peril – and we defend ourselves."

"Colonies, what!" slipped an underling.

Nan gave him a clear, empty look:

"Exactly, Spieck. But a guy like you sees colonies differently, if he has any ideas at all. You can get drunk within the laws of the mother planet or have kids with a native of Io – we'll put them in a zoo, and that's it. But an ozonator, on a globe devoid of atmosphere, cannot afford the luxury of nervous breakdowns."

"Beautiful, Nan!" yelled the big critic out of his cloud. "You have just the tone! Our space cohorts – the scouts of the solar system – duty, discipline, death, etc.! What do you think, free citizen DK?"

The Monk nodded gravely, already contemplating a luxury double issue. He rummaged in his pockets:

"This kid has the stuff, I've always said so. Here, baby moon, here's my star-girl, go and interview this odd-john, Heller... At the spacedock. You'll wait for him there. I read all the details: he likes neutral girls, like the one who was his girlfriend at Dome No 1... If he's a bit shy – it's a possibility – give him a hint; you're rather pretty, my little one... Ah! and then, you can sign – for once – that interview. 'Nangis' will do!"

And voila! She had barely listened to him: it was as simple as that – an order that was a once-in-a-lifetime opportunity. To refuse would have been to lose a hard-obtained job and to see the doors of all editorial offices closed... Viola suffered a crisis of great style and... Nan preferred not to foresee anything. She thought with some cowardice that they probably wouldn't have time to receive all the press. Mechanically, she exchanged her tattered cardigan for a rather presentable fur coat, with a furious blow of grapes that made her lips bleed...

"So? Shall we run there, girl?" hissed the political editor.

"And how! I'll go ahead of you, for once!"

On the stairs, she leaned against the tile, misting her burning forehead. Flames on the clouds outlined an intolerable face. I don't want to see him, Nan thought. "I don't want to. No, Lord!"

"Winged God – Titan – Archangel...," whispered the literary critic behind her. "I'll provide you with more – priceless – epithets when you come to see my micrographs, Nan."

"Thank you," she replied. "But you know, me and epithets... This Heller strikes me more like a handsome demon."

She was nonetheless at her post, with thousands of other tele-correspondents, a crowd stamping their feet on the starport.

The attack was nearing paroxysm. Of course, the spacecraft – K-1 – wasn't going to land in front of them in the picturesque state in which it left the continuum... It had carried out onto Neptune. But the wildest rumors were circulating. Nan's colleagues suffered – like all Earthmen – from spatial vertigo and recorded without necessity or urgency large slices of conversations, using portable dictaphones.

"The hull was completely twisted," assured an astrotechnician, "like this – you see? It looked like a Moebius strip. And all traffic tensors. As for the men of the crew, they underwent horrible metamorphoses..."

Nan squinted her eyes, dug her nails into her palms. In any case, she said to herself, "I'm quite at peace; he won't see me in this human magma. Later, I can always glean information, and I will not sign the article of course."

And then, as always, the unexpected had happened. When the luminous sphere rose to the horizon, there was a rush. The crowd ebbed first, with a 'ha!', and the shadow of the spaceship covered this high tide. Carried by a wave, Nan was lifted and deposited, despite her efforts, on the platform where the ship was diving in a spin. A thousand hands reached out – those of less privileged colleagues – someone passed her his stereo, a voice begged her to jot down "the first cosmically historic words..."

The huge monoatomic metal ball landed limply on the spot assigned to it – and it was a pandemonium: the loudspeakers howled, the speakers shouted their lungs out. Pressed against the grid fence that protected the landing field, Nan was surrounded by a thousand flashes. A trapdoor swung open. The interstellar guards lined up. Everyone knew that the companions of Arno Heller having been variously affected, so he would appear first. The Interplanetary Anthem swelled like a river. Through the tornado of hysterics rising from the crowd, Nan saw the access hatch open, a figure clad in metal and plastic emerge.

He... well, he hadn't changed much since the Escape from the Caverns. With a slight chill in her heart, Nan noticed that he hadn't lost a centimeter in height; his oxygen tank cast a shadow of wings on him and, under the faceplate, his eyes – like nocturnal lakes – smiled.

He raised his hand in greeting and said: "To this good old Earth!" The transmitters roared, the ceremony planned down to the smallest detail punctuated the human crowd, and Nan bit her wrist to keep herself from stamping her feet and shouting with the others, the delirium was contagious. With boundless anguish, she suddenly understood that HE TOO KNEW HOW THINGS HAPPENED: dark, dull eyes searched the crowd, bloody lips sketched a name. An imperious thought joined her, like an arrow of ice:

Where are you, Nan? I know you're there. Answer me. You're hiding. Isn't that a little cowardly, Nan?

But she was not going to discover herself nor especially to discuss! If it happened again, she would be lost... That's why he had chosen this term: "cowardly"; he knew she was sensitive to such a challenge. Nan buried her face in her hands and quietly squeezed through the living magma. She made herself very small and managed to get under a tarpaulin. The gates were there, she opened them and started to run.

This was how she had found herself before the windows of the starport...

"We have very little time," said Earl Stanley, whom she had completely forgotten, among the orange lights of the Farewell Bar. "But if we hurry, the commander of the spaceport, who's a friend, will obtain a special license for us. I happen to be the only single officer in the mission."

"Here," said Nan, landing back with ease in the present, "a very singular marriage proposal. We don't know each other..."

"Are you sure?" he asked, eyes meeting hers. Their sea light resurrected with such cruel fidelity the Happy Valley, the windswept shore and the original ocean, that Nan lowered her eyelashes. She answered like a simple earth maiden:

"I'm probably wrong. I would regret to cause you trouble."

"You're too modest," replied Earl. "I was going to spend an indefinite time in space, without female company, so that you can accompany me without remorse. Of course... (a slight sigh betrayed the anguish of a shipwrecked sailor, the desire to reach a firm shore as quickly as possible) it'll only be an interastral contract, so that when you return to Earth you'll be free."

(She read his mind and immediately copied the attitude of a young earthling girl – convincingly, of course.) She brought her two joined hands to her throat, gasped a little and murmured:

"You are very good..."

He shrugged:

"Don't overestimate me, I'll probably need your company more than you need mine; I am neither a hero, nor a martyr. But not a brute either. To be fair, I warn you: I like you terribly, Nan Nangis."

She plunged deliberately into the green wave of his eyes and her apprehensions vanished: she felt a boundless desire for rest, a soothing security. Silencing all her voices, she placed a small icy hand in his hand. She said sincerely:

"I like you too, Earl. A lot."

The licensing and marriage formalities took exactly thirty-two minutes.

CHAPTER II
Aboard the Daredevil

The spacecraft was called the *Daredevil*; it was a super-atomic rocket of great tonnage, but something else too. Stepping aboard, Nan stretched out her antennae and realized that she had never been part of such a powerfully tooled ensemble – all the new applications of electricity and magnetism were there, and the machinery used its own fissile materials. It was not a ship, but a colony marching into space; there was in the holds enough materials to reconstitute the atmosphere of a destroyed asteroid – as well as those of a station.

Perhaps, Nan supposed, venturing into the depths of the hull, gravity regulators, enough to attract meteorites into Andromeda's orbit, to compensate for its crumbling... The brains of the specialists offered her, on the way, the sight of an exploded Astral Belt, the debris of which could be used... A disillusioned atomized person saw a gaseous archipelago, like the Ring of Saturn. "But then," Nan thought, "they don't even know what they'll find, and they bother with this crowd! They are true Earthlings!"

The somewhat shoddy ceremony, which had taken place in the hall of the spaceport, had left her with a disappointing feeling. The captain of the port, slightly out of breath, had been waiting for them in a corner of the huge premises, a cirque to contain the masses. His shadow, superimposed, stood out just against the pink and silver rocket. A friend of Earl, he was a lion-maned titan... While Reverend Petrus (of the Interstellar Rite) spoke the usual words, Nan saw in the frosted glass, against the backdrop of the Milky Way, the same young girl – not quite Earthly. Nothing had changed in the image, except the presence behind her shoulders of this big young man, whom his loved ones treated with difference. Nan had a lump in her throat (As if I went back a million years – to come up with this!) and Stanley was a little pale.

She didn't dare to call him Neor yet...

Nan had vaguely feared that something would happen during the ceremony – hoped perhaps for lightning, shouting, for the irruption of some superhuman force; she would have seen without astonishment, as in the past, the marble pillars crumble and waterspouts rise. But nothing disturbed the order; the spaceport commander and the reverend had offered their good wishes to the young couple. When they had found themselves in the passageway, momentarily deserted, which led to the quay, Earl took a step towards her, as if crossing an abyss, and leaned forward.

"Do you want me to kiss you?" he asked, touching her for the first time. "It's up to you to say. You know very well that I wanted it from the moment I saw you, there, in front of that rocket, with blood on your hands and your pathetic little girl's face."

"Two hours ago?" she said.

"Or an eternity."

"Go for an eternity. Kiss Me."

She analyzed her feelings: it was hard to become an Earthwoman again, but Neor was helping her; she was rising from the abyss. she was cold, but he warmed her – there was not only swirling darkness and nothingness and stars, but a haven of calm, green earth meadows and waves caressing the silvery sand. And that kiss had nothing to do with the dressing of fire and ice his wounds had known...

They had arrived on the jetty and Stanley offered her his arm to cross the gangway. A flash of magnesium shot out – for a moment she felt caught, as in a net, in a pitiless gaze from the crowd. "Well, you're a little late," she thought, summing up the cry that rose to her lips, and she leaned, in defiance, on Earl's arm. A few lingering passengers and members of the crew climbed in after them.

Commander Georg Szubinak, a debonair giant, greeted Earl with visible relief: "I was afraid," he confided to him, "of a counter-order from authority. I get on better with you than with the rest of the team, you know..."

"Oh, no!" Stanley said, only smiling from the corner of his lips, "there can be no counter-order for me."

"What team was he talking about?" Nan asked a moment later.

"What, I didn't explain it to you? We're a few scientists attached to the Mission: Borelli the biologist; Karpov the atomist; Vere, who represents chemistry..."

"And you?"

"Oh! I do a bit of everything," he smiled, without gaiety. "Didn't you suspect that you were marrying a formidable character?"

The names were called from the deck of the first seats, a hall lined with statistics and screens, the size of a church. Crew included, there were on board 340 humanoid creatures – Terrestrials, Martians and mestizos; they had eliminated Venusians, too fragile.

Nan's hypersensitive antennae immediately established that this was no ordinary survey; the contingent, which was divided into two unequal groups – specialists and settlers – presented, despite its diversity, two common characteristics: there were the ambitious and the desperate.

The former belonged to the species she knew well: professional astrotechnicians, dry doctors of science, lanky astrophysicists and dashing social workers. A few characters had their suit pockets puffed out significantly, and Interplanetary Guard crest on their lapels. However, this privileged group differed from the *Spetz* that Nan had encountered on Earth: they were all marked with the signs "too much" or "not enough". Some, devoured by ambition, accumulated experiences and sought opportunities; they were a little young – or just too old – disqualified by a slight suspicion of heredity, nervousness or tooth decay, all of which make travel abroad a tragedy. Others had let themselves go at an imprecise time; they lacked an essential internship or diploma; under their normal appearance, one detected an anguish... A load just a little damaged...

They had refused mediocre posts in the terrestrial periphery, and were risking everything. Repopulating a satellite of the importance of Andromeda wasn't a sinecure...

The variegated mass of settlers was livelier, healthier, but Nan inhaled an imperceptible whiff of misery. Beneath the obligatory interplanetary outfit, she caught a glimpse of the heads of wolves, with uncombed locks, jaws that crunched a world, spindly adolescent elbows. Many of these adored adventure... Here, despair, inadequacy were the common mark. In a mechanized universe, the crowds passed under the rolling mill and the waste was expelled: there was the small craftsman, the ruined petty bourgeois, the worker who had opened his big mouth, and the vagabond. There were some Martians, in search of a larger status – and successful humanoids. Fathers of families in revolt against eugenics. Some strong heads, former relegates from Pluto, formed the hardest core...

For the first group, Andromeda was a change – and a risk. For the second, a lifeline.

Nan shrugged: she was probably wrong to be alarmed. It was the usual contingent of the first vessels, and the old colonists of Andromeda had been no better.

They had at their head an adventurous young captain: North Nangis...

She felt a little less at ease when Stanley introduced her to a rather formal group, under the aegis of the captain. She knew it was his clan;

here, all names were famous. Among them were scholars of world renown: Karpov, a quarrelsome and disillusioned character; Vere, who affected the air of a tightrope walker, wore long hair and bit his nails; Borelli, famous biologist and incorrigible charmer. Even better than the men, women also belonged to this brilliant group. Unless you were worth millions, you couldn't have afforded to approach solo practitioners as spectacular as Elisa Borelli, a doctor in childcare – at age fifty – with a complexion of roses and lilies. The stereo had popularized the ungrateful face and capable hands of Olga Karpov, psychotechnician. And Una Vere – well, she was Una Vere! A Calabrian chest and legs, the "most beautiful hip circumference in stereovision." Nan calculated that she had passed victoriously, thanks to hormone injections, the moral age of "cosmetic cream adviser."

Was it at this moment that a dull anguish that had been tormenting her for... (since when had that first glance been exchanged – the ceremony at the spaceport – or before?) came to the surface? Yet, she thought, this crew was normal, just a little more powerful, a little better suited to its task than the others... (Yes, but what task?) These settlers were ordinary people. Each serious expedition included several scholars, and these wouldn't be the least. Discoveries in the field of chemistry had made Vere famous, and his marriage – ill-suited – had forced him to leave a rector's chair... Of course, there were the bizarre ideas of Karpov... Borelli expiated without doubt some dazzling frenzy. Their wives had followed them.

And Earl?

No flaw in his armor. She had spotted in him a metal tension, a purity, a diamond hardness. Alongside these people, each of whom bore an imperceptible blemish, a slight crack, he was like the inhabitant of another universe.

Suddenly, she felt cold. "Earl has me," she thought.

"Honey, I must introduce you to my friends," said Stanley.

She wanted to please them. Not having had time to put on this interplanetary outfit, under which the passengers looked like glittering elves or bronze beetles, she managed just to raise her vital tone, instantly becoming like an angel from Perugino; she did shine her eyelashes and her hair with an unbearable brilliance. Such effects were sure to succeed, but didn't last. Her traveling companions greeted each other with enthusiasm. Una Vere complimented Earl on "that pearl, that eighteen-year-old wonder!"

"You'll leave her with us in her spare time," she added, turning to Earl with the graces of a waving snake, "in stereo, we'll make her a success – and our heroes have to be entertained, right?"

"I'm not photogenic," Nan stammered. She thought that they had never been able to photograph her: she was blurring the plates. For her identity papers, she had presented a skillfully made-up mask.

"We're going to have fun like crazy!" Elisa proclaimed. "Everyone's at the captain's table; we have a good Martian orchestra and, from tonight, we're organizing a party..."

"Yes, yes!" Una stridulated. "It's not because, for patriotic and solar reasons, we're going to live in a desert – in a desert! – that we must disguise ourselves as Saturnians! We will lead a life of heroic – heroic parties!"

She repeated each find at least twice. Earl dragged Nan under a plausible pretext: she had to put on her outfit. "But I don't!" exclaimed the young woman, arriving at the bend of a corridor. "Earl, this is crazy, I have nothing with me, not even a toothbrush. And this Una Vere must travel with fifty trunks of clothes!"

"Have no fear," he smiled. "Each of us receives a kit with essential clothing; I chose yours. Here is the key. Be quick. I must go up to the cockpit."

The key was No. 217. Nan found the cabin at the end of the corridor, a selenium and white enamel casket, with a narrow bunk, a polar bear skin on the floor, a folding dressing table and cupboards. From the threshold, the sixth or seventh sense of the traveler spotted, in the walls, magnetic currents that could be triggered, a thermal variator and a call panel.

Earl Stanley was no doubt a newcomer on board, for his personality had not yet permeated the smooth walls, but Nan felt an anguish and the presence of a terrible secret. She thought she heard his voice: "So you didn't know that you'd married a formidable character...?" She had to hurry. In the middle of the white booth, like a spacious coffin, she closed her eyes, stretched out her hands – fingers spread like antennae – and walked around the room. Not a book, not an identity paper, nothing. The first closet contained a bathroom and the second a set of space suits and interplanetary armor; on a hanger hung a dress of fashionable color. On the dressing table sparkled a slender diadem of platinum-trimmed pearls. Earl had chosen without hesitation the shade and jewels that matched her uncertain eyes, her moving pallor.

Fascinated, Nan instinctively made the gestures that every woman finds in front of mirrors and running water; she put on a quick mouth, brushed a smile even at the image of this foreigner, brightened by make-up, and more capable of struggling, of seducing... However, she was still feverishly looking for something else. Finally, her seventh sense led her to an invisible groove in the walls, a third door, closed. It did not open under her gaze. She walked on the recess and sent an individual electro-magnetic current through the lock. A serious shock sent her to the floor.

In this awkward position, she tried her mental waves and this time entered unhindered into a small room furnished with complicated instruments. There was no belino, no records to guide her, and – aside from her personal experiences – she was a mediocre physicist. She applied herself to reducing the radiations of objects to diagrams, capturing topological data and mathematical precisions – it evoked, from afar, her dazzling journeys in space-time, but in a mechanical, elementary mode. She picked up a term: Spatial Distortion... They called it Spatial Dimension? Poor idiots. Who had spoken of this at the spaceport? It was a committee...

She was there when the door slid silently on its hinges. Earl came in, dressed in white, haughtily handsome, and gazed at her with amusement. Realizing her humiliating position – she was still on the ground, a twisted, painful ankle – she tried to get up and staggered. Earl came to her aid and made her sit on the bunk.

"I knocked," he said, "but you didn't answer and I was afraid you would feel bad. It happens on takeoff. How do you find your installation?"

"Very pretty," she replied resentfully. "A bit narrow for two, maybe."

"Don't mind me; during first watch, I'll have a lot to do and I'll stay at the cockpit." His gaze swept over the smooth walls, the cupboards, and he added, between two tones: "I see you played Bluebeard's wife."

"Yes."

"And you couldn't open the third chamber."

"No."

She didn't like lying, and used omission.

He went to the door and inspected the false lock; a slight hiss rose to his lips. Turning abruptly to Nan, he asked:

"Who are you then?"

She shrugged wearily:

"I told you that I am Nan Nangis. Now I am also – probably – your wife."

"I'm not talking about that. To put this lock in such a state, you had to have electrical energy – but at the dock, you were x-rayed and you had nothing on you. I confess that I had suspicions from your first glance – also seeing the way in which you read surface thoughts. Then I saw that drop of your blood on the handkerchief..."

"And yet you brought me on board!" Nan said.

"I had to. I couldn't leave you behind and I was running out of time. I even married you."

"Yes. You don't shrink from any expense. Now you can still ground me, can't you?"

"Do you believe so?" he said. "Fifteen minutes ago, we left Earth's ionosphere. It's a non-stop trip. I think you'd better talk... I want something else, don't I?"

She didn't listen to him: so they were already gone! Space had taken her back, she was saved. Her ankle no longer hurt her... She smiled, inwardly, at open infinity, at the spirals of nebulae, at the dust of stars, and suggested with some humility:

"Couldn't we resume this conversation later? They're expecting us up there and I've got this ball gown. This long story is practically of no interest to you."

"We'll be expected," he replied. He pushed back the lock on the door and leaned against it, his arms crossed. As Nan smiled weakly, he added angrily, "Oh! I suspect that these are stupid precautions. You toy with barriers and currents. Now why do you think I'm going to Andromeda?"

"I don't know," she told him frankly. "Your mental barriers have held."

He answered curtly:

"I'm delighted. We, too, were taught certain disciplines. Listen," he went on with unexpected passion, "things are happening in the solar system right now that no physics, no chemistry, can explain: abominable, absurd and crazy things that are putting our universe in danger. Everywhere chaotic forces are unleashed; they mock our laws, our stability, our science, and destroy worlds as if it were a game.

"The Andromeda disaster is not a single fact, but a symptom; it leaves much out because it happened on an isolated satellite, where hostile action could not be disguised. So we have some chance of surprising our enemies who disguise themselves as elements, humanoids, and even cosmic powers. Other passengers are sent to Andromeda to recover. I go there myself to prevent further disasters..."

"So you're a spy," Nan said with disgust.

He lifted his head proudly.

"No, I'm the Space Distortion Commissioner and that's something else entirely. A spy is one who is sent to a foreign country and who hides. I stay in our solar territory and I fight with my visor up. The danger I seek to track threatens all intelligent races: those of Earth, Neptune or Mars. We all have a common enemy, a common cause..."

"I don't think it's mine," Nan said cautiously. "I didn't hide it from you: I don't like this world. My greatest desire was to leave Earth. And how could I help you? Psi faculties? Any Earthling has a good dose of it. Feminine intuition? If so, use Una Vere..."

It wasn't very clever, she realized that immediately; in horror. But Earl didn't care. "To hell with Una Vere"! he launched irritated.ly "You don't want to talk? Well, follow me to this little room you wanted to enter so badly; it's my study. I'll show you something and maybe that'll decide you not to lie – for once. Don't be afraid," he added in a softened voice, "I won't hurt you."

"What harm could you do to me?" she asked, heading for the third door, looking like a fallen young queen, dragging her sprained ankle and her time-colored dress. Her slender diadem starred the ashes of her hair and Earl wanted to take her in his arms, cover her with kisses, beg for her forgiveness – or even strand her on the first deserted asteroid...

Standing on the threshold, she questioned:

"Do you have these micro-films on you?"

"We can't hide anything from you. How do you know?"

"Because there weren't any in that closet," she replied disdainfully. "You know that I have gone around it, all the same. And these are the shots from the Astral Belt, aren't they? It's in the tradition of earthly authorities: you can't go back."

They took their places in front of the small individual screen and Earl projected images of the end of the world. They plunged into vast darkness, where cold white sparks flashed – distant universes that had not participated in the apocalypse. The reconnaissance rocket's camera hovered and captured – black on black – opaque shapes, debris so small that Nan thought: "There is no more Astral Belt." She knew better than anyone that it was once an archipelago of living satellites, remote outposts at the edge of the Solar System, where a handful of men suffered and struggled. The viewfinder swooped vertically toward a larger shadow coming toward it; a rough relief, white edges of craters, rocks proliferate. Nan realized that Andromeda had lost all trace of atmosphere, but the core was still burning, shaking with explosions.

On the surface, there was nothing left of a human domination, established for a century. No normal earthquake could have produced such damage. Orbital shocks, yes! They were planned and prepared. The domes of the three bases were cast in fireproof lecite and microsteel; yet they had folded "like a paper plane" (Nan still remembered the horrible words used by that last settler). Monoatomic structures rose up, crushed in spirals, as if they had been sucked into huge vortices. Here and there sprang crumbled cranes or shimmered lakes of molten metal. What terrible tornado had passed through? What had happened to organic life? As if to answer her question, the viewfinder began to search the funnels, like lunar craters.

It entered an excavation located under a dome and Nan almost cried out at the sight of a magma of fabrics and charred flesh: the servants of the atomic parts and civilian personnel of the small planet, with their families, had taken refuge there...

"So look," said Earl Stanley harshly.

The recorder craft was now flying over the unique globe city of Andromeda. All that remained of the master screen were a few superstructures like the vertebrae of a monster fossil. But this side of the satellite was more spared and Nan saw, under the pylons, the most moving sights: some ruins, veritable earthly ruins – vestiges of white colonial houses, smashed greenhouses and blackened gardens...

Human beings had lived there – not like space navigators who carry Earth with them, in the hull of their ship, striving to reconstruct their lost paradise. Here, human had built their houses on the atomic rocks and cultivated flowers on transported humus. Machines for reconstituting the atmosphere had expelled the vacuum. Men had erected a frail barrier between themselves and nothingness, and lit up enormous pink suns, to create day and night, because the human brain cannot bear the eternal, motionless twinkling of the nebulae.

The results had exceeded their expectations – the tourism prospectus had only been half-lying: the roses of Andromeda were as big as sundials and bursting with perfume; the intensive cultivation had produced mangoes that could feed a family, and grapefruits the size of watermelons. The terraced gardens, purple, blue and indigo, sloped gently towards a single lake whose emerald waters, saturated with organic life, was so still that they did not tremble.

A hundred years. Andromeda had existed for a little over a hundred years! Human beings had died there; others had been born. The young, whose eyes had opened under the bombardment of cosmic particles, knew no other horizon than darkness, no other homeland than this iridescent neon globe...

The viewscreen hesitated before a gracefully curving hill. It had moved away from the epicenter of the cataclysm, located at the level of Dome No. 1. It found the remains of a low house, built of earthen materials and which seemed very old for the station; sections of white columns surrounded it, forming a veranda and a peristyle. It had been crushed by the whirlwinds, but one still realized that its proportions were harmonious and its halls noble. The linear plane indicated a library and a reception. The garden was just a pile of ashes, strewn with mounds that were older graves. Other buildings, which had suffered more, profiled around their charred carcasses.

"This house," said Nan Nangis in a blank voice, "do you know what it was? It was the residence – the former residence – of my grandparents. I grew up there. Their graves were in this garden. My father didn't have his... I believe, Earl Stanley, that I will never forgive you for showing me these things!"

He replied, in the same harsh voice:

"You had to be taught."

The lights had come on again; she saw Earl's pallor, the corners of his eyes bloodshot. He added: "I think I understand you, in part. I was born on Earth, but I spent my childhood in the outposts of Mars, with my parents... Mare Chronium... it was a barren ground where many of ours fell. If someone had told me that their sacrifice was useless, I would feel a cold rage... Come, Nan Nangis, let me massage your ankle, otherwise it'll swell and tomorrow you won't be dancing with the Commander."

"I won't dance at all," she said stubbornly.

"As if! And now will you tell me all your guilty secrets?"

She raised her eyes to him with the transparency of onyx, of virid diamond, her inhuman eyes. His pupils widened.

"There is absolutely nothing wrong with my ankle," she said. "You can see for yourself: I restored blood circulation and deflated the epidermis. Now, you'll probably believe me if I tell you what you already suspect...?"

"Say it."

"I'm a KZ mutant from Andromeda."

A bell rang on the call board. Commander Georg Szubinak was calling in polyphony for the Space Distortion Commissioner in the third grade. The film – a little redacted – on the Astral Belt had just been shown, and the passengers took it rather badly.

"You'll have to give them a little lecture," the brave astronaut trumpeted. "They're a little disassembled, you understand? They weren't quite expecting that..."

"What were they expecting?" Earl asked point-blank. "To inherit the resort's greenhouses and palaces? Nothing predestined them to such facilities; they only wanted to review their individual files."

He was descending nonetheless, determined to use direct language and to send back to Earth, by first ship, those who flinched. A crowd was heaving in the warehouse of the third and Stanley's resolve wavered in front of the women who made up half of the crew, many of whom were cradling children: these could not stand a second trip. The screen was off, but it seemed that the shadow of the charred globe still loomed, like a threat. From the back of the room, Nan, who had followed Earl, admired, when he mounted the platform, his stature and his curled hair which sparkled. Interplanetary guards stationed themselves at the exits.

"The commander asked me to speak to you," Stanley said. "It seems that there are disagreements among you. Don't forget that you are all volunteers. You left Earth of your own free will; our homeworld was not hospitable to you; you were poor or vexed, you desired adventure or change, and no one asked for your reasons. The Federation took you for what you are – grown human beings who know what they are doing and are accountable for their decisions.

"Now you have seen what awaits you on Andromeda. I too saw it, at the same time as you. Ruins, yes, but work for builders, and also a free and fallow ground. The humus of this globe is among the richest in the solar system, still fattened by the residues of the cataclysm. Yes, it will be hard; we will first have to work in spacesuits and live in the hull of our ship. We'll have to rebuild everything, even the breathable atmosphere; rebuild an astro-station and a village under a globe; it will take months, years even. Only later can we worry about basic comfort. The principle wealth of Andromeda has always been its uranium content. Before the cataclysm, it was on the way to becoming the most important station in solar trade, and it must recover this position as soon as possible. It is for this reason that Earth has sent you, and given you the means to fulfill this task. This ship contains within it all the first necessity machines: transformers, atomic generators, ultrasonic excavators, all that the mother planet has done best in terms of modern equipment. And weapons, of course. Because we will need weapons...

"I repeat: living conditions will be harsh, but you knew it when you signed your contracts. Those who stay on will be rich after a decade, and they will be able to spread it among the rest of you. The former settlers preferred to stay; they lived and prospered – three generations were born on Andromeda. But no globes were spared from the astral cataclysm – Earth itself has retained a fear of comets..."

"Three generations," murmured a woman. "We heard that monsters were born there..."

Earl's eyebrows, which looked like brush strokes, rose sarcastically:

"Ask my wife. She was born on Andromeda, daughter and grand-daughter of settlers."

A murmur ran through the crowd. Taking advantage of this, Earl asked: "Does anyone have any specific questions?"

At the far end of the room, a swarthy man stepped forth; he looked like a former privateer – with a short beard and a thick Scottish accent.

"We would like to know," he said, "if the true causes of the disaster have been discovered."

"What were you told on Earth?"

"That there had been a series of orbital shocks, such as those caused by passage of a comet."

"And you don't believe it anymore?"

"No. Unless it's a newly-discovered comet, because the shaking axis doesn't match anything. Nor the devastation."

"Astrophysicist out of the lab, huh?"

The man blushed:

"It's not a crime."

("No," Earl noted, "only, you are registered as a Third-Class me-chanic... a detail to be reviewed.") "Well," he continued, "since you have a qualification, tell us first what has bothered you about the strikes in the devastation. This will interest your fellow crewmates."

"That's it," explained the man, growing bolder. "First, when a wan-dering star passes – we observed this in the case of Biela II – strong masses of water are sucked in and form tides. The highest points – buildings and rocks – are swept away. Finally, there is, almost always, a fall of meteor-ites causing fires. In case the comet comes closer, the atmosphere ignites and the oxygen in the air is quickly consumed. Finally, as a last scenario, if the two orbital axes interfere, the comet finds itself caught in the zone of attraction and falls upon the planet. The collision can cause the central nucleus to explode – which is the case for most novae... We designate, in technical terms, these phenomena under the letters A, B, C, the last being the symbol for a nuclear explosion."

"In the case of Andromeda, what letter would you say apply?"

"Well... according to these films, there's no longer any atmospheric layer – and yet there were only partial fires, which would not be apparent in case B. On the other hand, the water from the artificial lake and canals seems to have been sucked up so quickly that the tidal wave had no effect. And yet the superstructures, such as the domes and interplanetary cranes which, theoretically, fear only disintegration, have folded up, like leaves turned over by a current of air. Fourth point, the destruction is uneven; the epicenter is clearly located towards Dome No. 1 and the state of the star-port, on a planetoid of such relatively small dimensions, contradicts any theory of orbital tremors. In fact, I think that's all..."

"Fair enough," Stanley said. "Your deductions?"

The man hesitated a little. One could hear, in the hall, the gasping breathing of the mass.

"Well," he went on again, "I am only after all a former astrophysics student, so I reason by associations of thoughts. It looks like a huge whirl-pool started at the surface in front of Dome 1, and it gouged out a funnel, a titanic hole, if you follow me, and the whole edifice was sucked in that direction. But, as Andromeda only had a very thin layer of atmosphere, I don't see by what – nor how – such a hole was dug..."

"Good for an astrophysics student," Stanley smiled (and Nan, in the shadows, liked his odd smile – the serious eyes and quivering corners of his lips). "I can tell you that, indeed, something like this happened on the surface of Andromeda, something absolutely outside of normal physical standards, something I would characterize as man-made. This should re-assure you, in a way: this is neither a cyclone, nor a comet, hence no in-termittent peril. Do you know what we can deduce from that?"

"A spontaneous phenomenon...?" stammered the man from Nova Scotia.

"In matters of science, this doesn't exist. So far, determinism is king: every effect has its causes. It is a question of finding them and eliminating them, as far as possible. I won't hide from you that this is, personally, my mission – that of a commissioner for Space Distortion. Each of you must help me, and if it is up to us, there will be no second disaster on Androm-eda."

Nan thought that, on Earth, except for a few luminaries, no one knew the members of the Spatial Distortion firsthand. The moment was serious, since Earl Stanley had just revealed his function. The crowd understood it too – timid at first, a few rounds of applause rang out, then the uproar grew. Earl waved at the red-haired, swarthy man who made his way to the podium.

"You're called?" he asked.

"MacLeod. Category F3. Technician."

"Well, MacLeod, it seems direct contact is good; I would like to know from time to time what you all think and discuss the issues that concern you. Would you like to register with the commander as a settler delegate? The center will confirm."

He came down from the rostrum with a long step. The crowd opened up before him, with involuntary respect. After the ovations and shouts, silence reigned; people painfully realized, like the masses, in what conditions they would have to live and fight, against a faceless enemy – with this leader.

In the passage MacLeod caught up with Earl Stanley.

"Sir," he said with an effort, as if to give this title scraped his throat, "I would like to tell you that I am not qualified..."

"Oh! As if!" he said (and Nan searched his voice in vain for the joy of a tamer who had just left the cage). "I remember your file – work was conscientiously done. You were expelled from the labs for illicit experiments. You did three years of forced hibernation and seven years of uranium mining. Therefore you are the perfect iniquitous man to track reactions... Now get it into your head that only the Commander and I know your Terran past, and that it will no longer exist the moment you step down on Andromeda."

"Thank you sir," Jonas MacLeod said.

CHAPTER III
Nan Speaks

"And now," he said, "are you ready to talk, Nan?"

Earl hadn't had time to take off his white uniform and Nan was playing distractedly with her food. "You did very well," she said. "Quite the gladiator facing the lions, or the pirate captain leading his mutineers to fiery death. So, you're the future governor of Andromeda, I gather?"

"Just during the battle. Not for life, like your grandfather."

A flight attendant entered, with a champagne bucket and a bunch of Earth roses – from Commander Szubinak.

"Here," said Nan, "I forgot we had something to celebrate!" Earl silently filled the cups, and when the door had closed: "To our wedding," he said. "Whatever you may think..."

"But I don't think anything bad about it!" she protested. And she went on: "If I'm not mistaken, you want to know when and how I understood that I was a mutant...? Well, it came little by little... Listen:

"There are several theories on the controversial subject of mutations. You know, of course, that this is an action on the genes, factors of heredity. The 20th century already commonly employed, for this purpose, rays or chemical means, such as hyperitis gas, certain sulfonamides or certain phenols. Thus, by "chromosomic splitting", giant plants were obtained, experimental mutations were observed in fruit flies and mice. But as scientists worked hard to alter the number of nerve cells and project prefabricated intelligences, nature got in on the action, too. With a wise slowness at first, on the distant or poorly-known planets, islands, oases... Scientists have looked for explanations, and they undoubtedly found some. The most common, the easiest, was that of mutants born due to radioactivity: H-bombs or X-rays; long before the fission of the atom, prehistory offered us mutations; in the evolution of the human race there was a split between Neanderthals and their successors – similar and entirely different.

"The Tertiary was populated by small simians who were on their way to a more perfect form, but they disappeared without a trace, and humanity arose from a larger prototype that suddenly appeared. Darwin's transformism is only a somewhat outdated system of generalized mutations.

"However, most of the experimental mutations gave unfavorable results. Materialism is in play when it comes to making double dahlias or bayonet-tailed mice, but when it comes to brain variations, the Earth labs were failing. Nature did better; at least I believe so...

"On Andromeda first."

She gave Earl only a smattering of her thoughts. For the needs of the cause, she abbreviated or explained. In his colorless eyes rose the image of the incredible planet, created by men and which had revolted against their laws. Andromeda – so far from Earth that the epithet of extrasolar was applied to it – once again rolled its globe in black infinity, dazzling under the pink suns, its still waters and its floral fairytales. One can love a land that is not one...

Nan continued:

"This house, whose destroyed foundations you showed me, was mine. I was born there; I grew up there under the tutelage of two kind old men. My grandfather, at the end of a colorful life as a navigator, occupied the post of commander of the station; he was the very type of the astronaut of heroic times, that is to say, idealist and lover of the exact sciences. He had a fluvial beard and a limpid gaze; his subordinates called him 'Mister Neptune', and this nickname suited him well.

"Grandma was a little Creole lady, whose childhood was spent on Venus; I see her adorned with mauve silks and silver curls.

"This idyllic group took me in during my father's inter-astral journeys. Hothead of the family, he had married badly, he was soft and credulous, and his career was disastrous, without it being his fault. Here to him! (she rose her glass)

"I'd been brooded and decanted on the station itself, and Viola (so my supposed mother was called) followed my father everywhere, for she was fiercely jealous; I received from my grandparents a liberal education as desired.

"I said: my presumed mother. In fact, I have none of her hereditary characteristics, and perhaps no chromosomes or genes to recall this ancestry. Is this an effect of the intensive cosmic bombardment on Andromeda? Had the settling flask been irradiated? I do not know.

"I was a very ugly child.

"Don't say no, Earl, you don't know. Not a monster, of course, but a sickly, waxy being. Something unfinished, malleable... a little jellyfish. I suffered from all the diseases whose germs came to us by mail rockets – I felt so uncomfortable in my body! It was too small, inert, it hampered my essential functions – swimming, flying – I knew how to do it, but my body didn't obey me. My consciousness was waking up very soon, too soon, in that hypnagogic haze that envelops normal childhoods. A memory proves it; here it is: It was during a worrying twilight when the neon lights were failing; the room where I sat was full of shadows. My pediatric nurse, Agatha, a young person with rosy cheeks, stood facing a wall bay; she hugged me to her vast chest and, in her dismay, she let her antiseptic mask hang down. Me, I was wrapped in a brown shawl, not in my blanket (this one was in pink acetyl and lace: we knew how to live). Behind the plexiglass window, the artificial lights were dying, it was a blue and leaden half-light. I said to myself: 'But it's not the extrasolar darkness!' I lifted my head from the cup formed by Agatha's chest. And I saw, unfolding above the globe, like a torrent of rubies, the imperial tail of a comet.

"However, the only comet which passed in orbit of Andromeda was Halley's. At that time, I was ten days-old...

"However most of the time, I lived in dreams. The term is probably inaccurate, but the language of Earth has so few of them! There were two that repeated almost every night: it invariably started with a run in flowing black. Here writhed large luminous figures, rolled purple or blue balls, gently phosphorescent at the edges... In my first dream, the darkness was filled with flashing lights and, on one of the balls, something alive, organic in appearance, throbbed: it was composed of multiple particles, green and agitated, like mimosa flowers. I had to count them – and that required infinite patience, mountains of equations and logarithms... I woke up, drenched in a cold sweat. My repulsion for math dates from those nights.

"The second dream was more amusing: I descended in plane flight towards the balls and I discovered towns, houses and small characters, horrible or charming, who struggled there. They didn't see me, because I was fluid, scattered in space, like the 'force beings' of old science fiction novels, and I could only intervene in their lives in an irregular way. I tried to help them in their troubles...

"This dream gave me an acute pleasure in which entered a feeling of power and responsibility, and a morbid sweetness. I guess I loved those little humans.

"I was growing slowly. Agatha, of whom I have spoken, nearly played a disastrous role in my physical development. Probably because I only had old people in front of me and she was the only fresh face leaning over my cradle...

"One day this charming girl, who was very popular with the lower staff of the station, noticed that I was beginning to look like her. Strangely: a mole on the back of the neck, the curve of an eyebrow, the groove of a thumb... I had no other model! Like the ancient savages of Polynesia, Agatha imagined that I was stealing her soul – and fled. Fortunately! This pretty person was very vulgar.

"I now lived between a lisping grandmother who fanned herself with ostrich feathers and talked to lizards, and a very busy grandfather. He had just been appointed Commander of the Astral Belt, and we hardly saw him anymore: he traveled the archipelago in his little rocket, called 'flying needle', or sat on the Federal councils... I settled in his library, on the floor below, and I made contact in a way that I couldn't define, because I didn't know the alphabets, with Ulysses and Nausicaa, Oedipus and Antigone, Melisande and Pelleas... At night, I communicated with lower organisms: the dogs which had prospered on the barren plateau of Andromeda came to cry under the entities and I answered them. There was also a jackal and wolves escaped from their cages...We established friendly relations. But I was very discreet and nobody knew anything.

"I should probably tell you about my normal metabolism...? Grandpa was so busy and Grandma so distracted that they didn't notice. I poured the dreadful lukewarm milk they served me into the flowerbeds and I spat out the mucous boiled eggs; on the other hand, I lived on coarse salt and lime – one of our walls suffered considerably. They tried raw meat and grape juice – they went the way of boiled eggs. One day, I realized that by adopting the appearance of a chubby little girl, I would calm my relatives – and I did the right thing. Only domestic robots were not mistaken: I was, at times, a little transparent."

"However, I almost betrayed myself, out of thoughtlessness: one day, I quoted Euclid's postulate to Grandpa. 'Where are you getting this from?' he asked in his commanding voice.

" 'It's written in a book,' I replied, sulky, and as her eyes widened, I immediately corrected: 'You see, there was a drawing there...'

" 'No,' said my grandfather passing his index finger under my chin which he lifted, 'you can't lie! You read it, didn't you? How long have you been able to read? Let's see, spell...'

" 'I can read,' I admitted, 'but not spell...'

"As my grandmother entered the office in a whirlwind of perfumes and lace, he called out to her:

" 'Ambrosia! Ambrosia! This child's beyond me! How old is she?'

" 'Come on, North,' Grandma answered distractedly, 'when you scream like that, you scare the goldfish! You know very well that Nan was decanted on October 23, Earth time. She will be two in three months.'

41

" 'Two years! And she reads! Such a fragile child! I sure hope you haven't taught her anything!'

" 'Of course,' Grandma retorted. 'She knows how to read, without having learned it, like people of quality...'

"If I quote this incident Earl, it is that it is typical of the childhood of a mutant. There are so many ways to explain things! We ourselves never have the effect of being singular. But sooner or later...

"At that time I made music and poetry. I seized a green horizon and arms, full of roaring rockets, and then I placed on it the reason for departure in general – which could be birth as well as death, the anguish of the void and the unknown worlds to reach. I drew figures with eyes reflecting a house or a garden, and fingers in the shape of vines, ready to launch, to touch the universe. My characters were called Neor, the Disembodied Voice, the Singing Sword and the Dispenser of Perfumes...

"The warnings did not fail me. Grandma decided one day to enroll me in the best kindergarten that existed in the Astral Belt. She succeeded in touching, by polyphony, my grandfather who sat on the Astronautical Council... 'Imagine,' she would say, 'that the director refused to see Nan! She says her place is in high school! In high school!'

" 'Did you tell her that Nan is three years-old?'

" 'Sure, North. She fell in reverse. But then she pretended... Oh! you cannot know!'

" 'What?'

" 'That Nan is not human...'

" 'She is crazy!' cried my grandfather this time. 'What does that mean? Nan is the legitimate daughter of Viola and our son Nick, of course. Nick who would probably never have married Viola if... but enough! She has nothing to do with it! I have all the prenuptial tests and genetic diagrams in hand... Besides, the little one looks like Nick, doesn't she...?'

" 'Hmm!... Yes...'

" 'This director will hear from me!'

"I was sitting on the carpet and I pretended to play quietly with my cubes. In fact, I was trying to reconstruct the Tower of Babel. I said:

" 'What if you put me in the Colonial Mission?'

" 'She's crazy!' Grandpa's image cried.

"The Colonial School was a center of Catholic missionaries, people fit to go to hell if they counted on making recruits there. It took in all kinds of misfits, half-breeds more or less Martians, and the children of displaced people during the school season. Its teachers were excellent teachers, but

42

no one wanted to hear about it – and I was still the granddaughter of North Nangis, Governor General of the Astral Belt! Convenience was essential..."

...While, in the past, a little three-year-old Nan was struggling among earthly inconsistencies, the young bride Nan put her hand to her altered mouth and sighed:

"I'm thirsty..."

Earl put the glass of champagne to her lips, waited for her to empty it and said:

"Then?"

"In the story of a well-organized interracial case (repeated the eighteen-year-old Nan), similar events follow one another. But in life, it was something else. It was at this time that Viola Nangis presented herself, human to the tips of her pink nails, beautiful, with her small, rounded waist, her short leg and her round calf, throwing back her viperine head with blue braids – my mother. She came to the foot of our veranda, under the large flamboyant trees, because she refused to 'enter the dwelling of sin.' She had a citrine complexion, a statuesque low forehead, thin, slightly shaded, cyclamen-colored lips. Her eyes, green at rest, became almost white under a stroke of pride or anger. She had just had a resounding quarrel with my father and had definitely quarreled with the commander-in-chief of his astral sector, so that he was losing all chances of going up the slope. She joined Andromeda, all sails out, shouting that she was going to 'take back the child of her flesh from this race of monsters!' In the avenue where white lotuses and zinnias bloomed, she appeared, dragging a mauve acetyl tunic, selenite buskins, and head-dressed with Venusian gulls.

"She took me emphatically in her arms, while Grandma left her rocking chair and fled, stammering something about the 'madness of young men who, in the swamps of Venus, marry Earthwomen only good at scaring off galactic monsters...' I remember my own terror; I felt, in those soft, perfumed arms, like a trapped mouse... I was suffocating with disgust. Basically, when I think about it, it was the only normal aspect of our relationship between mother and daughter, this repulsion between two worlds, two beings of different formation and metabolism. It was... almost as if we had put in the same jar a very pretty frog and a fissile element... (I think all the sympathy would have gone to the frog.)

"But I didn't know – I still didn't understand what incommensurable pass this tornado came from!

"My mother took advantage of Grandpa's absence to transfer me to Passage House where the families of astronauts were staying. It was the first of the nights of terror that I had been given to experience – nights in which I used and abused my still unknown faculties, to make myself small, to make myself invisible – to escape. Alas, all this is not within the reach of mutants! Until midnight, my mother stuffed me with intolerable foods, candied lotuses, mangoes from the Canal, etc., and exhibited me in the middle of a yard of young pilots.

"As I stood up, she shoved me into a towel rack and forgot about me, for a moment. Father arrived next, very young too, tired with a copper red face like the statuettes of Jupiter. He no longer wore his badges – he was half fired and subsequently left Federal Navigation... (it seems that my mother had, at that time, slapped the commander general and accused his wife of recent ignominy). My father's visible dismay and his gullibility in the face of Viola's screams and threats affected me greatly. In fact, as soon as they had retired to their room, while I was rolled up in the towel rack, they had a dreadful scene. She rolled on the floor, reproached my father for creating a monster, declared that she was going to poison herself – and she waved a small perfume bottle at arm's length – then that she would simply throw herself on the ground, without a suit, in which case 'the stale atmosphere of Andromeda would suffocate her dead.' I really wanted to tell my father that the Globe was watertight and the atmosphere constantly renewed by ozonators, but he didn't hear my mute cries. So I emptied myself of all vital energy and, falling on the floor, I began to roll beside my mother, imitating her contortions, and we both screamed so well that my father covered his ears and ran to fetch a doctor.

"When he left, my mother sat down, in the middle of a fit of hysteria, and laughingly showed me that the little bottle was empty.

" 'Imbecile,' she told me, 'you can't poison yourself with that!'

"That's how I learned you could lie...

"The next day it was pure. The nurse from Passage House was taking me for a walk in the public garden, dressed in the only little dress and the red anorak which we had taken away, my mother seemed surrounded by her court and cried: 'The red nightmare! The red nightmare!' She jumped on the nurse:

" 'She's not my daughter!' she proclaimed. 'She was stolen from me, she was replaced by a Martian with cat's eyes!" She grabbed my collar with both hands and laced the little garment up and down. I was shaking and chattering my teeth. Back at home, the nurse had the unfortunate idea of offering me milk – the consequences can be guessed... the broken cup rolled at the feet of my mother who declared that she would teach me to live! The nurse was dismissed, and Viola took me on all fours around our room, she cracked her lowlon belt like a whip and yelped: 'Go live under the table, stupid! You're just a Martian – no – Saturnian beast...! You'll live there with the dogs and you'll eat in a wooden trap! You would live on all fours until you die!' Luckily, she was asked for by polyphony – 'an admirer,' it said, immediately laughing and reassured. She put on her prettiest headdress of Riim feathers and ordered me to kiss her; I obeyed, then, as soon as she was out, I slipped quietly into the bathroom and threw up.

"I slept that night in the little dog's basket, very comfortable – the Passage House was a first-class hotel. When I first awoke, my eyes were so swollen with tears that, through the darkened lens, the flowers in the garden had assumed fantastic shapes and proportions, swirls of palpable perfume danced down the paths, and neon lights imitated the moon on the floor. I sat in my basket and imagined a journey into infinity, a blue and green planet and winged beings ascending towards the sun... It seemed so pretty to me that I pulled from the lining of my torn anorak my school notebook, which I carried everywhere with me, and I wrote, pell-mell, musical notes and rhythmic phrases, a whole somewhat delirious poem.

"The second time I saw my eyes again, the night was late and half the neon lights had gone out. My mother was standing in front of the mirrored wardrobe, completely naked, shaking with gasps of laughter, and admiring, as she said, her 'virgin belly'. She put her pretty foot, very small, under my nose and exclaimed: 'Kiss it. Isn't it carved out of marble?' As I stepped back, she uncovered my notebook and seized it; in the front row, she began to giggle and declared that it was a bunch of lies and madness... They had told her in town that I was not a normal child, but she would know how to train me!

"At that moment, she put on her dressing gown and forced me to tear my notebook in four, then to sew it edge to edge: 'So that no one in the world can know how stupid and bad you are.' The notebook sealed, she then dragged me, under my lacerated anorak and my nightgown, to the landing stage of the rockets, at the entrance to the gardens.

"It was very dark, I was shaking, and all along the way she threatened me to take my notebook and read it aloud, to show the whole world my ignominy. I had to get on my knees and ask her forgiveness for being a stupid, lying, proud girl... By dint of crying and because I forgot to give a precise shape to my features, I had almost no more face...

"At the top of the dock, it was very solemn – she made me swear never to write anything again – or only sensible things – things that I would have seen and that everyone would know.

" 'But why write them?' I asked between sobs.

" 'To avoid lies and vice. You know what happens to vicious liars? They bend over a black abyss – like here – and they fall. They fall and their fall has no end.'

"Thereupon I dropped from the dock. Not without throwing away my notebook first.

"I don't know why I did this stupidity. I knew I couldn't really go down – the gravity was almost zero. The notebook flew away, fluttering like a white bird; I no longer looked at it, I was too ill. My whole nervous system was falling apart, I had enough – enough – enough! I simply released my blood and caused a monster nasal hemorrhage – I hadn't reached the ground when my clothes were soaked through.

"I wasn't at all frightened at the sight of this emerald-green arterial blood, of these two little fountains which froze, as I sank with delight into a black void. No doubt I had ended up on the waste ground, on the other side of the dock, a cemetery of old rockets, where scrap metal was piled up and where wild grass grew between dislocated propellers. They could have searched for me for a long time there, if an interstellar guard hadn't seen us pass, my mother dragging me and me crying, high up like two ridiculous Chinese shadows. They rushed towards the Residence... but this is a sequel to the story.

"I came to, because someone squeezed my nostrils very hard. At the same time, a steel key had been placed on my neck. I probably didn't have more than a liter of blood left in my veins, I felt surprisingly light and ready, only I couldn't lift or move this useless envelope of flesh... My first idea was to chase away this rest of liquid so that I could escape in peace – and I made an effort. Someone cursed me, someone pressed to my lips a hot spring that I was forced to drink – and which was also blood.

"My unknown savior was not tender. 'Ah! You want to die!' he said, keeping my mouth open wide under his gashed wrist. 'Dirty little girl that you are! Well, no, you won't die! If we find you here, they will still accuse people of the area!'

" *I would like to know*, I thought, *who could prevent me from dying?*

" 'Me!' answered my savior. I realized that he was reading my thoughts and, at the same time, I felt that the flow of my blood stop dead and that a little warmth came to me from his other brown hand, placed flat on my body, at the approximate location of the solar plexus. I tried to fight against his will, but I was weak and numb – yet I felt that with a little effort I would break down this frail barrier: I was already establishing a scale of comparisons...

" 'It's useless to make me drink your blood,' I said. 'It doesn't help, that's not how you transfuse. And it tastes bad.'

" It can't hurt you, anyway,' he said. 'It has the same color as yours. Presently, I'll stop it dead.'

" 'I didn't know there were more like me,' I said flattering him. Now I saw him, more in thought: a little boy from the zone, wild, dressed in patched overalls – a brown and silver being. 'There aren't many of us,' he replied, 'you're the first of this kind that I've met, but since there's already you and me, there must be other mutants.'

" 'What is a mutant?'

" 'Oh! Don't be silly, please! They must have told you that you're not quite normal? You let your blood flow at will, you stop it when it suits you – and it's green – you read people's minds, what's good for them to eat gives you colic, etc... These are symptoms of a mutation. It seems that it happened because of radiation or ultrasound, that's what they told my mother, when she took me to their hospital. To get me 'vaccinated', the fool! They put me under observation, but I escaped and live here.'

" 'All alone?'

" 'All alone.'

" 'And your parents?'

" 'They are very happy to be rid of me, they still have six lays – normal!'

"He was looking at me through his tangled curls. He said again:

" 'You thought you were unhappy, didn't you, when you jumped off that thing? Well, you see, there's someone more unfortunate than you...'

" 'Where do you sleep in the extreme cold?'

" 'Over there, in a cabin. I unscrewed a little and recast all that with my individual current. It makes me a nice house, with a spring berth again.'

" 'And what are you eating?'

" 'Bah! – And you? Probably also things that make others wince? Iron rust, if you want to know. It's not bad, look at my muscles...'

"Without transition, he asked:

" 'What are you doing here? Are you granddaughter of 'Sir Neptune'? I saw you in a nifty chopper the other day – like a silver pole. But you're

47

not pretty,' he added, inspecting me curiously, 'yet it's easy for you to be pretty...'

" 'I don't care!'

" 'Well done, girl! Get it into your head that it'll come in handy one day. Isn't it nice to have hair and skin like light, and long legs like they always say?'

"I thought of my mother and said:

" 'I hate beautiful women. You, later on, what do you want to do?'

" 'Oh!' he replied passionately, 'fly! But not as you think. Not with those stupid big airships, which are like heavy fish. But almost we can do so much with our body – how do you say it again? With our reflexes – it also seems to me that we could – didn't you feel that when you were falling? Change us into vibrations, into waves, into light... and then, there would be no obstacle, no space nor time.' "

Nan broke off: her clear eyes were staring at an invisible point, beyond the smooth walls, and Stanley realized that she was there, in the middle of the rocket graveyard, on intact Andromeda, under the rosy glow of the neon moons. Alone, with the boy who looked like a silver figurine and said some big things. Beginning to understand that she was not like everyone else and that nothing would bring her back to the Human camp

Earl's hand gently circled the green-veined wrist...

CHAPTER IV
"Those so good Earthlings..."

Nan continued:

"The boy fled, hearing a patrol coming. Warned by the interstellar guard, Grandpa arrived like a cyclone. He was ahead of my mother, who was breaking her heels on the scrap metal and moaning; he wrapped me in his interplanetary jacket and carried me away, without paying him an atom of attention. They gave me several transfusions in a row.

"I didn't die.

"However, my 'case' was now brought before who-knows-what high authority. My grandparents were forced to place me on neutral ground, that is to say at the Mission. I will never forget the morning when I presented myself at the convent, located on the outskirts of the Globe and so miserable that, without Grandfather's subsidies, they would have been deprived of air! I had put on, like the little girls in the area, a coarse cotton dress and espadrilles, and I had on my back a little antediluvian mask, with a pig's snout.

"The superior being absent, I declared to a bewildered sister that I had no time to lose; Viola threatened to take me back and I had to finish my studies before. At least, what I heard then, not 'studies'.

" 'You will enroll me in your highest class; I have to take the exit exams in a year.'"

"The sister had just landed on Andromeda; she was English, from Shropshire! She was wringing her hands! She gave me a little dictation – hell if I knew such exercises existed – and winced at my thirty-four spelling mistakes. I asked for the books for the grown-ups – all of them, please.

" 'My child,' she sighed, weary of the struggle, 'you give them back to us if you don't use them!'

"The Mission ignored the hypno-teaching and belinography courses, so I returned to the Residence laden with grimy textbooks. I returned to the library with its harmonious lines, which smelled of Grandpa's blond tobacco and sandalwood, and there, under the table whose fringed carpet concealed me from the rest of the universe, I made contact with a scholarly science – narrow and methodical. I spent the last three weeks of vacation, God forgive me! Without combing or washing. A clever doctor prescribed me arsenic pills, so I took a handful of shiny little balls with me and chewed them like candy. In a few days, I learned a bit of French and Russian, a bit of earthly geography, a history stuffed with crusades and crazy kings, and stories of taps and spaceships crossing each other. Back at the convent, I repeated the same dictation – with only three mistakes. I was summoned to the Superior, a woman still young, with a pale and puffy face that betrayed a lack of hormones, with prominent transparent eyes, friendly frog eyes – to tell the truth, not quite human either...

" 'Well,' she said, inviting me to sit down with a gesture, 'it seems that we should accept you in the upper class, my little girl. At four years-old! Do you realize, I hope, that this is a little worrisome?'

" 'I can't help it,' I replied. 'And yourself, I think...'

"She interrupted me, quickly:

" 'Nan, I wasn't so good, and besides, in my time, we didn't hear about mutants, that's all. So you left your faculties fallow. Do you plan to report to Solar Education?'

"She looked at me for a long time, before asking me:

" 'You don't mean any harm, do you, little girl?'

" 'What do you call harm?' I asked. 'If that means I want to break things or hurt people, then of course not. But you have, on Earth, such strange laws that one doesn't know on which foot to dance.'

"She sighed and said:

" 'We are all creatures of the Good Lord. Strive to do your best. We will keep you.'

"They created, a few days later, a class for me alone...

"Now that I knew I was being watched, the idea that I was of a non-human race was slowly anchoring itself in me. It didn't bother me at first. I had to take some precautions to spare the electric lamps and not blow up the Geiger counters; it was not difficult. I spent time under the flamboyants and the pandanus, the wild gardens where the climate of Andromeda made the pink rockets of the nielloes bloom and the enormous purple bells of the aconites. This land was rich and fertile. The house was a former blockhouse, founded on a cemetery of early settlers before the establishment of crematory ovens. All those dead who had not been burned were there, I could have called them by their names – the terrible dead, throats of blood, crushed in the rockets in full flight, asphyxiated by ozonator failure, riddled with bullets in brawls, and others, frightened women under their heavy spacesuits and who, even in the great darkness, hugged their children to them.

"I thus communed with Andromeda's past.

"But did this dimension of time still exist for me? A new faculty was ripening in me; it scared me. The world now appeared to me, not through a frame of time, but in the form of radiations or waves; I could, if I wanted to, see the forgotten things or those which were barely announced. The imminence of a danger, death, the failure of an enterprise provoked nausea in me, boredom was dizzy and despair an oppression. This is how I escaped the fall of an aerolite and was able to rescue the superior from a fire that was about to be started..."

("Have you met any other mutants?" Stanley asked, briefly.)

"As far as I can tell, no. Pupils of all colors and bizarre appearances – Martians, Venusians, mestizos – frequented the Mission; they arrived by helicopter or by aerobus, sometimes by rocket, because other islets of the Astral Belt didn't have a high school, and they took off their suits at the school entrance. They were given little tunics and white veils; it was a pretty strange sight, especially when the humanoids were green or scarlet, or had three eyes or four arms. The prayer common was said. My companions were charming girls, a little obtuse and full of goodwill; I had fun scrambling their brains and poking around in their ideas, none of them could read minds or walk through walls."

("Did you see the boy from the Rocket Graveyard again?"

"Yes," she replied. "Once or twice... what does it matter?"

"That's what I wonder. Carry on, Nan.")

"The first time, he came at night to sit on the crest of the wall, astride. He had grown a lot; the artificial moons made his profile, the tips of his eyelashes and arch of his mouth gleam like silver. He told me that the human boys in the area were throwing stones at him, and that the stellar guards had sprayed the graveyard with flamethrowers. But he had dug a hole in an old mine gallery and had transported his treasure there – all sorts of used machinery parts, with which he hoped to make an engine. I proposed to him to go and see Grandpa and I promised to tell him that he had saved my life.

" 'Do you think! he exclaimed. "'For them to take my blood pressure every ten minutes and lock me up – like they locked you up! Very little for me!'

"He added, absorbing my thoughts:

" 'Those cretins of the zone! They don't even understand that they should adore me! I could, in a few years, give them everything they want: jobs, money, girls! But lo and behold, I myself come out of the under-

Globe slum, so they can't swallow it, and they bark at me like dogs of the astral militia! Pigs!'

" 'Maybe' I said, 'it is because you won't, in fact, give them any good things?'

"He stopped licking an open scratch on his wrist and looked at me with interest.

" 'You know that, do you? I've always thought that girls were precocious... I can't see anything – at least not yet clearly. I guess my parents' Earth blood was too heavy. If I want to move, it has to be concrete, and then it causes damage...'

" 'Are you happy,' I asked, 'that the militiamen burned the carcasses you demolished?'

"He laughed darkly:

" 'Demolished! Can we say it! It was the day when those minks from the zone threw their dogs at me... the most obtuse creatures after themselves! Look what they did to me!' He showed me his arm covered in a network of burst veins: 'The bone was broken in three places – I had to put it all back together, I assure you I had a fever! But now it's okay and I'll take my revenge... No,' he cried suddenly, 'you don't understand anything, you're just a stupid girl, you'll be married off to an official from Saturn or Jupiter, he will give you lots of children – and you will forget that we had wings...!'

"He jumped to the other side of the wall with inhuman lightness, while I went to offer him belladonna clusters or balls of arsenic, and I heard his laughter shiver in the night. Not a dog dared to bark! I ran to the window and shouted:

"I ' will never forget!' "

("And the second time?" Earl asked, ruthlessly.)

"Oh...! It was at the time of my departure for Earth. Ten years had passed. I was registered at two land-based universities, by correspondence, and I wondered if the presentation of a thesis, at the age of fifteen, wouldn't cause me new disagreements. Suddenly, my grandparents died, in the space of a few days, of one of these strange astral epidemics, whose names are still unknown. I was a minor – my Earth family claimed me and Andromeda sent me back... with pump! The music from the starport was playing and there were flags, I found myself quite stupid with my skimpy black dress, under my spacesuit.

"As I climbed the ladder of the spacecraft, a young native mechanic, one of the crawling ones who serve in the astronautical relays, pretended to want to rush towards me... he was pushed back by the guards. Rather roughly, he fell face down on the stones..."

(Nan licked her lips with a dry tongue – saw again the beautiful convulsed features, spattered with almost green blood...)

"Yes," she said, "I think it was that boy..."

("Then, Nan?")

"Then," she said wearily, thinking it really was a strange wedding night – a third-degree interrogation – "then it was Earth – and those so good Earthlings...

"Because you're really good, aren't you, Earl? And virtuous, and prudent... only, you have a terrible inferiority complex. It seems inadmissible to you that an inhabitant of Earth juggles with electromagnetism or composes sonatas at the age of five! But I'm still anticipating. Two pieces of news were waiting for me when I landed – my father had perished in an inglorious shipwreck – and it was Viola who was waiting for me at the starport. Horrible, slouched... God knows what she had done with her tea-rose complexion, she reeked of whiskey and complained. She hadn't yet received her pension! It was claimed that Nick Nangis had scuttled his lunar freighter! Then she remembered that I had learned that she had decided to sell me to the first bidder or to some Barnum.

"A decree that forbade exhibiting mutants on the boards saved me from the worst. Viola never ceased to reproach me for it. If only I'd taken the trouble to be pretty! I could have looked like Venus, like Cleopatra – and I was just a pale little girl! No matter how much I explained to her that the face and body of a mutant are stabilized from the first decade, she didn't want to hear and dragged me to beauty salons. They kicked her out, politely, because she didn't want to pay, she offered me as a subject for experiments!

"In the meantime, I was looking for work. My college degrees from Andromeda weren't worth much. I was a cashier in an oil consortium, assistant to a shady beautician, I would have done housework if the employment office hadn't found me too frail. I gave lessons in literature and Latin. My earnings barely covered the rent of a filthy hovel and Viola's daily alcohol ration. She took to drugs and cursed the ungrateful girl for whom she'd lost her youth and her beauty. She wasn't even sure that I was really her daughter – there was a lot of traffic going on at the station's genetic labs! At nights, I made music that I tried to sell, and an Astral Belt memorabilia book. I adopted the particular wave of Andromeda and recorded it, such as it was, with the anguish weighing on its globe, its isolation, the struggle of men lost in the void, their excessive desires and their failings. It was hard and raw, it was a shred of living flesh, torn from humanity. The manuscript was, of course, rejected by a hundred publishers... 'You never wrote that!' 'Such things are not possible – it's too realistic, too awful.' 'It's too romantic!' I asked for reports of the reading committees and they made a collection of bewildering nonsense.

"At the fiftieth publisher, a pale reader under the harness and who had formerly composed a *Handbook of Living on the Planets* offered me outright to make some alterations to my manuscript. We would cosign the work together. 'Me first of course, for I have a name – yours after, but you would also be in the credit...' "

"I was fifteen, I refused. I have repented of it more than once. Other proposals were more direct... And everywhere the same refrain: 'You say you wrote that? All alone? It's impossible.'

"I took part in a contest for a stellar drama which guaranteed the anonymity of the candidates. The prize was one million credits... One fine morning, I nearly fainted with joy while buying a newspaper: my manuscript had won the prize, its style evoking that of a world leader had misled the jury. But, the same evening, the jurors had learned of their blunder and they changed their minds: I received nothing at all. A caustic secretary, who was responsible for dismissing me, explained the matter to me very well. 'You understand,' he said, 'if you start making Shakespeare or Faulkner, you're a public danger. We cannot afford masterpieces. Besides, you're too young, perfect success is characteristic of the old or the dead.'

"With each failure, Viola made terrible scenes for me...

"From then on, I ghosted for comic book writers, copying music, adapting silly lyrics to even sillier music. I was badly paid, or not at all. 'But anyway, my little one,' they told me, 'admit that you plagiarized that!' I was simply robbed by a commercial printer who took my two books of *Astral Adventures*, threw them out in the market and never got back to me.

"Do you remember, Earl, the last four fairly painful Earth winters? I was coming from this hothouse, Andromeda. My dresses and coats, ten times older, were no longer presentable and hardly warmed me. One evening, returning empty-handed from an errand to work, I lost a glove in the street. I wept with rage and desolation!"

"Why didn't you just search for it? Earl asked harshly. "Or sue these people?"

"How?" asked Nan, "I didn't have enough to pay for my aerobus! In addition, upon the denunciation of one of my employers, I had been summoned by the militia. I was told, without hesitation, that in a year or two, 'all my peers would be reclassified in the norm' and I already knew what that meant. I was given a KZ mutant card, and it was that night that Viola jumped down my throat."

She passed an uncertain hand over her forehead, suddenly covered in large drops of sweat, and wobbled.

"Excuse me, Earl," she said, "but I've little earthly patriotism. For me, this is Earth: endless winter, mud, wet snow, closed doors, rude police officers and a drunken Viola. Now you know all about me, and I'm at my wit's end. You understand, us non-humans..."

Nan never quite remembered the moments that followed. Stanley lavished almost feminine care on her; he laid her on the bunk, wrapped her in a soft vicuna plaid, asked for an electric blanket and some coffee. He gently caressed the closed eyelids over the terrible eyes and thought she was finally asleep. Then he left.

The experts had gathered in the captain's cabin. On the desk were piled the films of the Astral Belt.

"It's boring," said Karpov.

"Even more for Stanley than for us," sneered Borelli.

Earl looked at them, distractedly: "I called you," he said, "so that we could share my data. The sooner we know where we are, the better."

"Let's come up with a working hypothesis," Vere suggested. "A quantum of energy was released; it's a question of knowing for what purpose and not by what means. Over to you, Karpov!"

"Let us first eliminate the absurd," said the atomist. "Andromeda is of no interest to an attacker from our system. Too far, too small. Of course, we can always assume an outside attack, for all we know! But that would be an assertion to prove. Consequently, it seems – and the study of the epicenter of the cataclysm corroborates this hypothesis – that the blow was struck from inside the station."

"Do you know," Borelli asked pointedly, "the usual population of satellites? A few minor specialists, a good contingent of manual workers and, to hold it all together, a handful of interplanetary guards. The general level hardly exceeds that of F3 astrophysicists..."

"Do you know," Vere went on, in the same tone, "an energy that can bend microsteel and crumble quartz rocks in a third of a second? On an asteroid? Not me!"

"But," Karpov sighed, "regretfully, that's your business, Stanley! I'm sorry, yes, but where are the experiments on hyperspace warping? Was an isolated attempt possible?"

"Well," Earl said, nervously cracking the knuckles of his hands, beautiful and long as a woman's, "nothing stands in the way, in the current, brilliant state of science. We know that, in principle, reversibility from one dimension to another's possible. However, I can assure you that no practical application has been given to these theories: it would make too much of a mess to begin with."

"The mess," Karpov observed, "is what we saw on those tapes."

"I give you the Federal Labs version."

"That means, by civilized people, but what if there were others? Reckless experimenters who wouldn't be frightened by a hecatomb? Would they know... I mean, does such an experiment require unlimited resources? Could an organization other than the Solar Federation undertake it?"

"Anyone could, if he possessed certain knowledge, or rather certain abilities, which fortunately are rare," answered Stanley with great clarity. "The theory is in the public domain; it is only the application. You know that great discoveries are sometimes the sum of immense labor, seconded by chance. As far as I know of this matter, the work has already been done; the counterpart which can also be called genius, remains..."

"Let's think," protested Karpov who didn't take offense at anything. "Aren't we going beyond our thoughts here, Stanley? Let's admit the hypothesis of a maverick scientist who would've worked on his own behalf on an artificial satellite and made a discovery of which federal organization were so far incapable. But was this man... this being – we don't even know what form of intelligence it is – unaware? He was running a monstrous risk; he must have known that he was going to sacrifice millions of lives, entire globes perhaps, and that he would be the first to perish... How could such intelligence, such genius, be reconciled with such lack of foresight?"

"Risk," Earl said coldly, and they felt for the first time that evening that he was weighing his words, "risk is our common lot. Any interplanetary freighter pilot goes for broke, all the more so when the freighter is worn out and the pilot drunk. You also know that once the probability of individual death is admitted, the rest lose its importance. I can imagine pretty well who this madman could be..."

"Only half a madman," said Borelli.

And Vere said: "A monstrous egotist!"

Karpov dropped: "A fanatic, perhaps?"

Stanley shrugged, thinking:

Try to imagine it yourself, because I am getting tired of this. You think my job is easy? You people are only dealing with harmless organic matter, reactions and other trifles...

But he only said:

"You will be annoyed when it is uncovered."

Vere asked, worried: "Do you seriously think that he's going to...?"

"To do what?" asked Earl. "To blow up the globes or cross the continuum? I'd rather not think about it. The being who triggered this experiment broke down obstacles that have held back humanity since the year 2000. He is undoubtedly a genius, but he is also – certainly – the greatest criminal of all time. Now remember, if he survived, which I'm not sure about, he holds enormous power in his hands. I don't doubt that he would use it again."

CHAPTER V
Nan dreaming

I didn't tell him everything. I couldn't reveal the essential – nor what constitutes the secret of others...

On the narrow berth, in the spacecraft heading towards the unknown, Nan was dreaming. But it was not an extraordinary dream. Formerly the Atlanteans, from Earth's long ago past, could "remember" the future. Nan had reclaimed this ancient power, and had sharpened it. She had sworn "never to forget."

Earl got me to assure him that there were only those three encounters... On a human level, of course. I don't know what cycle to attach this one to...

It was towards the end of my stay at the Mission. I was becoming cumbersome, and the nuns could no longer take care of me. One night (I lived mostly at night), I was in the bathroom, a prosaic place if there ever was one, and I was refilling my hot water bottle. I heard someone call my name, but I saw no one. I ran down the hall – I opened the doors and cupboards. Everything was as usual. But a cold laugh burst out, I didn't know from where.

"Don't look," said the voice of the one I still called the "wild boy." "You won't see me – and it's better for you. I am not presentable."

"Where are you then?"

"At the popular clinic, on a pool table. They've anesthetized me, you understand – so I take advantage of this to escape."

"They've caught you, after all!"

"And how, the bastards! They put sleeping pills in my dish of rust – I slept like a beast and woke up under the hypnotist. But all of that is trifling. Listen, Nan, I came to warn you: get the hell out!"

"Wh... what?"

"Sorry, I forgot you don't speak a man's language! I said: leave Andromeda, embark for anywhere, take off... They've finally realized that we are a danger to them – us, the mutants of the four dimensions and the three realms, who are born with skills superior to these earthworms, with vision of the past and memory of the future... And the best thing is that they don't anticipate anything, they simply fear our primacy...! A primacy, damn it!

Get the hell out, Nan! If they ever catch you, you don't know how awful it is!"

"But they didn't kill you..." I said, my lips frozen.

"No, not yet. I would prefer it if they had. They got it into their heads that they could 'bring us back into the norm' because we are so human! So, they first submitted me to hypnotists, to ram their short ideas into my head, and then a little stupid doctor noticed that I was cheating! I answered their thoughts, of course! So they X-rayed me from every angle, they concluded that there was in my medulla oblongata – or in my cortex – an additional center, which they will try to remove later."

I think I shouted: "Oh no!"

"Oh yes!" he parodied faithfully. "They believe that, this way I'll forget everything and become a useful social element – a rocket mechanic, or something like that.

"But I'm not as dumb as they think, do you hear me? I myself operated on a cortex transplant – and when they have scraped my cranial cells, there will remain in my body a shred of living tissue, a germ... Oh! I know, adaptation will be long, I will seem stupid, but so much the better, since that's what they are asking for! That's also why I contacted you, Nan. Any operation has its risks... Don't forget! Can you hear me? Do not forget! You're the only mutant from Andromeda that they haven't been able to spot, shrink..."

"But," I said, appalled, less by the news than by the anguish concealed in this cry, "why are they so mean to us? We didn't do anything to them!"

"Not yet. But we could..."

"How can they know...?"

"What about Atlantis, my dear?"

"What, Atlantis?"

"Look, Nan, I've got no time to waste, I think they're starting to mess with my brain. You will eventually learn how our island perished: humanity has retained an unnamed anguish about it. Know only that we can do evil as well as terrible good... The terrible fusion of our faculties, which reach all planes, can cause the fission of an atom as well as the bursting of a star. We haven't tried it, in this life – not yet, but it will come. In this sense, Earthlings are right to tremble... Oh, Nan!"

The panting voice died away – and there was silence. I stretched out my faculties in vain, my invisible antennae, to feel the void. Suddenly, a heart-rending cry came to me – such that I suddenly remembered that Arno was still only a child.

"Oh! Nan! They make me suffer! We will meet again and we will take revenge, Nan!"

This is how the only friend of my childhood was suddenly snatched away from me. The boy in mechanic's blue that I saw later on the starport looked nothing like the little faun dancing in the moonlight.

Nor, of course, the one I met on "our island" – in a scary past...

Because I have descended into the past. I have always kept my promises. To understand everything and forget nothing, I had to develop my mutant faculties to their limit. At least, the ones I suspected...

I believe that this faculty, incorrectly called "time travel", ancient humanity possessed it, but they lost it, following who knows what cataclysm... Hence, no doubt, the notion of sin and death. Because, as far as I know, death does not exist, and the Ancients also knew it: one does not die, when one is in possession of an indelible, invariable and open past, shining with a thousand colors, and a fluctuating and multiple future, made with the shards of the present.

A human being moves every hour on this road; he is simply more attracted to the time sequences where his material body is there to receive him. Because in this closed universe, nothing is lost and nothing is created, and sooner or later, through millions of various combinations, the atoms of our bodies, which seek and attract each other, are reunited, until the purification is complete. This is what some have called reincarnation. The rest of us have another name for this: stopovers...

One night, I was lying, as I am now, on a bunk in the dormitory. My companions were sleeping. A little Madonna by Bernardino, for whom I had taken a liking to the point of borrowing her sharp features and her linen hair, smiled next to the blue window. Closing my eyes, I let myself slide limply into the void. I'd hung up, in passing, some pictures of Andromeda, the history lesson of the day... Then, I began a vertical fall and... when I think about it, I still shudder! I understand now what we risk by falling so far. Half of the madmen in the wings are "fallen dreamers" who couldn't come back up...

But I wanted to know, didn't I?

So it happened that I was no longer Anne Nangis, but another me. I was no longer on an artificial satellite, but on a royal planet, with vast horizons. I was standing on a promontory of blue opal, and in the sky there were two moons.

At my feet rustled the original ocean. Just by its smell, I knew it was younger. Creatures of strange shapes, phosphorescent milled within it. As I turned slowly, I discovered behind me a valley full of incredible vegetation, of immense flowers which opened and closed, like shells...

Although the plants were gigantic and luscious, and the sea limitless, I didn't feel overwhelmed by their majesty. I, too, was taller, stronger; an intense life, a rich sap circulated in my veins, and I knew – and I could do – brilliant, inconceivable things, things that no one had realized before. I commanded each of my muscles and I ignored weakness, humiliation and fear.

I straightened up and felt a cool, shiny mantle of blue-black hair move down to my legs, and my shadow loomed on the white cliff, a fairly slender, flexible and free waist and long folded wings... I was going to cry of pleasure!

They were not the feathered wings of an angel, but vast and powerful membranes which, when at rest, creased finely, like the wings of a silver bat. I raised my hand to caress them, and behold: my long efficient fingers were webbed at their base, and I realized that I could fly and swim perfectly. My grip on this world was ideal.

Although the place was deserted, my refined hearing perceived multiple currents that I knew how to read. A tide: human and animal thoughts, and even the deaf and powerful cogitations of plants. Two stars lit up above my forehead; they crowned with undulating antennae the mental diadem that humanity would later lose.

Never in my present life had I experienced such intoxication. It was good to live; the planet I walked on was young, and I belonged to a triumphant world; on the valley filled with vast camellias like cups, with azaleas the color of flesh, a luminescence betrayed the presence of a big city. The image of the Megalopolis immediately fixed itself in my brain: buildings and avenues of opal and onyx, which were to be the material of the country, pyramids storing light and heat, mysterious zodiacal wheels...

The civilization of this island (because it was an island) radiated. However, not all of its inhabitants were winged or provided with antennae, for I saw the crowd walking and not flying, and individuals communicating in melodious language. White silver or azure, what was their country? And my own name? These notions came back to me slowly, they emerged from my subconscious, like the vestiges of a vanished continent.

I knew that my country was powerful and that it dominated this planet, still in the darkness of a barbaric age. Our ascendancy, based on science, was limitless; like the moderns, we had lightning and the atom, we exalted plants by virtue of hormones and obtained giant species among the sacred animals.

I learned that my name was Atlantea (an Atlantic name, distorted by euphony), and that I was not the only one of my race nor of my time. Incomprehensibly, these facts constituted the most terrible of dangers. My fellows were brilliant and hard beings, of a pitiless perception and whose wills knew no obstacles.

The most well-known, those connected with my destiny, presented themselves to my mind as disembodied voices – musical phrases. I recognized the sweet marine melody, a little cold, which was called Neor; then a rhythmic wave, olfactory as well as auditory, rose to attack my nerves – I knew the patterns scattered over many female beings, harps and cymbals, waves of musk and rot – they signified Love and Death and were called Queen Nellare, the Dispenser of Perfumes... But a violent screech, sparkling like a blade of crystal, then hit me in the chest and I staggered: this last comer was called the Sword that Sings...

"Grandpa," asked an eight-year-old Nan perched on her grandfather's knee, "was there a time when men had wings?"

He fixed her with his vague eye.

"Physically, you mean? Or do you take this as a symbol?"

"In my dreams, I see beings with bat wings. Often."

"Paleontologists admit it," he said cautiously. "They even place a race of flying lizard-men around the middle of the Tertiary..."

"It's not about lizards," Nan decided. "My Earthlings are beautiful and civilized; they live on an island, the ground is made of opal and quartz and dug caves, all in mauve and blue stalactites. The whole island is excavated in depth; it looks like a honeycomb. The sun sets on the right, and at night there are two moons..."

"God forgive me!" cried Sir Neptune. "Have you ever read Plato? A work called *Critias*?"

"Let me tell you, it doesn't exist on Andromeda."

The sea god cradled her for a moment, in silence, then he began:

"Once there was an island called Atlantis..."

That, thought Nan, I already knew. It remained to learn how this world perished.

It was an island with a planetary civilization, based on astronomy, and subject to a matriarchal order. It seemed that the rest of Earth lived in the beginnings of the Quaternary, an obscure panic often evoked the external darkness where thrived simian humanoids. I don't even know if my Atlanteans were really human: their wings and webbed extremities make you think. Did they come from a more evolved planet? Or was it an intermediate species between man and bird, which was already beginning to decline?

In any case, it was a people in full decadence − of a mind-blowing, paranormal civilization, of an exquisite and cruel refinement. I believe that these beings had all the vices and that they played with obscure or forgotten forces to excite their already jaded senses. There was much talk of the Ancients, of their science and machines, the use of which had been forgotten, and others, which were used without discernment. It was lightning in the hands of blind children, on a young planet, which had its own future and its own laws.

However, these Ancients who had been wise had left to their descendants the means to dominate this world in peace. A system traced long ago still ruled the doomed island; a strict framework of physically dissimilar castes, no army, but a militia, to maintain internal order, squadrons to contact the rest of the globe, and a College of Priests to lead. As far as I could understand, these theocrats were no longer scholars, but mages. The pyramid was at its summit a hereditary queen and an elected conjurer. The last of the name was called Atlantea.

My two lives had nothing in common, not even me. The strong and supple, winged and shiny girl of Atlantis had nothing to do with the current runt of Andromeda. My real life, which I was able to tell Earl, was a dull but continuous life − the other, bright and terrible, presented itself as a series of fragmentary images. I plunged into it like an earthquake, a landslide, a hot maelstrom.

My dreams did not observe any chronology; they got tangled up, overlapped, so that today, when I try to put them in order, I am forced to classify them in "happy days" and "hours of dread". I believe that the first preceded the others. I believe that I have been happy for years, in the midst of threats and perils.

At that time, I lived near a village apparently called Dea, a small circular temple of rose quartz. The walls shaped by the Ancients displayed idyllic frescoes, cherry blossoms and a lotus creek. The vault was an Astral Stadium, bounded by the Milky Way. Except that the corollas were as big as basins and the scents palpable, I could have imagined myself at Nausicaa.

I had a large garden for my games. It sloped gently towards the ocean and I was never to cross its enclosure of azaleas. The village was nestled in the hollow of the Happy Valley; at dusk, I heard the voices of other young girls singing, forming circles, and I knew that I raised my voice halfway, it would cover, like a bronze bell, any tone – gold or crystal. But I shouldn't sing.

Once, while playing ball – still at Nausicaa – I dropped it on the other side of the enclosure.

I couldn't go and get it.

I had no family. The old priest Isides came to teach me the names of the stars and the easy myths, like that of the virgin whom the Swan loved (and their progeny has wings and webbed feet) or that of the giant, the color of lightning. But at night the warm walls spoke, insinuating voices poured science into my numbed mind, and I learned things horrible or magnificent – the coexistence of various modes of time, and the Sixth Space which encloses them all, or the one can walk as in an orchard where one can touch everything and pick everything; the interdependence of the stars and the art of charming monsters. I also learned that there were black and creeping dangers; I believe that the beings of my species, carrying within them their own morality and the germ of Truth, could be killed, with impunity, as long as they had not reached the plenitude of the revelation – and their fifteenth year, because they weren't quite human. But an ancient law said that Atlantis would exist "as long as there were Conjurers". Each time an elected Virgin was about to die, she designated the latitude under which her younger sister would be born, and signs of recognition, and the royal guards scoured the country.

Also the cities and hamlets, which had the honor to arbitrate a predestined child, concealed her, piously. Such was my fate.

However, I almost died of a natural danger, and it was Neor who saved me...

This happened during a festive season, perhaps even at the time of the accession to the throne of Queen Nellare II. Surveillance around me was weakening; the hypnotic barriers were very old and, at times, crossed by waves of rare violence. A few stages away, the Megalopolis gave itself up to feasts, orgies, combats of monsters and gladiators. It seems that even then, the crown princess liked to use old mechanics, to magnetize the wretches thrown into the arena or to cause sunspots by currents of radiation. The seasons were strangely shifted and annual migrations of insects took on strange proportions.

One night, I was awakened by a flight of giant moths which had overflowed into the Happy Valley. I called – no voice answered me, my thoughts dulled against a wall several leagues advancing, wings shedding their pollen, soft brown bodies pressing together in a rustle of rings and chitin and were about to expire on the stormy sea. The air was saturated with a bland smell of flowers and corruption.

I groped my way out of the temple and ended up in a valley already half full of beating shapes; my foot sank into living magma, throbbing ocellus blocked my path and I was suffocating... I managed to extricate myself from this trap and flew, on my still weak wings, over a plain where light whirlwinds passed. I saw, without taking fright, that I had moved away from the sacred prison; the agitation of the moths still blurred the landscape – the smallest insect measured two cubits – but I distinguished under my feet the white manes of the waves, an enormous scintillation, the stars which were reflected in the sea. A human voice called out to me and, leaning forward, I saw the most beautiful thing in the world: a slender sail, almost lying down to leeward, and a slender dancing boat.

Like a figurehead, a man towered over the abyss. Everything about his figure, his golden profile, his slender hands, called for comparisons of flight, of momentum – but he had no wings. This detail, despite his obvious physical strength (he was driving his skiff in the middle of a double storm), gave him an appearance of vulnerability. I had never seen him so charming... I spread my wings and sniffed him a little high; he's laughing:

"I didn't think," he said, "that Dea's moths had dream faces! Descend: the wind will carry you out to sea."

The starry antennae lit up on my forehead as soon as I stepped aboard the nave. No doubt the navigator was aware of these illusions, for he bowed so far as to kiss the ground, but his voice, when he spoke, was still stamped with irony:

"You must forgive me for my mistake, noble princess," he said, "I thought you were in danger; I see now that it was not so. But I have come so far! I am Neor, son of Isides and Navarch of the Queen. I didn't know that a *real* Atlantean lived here..."

The very deck of the boat was strewn with expiring moths. I shivered. I said:

"My wings are weak, I fought with these monsters and I'm tired..."

"My boat is only a nutshell, but I have carpets in the steerage, you can rest there, if you deign."

"I lost my sandals and the ground is strewn with shells..."

"I'll carry you."

He was already approaching, arms outstretched, when I shouted:

"Don't step on my shadow! You'll die..."

This is how he understood that, off the Happy Valley, he had met She whose very shadow kills. The Chosen One. The Conjurer who speaks to the Disembodied. He didn't look away, and I liked the way he yanked off and threw his coat at my feet. Our hands did not touch. But the sea breeze enveloped us and my fragrant hair swept over his mouth and his nostrils. Like the sponge soaked in myrrh offered to prisoners condemned to death.

In the category of "terrible dreams", most often, I found myself at the point that I dreaded the most. No doubt my nervous cells had been impressed by this moment and the trace of it remained through the ages. Invariably, I was plunged into a cataclysm – a raging earthquake, tidal waves invading the hills, onyx columns and marble altars crumbling. Raising my eyes towards a black or purple sky, I saw a star that filled the horizon and ignited the darkness. The huge profile of the satellite stood upright on my eyes – I saw it dazzling white, then purple, finally black... My astronomical knowledge told me that Earth had drawn one of its moons into its orbit. The disk, hideously split, rained down its shards in chaos...

For the first time, I was going to appear to my people. The foundations of the world were shaken, but, in an immense creek, in the very heart of the Megalopolis, the crowd laughed and gorged themselves on blood, the octopuses hugged and trampled human prey. Years then separated me from the Valley Fortunately and from the Ocean, I was no longer the free and flexible girl who flew over the waves, but a priestess sheathed in gems, like an idol. A nacre mask and make-up clad my face, elongated my eyes slanted with antimony, and my mouth, tinged with anemone juice, was bleeding like a wound. A tiara of emeralds in the shape of a wheel bruised my temples... I was in solidarity with this crowd, these crimes and its majesty...

Internally too, I was different. Not corrupted, like these people, but burnt, petrified. I had renounced everything that made this Earth so sweet, and I knew that name Island was going to perish. I had never sung with the young girls of Dea, I had exchanged my shore and my temple for a prison of jade... The hatreds which I had excited, the monstrous jealousies, insulted the sky... I was the Chosen Virgin, She Who Speaks to the Dead, the Salvation of Atlantis. And Atlantis was ending...

No doubt, I had, by my renunciations and my pride, fulfilled the Dispenser of Perfumes, for the queen, in her violet veils and her orb of musk, prostrated herself on my passage. Her mouth whispered to me: "Be blessed, Atlantea! Whoever insulted you is going to die."

I was left and distracted, a jewel of the tiara hurt my temple. The queen added again, as if she were sipping black wine: "I caused his wings to break. He will die at your feet."

...In the arena, a small octopus was gorged on the viscera of a human child. I looked at Nellare with keen attention: she was everything I hated. Later, I would find shards of her triumphant femininity in the beings who would hurt me the most – Viola, Una Vere... But Nellare would remain for me the synthesis of evil, with her bluish skin, the nocturnal sheet of her hair and her body so visibly modelled in a single drawing... Her essence was opposed to mine, as matter is irreducible to spirit. She was the queen of this island, that the one she was going to deliver to torture was her brother, of the same blood, and whom she would have to marry according to the laws. Had he hurt her? And me? What insult was that? Horrible ties united the three of us, but I sat up with wild pride – yes, I was guilty in their eyes only of having foreseen this end of the world, of warning! In vain. Nellare and Hellemar, the two sovereigns of my island, had remained deaf to my opinions, one hated me and the other... Suddenly, I felt an unspeakable shame. More than filthy: beyond unhealthy...

The other had loved me and he had wanted to possess me.

He was going to die.

It was at this moment in my dream that there was a jolt, so strong that everything was mixed up. The columns of the circus crumbled, the monsters escaped from the vivariums and a torrent of bodies devastated the bleachers. Falling at my knees, Nellare embraced me: "Anything you want!" she moaned. "My crown, my power and him – if you want! But pray! Speak to Heaven! It will listen to you – maybe!"

I pushed her away in disgust and my outstretched wings knocked her down. I left the crowd, in a flight terribly hampered by the weather variations, and I flew over the boxes and the arena. Of course, I had no idea of the prisons of Nellare, but I glimpsed the most horrible sights... Splitting the air, rolled by hurricanes, I arrived at a trapdoor, all smooth angles, of a geometry that was not of this world, as the feelings of this crowd did not belong to an ordered universe.

I fled the smell of the beast exhaling from the crowd and the musk of the Dispenser of Perfumes. Beneath her feet, a vertiginous staircase had been dug…

(At this hour, I was already the terrified earthling child who, in millennia, would flee in horror from all the grip of flesh and release blood, in the darkness).

Sometimes, I woke up at this moment, for good. I came back to life, smug, ready to scream. Sitting on my bed, my skinny arms hugging my knees, I would feed myself a thousand times. But mutants don't die so easily, do they, Arno? Night was closing in and I found myself before the octopus pit.

It was a kind of well, in the shape of a funnel, with a jade rock as a backdrop. (We see such landscapes in nightmares.) A partition of large selenium mesh – resistant to what degree? – protected a kind of altar. The wells teemed with atrocious shapes, tentacles, suction cups, horny beaks; and an eye that shone with atrocious cruelty. Ten or a hundred monsters stirred, heaved themselves up, threw their slimy limbs against the grating; sometimes, passing between the meshes in a burning jet, they reached a human silhouette, nailed to the rock.

In a face of silver, dark eyes lived alone. They said to me:

"Here you are, Atlantea. I knew you would come. Do you think I couldn't die – before? I just had to release my blood. But I waited for you."

This moment of horror was followed by a fall into nothingness, probably an earthquake stronger than the previous ones and punctuated by explosions. A brief half-conscious sequence showed me the rim of the collapsed well, the unspeakable remains of the supernatant monsters…I must have struck during this time, burned, disintegrated, because I still held a smoking weapon in my hands, but I was sitting on the floor and I think I was crying.

The head of the condemned man rested on my knees and I was frozen with repulsion, anger and pity. He might not be dead, but his wings were hanging down, badly grazed, and his chest was scorched with corrosive venom. Here and there green blood oozed out – that of a vegetable creature. The dark eyes opened. I met an icy smile.

….Later, much later, we fled into the underground passages on which the Great Island rested; there were only grottos and caverns, inside which an interplanetary rocket would have looked like a toy, walls of jasper and stalactites of moonstone. Huge black lakes furiously licked the quartz shores. Abyssal monsters, which my race had driven back into the darkness, held out their flat heads and their blind muzzles. Colossal toads who had lived for centuries in the thickness of the rocks, perceiving the outside world only through the taste buds of their dermis, tried to leave their asylum... but in vain, in vain! Like the luminous civilization of the heights, this dark world was doomed.

A hundred times, a thousand times, I would have liked to close my eyes, fall into this white sand and sleep, so bruised were my limbs, so drunk was I with fatigue. But I couldn't. I wasn't the only one looking for an impossible salvation. The being who fled with me, and whom I was obliged to support, whose wounds I stanched and washed, thank heaven, was not Neor. I had the consoling idea of having saved Neor by sending him far away, to the other city of Earth, on an ocean perhaps preserved.

The one who accompanied me was my worst enemy. I knew he had committed monstrous crimes; only this cataclysm preserved him from a just punishment. However, I had saved her from a fate worse than death. He was very tall, his Atlantean wings hung broken at his shoulders and hampered his walk; he too seemed, like the rest of this vanished world, made of imperishable materials – marble, onyx – and his eyes were nocturnal lakes, but all this beauty emanated a presence of death.

Several times we had to face the saurians. The one I called Hellemar – or the Singing Sword – had picked up my broken sword from which a light sprang... (Wasn't that like a modern disintegrator?). But it happened that an unpredictable leap of brontosaurus snatched this weapon from him and I had to intervene in the melee, in a cerebral and rapid way. Sometimes we were so weary that we took turns sleeping on the sand, while tremors tossed the darkness and Death howled. He who was valiant was not sure that the whole Earth had not been damaged and that they would not roll together in their prison of the rich, through an icy space. Often I was forced to stop because my feet were bleeding and I forgot, in my haste, to command my blood vessels...

But more often still, I had to close the wounds of his wings. The membranes were cut at the level of the clavicles and hung without force; they would never come together again to carry this great body. I then felt like carrying out their complete ablation, but the terrible dark eyes stared at me and I dared not strike.

"You think I'll never fly again," he observed once.

"Oh! I say, how important is it? If you wanted here, once."

"And that would give you a sense of superiority, wouldn't it?"

"That, my little one, I don't need to see you ready..."

"I say, you are pride itself."

"This is a subject that we have tackled without success."

"But anyway," he cried, "are you finally going to forget who you are and who I am? So you need more than an end of the world? Yes, you are the chosen one and I am a wretch, crawling in the mire of my vices. But what after? What does this get you ahead of? What has your sky done for you more than for us?"

"He gave me the foolishness to set you free," I replied sourly. "And also the occasion."

"You repent, don't you...?"

With each fall in Time, these disputes resumed, with increased violence. We were both bleeding from it... I admit that, at times, I was tempted to abandon this recalcitrant, wounded man and continue on my way alone, in the night. He approached me:

"You sent him back in time with his squadrons. The rest didn't matter to you. Perish Atlantis, if Neor survives!"

I protested:

"My warnings missed no one. No more to your sister than to you or to your senate. Neor was the only one to listen to me."

"Yes, Neor was perfect! But don't be afraid, he'll be back here at the first sign of disaster – I know Neor's species well enough! His people amputated their wings to be closer to a suffering humanity. He will return, because this island perishes – and you with it..."

"It has nothing to do with my fate."

There was an unfortunate softness in that retort, so my opponent propped himself up on one elbow. He was stretched out on the sand, at the edge of an underground lake, and his dead wings covered him. A resin torch smoked in the darkness.

"Nobody has anything to do with anybody's fate. If you allow me, O Chosen One, it is indeed stellar selfishness that you have reproached us with! It makes each being a closed microcosm and this conception, according to you, will be the basis of our crimes and our loss..."

"Selfishness alone would not have diverted the comets from their course. It took your insane experiments..."

"We only wanted to vibrate in contact with the universe."

"Shut up," I interrupted him. "You are insufferable, you are generalizing. Ah! You can boast of being truly human!"

He looked at me amidst the flickering of his antennae – and I found in his dull pupils, which had seen so many things, which had closed under the influx of too great a sweetness or of a frightful voluptuousness, something the gleaming gaze under the eyelashes of little Arno who leapt over the cemetery of rockets...

"I admire your pride," he resumed. "Here is probably the only force intact in the general collapse. You never cried, moaned in pain or longing! You are unaware of the burn of the intertwined bodies, their sweat and their sanity. However, hear me, Chosen One, a force pushed you to deliver me. In your eyes, I was that necessary evil: Life."

"I hope," I say haughtily, "that at the end of this cataclysm, you will have time to procreate a dozen children with a passing monkey. You could not do without it and nothing would be definitively lost for Earth."

He closed his eyes and said with disarming sweetness:

"You are a monster, aren't you?"

I was there in my lived memories, when my grandparents from Andromeda went out one by one, like flames that one blows out, and they are buried in the garden of pandanus. The new governor of the station summoned me to present me with a radiogram which claimed me, in the name of my family, on Earth. I was very distraught. I had loved Sir Neptune and Grandma very much and I felt dully that I would never find the freedom and indulgence that I enjoyed in their shadow. After all, I said to myself, Earth is our motherland, to us Earthlings! The date of my departure was fixed.

However, before that, I tried to contact the "wild boy" who was no longer wild.

I learned that he had been discharged from hospital, that he was physically "doing very well", and that he was working as a mechanic at the station. And also that his name was Arno Heller, a name which then meant absolutely nothing. Only, I believe that I had lost my present life, I still saw him under the aspect of the statue with the broken wings, of the big black and white lily. I came to the station under the pretext of registering my bags and I surprised him – yes – in the arms of a monkey.

The scenery was worth the scene; it was a miserable shack where half-breeds from check-in and passing pilots took a glass of deadly Venusian alcohol, or a jug of Martian seghir, on a counter. Fiber cement walls, a tin roof, a few poisons at the bar, a slot machine and a stereo-music device. The benches were gleaming from the backdrops of interplanetary suits and the chrysanthemum-headed Martian serving had heard just about every 'good story' about the solar system. There were also waitresses – here's why...

Some pilots were returning from a multi-year flight; they looked like the sailors of yesteryear, capable of taking a sea lion for a mermaid. I learned later that the establishment had rooms upstairs.

A minion told me where I would find Arno Heller at the Martian's. He allowed himself a sidelong smile, which I disliked, so I ventured into the vacant lots, with my latest interstellar suit and my first high-heeled shoes. I forgot to mention that, for the past few years, I now looked like a long, thin Earthling ingenue. And then I was the granddaughter of Sir Neptune, that is to say, on Andromeda, someone famous... The navvies followed me with admiring glances.

In front of the bar door, I projected my antennae. Sure enough, Arno Heller was there – and he looked quite like his black and white self. The girl who kept him company was a very ordinary crossbreed, what is commonly called a bitch. They were upstairs and I prefer not to say in what posture.

I knew (in theory) Nellare – and all the vices, and all the enchantments of Atlantis – so I fled...

I still remember the laughter of the navvies.

CHAPTER VI
Circular Nightmare

The second stage of destiny – the ineluctable event against which we stumble, because it was prepared from a long way off – was this circular, or rather its disappearance.

Its dizzying course had carried the *Daredevil* to the limit where Earth stereograms could reach it directly; it was therefore going to receive the last mail before it landed. In the radio set with compressed-air partitions, a fairly simple depository collected news and belinos. It all came through the usual channel – photosphere radiation and irradiated photoelectric cells. They impressed the display board: a screen fifty centimeters-wide and extended by a ten-centimeter microsteel cage. The screen reproduced each wave in seven copies, the last of which remained projected, while others fell into the cage. The copy in preview remained on the board until other news arrived and it was all perfectly synchronized.

At the time Circular SZ 928,000 entered, the post was held by two radio officers: Anton Freade, Specialist 1st Class, and his deputy, Walter Cross, a rookie. A third person arrived who, in fact, should not have been there: Dr. Borelli. She was going to send her report to Earth or something like that. Of course, her presence was not regulation and only underlined the confidence of the crew in all that touched the members of the brain trust.

The lights on the call board came on when the doctor crossed the threshold of the post. What followed was commented on in various ways. It seemed that, as soon as the first lines of the text appeared on the screen, one of the officers (but which one?) tried to break the protective ramp. A savage fight ensued, during which Dr. Borelli thought she had been transported into the screen of an old western motion picture; she received a punch on the head and collapsed on the carpet. She still saw, as in a dream, the older of the two officers – Freade – assail his fellow officer – like knocking out an ox. Cross bent and fell. A second later, Elisa Borelli thought she was witnessing a physically impossible scene: under the two men's feet, the exterior trapdoor had opened – and they seemed to be struggling above nothingness. At that moment, she fainted. It must be added to all this that her memories were vague when she came to after ten minutes, nauseous and her mouth full of blood.

Second Officer Walter Cross was lying a few feet away from her, his temple open. The bulletin board, split from top to bottom, left only a weak luminescence, and the microsteel cage was gaping. It was freezing cold; the air was barely breathable, but the hatch was closed and the rug pulled down.

As for the circular which had provoked this incredible fight, Elisa Borelli had no idea of its content. Or so she said. It was a note about genetics – or something like that. This made the altercation even more inexplicable.

Walter Cross's version differed in detail. He reported to Commander Georg Szubinak and the latter presented him to the brain trust. Following Cross, at the time of the reception, Anton Freade was facing the scoreboard, with Dr. Borelli at his heels. "He was explaining something to him and maybe he was getting angry," she reported. "Him" was Cross, in the background, manipulating the X-rays. Nevertheless, although being the farthest from the screen, he had been able to read the first lines of the text. He believed it was a pilot's instruction, regarding disturbances in Jupiter's ionosphere.

Suddenly, and without any warning, the first radio officer had jumped on the board and broken it with his bare hands. Believing in the onset of space sickness, Cross rushed to hold him back, but Dr. Borelli found herself between the two men. Freade pushed her aside. He grabbed his thermic gun and started punching.

"I must have been hit in the temple," said Cross. "Afterwards, I don't remember anything. I came to in front of the broken screen, the gutted microsteel cage, with the doctor who was examining my wound and crying all the tears in my body. It was very cold and there was a lack of oxygen; we would have rushed to Pluto... I screamed – and I fainted again..."

"No wonder," said the major, "Mrs. Borelli has told us that your skull was split..."

"Oh!" Cross exclaimed, "ladies do exaggerate, don't they?"

There was no report from Anton Freade because the First radio officer had disappeared, without leaving on board the spacecraft a trace of tissue or a living cell – only a little blood on the board – it had to be his, if he had hit his bare hands.

It was a strange blood, fluid, and of a vaguely greenish color.

Commander Szubinak examined Freade's file: he was an old navigator, he had had a number of spaceflights, and various posts on Mars and

Venus. What one might call a "boring colonial." But a bout of space sickness cannot be ruled out...

The brain trust was gathered at the cockpit; Karpov was biting his nails and groaning; Vere was wearing a distracted look that signified his detachment about a row between subordinates; and Borelli sneered unpleasantly at the thought that his wife had participated in a fistfight.

"To sum up," said Earl Stanley, "we're in the presence of two facts: the brawl between two crew members and the disappearance of Circular SZ. The first concerns only Commander Szubinak. Space sickness, if it is a condition, isn't contagious; however, Professor Borelli is at your disposal, Commander, to examine the rest of the crew and, possibly, the passengers. The second fact – that's to say the disappearance of the circular – is our responsibility..."

"I don't see," said Vere, suavely, "why these young people would have been knocked out by a whirlwind in the ionosphere. Or a genetic issue: both were unmarried. The attack of space sickness seems proven by the absurdity of the situation."

"Sorry," Karpov interjected, "but let's not make the mistake of taking lightly a case that... There's still another aspect of the problem: you said that the microsteel cage had been gutted? Wasn't there a key to open it?"

"Yes," replied Szubinak, "I never part with it. Here it is."

"It's a good precaution," Karpov said coldly. "But insufficient, I see. Did we find a pick, a blowtorch, a tool with which we could smash this cage? No? Besides, microsteel is not easy to cut, by definition. We may be able to break a screen, with our bare hands, but not to rip open this partition. Do you agree with me?"

Everyone bowed.

"Another absurdity, which I like to underline, as a – hum – physicist... The question of the open hatch door. Doctor Borelli could have had, under the effect of the shock, a hallucination, and Cross admits that he 'doesn't remember anything anymore' about that moment. But the rescue team noted, upon arriving, that the air was unbreathable, rarefied and icy. Is there an outward hatch door in the radio station, Commander Szubinak?"

"Of course," replied the latter. "It's an emergency exit with electromagnetic opening."

"Does it open easily?"

"No more than the microsteel cage," Szubinak growled.

"Do you have the keys?"

"Here they are."

"Are there others?"

"Yes. As this exit ensured security of the radio station in the event of a sudden landing or a fire on board, the officer at the post with the highest rank has a complete set of them."

"And this officer was?"

"Anton Freade."

Vere's mouth rounded, as if he was going to whistle.

"Good," said Earl. "Could he have opened this trap door during the struggle?"

"If we accept the testimony of Doctor Borelli," said the Commander, "it would seem so. There was a moment during which Cross and her were unconscious... As for the hypothesis of the struggle above nothingness, it's absolutely impossible. The rocket is spinning at maximum speed, there is no air around us – well, it's against all physical laws... it must be a hallucination."

"One thing remains," said Borelli, slightly shocked. After all, it was his wife's testimony which had just been questioned. "Freade has disappeared."

"I would like," said Stanley, "to question this man, Cross..."

An imperceptible change had occurred. If Nan had been present, she might have appreciated it. Earl hadn't yet been officially given his title of Governor, nor that of Commissioner for Space Distortion, and yet everyone seemed to defer to him...

"Nothing could be easier," said the Commander. "This boy, whom I don't know very well, but who has excellent references and all the required diplomas, is at his post. He's our only qualified radio officer now and, despite his injury, he's keen to serve..."

He pressed the intercom button and the polyphonic screen lit up. To everyone's surprise, it remained white. A young voice said aloud:

"This is Walter Cross, second radio officer. Something happened to my receiver, free citizens. I can't see you."

"Neither can we," Borelli decided, "Please briefly repeat your statement regarding Circular SZ."

A silence. Then Cross's voice:

"Listen. I have no way to verify your identity. The device distorts voices. This circular was secret."

Borelli fumed. Vere raised his eyebrows. Karpov said:

"The boy is careful."

"How are your hands, Cross?" Stanley asked in a clear voice.

"My hands?" the voice wondered. "Ah, because I bumped into Freade? Of course... but not enough to damage them. Should I report to the onboard doctor?"

"No need," Earl said. "See what's wrong with your device."

And he cut off contact.

"You wanted to know...?" Borelli began.

"If it was indeed Freade who smashed the frame with his bare hands. The report did not mention the hands of the second radio."

"He wore gloves," Szubinak said. "Just before the fight, he was handling magnetic cards. Do you want me to summon him?"

"No," said Earl who seemed to be disinterested. "This boy seems to have a keen intelligence; there certainly is nothing wrong with his hands. We face a problem that Karpov has reconstructed, for which I thank him: a vanished circular, a missing crew member – and the physical impossibility that they left their post. What did you deduce from this, free citizens?"

"Nothing," said Vere, "except the importance of said circular. One doesn't break a screen, rip open microsteel and even a ship – for nothing."

"Even in case of space sickness?"

"But what is space sickness? A madness which, by the constant changes in gravity and nervous wear, affects overworked astronauts. A kind of epilepsy, isn't it, Borelli? I don't see a madman smashing through microsteel or forcing an electro-magnetic hatch open..."

"And of course," said Karpov, "there's no hope of contacting Earth before we land to sort this puzzle out?"

"No hope whatsoever," the Commander said dryly. And he turned to Stanley and asked: "Should we look for Anton Freade?"

"Of course," Earl replied. "But with the utmost discretion – there's no need to worry our passengers. And, if you want my opinion, watch Walter Cross too."

"You think that...?"

"The way the screen scrambled seems... odd."

For Nan, on the contrary, this first day in space had brought only a feeling of security, of lightness; she woke up a little late in her selenium setting, laid out like a mutant who is reborn at each dawn, took the latest news from Earth on video – they no longer received any direct news now. Nothing transcendent – an interplanetary peace congress, a Mars-Venus match. A fashion update about in parallel footwear – it looked odd to her, but women would manage. Arno Heller, who had received the title of Galactic Hero No. 1 from the Solar Federation, had disappeared, as soon as he had arrived at the starport, but in gallant company... the journalists were on their toes...

Nan turned the news off. The intercom soon announced a meeting of female specialists on board and a dinner dance at 10 p.m. She decided to go to the meeting; honest in her way, she played the role of the conscious and organized wife.

The freight elevator had brought forward a lunch which she submitted to the examination of her sensitive sense of smell; she tossed back the bacon and eggs, tasted the vitamin pills, and savored a small jar of marmalade. Then she went down to the third steerage, to the clinkers as they called it. The meeting was held in the radio room.

Elected president unanimously, Elisa Borelli sat there, a black band over her left eye. Before the pediatric nurses, geneticists and pedagogues of the *Daredevil*, she pronounced a short speech. And despite her baby complexion and huge diamonds, her words exuded wisdom and even indulgence. She admitted that a medical examination ordered by Commander Szubinak would be scheduled in due time, not because he had found a single case of space sickness, that of old astronauts' fame, but because the no less worrying void sickness that had just made its appearance. A normal phenomenon on a vessel whose passengers were almost all on their first crossing, it consisted of convulsions, accompanied by fever. Children were said to be particularly sensitive to it.

"The usual therapy," Elisa Borelli said, "consists in showers and sedatives. Don't be scared. This disease is common and heals quickly after landings. This is the price paid by the protectors of humanity."

She asked free citizens to join a voluntary watch list – there might be a shortage of nurses and, in any case, the fact that the "elite specialists" took part in the common miseries would produce an excellent effect on the migrants.

"This is only the beginning, alas!" resumed the doctor, leafing through her papers. "We'll have to fight against more serious evils... The *Daredevil* transports an unusual human cargo in the annals of migration – and God knows... The recruitment was made during a state of emergency; we had to grant travel permits to many couples in – ahem – irregular situations, having lived under an unsanitary regime. Many of these young women are – er..."

"Pregnant," said Olga Karpov, flying to her aid.

"...Yes. Not only did this happen without medical preparation, but Andromeda, at the present time, has neither genetic labs nor decantation centers... These poor women will have to bring their pregnancies to an end and give birth in natural conditions —which is very painful. Of course, women before the year 2000 did the same, but we must realize that generations separate us from these robust femininities and many variations have occurred since in our organisms! We can't even be sure of the biological results – I mean that, by necessity, premarital examinations were superficial. Some accidents have unfortunate consequences..."

"Heredos and all the rest," growled Olga Karpov, realizing that the president was sputtering.

"Yes, yes, that's the word... but I had the impression that there were also details relating to the uranium mines where these young people worked, and to cosmic dust... Finally, one last thing. You'll excuse me..." (she touched her eyepatch) "...I'll explain all that to you later. I've a very bad headache... A stupid accident deprived me of part of my faculties..."

The room quietly applauded. Nan, in her corner, had icy hands and tried to smile. What she discovered, under the hypnotic influence that paralyzed Elisa Borelli's memory, was frightening... So she wasn't done with Earth! She slipped discreetly towards the exit, before the end of the session, and stumbled in a long corridor, cluttered with frail shapes stretched out into makeshift bunks. Nan realized that she was in a waiting room, where the patients suffering from void sickness had been isolated. A concert of fine and discordant voices repeated a single sentence:

"I'm falling! I'm falling!"

These crises resulted from the first shock, the first contact, with outer space. Some children were delirious, they spoke of a "black hole", of "shooting fires", of a "ceiling which was also a floor", and sank into vertigo and nausea. They had to be tied with straps so much they were struggling. Others were in comas and disheveled; their mothers wiped the foam from their mouths.

As Nan passed, little feverish hands were stretched out; fingers gripped her white dress. A boy dug his nails into his elbow. She leaned over and saw ahis hot little face, his rolling eyes, his small teeth clenched in tetanic contraction. Was it necessary that in all the suffering children, she saw the Other, the little mutant from the cemetery of rockets...? She took his head, smooth like a fruit, between her hands and the child immediately softened. The faint cry shrilled: "I'm falling! I'm falling!"

"Well," she said in her most ordinary voice, "have you ever fallen out of a tree? What a shame! A boy of your age who moans like an baby!"

"I'm falling!"

"But it's over now, isn't it? You can't always fall. You were on the third branch of a fir tree; you slipped on resin. There are stories for nothing!"

The raspy and soft voice, the magnetic waves which Nan radiated, produced their effect. On all the berths the blond and dark heads calmed down in the hollow of their pillows; the tetanic tremors became less distinct and arms relaxed. A boy's voice pronounced, astonished:

"Wow! I'm back in my bed!"

"Of course, you are," said Nan. "You had one of those bad dreams..."

"But just now, I was suffocating!"

"You ate too much pudding. And you, little blonde boy, you twisted yourself in your blanket... Here's the proof."

"But we were falling! We were falling!"

"You relived it all. You're not falling anymore now, are you?"

"No, no, no!"

"Now, who wants to hear a fairy tale? A true tale of Earth – with a blue star where dwarf-birds live – the story of a crystal crown and a princess all in gold?"

"Me, me, me!"

"So listen. But first, all on their backs and hands crossed. You, who are under the light bulb, you can turn on the right side. Now listen: Once upon a time, there was a princess so beautiful that the roses paled with envy, and whose foot was so cute that she could put on a kitten's slipper..."

When she left the room, all the children were asleep. She experienced some difficulty in making her way through the crowd of mothers who were trying to kiss her hands.

At the top of the passageway, the white light of an intercom screen lit up and an official voice called out to her:

"Free citizen Stanley, to the cockpit..."

"It must be Earl," she thought. A light, delicious pang of heart revived the green meadows, the Happy Valley, a dancing boat in the middle of the spray... "If I fell in love with him, I would be saved," thought the very young Nan from 2500. But her optimism waned when she faced the viewscreen. "Hello?" she said.

The official voice inquired:

"Free citizen Stanley?"

"Yes. Can't you see me."

"You forget," said the voice, suave, "that you are scrambling the system. Nan, beware: you have hypnotized these children..."

"For their own good!"

"I have no doubt about it. But their mothers will remember. Hypnotizing, like picking a fruit, is a trait of the KZ mutants... Not that it does any harm... I would like you, Nan, to hypnotize someone. It's about this lost circular..."

"What circular?"

"Right! You don't know about it yet. The one that Elisa Borelli forgot. But you know how it is with a non-continuous treatment: she might end up remembering. This circular was about mutants..."

"Who is speaking?" cried Nan. "How come I can't see you? Answer me!"

A haunting note reached her: old, forgotten music. Something like the beginning of Liszt's 2nd Hungarian Rhapsody.

They had hung up.

The dinner dance at the premieres was successful like all meals of this kind. It was served at small tables, and the room, for the occasion, had been transformed into the hall of a large restaurant, with veiled candles, crystal glasses and greenhouse flowers. Serpentines traced graceful arches; the women showed off their No. 1 outfits, "8/10 short," Karpov said, and the men were dressed in shimmering interplanetary uniforms. The dishes had been renamed, there was a *crème of Astral turtle* (and only the chef knew where such an animal was nesting), an *Andromeda pheasant* – which did not exist – and an ice cream bomb concealing within it some sour cream and red currant, which was simply called *Orbital Shake*.

Elisa Borelli was conspicuous by her absence, because of her black eye, but Una Vere, in a gown cut low to the loins, left a trail of flame velvet behind her. Nan was so beautiful under her pearl diadem that she took Stanley's breath away.

The orchestra was very good; the Martians hardly abused the brass. Earl invited Nan to an old, slow dance, a 20th century dance called the *bolero*. When they were away from the presidential table, while breathing his amber hair, he asked: "Have you ever looked at the void?"

She shook her head.

"Do you want us to do it together? I thought," he added, "that the ceremony of our marriage was cancelled, and that, to begin a new life together, it is necessary to do something exceptional. It seems that the vision of the void drives ordinary mortals mad. But we're used to it, aren't we, Nan?"

"Yes," she said.

He took her by the hand and led her through the white corridors, totally deserted, because this part of the spacecraft was watched over by photoelectric cells, towards the pilot's cabin where a radiant screen was embedded in the torque. Commander Szubinak in his mobile seat saw them pass and gave them a friendly wave. They climbed into the turret. Thoughts and feelings rushed at a dizzying pace: Not that everything here had gone very well or at least according to certain rules, but this vision...

Suddenly they plunged into the starry blackness – millions of stars sparkling and cold. Nan felt the pounding of blood in her arteries. The overriding impression was one of incredible darkness. These surrounded the transparent couple from all sides...

Cold lips touched Nan's, two hands took hers. Earl felt a reluctance for a second and asked:

"Are you my friend, Nan?"

"I believed you," she said. "You brought me aboard this ship..."

"I wonder if I was crazy... But I couldn't leave you alone on Earth and we were running out of time. Why did you agree to follow me?"

She looked up and noted what was dear to her, all that she had recognized in the handsome manly features, tense and refined by worry – that shine under the too long eyelashes, that trembling sigh, on the lively mouth of a hasty voluptuousness. She said:

"I came to you, because I was left to die and I was malleable like wax and an abyss was opening under my feet. I was ready to leave and erase everything... I was the fox that has forgotten its kind and hunts with men..."

"So you knew...?"

"That he was there and that everything was going to start again?" Nan said briefly. "No, I'm not talking about an end of the world and, besides, that doesn't concern me. But you already know that I penetrate the past and – a little – personal future. This being, this man who made me suffer so much over the centuries, I no longer want to meet him. I know that, when the time comes, it shall be unacceptable... because it has already happened. I was scared..."

"Just scared...?"

"Why are you asking me? this"

"Because I love you, Nan."

She laughed without gaiety:

"Do you like a mutated creature – one that has green blood and feeds on arsenic?"

"Yes. And who has ten senses instead of our five. Who could arrange chain reactions... and who remembers things from the future, still formless, nebulous, similar to the monsters of the great depths – horrible things – and who relives, in indestructible dreams, a past that contains the causes. That's where I am, Nan, and I just wanted to do my duty."

"Do you regret it?"

"No. If you could love me..." Mentally, she wished to be loyal and faithful, to be human, and God knows! She reached a blank. Everything could still be saved! She didn't really want to be a phenomenon, and wasn't it still a beautiful and soothing destiny that an Earthwoman who devoted herself, trembled and waited...?

From very far away came a flood of old music in star velvet; it was sweet to soften in his tender arms, to sink into an accessible abyss, peopled with earthly islands, flowers, and open to a warm ocean. Nan was going to agree to accept and return – with anger – the long kiss that would seal everything.

But in the tide of chords a discordant note emerged, coming from she knew not where – which spoke of an ungrateful globe, bathed in artificial light, and of the miserable creatures that inhabited it. There was an area, a hospital and a rocket graveyard. There was the barrack of the Martian's, where one evening, after the last spacecraft had taken off for Earth, a boy with his forehead split by the scar from an operation, with a mug of stiff alcohol, would murmur: "Nan! Nan!" and wondered with horror that he had forgotten nine-tenths of his life – until that evening.

"All this is only fair, perhaps," Nan Nangis struggled to think. "Earth doesn't need monsters..."

She heard a cold laugh and clearly heard a voice saying:

"There would be billions of monsters to plant on other planets... And these monsters would be human..."

At that moment, Nan stopped thinking. An imperative wave had just reached her – an unknown voice. She shivered under the anguish of the being who called her to his aid. Obeying obscure laws, she pressed a handkerchief to her mouth and said:

"It must still be my metabolism. Forgive me, Earl..."

The rest was a well-conditioned nightmare.

She ran down corridors and stairs, in a pitiless light. (Centuries later, in a later existence, she would dream of that escape—among bright whites.) She reached, without hesitation, the radio room, where Elisa Borelli sat enthroned among X-ray machines and tables littered with complicated statistics. The doctor was there, her blindfold over her eye, like a dark streak – and Nan understood what made the charm of this sweet creature: she embodied exactly what toddlers dream of – safety, a warm breast...

A little red-haired girl, wearing dancing curls, was perched on her stuffed knee. She looked like a squirrel. She sucked on a peppermint and regarded the newcomer with intelligent frog-green eyes.

"My dear," said free citizen Borelli, turning her wild blue eye towards Nan, "I think I remember the contents of this circular. Or at least, I'm beginning to remember... It was really a note about genetics – I don't understand why this delicious boy – Walter Cross – is talking about the ionosphere. These were KZ mutants, known as 'Andromeda mutants' because the most striking specimens were spotted on this satellite..."

But it was not the free citizen who had called Nan for help. The young woman was sure of it now: it was the little squirrel girl. The frog-green pupil had peculiar pulses...

"I'm really happy," Elisa Borelli continued in a lamenting tone, "that you're here, my dear! I need some advice... The others are full of preconceived ideas; they come from the Lysenko Institute or the University of Elmsworth, and only think of doing vivisection. Do you want to question this little girl in front of me? We will see..."

Nan gazed coldly at the child who was sucking her lozenge and she bombarded her with imperative waves: "You're happy now, aren't you? You couldn't resist the pleasure of parading in front of your boyfriends – and here we are, in trouble... Now watch yourself. I'll try to get you out of there, I'll ask you questions, very simple ones – try to answer them like a real Earth child. Can you?"

"Of course," answered the little one on the same wave. "I'm not completely stupid! All that is the fault of the acoustics in this Noah's Ark..."

Thereupon she sobbed, looking like a normal baby with colic.

"Don't be afraid, little girl," whispered Nan, with fearsome sweetness. "What's your name?"

"...Lizzy."

"Sweet Lizzy." (She's not afraid.) "Lizzy. How old are you?"

"One – and then ten."

"Ten what?"

"...months..."

"Almost two years then. Lizzy is a big girl now. And your mama is?"

"Mama MacLeod... And then Dad MacLeod. And then me, Lizzy."

"Well," said Nan, raising an intense gaze at free citizen Borelli, "her voice is that of a child not too advanced for her age. But she has good rosy cheeks... Is this experiment enough for you?"

"You cannot know," Elisa exclaimed, "what a relief you bring me! An impartial witness, that's all I needed... I was going crazy... Go back to your mother, Lizzy, here, take that lollipop again... go..."

Lizzy slipped off her knee and disappeared like an elf, dragging her oversized man slippers.

"But," Nan hazarded, "I don't see what worried you about this kid!"

Elisa Borelli shuddered, looking back.

"Imagine," she said, "a while ago, we were getting the vaccinations... This little girl was at the back of the room with a boy her age, on this bench. Suddenly, the fans having slowed down, there was a partial silence and I heard her say: 'Hands off, sparrow skull! The dumbest animal after the sea lion is homo sapiens!' Awful, isn't it?"

Nan suppressed a smile: it was the language of a two-year-old mutant who imitated the scholars and thugs around her...

"Above all," resumed the doctor, "there is this circular which finally came back into my memory, and which was really worrying, do you understand me? It was about their immediate destruction... I should report to the Commander..."

"Whose destruction?" Nan asked, to save time.

"KZ mutants," said Elisa. "On board interplanetary vessels and on artificial satellites... that was the terms employed."

"Are you really going to bother the Commander with such a small thing?" Nan asked, raising her slender eyebrows. Beneath her diadem of pearls, bathed in uncertain lights, she looked like a young princess embarrassed by questions of etiquette. "It seems to me... I could be wrong, of course... that such an order is so trivial! We have no mutants on board."

She suddenly felt fresh and light, free from hesitation and ready for battle. The enchantment had fallen; she was no longer the "fox that hunts with men".

Elisa Borelli only wavered only for a moment, she said:

"That's irrelevant, my dear. During all these hours when the content of this radiogram escaped me, I felt, how can I tell you...? In a state of inferiority. It was the first time in my life that such a thing happened to me – I have, in general, an excellent memory. Of course, there was this brutal shock…"

"Are you really sure you feel absolutely fine now?" Nan asked. "Really good? You could be wrong. Consider that your report would have serious consequences and would lead to the destruction of living beings…"

"Oh!" said Elisa, "those monsters? These fake people…?" And her naive eyes beamed.

Coming out of the radio hall, Nan saw two things that a quarter of an hour earlier, she would not have recognized. She went to the first intercom and asked for the cockpit.

"This is the cockpit," announced the official voice. "Second Officer Walter Cross has the device."

Nan threw out, quickly:

"You were right this morning, the hypnotic treatment didn't last, she remembers. Not everything yet, it seems, but snippets. She's going to report to Commander Szubinak. I'm talking about Elisa Borelli, of course…

"I don't understand, free citizen," said the metallic voice. "What is this about?"

"If you are Walter Cross," she answered in a mocking voice.

"Thank you all the same, Nan, my dear…"

A sharp snap. He had hung up. And she heard the same haunting phrase from the 2nd Hungarian Rhapsody…

Nan stood there, shaking – she thought she recognized that voice. But she had to act. She slipped into the first walkway she came across; her sense of direction guided her; she moved like a sleepwalker. A quarter of an hour ago, she was going to swear her final engagement to Earl, facing the stars; she had followed almost lovingly the moving outline of his lips; she was the fox who had betrayed her race… – this species – until the appearance of a very small red-haired girl about to be persecuted had made her go back thousands of years back…

Nan – Atlantea – was again responsible for her own.

She crossed the dormitories of the third floor where a motley humanity was crammed. Children slept in hammocks and mothers breastfed, as at ages when there was no genetic institute. Squatting between the beds, the hairy men, like satisfied cavemen, played dice. Teenagers stared amazed at the wake of her "time color" dress…

Although there was little difference in the installation, Nan plunged into a lower world. She caught an atmosphere of insane hopes, of frustrated efforts, an incoercible smell of sweat and cabbage soup. At the bend of a hallway, Lizzy MacLeod was lounging in the arms of a bearded guy who was obviously Jonas MacLeod.

"You left Earth because of her?" asked Nan abruptly.

The man hesitated, clenching his huge fists, but the little girl piped:

"Speak, Dad. The citizen knows a bit about it: she got me out of a strange mess."

"Well yes!" MacLeod threw. "I worked in the uranium mines, free citizen. I had six children and Lizzy was the only one who survived. We were well paid – only the children couldn't stand it – or they were born flawed, deprived of an essential organ – poor little rags, what! – they all died. This one, you see how holy she is – a real little Mona Lisa – and precocious, like a hothouse melon. So when the race relations inspectors came to snoop around her, and run some tests, I took to the wind, picked up my togs, and ran...

"My wife and I agreed to die on a satellite, because Lizzy said 'Andromeda, it was good for him'. But just as it is true," he added, raising his voice, "that I am one hell of a Scotsman, I would strangle with my hands anyone who touches my Lizzy. We're not doing anything wrong; we're a family of ordinary Earthlings, and if any sparrow-head..."

"Don't say 'sparrow-head'," advised Nan mechanically. "Lizzy uses too much imagery..."

He had placed the little girl between his knees and he was shaking his fists like beaters.

"Dad, it's not about that," Lizzy corrected in her high-pitched voice, "since Doctor Borelli knows that I exist and that, in addition, she unearthed an official document, she will alert the ship, and you cannot strangle everyone. Listen to the free lady instead, she might find a solution..."

"Lizzy," Nan said desperately and trying to reassure herself, "you're alone on board in your case, aren't you...?"

The little one shrugged her pointed shoulders:

"I can swear to nothing, but in dormitory 6A, we are fifteen or sixteen..."

So the danger was there! It had risen, this generation of mutants – monsters good at repopulating the planets – that galactic expansion now demanded; beings who could endure everything, adapt everywhere – from children born in uranium mines, on isolated satellites, to the outposts of inhuman planets. And Old Earth, terrified, was set against them!

Nan clenched her hands violently; she clearly saw thousands of little bodies tied to operating tables, slender burning faces, rolling eyes and those tiny teeth, clenched to a howl of terror and pain... Her own species! She had to save them!

Her mind worked with torrential rapidity. "I'll take care of Doctor Borelli – this chatterbox, this traveling ship's transmitter, even if I lock her up in a closet!" she decided. "As for Lizzy and the other 'precocious children', let's spare the tests. Everyone in bed. Looks like you're suffering from void sickness. Can you imitate it, Lizzy?"

"Of course," affirmed the small girl, jovial. "We're Earthlings enough for that. Look!" She braced herself, seemed to break up and yelped: "Ouch! I fall!"

Jonas blanched.

"Try to look less like Picasso's women," said Nan.

The last image she received and kept preciously, like a justification, was that of a powerful Earthman who, in the very heart of the ship, hugged a red-haired squirrel child.

CHAPTER VII
Faceless Enemy

Elisa Borelli was operating the intercom for the third time. The cockpit had sent her back to first steerage, and cabin No. 1 to the Commander's private office. So this Szubinak was nowhere...? Gradually, the text of the SZ circular came out of the darkness and blazed in her brain. It consisted of three paragraphs in all. In the first, a brief statement from the Space Distortion Committee announced that the "Andromeda disaster" was caused by an "attack contrary to all federal laws". The second paragraph stated that the Committee was studying the above case closely: "One of our agents is currently *en route* to the Astral Belt, armed with secret instructions and full powers." It gave the first results of the inquiry; it was a nuclear-based reaction, caused by a human-looking phenomenon. This paragraph included a *nota bene* three times longer than the main article.

According to these results, the phenomenon in question had a different metabolism, incredible energy capacities and caused chain reactions. So he was a mutant. It could be, added the NB with praiseworthy exaggeration, that this was an adaptation of the human being to the new universal conditions. In this case, the formula would soon stabilize. Currently, it was not so. Such phenomena threatened the globe and possibly the entire solar system. No one could claim that they weren't the normal result of a mutant organism's functioning... Therefore, these beings were dangerous, and had to be exterminated as soon as possible. The third and last paragraph included a list of names of mutants that might be on board interplanetary ships...

Elisa Borelli understood that she had committed an enormous folly. But how could she suspect? This Nan Stanley looked so calm! And that friendly radio officer! Not to mention the little girl, all the little girls and boys... Who would have thought the *Daredevil* was carrying such explosive cargo? She'd have to talk to the Distortion Commissioner...

Suddenly, her hands froze: wasn't he Nan Stanley's husband? He wouldn't take her seriously, and she would have Walter Cross' testimony against her. However, there was an immutable rule, motivated by frequent nervous incidents which devastated space crews: "On an interplanetary ship, the testimony of a single person should not be ignored..."

One would argue that, from the shock she had received, from her momentary amnesia, her word did count. What if her husband... but no, he wouldn't intervene. The couple's relationship was strained and no trust existed between them. Elisa reproached her husband for his weaknesses for pretty assistants, and Borelli despised his wife, her lies and her puerilities. "He'll tell me again that I have exhibitionism in my blood," she thought bitterly, recording the slow music of a funeral march.

"And it's true, I can't get over it. I feel ridiculous with my make-up and my rings – but I can't give it up... I take care of my health and I steal pastries from the refrigerator. Me! I used to be a sylph in stature and the best dancer... I used to run barefoot in the dew and now I can barely lift my elephant legs! We must have faked the medical tests, otherwise the *Daredevil* would never have taken me on board. (A funeral music swells like great organs, filling the radio room and – perhaps – infinity...) I am irremediably sick. I wake up every morning with a bland taste in my mouth – I'm definitely making sugar and I'll never have kids. And Borelli hates me. This ridiculous story that comes on top of all that – and we will have to stay maybe ten years – or more – on Andromeda, in the midst of a population that hates me – without air, without sun and without flowers..."

Suddenly she saw that she had risen to her feet and was about to scream with terror.

"Nothing can stop this rocket – or reverse it," she thought. "However, it would be easy to fix all this – to put an end to this anguish and this disgust..."

The hypodermic syringe was stored in the cupboard on the left, and the morphine capsules were within reach of her hand.

"How soothing is this funeral march and what majesty there is in human death! How did I not think of that sooner? Yes, this is all easy. And after all, it will be a good ending..."

The interplanetary guard Spriegel would have fallen asleep at his post, at the corner of the passageway, but the patrol had spent the whole day looking for Anton Freade – who was seen everywhere and nowhere – climbing the hatches and rummaging in the holds.

Spriegel was a heavyset giant, and in the end, he grew disgusted with these games. So, assigned to a quiet position, he placed himself at the intersection of the two corridors – so anyone moving from second to third would pass in front of him – and he resolved to take some rest. Oh, not even a nap, he would just lean on a ledge, he would lean on his weapon and close his eyes...

When he opened them again, the lights had barely faded and he felt a cold breath on his face. He looked at his stopwatch – well, he had slept for six minutes... It wasn't too bad. However, he had the irresponsible, concrete impression of someone or something passing in front of him – not a silhouette, rather a trail of shadow. It came from the radio room and it ended up... where? Someone was there. The radio room... He shivered. What if it was Anton Freade? A cold sweat beaded on his temples and, without taking the time to think, he rushed into the corridor of the third – only to bump into a closed door.

The hallway was empty and the stairs too. Had the passing shadow moved in the opposite direction? In the air floated a musical phrase, solemn and slow, coming from above... Spriegel was about to call the patrol – but what would he say? That he had fallen asleep and thought he'd seen a ghost? That was enough to retrograde him!

No. The best thing was to knock on the door of the radio station and call out to the officer who was supposed to be there. He would see if it was Anton Freade... And if it really was him, what would he do? He was supposed to be a dangerous madman... In any case, he would ask him why he moved around at night. Yes – and at a trot!

Spriegel checked his gun in its holster. He moved towards the radio room, feeling in all his nerves the slight excitement that precedes a fight.

Slow, funereal music accompanied him.

"If he doesn't answer immediately, I'll shoot," decided Spriegel. "We don't argue with that species... They say, in the holds, that he is a KZ mutant..."

He stepped forward. It was a matter of half a second...

At the threshold of the radio room, Nan froze. She had come back with the firm decision to argue with Elisa Borelli, although she knew it would be quite useless. "She must already know who I am and won't even want to talk to me. But honestly, I have to make this attempt." She was ready for anything, even to lock fat Elisa in a closet. But no one answered her repeated knocks and, when she entered the shiny white room, she saw an enormous doll-like figure slumped in a chair, her head and arms dangling.

Without moving from the threshold, Nan realized that Elisa Borelli was dead. Completely dead. There were no traces of violence, but on the ground, close at hand, she saw a broken hypodermic syringe. Nan leaned against the wall; she had the incoherent impression of living in a detective novel. Did she have an alibi...? Yes... no... everyone had seen her in the third hold and Jonas MacLeod would testify to that... What could she do now? Nothing that might help poor Elisa... A heroine in a novel had to, depending on the genre, vomit in the nearest sink, faint with a distinct little cry, or call the police.

But...

She remembered her communication with Walter Cross – or the one who was not Walter Cross...

"Thank you all the same, Nan, my dear..."

She felt suddenly very cold. Yet, this syringe was, it seemed, an indication of suicide? She closed the door softly, remembering that she herself had come there with the intention of "stopping this chatterbox"...

Under the very door of the Command Post – a calm and serious place where a space light shone and the waves of delicate instruments crisscrossed, she stumbled into the second corpse of the evening. It was Guard Spriegel – who had received an electromagnetic shock in the face – and wasn't a pretty sight.

But Nan didn't look at him – her eyes were fixed on the radio station through the gaping door. Three men were there... no, two. What she had taken for a third figure was an empty astronaut suit. Earl Stanley and Szubinak leaned over it. Nan didn't scream, didn't fall, she just sat down on the ground and as the two officers looked up, she said politely:

"Thank you, I'm fine. I just came from the radio room – free citizen Borelli is dead..."

The cabin began to spin; it was like the time when she'd fallen from the landing on Andromeda. She found, with satisfaction, Earl's arm bent under her neck and felt that a flask was brought to her lips. She took a mouthful that felt like fire and coughed. At the same time, singularly lucid, she realized that Elisa's death and that of the guard had nothing to do with her failure. It was this armor... Even empty, it retained the arrogant grace of a body.

Nan sat down and wiped away the tears that tingled her eyelids. "I am very ashamed," she said. "I am useless."

"We would be too, in the same circumstances," said the major, with indulgence.

"What is this?" She pointed at the space suit.

"It was Ensign Walter Cross's suit," Earl replied. "Only, as you can see, he's not in it."

"It's pierced with thermal jets at chest height..."

"Yes. Spriegel seems to have shot first."

"Who's Spriegel?"

"The guard."

"But he is dead! Where is...(she struggled to speak, but each word was like a block of stone) where is – the other corpse...?"

"You mean – Cross's?" asked the Commander. "Well, here's the rub – it's not here. The jumpsuit has blood on the neckline, but..."

"With all those bullets in his body," Nan said, fighting against an insane hope, "that boy couldn't have survived!"

"It seems so," answered Stanley, coldly. "But what you just told us... What happened to Dr. Borelli?"

Nan found her voice to pronounce: "I just found her in her office – she fell headfirst on the table. And – Oh, Earl! – She had a hypodermic syringe ready..."

"Suicide?"

"Yes – no – I don't know. (It was better not to assert.)

Earl turned to the Commander. "I believe," he said, "that we must look the truth in the face. We have two dead and two missing, and I don't believe in coincidences. It seems that we have on board a being dangerous for the community."

"A madman?" asked the Commander.

"I'm afraid Earth's conventions don't hold true in space – especially in this case. The doors of the station were closed, held with compressed air, at the time of the disappearance of Freade, and in this corridor, no photoelectric cell reacted. This assassin, Commander, doesn't care about the laws of physics..."

"So?" Szubinak asked, straightening up. "You understand, me, I'm an astronaut out of the ranks, I drive my clunker, that's all. These stories are beyond me. We've searched the ship from top to bottom, by the usual methods, without finding a trace of Freade, and as far as I'm concerned, he is no longer there. Here's the same thing happening to Cross... My training is not sufficient to face a ghost."

"All right," said Earl. "I understand, Commander."

"I place my powers in the hands of the Space Committee..."

They seemed to have forgotten the presence of Nan, curled up at their feet, very small. Earl gave orders in a dry tone:

"Can you energize the walls between the floors? Yes? Perfect. Post guards at all the exits. Order the passengers to return to their cabins and stop anyone lurking in the corridors. Ask for identification documents and photos."

The night continued. Nan returned to her cabin-coffin. The commanding officer's order had come in the middle of the party and a crowd of first-class passengers was returning to the steerage, talking feverishly.

"An escaped madman, really?"

"For God's sake, Francia, talk about something else!"

"They say he knocked out Dr. Borelli..."

"No, just one of those frail interplanetary puppets..."

"Milos, you're talking nonsense – even a mad dog wouldn't bite a guard – by the way, it seems that they're going to energize the floors, it's not a precaution to take against an ordinary man. It must be one of those interplanetary monsters..."

The rest was lost in the laughter of excited women and the slamming of doors and bolts.

Nan saw Earl coming, like fate.

"Well?" she asked.

"Well," he replied wearily, "as far as we can tell, she committed suicide. No signs of violence. She was perfectly healthy – a little sugar in the blood, perhaps. It just seems like, all of a sudden, she decided she'd had enough – and she injected herself with a massive dose of morphine."

"She didn't leave a letter?"

"Only scribbles on the blotter. She wrote 'SZ 892000' two or three times – then: 'Thinking about baby bottles' – and drew a radio badge. Ah! Yes, there's also a staff of musical notes – an old piece from the 19th century, Liszt, I believe... It's not very explicit."

"Do you think they killed her?"

"Yes. But I have no proof."

"Cross or Freade?"

"One of the two," Earl nervously knuckled his beautiful hands. "We'll soon know. We've placed energy barriers so powerful that the walls support them with difficulty, all living beings are therefore prisoners on their floor..."

"In short," said Nan, stiffening, "this being, what do you accuse him of? Until proven otherwise, Elisa Borelli committed suicide and the guard Spriegel attacked first. It seems that his adversary acted in self-defense..."

"Yes," said Earl. "But there's this circular."

"A scrap of paper!"

"...Other information preceded it. It is, without a doubt, about the disaster of Andromeda."

"I don't see," Nan said with a certain impudence, but she was going all out, "why a note regarding disturbances in Jupiter's ionosphere or the orbital shocks of a satellite could have caused this series of disappearances and deaths?"

"Not even," Earl said, blushing, "if our ghost was a KZ mutant? A being who might have followed you on board this ship?"

Now they were challenging each other. Nan abruptly placed both hands on her knees – it was only a gesture, but it lightened the tumult of her blood. Under her gaze whose emptiness widened, Earl felt on the edge of the abyss and hated his job.

"So," she said, "that was it, this love confessed before the stars...? As I fooled around – stooped to Earthlings – was I bait or hook? You knew that I wouldn't board the spacecraft alone. You used me – and I gave headlong into the net!"

"Nan..." he said, tortured.

But she interrupted him violently. Her hair was phosphorescent and her knuckles creaked, sensitized by danger.

"What, Nan? I don't want to hear you talk about loyalty or tenderness anymore! Truly a beautiful affection that leads to demoting its object to the rank of a decoy, or of a beast attached to the entrance of a trap, to attract another beast of the same species! Ah! I should've remembered what we are to you: half-apes, ersatz men!"

"I swear to you, Nan," Earl said with unexpected violence, "that I never thought so, nor had I such intentions! And if you don't believe me, do you think I was crazy enough to bring such calamity aboard this ship? Only, I'm afraid, that's what happened. And now I have to do my duty – just my duty..."

"Do it," answered Nan with exquisite courtesy.

Three interplanetary guards were chatting at the turn of a first-row corridor. Hazel said:

"The drill we're being given – it's rubbish, and I'm being polite. You can't even interrogate the bigwigs, and IDs are manufactured. Another thing, this energization! What is it for, please? If we're dealing with a humanoid, heat guns are enough. But if it's a draft or a chemical combination, what do you think we'll be doing, the rest of us...?

"What if it's a person who can turn into a draught?" said the oldest of the guards, whose name was Jan Mudds, peacefully. The man had twenty years of astral navigation and was not surprised by anything.

Shurst, the third guard, turned his bovine head. "Bullshit!" he repeated. "Such things don't exist. It's as if one wanted to move by making holes in the hypersphere. In the past – I was then doing my service on Andromeda – I knew a boy who only dreamed of this... Hank or Henry, he was called – and you had to hear him – he only blabbed about those hyper-vortices..."

"Hyper...what?"

"Holes through nothing."

"Hank or Henry," Hazel said, pulling out his toothpick. "When were you on Andromeda? Two years ago? Me too. Wouldn't it be Arno Heller?"

What happened next was strange. Old Mudds had just enough time to step aside to stuff his pipe with that Venusian tobacco he couldn't get out of the habit of, a kind of marijuana that sometimes gave him delirium, but which made him jovial and without complications...

And then, the next moment – the passage was empty. Mudds was alone. There was neither Hazel – nor Shurst.

The old navigator widened his eyes and nodded. Where were the other two? He had indeed perceived a spark, but it was doubtless that of his pipe, on which he was blowing. Had he then dreamed? Shurst – Hazel... A note of tropical music sang in his brain and he saw the soothing images of the Venusian forests, a swamp blooming with lotuses, this hill of orchids where he intended to retire...

"They were there, they were talking... the devil knows about what," he decided. "These young people talk without consideration. And then they took off. I still have to report..."

Borelli was pale, with bags under his eyes.

"I know," he admitted, "that Elisa was perhaps not very happy, but for her to commit suicide – no!"

"Yet, the facts are there," remarked Commander Szubinak. "The hypodermic syringe bore only her fingerprints..."

The staff sat in the Commander's office. Many people had come and gone; there was an odor of dead parties in the air, of faded flowers; they walked among the garlands and streamers. As the neon lights tired the eyes, Szubinak had brought one of the shaded chandeliers, and the light softened the rough-hewn face of Olga Karpov, who was stenographing on a corner of the table. She raised her sharp chin and her Mongolian cheekbones to Borelli.

"Elisa was jealous," she said. "This is not slander but a diagnosis. And too feminine to admit defeat. She loved you, Citizen Borelli. Besides, what intelligent woman, at her age, hasn't wanted to kill herself – once or twice? It's the little things that hold us back: details... the cats or the geraniums that no one will be able to take care of like us... The new windows or the carpet in our room... On board the *Daredevil*, none of this existed..."

"Do you think she killed herself?" asked Earl Stanley. "Yet Borelli who was her husband doesn't believe it."

"Husbands know nothing of their wives. On reflection, she could have killed herself."

Always like in nightmares, where suddenly a burst of laughter underlines the most horrible situations, free citizen Una Vere made a dramatic entrance. She asked to testify! Ostrich feathers fluttered gently above her head and she curled her fiery train like a mermaid's tail. She sat down in a low armchair and lit a cigarillo in a jade cigarette holder.

"I'll come straight to the point," she said, dancing her sharp-trimmed slipper to the end of her feet. "I believe that all of you, both the Commander and the members of the Team – forgive me – are making a mistake of intuition. Feminine sensibility, here is the essential point! So much of poor Elisa lived, I had refrained from any interference in her affairs – it's such a delicate case, isn't it, free citizens? But right now, I have to speak!"

"Speak," said Szubinak, "please – no circumlocution, free lady!"

"This is just an introduction," Una Vere fluted. "Don't you think that poor dear Elisa's visit to the radio station the other night had some connection with her death?"

"It's possible," Earl Stanley conceded.

"It's obvious!" cried Una Vere. "How many times have you seduced me with this truth: when two exceptional cases arise, at short notice, involving the same person, there is a relation of cause and effect!"

"I was talking about chemical compounds, my dear!"

"Life as a chemical composition? But it doesn't matter... Did you ask yourself the reasons for this impromptu visit? No!"

"There was nothing out of the ordinary about this visit," Szubinak corrected. "Any member of the team can enter the radio station and give their personal message..."

"Yes, but he doesn't always get punched in the head! This is the exceptional circumstance, and not the visit itself; besides, the courier was used as a pretext..."

Una Vere shrugged her bare shoulders indulgently.

"Do you, by any chance, know more than everyone else, dear friend?" Vere hissed.

His wife gratified him with a thin thread of filtered gaze between the artificial eyelashes, appreciated the tension which reigned over the assistance...

"Of course!" she said. "Anton Freade was Elisa's lover!"

"Wh-what?" gasped Borelli, rising in his seat.

"No antediluvian demonstrations, dear! Elisa was your wife, of course, but she was also just a woman... and I never heard that Don Juan's wife had to be beyond reproach..." She flashed a bewitching smile. "Elisa, dear friend, frequented the Turkish baths on 500th Avenue."

"It's not a crime!"

"I never said so. She met Freade there..."

For a moment, an indescribable agitation reigned in the post – not that Borelli's misfortune had really affected his peers, on the contrary, people were trying to classify the revelation and Una Vere was intensely amused.

"I am sorry," she said, playing with her cigarette holder, "to give your riddles a news ending: Elisa, poor soul, was no longer young, she clung on. Freade knocked her out. He resisted her, she killed herself – or something like that. Don't make that face, Borelli, it's from the 19th century, it's arch-classic..."

"But," Commander Szubinak protested, his feet firmly planted on the ground, "that explains nothing! There was the destruction of this circular..."

"Merely an excuse!"

"And Cross' testimony..."

"You wouldn't want a charming boy to betray a lady! Besides, Commander, this Freade is capable of anything. He's a monster – my intuition cannot deceive me. He's hiding on board and he's committed other crimes. He's paranoid!"

"Oh! My head!" moaned the Commander. "So you accuse Anton Freade...?"

"Perfectly!"

They were all there, when the actress let out a terrible cry that had nothing to do with her repertoire. She was gracefully stretched out facing the viewscreen, and the whole brain-trust saw her features decompose, her face turn into a leaden mask... Olga Karpov threw her long arm towards her and slapped her. The five men, following the direction of her gaze, took refuge in front of the screen which reflected the night outside. A dreadful pale disc floated in the darkness: the frozen face of a dead man. In the vacuum of space, dragged into the orbit of the ship, a grotesque puppet followed the course of the *Daredevil*. His eyes glazed over and his mouth opened in nameless horror.

The Commander took a few wobbly steps towards the shiny surface and shouted:

"Freade, is that you? (His voice was terribly hoarse.) What are you saying? What are you doing there?"

This was Commander Szubinak's only failure; he passed a half-hand over his forehead and apologized: "He was my comrade – and he moved as if he were alive..."

The dislocated body rotated in a vacuum and disappeared from view.

"In any case," said the calm voice of Earl Stanley, "we no longer have to search for Anton Freade..."

It was the moment chosen by Jan Mudds, of the interplanetary police, to burst into the room. He had just attended the call of the guards. Pale, at attention, he recited like a lesson:

"Floor 2, hallway OXX, section B: two men lost, Commander – Shurst and Hazel."

"Killed?" Szubinak asked.

"No. Disappeared. Volatilized. Yes, that's the word..."

With the appearance of Freade's corpse, already, the most balanced of humans were starting to live on the margins of normality – but this declaration put the crowning touch to the horror. The group were frozen in the posture of automatons – Una Vere was panting, her mouth open. Olga Karpov had stopped in the middle of the room and, among the men, only Stanley kept his composure. He listened to Mudds' report and ended up extracting the truth from him in bits and pieces: the two men seemed to have been disintegrated, under the very eyes of the old astronaut...

"In short," Earl said, exaggerating his icy calm, "let's sum up: he's on the first floor, armed with a disintegrator. It would be a waste of time to oppose him with more men. It seems, however, that the energization of the walls holds him prisoner. Can't we increase it?"

"No," said Szubinak, "the walls wouldn't support it."

"Do you have another suggestion, Commander?"

Szubinak thought for a minute, then offered:

"Yes. It's necessary to consign the passengers to the cabins, to remove the guards from the exits. Then, we could bring our mobile blasters set to infrared – the heaviest setting – and scan all the available surfaces."

"Let's do it," said Earl Stanley.

CHAPTER VIII
Manhunt

Una Vere burst into Nan's cabin, one cheek redder than the other, her pink nylon negligee concealing nothing of her black lace underwear. She was trembling, like a frog seized with galvanic tremors.

"They located him!" she cried. "They have him! To arms! There he is, on the first floor, where he disintegrated two guards! My dear, this is thrilling! A real manhunt has begun... my cabin's next to yours and we'll spend these exciting hours together! Do you have any whiskey?"

"No," Nan replied dully. "And no gin or Venusian Shraoui either."

"It doesn't matter," said Free citizen Vere. "I'll suck on an pill, you know, one of those wonderful 'aphrodisiacs for reasonable use...' But now that I think about it," she added oddly, "it was Walter Cross who provided me with them."

"How?" asked Nan. "Did you know Walter Cross?"

"Of course," returned the astonishing creature. "Quite well. I slept with him the night before boarding."

Nan sat down on the bunk and took a deep breath. So, ultimately, there was a Walter Cross! It could not be this white and black fatality, adorned with the seductions of a fallen angel... For the night preceding the departure of the *Daredevil*, a spaceship rejected by infinity hadn't yet touched Earth. For hours, centuries, she had shivered with fear – she had believed herself to be pursued by superhuman force... intelligent, for whom it was the first cruise and who had pushed his naivety so far as to celebrate his stripes in the arms of Una Vere...

"Tell me about him," Nan said.

"Oh!" said Una, "about Walter? He was a delicious kid – one meter eighty of fresh flesh – and humor! We met in a Chinese restaurant and it was love at first sight! We left for the beaches of the South, by helicopter... My ancestors, what a guy! Do you believe we were going to do this madness – stay on Earth together! But Algebrant Vere kept my papers – and there was, of course, his bank account... So we came back..."

"Aboard the *Daredevil*?" Nan asked.

"No! In a bistro at the spaceport... And here's where things get complicated: I went to talk with Vere at his lab – and left him at the bar... When I came back, he was royally drunk – he told me things that I can't repeat –

despicable things about my age and old people in general. Poor kid – those Venusian cocktails are deadly...! I left him – he couldn't take two steps..."

"My God!" said Nan.

Without knowing how, she was standing. At this moment, behind the shiny doors, amplified by the loudspeakers, the voice of the Commander thundered:

"Alert everyone! Alert everyone! The Commander of this spacecraft is obliged to warn you that a dangerous criminal is on this floor. We are resorting to emergency measures. We're checking the tightness of partitions. Let no one leave their individual cabins. Don't let anyone in. Infrared blasters will sweep through the passages at 320 and all organic life will be destroyed. Alert everyone!"

Nan ran to the door – an interplanetary guard in battle gear was already blocking it. As imposing as a cupboard, he brandished his thermic pistol on the stop switch and turned a face of granite towards the young woman.

"Do not go out into the corridors," he repeated. "Block your seal adjusters. If you need information, contact the Command Post by intercom. It is forbidden to circulate in the corridors which are a danger zone. At the first movement, I shoot!"

"But I am Anne Stanley!" cried Nan. "I'm the Distortion Commissioner's wife."

The guard replied:

"Those are my orders, free citizen."

Leaning against the folding wall, Nan closed her eyes. She felt the commotion of the ship in her body, her veins echoing the footsteps and cries of the crew, the brief orders given by Earl and the powerful flows of energy that reinforced the defenses. In her temples rolled the blasters which one maneuvered.

"Are you blocking them at the incandescent index?" questioned a voice she recognized as Borelli's and in which she detected an unhealthy excitement.

"Yes," answered Szubinak. "Nothing escapes it. Refrigerators are turned on to protect floors and walls."

"Nothing... nothing can escape..." Borelli stammered. A silence followed, during which the commander reported to a higher authority. And Nan clearly heard Earl's voice:

"Fire!"

Una Vere had just leaped like a flame: it was her turn to understand "But," she cried, "it's insane! They're trying to get Walter Cross... but there's no Walter Cross on the *Daredevil*!"

"Ah!" said Nan, "you got it... I was wondering..."

"But I must warn them... It could be anyone of them! Walter never boarded; he was too drunk for that! The other is an impostor – he's probably some kind of mutant – one of those half-apes – and he's all the more dangerous! Quick, I have to contact the Commander."

"You won't," Nan said with her fearsome gentleness. "Do you think he doesn't have enough dangers to face?"

On the control panel, the thermal index jumped several degrees and a dull pulsation, the hum of tide in motion, announced that the ray blasters were going off.

Una's pupils widened and she licked her lips with a thin tongue.

"Let's see," she said, "let's see, if I understand correctly... You want to give him a chance? It's very sporty, very... but anyway, we won't see anything. But if I communicate with the Commander at this time, it's possible that we'll be summoned to the cockpit... They have interior sights there... What, is that not what you're thinking? There's nothing to be ashamed of, my dear. I love gladiator fights..."

She was heading for the intercom device, when Nan stepped in – and it was a struggle. Una Vere struggled and screamed, Nan managed to jostle the device which fell to the ground and she stepped on the wires.

"Young woman," cried Vere, "you would make me suppose the worst things!"

"As you please," Nan replied courteously.

"You take the side of this monster and who knows..." She banged her bony fists on the door and let out frightening cries. Nan's tense nerves heard the increasing hiss of the batteries – full incandescent infrared rays bathed the walls – she counted one-two-three blaster discharges. "Help!" shouted Una Vere hanging from the lock. "Beware of the mutant – the ape – the monster!"

Nan grabbed the rowdy girl; she was young, sporty, but her adversary's rage increased tenfold – they fought and both rolled under the bunk. It was, Nan thought, perfectly synchronized – a laughable little whirlwind, at the heart of a cyclone... The free lady spat out two or three teeth and managed to reach an ebony casket on the dressing table; she threw it at Nan's head. A red veil rose, concealed the world. Outside, incandescent hell was unleashed...

It was at this moment that the door of the secret cabinet slid on its hinges without noise. Una Vere, who had already reached the intercom, spun around like a puppet with a broken spring and went to lie down on the white bear skin. Her neck twisted oddly and a bit of pink foam wet her lips.

"Don't kill her!" Nan yelled. "I beg you – not in front of me!"

"It's not my fault she's epileptic, after all," replied a subdued voice. "You should have sent her a paralyzing wave, instead of fighting... You didn't think about it. We get dirty, among humans."

He stood in the doorway of the lab, and he laughed, pitilessly – like, as of old, a brown and silver young god. Him. Walter Cross, for others – probably. In fact – Arno Heller.

He descended into the cabin, with his feline grace. "I would have come sooner," he confessed, "but there was this horde of guards in the corridors and I didn't want to compromise you. So, I went into the next cabin and tampered with the walls a bit. No one heard anything. And humans always miss monatomic structures..."

She wanted to yell: "Go away!" But no sound came from her lips.

"So don't struggle like a trapped thrush," Arno said with a sort of unexpected sadness. "I didn't ask you anything, did I? I just couldn't live without you – so I changed the structure of the atom, you know. My spaceship exploded and we went through the void – it's as simple as that."

He wiped the blood from his cheek and Nan said, fascinated: "Did Freade hurt you?"

"No. That wound, I've already healed it. It's Spriegel's heat gun." He added, with courtesy: "If you really want it, I can leave."

"You will be shot on the threshold!" Nan said harshly.

Perfectly arched eyebrows rose: "Do you believe it? We mutants don't die so fast."

A silence fell. Nan came to lean against the cabin door. Arno Heller had not moved. Above an oddly twisted Una Vere, he shone with his wicked angel radiance.

"Do you remember our last conversation?" he asked. "On Andromeda, in the pandanus house...? It was so difficult, Nan, and so painful! What they were doing to my brain was unimaginable – the finest butchery job! It took me years to undo that. There were days when I truly believed that there never was an Atlantis – and that I was just Arno Heller, the rocket mechanic...

"But I managed to survive and I think I've changed less than you, Nan. You have become so human! It seems you have all the virtues of a good Earth wife..."

Motionless, against the wall that bounded hell, fascinated by this blood whose flow disfigured the beautiful face, Nan murmured:

"I have to heal you, don't I...?"

"It's not necessary. I wouldn't want to inflict this supreme disgust on you: touching the wounds of a mutant!"

She cried: "You're crazy, Arno!" It was like a dike that had broken, she knew that nothing would hold her back anymore and that they were on the same side. Earl Stanley's face, his tenderness made of security and reserve, were already fading. A flash of gentle irony shone in the mutant's eyes, and he allowed himself a moderate triumph:

"Are we on familiar terms or not? These constant changes tire me..."

The loudspeakers thunder again:

"Alert everyone! Alert everyone! The infra operation is over, but no one can move outside without a suit. The interplanetary guards have taken up duty at the doors of the cabins, of which a commission will control the occupants. Prepare your identity microfilms. Anyone who flees will be shot. Alert everyone!"

"What are we doing, Nan?" inquired Arno Heller. On his lips, her mere name became a caress, and the inextricable situation, a game. "Of course, you could deliver me to these earthly brutes; they're numerous and I'm hurt. You might be rid of me. But I don't believe you're going to give me away..."

Flabbergasted, she threw: "You attacked Anton Freade...!"

"No," he said, "although I don't see the need to justify myself. It was he who attacked me when I broke the viewscreen. We fought – and he managed to knock me out with the butt of his thermic."

"So what?"

"So nothing. As I fell, I managed to open the hatch, using my electromagnetism. He got through it, dragging me along. You know that us mutants don't follow the laws of gravity... I went back."

"You killed Elisa Borelli."

"Not even that. I simply released her inhibitions and complexes – and she felt unable to live. She was getting dangerous, you know. Admit that I acted in self-defense."

"Yes," she said. "But why destroy this accursed circular?"

"Because my name was on it. And also yours."

Knocks echoed behind the panel. With a sudden movement, Nan pushed Arno towards the secret lab. Then she opened the door. Commander Szubinak was there, a gun in hand – he was about to apologize and recoiled at the sight of Una Vere...

"She wanted to go out during the infra operation," explained Nan. "She claimed to have a communication to make to you – something about this Cross whom she knew intimately. I opposed it, because, really, it wasn't the moment. And then she had a terrible seizure – I didn't know she was prone to epilepsy..."

"Me neither," Szubinak whispered. In his heart of hearts, he cursed Vere: an epileptic on board! All that was missing! As the interplanetary guards relieved Una, she struggled wildly. Nan backed up to the lab door and bombarded the energy with imperative waves. The partition moved slightly and the young woman, who had crossed her arms behind her back, felt Arno's fingers curling around hers. "I can still call for help," she thought. "I can shout: 'The criminal you're looking for is here!' I would have broken all ties with the past, I would be free... He would die." But with terrible lucidity, she understood that she would not survive Arno.

Lips rested on her icy wrist. She begged: "Hurry, citizens. I think I'm starting to feel ill..."

The guards rushed in, understanding.

They soon retired ,carrying Una Vere, foaming, over whom the Commander had mercifully thrown his cloak. A hundred times, a thousand times, Nan saw (as the Perfume Dispenser had promised in a terrible past) Arno Heller dead at her feet, and she almost cried out in anguish, released her blood and died too.

The sound of footsteps died down on the stairs, she ran to push the bolt and Arno received her in his arms, like a wreath of lilies. She pulled away violently. He observed: "You saved my life."

Rising like a snake, Nan hissed: "Yes, I owed you, didn't I? But now I've paid my debt, it's over between us – I love Earl!"

"It doesn't matter," he said distractedly. "You already thought you loved Neor. He was good and I was bad. Yet, it was in my arms that you died..."

"Did you see the end?" she asked eagerly. "To say that I wanted so much and that I couldn't! No doubt I was half-mad when I died. It was during the escape in the caves, wasn't it?"

"No, it was coming out of the caves. The ocean was rushing through the cracks in the rocks and we managed to climb to the top of the island.

You weren't mad, but unconscious, and so as not to get carried away by the waves, I tied you to me with a vine. But the water was still rising, and that's how we died."

"Does this mean that we will remain linked for eternity?" Nan almost yelled. "I don't want to! I have nothing to do with your follies and your crimes! You are the most monstrous being... You destroyed Andromeda and all those unfortunate folks..."

"Oh!" he said, "you call that a crime? Their life and their death were equal. Spoiled granddaughter of Sir Neptune, what do you know of the miserable ones? I was one of them myself. They lived a vegetable existence, on an ungrateful rock, where the very air was artificial – and they only left this empty hell, for succession took place every twenty years! And so, they received a nice retirement and they were going to spend on Earth, after two or three months, because they had lost the habit of breathing nitrogen or earth bacteria – and their family being dead, or remained on Andromeda, no one even knew where they were buried!

"I gave them a dazzling adventure and a beautiful death: Earth hasn't finished singing their glory! Because I opened to it – to this frenzied planet – a window on infinity, I put within its reach all the immensity of worlds and galaxies – all different, all magnificent!

"If it was a crime Nan, I don't regret it!"

He was telling the truth. Nan remembered the last night on Earth, its crimson light, that delirious crowd, and the face of the Dark Angel in the clouds. This crime, she said to herself, it is for this crime that they have divined her! Distractedly rubbing her wrist, as if to remove the burn from a kiss, she questioned:

"Why did you board the *Daredevil*?"

He smiled. And everything was immediately simplicity itself...

"Come on, I couldn't just let you run away again?!I was no longer a moron, a brain amputee, like on Andromeda. I saw you get on the spaceship and I think you saw me too. I ran out of time, desperately. I picked up a decaying radio officer from a bar, made him drink liters of gin, after which I grabbed his papers and introduced myself under his name. He was a certain Walter Cross..."

"They could have recognized you!"

"It was a risk to run..."

"Come on," said Nan, "come on," and she clutched her temples in her hands, like every time an excess of notions invaded her brain. "I still don't understand! How come your name was on that flyer? No one suspected your presence on board! After all, you're Arno Heller, Galactic Hero – Earth gave you a delirious reception... The stereo transmitters told about your childhood, enough stories to make a diplodocus cry – and I felt like I was going crazy! So?"

"So, it's very simple, it's not Arno Heller, it's Walter Cross who appeared on the flyer. This takes nothing away from the charm of the manhunt."

"I don't understand. Was he a mutant too?"

Arno shrugged. "The smartest woman – and you are that, Nan – will never swallow human baseness. No, Walter Cross was a perfectly stupid young stallion... But there are cells on Earth and throughout our solar system of a powerful organism called the Space Distortion Committee..."

"I know," Nan said. She had read enough, despite his defenses, into Earl Stanley's brain.

Arno showed his young wolf teeth, smiling: "I think so too," he said, "you are well placed to know too... This terrible machine was set up, like all organizations of this kind, for an excellent reason: by the fault of the inventors who were too reckless or too hasty, this good old Earth was in peril; it was necessary to put a brake on the games of the sorcerer's apprentices... The goal of the Spatial Distortion Committee is twofold: first, to study the means of defeating hyperspace, under all security guarantees; second, monitor any penetration into our galaxy, as well as any individual attempts. You see that this can go a long way! This organization is their Inquisition, a legal mafia, singularly more powerful than ministers, parliaments and billionaires, so much so that, if the federal president came up tomorrow to build his little hyperspace machinery, it's likely he would die of an embolism within a week. And we would bury him with honors that would be due to him..."

"Yes," Nan said. "But where does this unlimited power come from?"

"From fearful panic," replied Arno. "From what they call the 'Year 2000 Terror', the age from which, for fear of disintegration, humanity accumulated its legacies and directed its best minds towards a controlled science. Me, I was – I still am – a maverick... Well, while Earth, as you say, gave me a delirious ovation, the Space Committee didn't let me down: they knew how Andromeda had ended. I guess they already knew that when I landed on Earth. They should have arrested me then... Yes, but to seize Arno Heller whom the solar system carried in triumph? Getting your hands on Hero No. 1? The thing was risky, and the Committee is composed of cunning minds.

"It happened, however, that I lent my flank to their enterprises, embarking under a false name... They jumped at the chance. It is therefore Walter Cross who was the game to be killed on board the *Daredevil*. Later, they will pretend to find, in a mountain crevasse somewhere, a corpse which will become that of Arno Heller, and Earth will preserve a dazzling memory of him!"

He passed over his open wound, the transparency of which gleamed, an uncertain hand, and pronounced between two tones: "Let's not forget that your husband is Hunter No. 1, Nan. What time does he come here?"

She restrained herself to answer: "I don't think he will come tonight. He has too much to do in the cockpit."

The dark eyes had again an icy flash: "In short, why did he marry you?"

"Pity!" she threw dryly. "Because I was alone on Earth, and, unfortunately, not human enough. Because I knew you'd come back, ruining all my chances, wreaking havoc on your way – and I wanted to run away from you again. Earl picked me up like a rag, at the starport docks..."

"Strange pity!" said Arno. "But he does look like Neor. He would find a single pearl in the mud and pick it up – out of pity, so that it would not be trampled on..."

"Shut your mouth. You're not worth Neor's little finger!"

"You've already told me – and not just once. And also that my lips sullied his name, just by pronouncing it... What torture to be bound by timeless ties to an idealistic girl who has the mentality and the prejudices of a Great Conjurer of Atlantis!" He dropped that taunting tone to add: "I'm afraid to embarrass you, Nan. I am, for some time, a prisoner in this cabin – the walls are still energized – I guess they're preparing a new operation and I've exhausted all my static energy..."

"I didn't ask you to leave," she replied.

CHAPTER IX
The Truce

The Commander made his report to the brain trust: he was out! By energizing the structures of the spacecraft, he had risked his ship – a beautiful ship, which he valued more than the apple of his eye. He had swept the floors with infrared, arousing protests which would go, he said, to the Interplanetary Council, especially in the third hold, where the passengers could not manage to hold their children and where there now was a recrudescence of cases of void sickness. Two steerages were delirious...

At this time, the guards were still walking the holds, in an atmosphere of "Last Judgment"; blue smoke darkened the air and a suffocating heat, despite the fans, had invaded the upper corridors. Szubinak himself, the encephalograph in front of him, had checked the declarations of passengers – and he had found nothing. Una Vere kept yelling at the nurse claiming that her brain had been stuffed with electrons – and there were times when the Commander started to believe it!

"Do you think," Vere asked, coming out of his group, "that my wife received a blast of mental energy?"

The Commander planted his honest simple navigator pupils in the evasive eyes of the chemist:

"She's not epileptic, is she? At least, that's what you said in your applications: *Vere, Una Stephanie – nervous diseases – none...*"

Vere stretched his lean body. "No," he said. "She's never been sick, but she's an artist, hypersensitive. If it didn't seem... paranormal, I would say that she reacts to certain, er, presences..."

"Perfect," said Karpov, "I think we're cooking. We're on the trail of a being who makes fun of electromagnetic energy and plays with microsteel, an invisible being – or nearly so – since encephalography does not reveal his clandestine presence, but who acts on the nerves of sensitive women... By the way, this encephalography, did you use it everywhere, sir?"

Szubinak hesitated a moment: "Except in your personal cabins..."

"You should have," Earl replied, icily. "Nobody is safe from suspicion. I am not telling you that we are betraying you, but it is easy to upset a being's mental equilibrium by plunging him into an environment of harmful associations of ideas, or even by hypnosis or electro-shock. In the future, as far as your research is concerned, treat us as mere passengers, Commander Szubinak."

The others nodded.

"Let's continue," Karpov went on. "However, this being, however paranormal in his manifestations, also has an organic action: he killed three interplanetary guards as well as Freade, and unbalanced, to varying degrees, two members of our team: free citizens Vere and Borelli. Incidentally, a chance for you, Vere, that free citizen Stanley was present: without her, your wife might have gone under the infrared!"

"But why women?" Olga Karpov asked.

"For the obvious reason," replied her husband, "which your very presence here underlines again; because those two were the most impressionable. This doesn't mean that others are safe: a corrosive acid first attacks fragile materials, and acts gradually."

"This is but one aspect of the matter!" Vere protested. "The being we pursue is not pure energy. I had the blood stains on the radio screen and the spacesuit collar analyzed. Here are the conclusions of my chemists: it isn't blood, but..."

"What?" Szubinak asked.

"A vegetable sap, strongly added with hemoglobin. The being we are dealing with is therefore not quite terrestrial, let's say – not quite human..."

"I like this better!" sighed the Commander. "Weren't there a species of thinking plants on Saturn?"

"Yes, but they didn't move out of their soil. Make no mistake, this phantom does look human. Don't your charts, Borelli, mention a green-blooded humanoid species?"

Borelli made a helpless gesture: "Only when it comes to degeneration..."

"It is a mutation," said Earl Stanley. He looked up at the team members with a stricken face, but his voice was calm. "I should have told you about this from the start, but I hesitated – after all, these were secret documents of the Space Committee. But the *Daredevil* is out of the communications range; it's up to each of us to take our risks. Remember, Borelli: at one time, the Biological Institute gave us reports from the Astral Belt – these were phenomena involving several planets, but Andromeda took precedence. Here and there, we noted the births – normal – of children with green blood. These little non-humans were gifted with unique abilities..."

"The KZs," said Borelli. "I thought that they had been operated on and that they suffered badly from the ablation of certain cervical centers?"

"I vaguely remember some grim stories," Vere said. "These children had strange abilities..."

"...Like adapting to any gravity, breaking down electrical energy – and God knows what else. They were, in short, monsters, well prepared to repopulate any planet, better conditioned than humanity in general, and that made them extremely dangerous... It may be that the radiation of the solar system being understood, we would later need such a race, but these spontaneous 'Hyperspatials' came too soon. They upset all the laws... We tried to bring them back to the norm, and the human mass believed, in fact, that we had destroyed them all. It seems that this is not the case..."

"We would therefore," Karpov said slowly, "be dealing with a KZ mutant from Andromeda. That's what you want us to hear, isn't it, Stanley?"

"For my part," said Earl, "I am convinced of it. And that worries me."

"You mean that...?"

"It is a danger that we cannot limit or conscribe on a single level. I am under no illusions. Your wife was not neurasthenic, Borelli, and I doubt that free citizen Vere ever exhibited symptoms of epilepsy; they nevertheless succumbed to an insidious will which replaced their own. I believe that from now on, we will all have to watch not only the corridors of the *Daredevil*, but our own thoughts."

"I have an idea," Szubinak said, listening to Earl intently. "It's not, of course, a scientist's idea – but I have traveled a lot – and on some planets we have encountered such strange life forms! The hypnotizing birds, and others... So here it is: to take this paranormal creature alive, we need organic, living agents, that his presence can impress... Thank God, he's not human, right?"

"No," Stanley said vigorously, "he's not quite a human creature. Your idea, Commander?"

"Here it is: we have on board this ship a zoo which includes, among other things, a dozen wolves, hyenas and jackals; these beasts, good destroyers of waste, were to be landed on the asteroid. We could make them smell Cross's armor and release them."

"All right," said Earl Stanley. "Do it."

As the scientists withdrew, the Commander, with an imperceptible sign, held back the Distortion Commissioner.

"Free citizen," he said, "we've had our first contact with Andromeda. And I would like to tell you that I am bored already."

It was huge for Szubinak who hardly trusted himself and expressed himself in euphemisms: his profession wanted that. He led Earl to the safety screen and used the brain adjuster. "We can't see anything yet, normally," he explained. "We're receiving radiation from asteroids here. The glow projected in front of us is infinitesimal, which would be nothing, since Andromeda is an artificial low-density satellite. But it's double or triple, which means..." He didn't finish. He rummaged through the microfilms received from Earth. "We believe we have a complete picture of the disaster here," he added. "It was understood that there was no longer a trace of atmosphere and that organic life had been annihilated. But there was no indication that tremors were continuing!"

Earl adopted his adjuster on the small stereo screen and stared, without turning pale or changing his expression, at the fluctuating spectre that heralded the worst of things. When he turned to Szubinak, his face was inscrutable and his eyes clear.

"It's not about orbital motions," he noted. "Simply a force of inertia. But that doesn't advance us."

"You conclude?"

"That gravity acting, instead of one Andromeda, we'll find two or three. God knows them to be habitable!"

"But," murmured the Commander, "you believe that the Committee..."

"The function of the Committee is to foresee the worst catastrophes. It's not for nothing that we loaded twenty separate ozonators."

For a moment Szubinak did not realize the threat in such a statement: already an artificial satellite devastated and reduced by earthquakes presented a well-conditioned hell, but to suppose that Earth was going to swarm its colonists on fireballs – it there was a step, he hesitated to take it. However, he advanced the monstrous hypothesis:

"Do you intend to disembark all the same...?"

"Listen, Commander," Earl cut in, "I won't waste my time explaining this to Borelli or Vere. But an astronaut is placed under the same laws as a federal astrophysicist; we belong to the same organism, of which we're the brain and you're the arms. Therefore, you know that an order is not to be discussed. Do Earth and the Sol System need the outpost that is Andromeda? This is obvious, and the disaster that has befallen this satellite only confirms it. If it was an extrasolar attack, the Astral Belt is blocking an invader. If, on the contrary, as I believe, this position served as a spring-board for illegal tests, we must study the danger on the spot."

"Heavens!" Szubinak whispered.

"It is visible here," Earl continued, "that the satellite is fragmented into two or three unequal bodies which rotate on the same axis and that erosion threatens. We will have to establish the artificial gravitation devices and to hold until the moment when they will have welded these together. The operation will cost less than the creation of a new satellite. It will make the task of the first settlers harder than we feared, however. I will be the first to break the news."

The Commander bowed. Earl asked again:

"When do you plan to launch the wolves?"

Szubinak consulted his chronometer:

"The folks in the steerage below are a little too excited – we'll give them two more hours to rest before we do. Let's do it at six o'clock in the morning – solar time."

And Earl suddenly realized that it had been hours – centuries – since he had left Command Post or seen Nan.

"I think I fainted," noted Arno Heller, propping himself up on one elbow on his polar bear skin.

"Idiot," said Nan, "don't you know that state? It is one of complete relaxation. When we're at the end of our rope, we recover, and during this time, Earth could split open. I think death for mutants is that. And one day, we wake up and..."

"Even if it means reuniting the scattered atoms of our envelope. And if something is missing, we are terribly hungry."

"Are you hungry?"

He grimaced: "It's been three days since I've eaten anything."

"What are you eating now?"

"Alas! Neither rust nor nickel. Their operations succeeded in damaging my digestive tract: human food is not needed. Annoying, isn't it? Can you let me rest for two more minutes? I have in my carcass two or three of their thermal projectiles and it tires me a little..."

The infrared radiator, which in no way recalled the threat of scarlet death, bathed the pale face and the long-lowered eyelashes as if on a haunting pleasure. Nan clenched her fists and ran to the cupboard, looking like Judith about to finish off Holofernes. She remembered that the lift still contained her breakfast that she had forgotten and sighed in relief. The mechanism only started to work when the tray got lighter. She was able to bring back a solid ration of ham sandwiches, eggs and oatmeal. Hot coffee was in the thermos. She watched Arno gobbling up these foodstuffs; his face expressed a slight disgust. He laughed:

"Do you despise me for feeding myself like everyone else? Are you still on arsenic and lime?"

"No," she returned, oblivious and distinguished. "I have a little jar of bitter oranges that taste delicious, like almonds. But they look like cyanide..."

"And how do you do at a table?"

"Oh! I got used to it... I spit food out without difficulty."

After a moment of silence, she asked: "These thermal projectiles... there's nothing to remove them?"

"Not for the moment. But they're not dangerous, only troublesome, they wander off my diaphragm. One of these days, my muscles will eventually eject them. It's not the first time, as you may think..."

"You had a difficult life...?"

"Difficult enough. Do you remember that already, at the rocket cemetery, the Earthlings accepted me with little grace? And I'm not talking about cross-browser brawls. Remember this, my child, we can only be killed quickly by a bullet to the heart, which takes away control of our circulation. The rest can take care of itself. We even scar the cervical tissues and, if removed, our gray cells proliferate. I know a thing or two..."

"How come your blood is... almost red?" Nan asked, lightly touching the wound on his forehead.

"Transfusions, I guess. My vegetable blood disgusted those damned nurses from Andromeda. Deep down, I've always hated Earthlings, ever since..."

"Yes," replied Nan, acerbically. "I saw the proof of it, at the Martian's..."

A fleeting, amused smile restored Arno's face to its youthful grace. "So," he said, leaning on his elbow, "was that it? I always wondered which of my 'crimes' had offended you so much... Was it because of this stupid affair – having sex – that you ran away, cursing me? Shut up, don't protest, for once! Note, I suspected your presence – but I was so dazed by their operations, and my blood was so heavy! These foreign tissues, these glands that they had transplanted into me – they weighed tons! It took me a long time to assimilate them... But you, Nan, free and brilliant, whom I had warned, you should have understood! I had so much hope for you!

Whenever I was in too much pain, their anesthetics weren't taking – three out of five times – I was screaming, 'Help me, Nan!' I was screaming inside myself, of course. I was too scared to drag you into this mess – in fact, you were probably the only one from Andromeda, the only one from our race of mutants, to escape it... I thought to myself: 'It's fine since I warned her, she won't forget, even if I forgot everything. If she meets me one day, in a crowd, she will call me by my name – and I will wake up from this nightmare!'"

He too was clenching his fists, biting his lips, and Nan understood that he was reliving the terrible moments...

"Remember," he continued, "I never knew much of Andromeda. I knew nothing outside of this closed world, I had read no books... And it contained this shelter – the rocket cemetery, the garden of your convent with its wall of ivy, where I came up to see you. Your house that I admired so much... I lost all that, because I wanted to see you again. But I still have to thank you. To exist, first. To be the free mutant, the dazzling Nan who despised me, when I was trying to acclimatize myself, to fit in with the masses... Oh! Nan, you don't have to have your eyes on the starport, to address that pathetic boy who dared to look up at you!

"You were right: the mechanic Arno Heller was not entitled to it: he was a loser, he lacked courage, even to commit suicide. In his life without horizon, he had, like many stars, only a roof of sheet metal, far from the ozonators, and the wages of his day which he drank, the sad brute!

"You almost reproached me for this sordid adventure at the Martian's... Oh! Nan, how happy I am! Do you know that was the first woman I touched? She was boorish, ignoble, and stank of rancid oil; me, I closed my eyes, I clenched my teeth – and I thought of you.

"That was my 'betrayal', if you want to give it that grandiose name – and those that followed were hardly better!"

Now he fell silent, but Nan had slipped to the ground, near the wounded man; she no longer knew if she was once again supporting, in the caves, a heavy and feverish body, or if the giant with dead wings was carrying her over the rocks. She tore herself away from this heartrending sweetness to throw out:

"It's all the same. I wanted to kill you. You disgust me too much!"

"Nan, you're a monster. Don't you realize that you're even more monstrous than me?"

"What did you say? Repeat it, repeat it!"

She dazzled him with her snow whiteness, her colorless eyes. "Didn't you mix everything – the good and the bad, the pain and the pretty – in an inexpressible mixture? You don't know how to hold your blood or speed up your circulation? Oh!" she cried suddenly, digging her nails into Arno's shoulders, "why can't we talk to each other without hurting each other? Why are you calling me a monster, for the second time...?"

"Admit," he said gravely, "that the first time was deserved?"

"I don't think so. I don't believe it. I never understood all these stories of love and hate – nor the ties that united us, you, the dispenser of perfumes, and I. I guess my island perished because you unleashed all your senses, not just the human ones, but those outsized abilities – electromagnetism, atomic fission, what else do I know? For the sole purpose of possessing the world and extracting a few black drops of voluptuousness from it. I don't know... Probably, at the time when I lived by your side, was I too young to understand..."

"You're still too young, Nan."

"But I would like to know..."

"For what reason?" he asked with deep sadness. "You see, I don't regret anything about that life: we were new then, in the fullness of our faculties and our strength, and filled with faith in ourselves, that same 'faith that moves mountains'. I believe that, having returned to the same point, I would have acted as before. Now, whoever we are, we belong to an old world and a different civilization.

"You would tell me that Atlantis was highly civilized – yes, but in another way... Just think of its laws... Just now, you asked me what ties united me to the dispenser of perfumes: she was my sister and was to become my wife – sacred incest does not date just from the Pharaohs. We belonged to a race which asserted itself through death and pleasure; an Atlantean could not have relations with an ordinary Human, without killing him! And we developed within us the faculties of destruction which, spurting out all at once, like sheaves of flame, created a terrible void around us.

"To kill, to love, was like one. It is possible that identical civilizations, more likely of insects, still exist on distant planets of our galaxy. Everything shameful, carnal attached to human unions, all ancestral terrors come from there... Our so beautiful Island was a world of triumphant criminals... And you were no better than the others!

"Worse no doubt, because my sister was Nellare. Fearing no ascendancy on the winged Atlanteans, she did everything to weaken my will, to

117

rot me... That's the correct word. I was obnoxious, Nan. My only normal, avowable feeling, according to our current moral code, was my love for you – but the laws of Atlantis made it the darkest of crimes.

"It is moreover for that crime that I was to be tortured when the providential cataclysm arrived. I had, three times, disobeyed the queen, and you yourself had pronounced my death warrant."

"I don't understand!" Nan exclaimed again, clutching her temples with both hands. "It seems to me, however, that I was mad about you... Wait, don't touch me! It was in the other life."

"Do you want us to relive it, for a moment, together?" muttered Arno. "It was such agony and such delight..."

CHAPTER X
Falling Star

They plunged back into Time.

And again, it was the Divine Island, the original ocean, the cities of onyx and jade, the vast hanging gardens, with the strokes of azaleas and magnolias – drunk with perfumes... A world of deaf and powerful pulsations of universal life – and the palace of blue opal, on the hillside.

Two moons stood behind the golden colonnade. Nonchalantly stretched out at full length on the snow leopards' furs, his black wings folded, Arno – Hellemar – the Singing Sword, royal prince of Atlantis, listened to the recriminations of Queen Nellare, his sister. The panics that seized the Dispenser of Perfumes from time to time were foreign to her. One would have said that the blood of this princess, turned black, poisoned by all her excesses, was swirling in her veins; she trembled, she came to wake him during the night, naked and adorned with all her jewels, her heels and palms stained with anemone juice – and she walked through the rooms, twisting her hips and her hands.

"So you don't understand!" she cried. "Stupid race of men worse than apes! This Earth where you have prospered has so stupefied you! What are your antennae and wings for? Besides, I will break them one day! There is a prophecy of this world: this girl will be the last Conjurer of the Island, after which Atlantis will pray!"

"Well," asked the Singing Sword without leaving his cousins, "maybe this will be a fun experience? Humanity perishing in a single night... Nellare, you have never attempted such great carnage!"

She stared at him with her white eyes of anger and terror:

"You are mad! You don't have any more sap in your veins – and that hardly surprises me – but I want to live! I want to crush, trample the human anthills, rummage with both hands in the palpitating bodies!"

"Lovely program!"

This power of irony went beyond Nellare; she stumbled against it, like a monstrous ant on a piece of glass. Without trying to understand, she hissed:

"It is said that on a distant planet there are beings invisible to the naked eye who visit us, and whose tentacles – digits – plunge into our brains. They extricate or create images at will. I would like to be one of these creatures. I would like to knead your brain!"

"Yes, but you can't help it, we are of the same race. As for shaping brains, my poor friend, I really don't see what you could create that's new? A few visions of orgy or butchery? Go, don't regret anything, I'm better off without you."

Nellare struck the flagstones with her bare foot:

"Everywhere," she cried, "these absurd barriers! Only an Atlantean can destroy an Atlantean! Not one of those fat wallowing pigs can deliver me from that girl! She is however not well hidden; her radiation breaks my nerves!"

"I really don't see why you would want to kill her so much?" Helle-mar muttered, wearily. "You've never seen her; she's not old enough to bother you. Besides, as far as I remember, there have always been Conjurers in Atlantis; these pale virgins have interrogated the Heavens and their virtues will make counterweight of our lusts. They die young; this double burden must be unbearable. This one will perish like the others."

"Let your Atlantea drag out her anemia for twenty years; you will receive no more remonstrances than the other sovereigns of this island and, since you promised that she will be last prophetess, at her death you will heave a sigh of relief..."

"So you didn't get it?" Nellare shrilled. "When she dies, this world will cease to exist!"

"Well, if it's going to produce such a burst of cosmic energy, I don't see what you can do to oppose it? This prophecy is very old."

"I want to kill her. Just before she reaches the age of Revelation... I can make sure that Atlantis does not have a Conjurer called Atlantea... And since the prophecy will be disproved on this point, I'm sure that cannot be realized on others!"

"Oh!" said the Singing Sword, interested, "you talk about this dead woman as if you were going to crush a little lizard! But never will an Atlantean raise their hand to this white shadow that holds the destinies of their island. I'm not talking about the others – they couldn't cross the mental barriers. Under these conditions, who will be her killer?"

"You!"

Here. It was as simple as that. The imperatives of an Atlantean queen could not be eluded, any more than an arrow returns to her quiver. Helle-mar stood up and stretched out his silver, feline body into the white glow. This mission bored him, nothing more. He had never killed his victim.

"A child," he thought with disgust. "She'll probably run and cry, and I'll have to try several times – or talk to her sweetly. Disgusting. Why does Nellare always burden me with odious and easy work? She entrusted her ships to Neor, she could have chosen me, but no, she keeps me on hand for her dirty deeds..."

He was not thinking of the Atlantean people, capable of lifting up and defending the child-priestess. Neither of the priests nor of the mental barriers that defended the sacred domain. The matter is settled between him and Atlantea.

"When will I leave?" he asked without looking at the queen.

Perhaps she was hoping for his presence. She stood in the lunar flow and her azure body, supple as a vine, was a call. The invisible presence of this child, promised to death, could have enriched their night of love.

But Hellemar had already chosen a perfect weapon from a panoply, a dagger of sparkling rock crystal...

"You will strike tonight!" decided the queen.

The second image that presented itself was that of the Happy Valley. The rose quartz walls radiated a peace, a gentle, disillusioned wisdom. No barriers were erected; the Priest-King gave the keys to Hellemar.

He descended towards the beach, by the path of lilies. Each sharp thyrsus, each clump of azaleas was a canephore which throws its floral load under a triumphal chariot or on a tomb. The largest moon, the one that had the appearance of a silver shield, rolled among the clouds and its light traced a road of opals to the waves; the other, furtive and blue, danced on the giant ferns. The ocean was calm, solemn and shimmering with its millions of scales, already in the East, the sky was turning green.

She stood above the waves, in her white tunic, and her long, shiny blue hair touched the water. Her eyes were two glaciers, two polar stars; it had taken millennia and generations of purer Atlantean blood to create this fearsome and perfect jewel. Hellemar knew she was going to be fifteen at dawn...

A triple circle of snakes surrounded her with a rustling enclosure. All the friends of the little Conjurer had arranged to meet; gold, turquoise, emerald, they had left their covers, their stones warm in the sun, and they undulated to the rhythm of a strange music. A melody that was not of this world: Atlantea had made its own pipe, with a wicker rod, and she stretched out crystal fibers. A held note evoked flight in space, a fluid and deep universe, spirals of stars too perfect to be alive. She realized this miracle: to make herself heard by snakes as by men. Triangular shadows, the heads of reptiles swayed on the white sand. Hellemar had jumped from his chariot and was advancing, without feeling that the biggest of the pythons had relaxed like a whip and was embracing him. He had not taken ten steps on the beach when he was already paralyzed, reduced to help-lessness, and he despised the danger; he gazed, as if drawn by a magnet, at Her whose smile gives a Happy Death. He wanted this death. And the dance of the snakes surrounded it with its volutes.

"Are you Prince Hellemar?" sang the musical wave. "How handsome you are! At the dawn of this great day, does the queen send you to pay homage to me or to kill me?"

"Choose, Atlantea."

"Look, the moons are pale, in the East stretches an emerald lake. Pres-ently a bar of silver will sink into the sea... I am fifteen years-old and no mortal can touch my shadow. I choose to believe it was a tribute... it's the best she could have done."

"It will be what you wanted."

"At the dawn of this day, I can choose a victim..."

"She's there."

"The sun is rising, Sword who Sings! My friends are in a hurry to return to their homes. Are you really happy to die before my eyes?"

"I do not ask for another fate. Even dead, I'll follow you everywhere, Atlantea..."

She shrugged her shoulders: "My first liege man, my herald! Of course, I won't kill you..." The music faltered imperceptibly and the mon-ster released its grip, the brief triangular head slid down to the ground. Already a gleam was flashing – Hellemar had freed his arm and the crystal dagger was finishing the beast. "Too bad," said Atlantea, without moving, "such a beautiful python!"

The reptile had detached itself like a dead branch and was lying on the sand. But the dancing forest surrounded Hellemar. "Would you have preferred to see me dead instead?" he asked. The girl shook her head:

"If I wanted to, you would be..."

It was at this moment, in the first rays of a triumphant sun – gold and honey – that he clearly struck, carried by the wild waves, the voice – the cry – of Nellare: "Kill her! Kill her!" cried the queen. "Because no one will know! I command you! Hellemar, I will make you pay dearly for this betrayal!"

"Has anyone told you," asked the prince, "that you are beautiful, Atlantea? Is it pleasant to be the last Conjurer of a doomed continent, when one is fifteen years-old and has the face of an azalea...?"

"Oh!" she said, "a Conjurer has no face. For a second I have no more eyes, no more mouth; at the coronation, I will put on a golden mask, so that no one sees the features that are no longer... You will accompany me to the City, will you not, Singing Sword?"

"Yes."

"Shouldn't the queen grant me the first three temporal pardons that I will demand?"

"The Queen...? Yes."

"Even when it comes to his blood?"

"The law is the law."

"So I will ask her that she gave you to me, Hellemar. You will be my vassal, my guard and my shadow. Don't be afraid, you won't have to do anything, Isides will take care of the Temple and Neor of my people. But only I have rights over my liege-men. No one on this island can touch their hair: it is sacred."

He accompanied her in his chariot, among the rustling carpets of snakes. Beneath the terrible glare of ice, he felt devoid of all strength and all desire, happy as a drowning man who lets himself be carried away by the wave. For a single moment, the sea breeze playing with the flowing hair of the Conjurer, had enveloped him in a shroud of perfumes in which he thought he would faint.

He could never forget that triumphant morning – the huge orange sun bursting from the sea, the murmur of the priests and the murmur of the people. His place, on the chariot with the golden axles, at the side of Atlantea – and the purple mantle with which he had covered her frail shoulders. The gates of the City which opened before the Last Conjurer, the onyx and diamond threshold which they crossed together, his heart too big his chest and the touch of a small hand which pierced him with an acute delight.

Hellemar's second crime was simply to refuse the throne – and the bed – of Nellare.

It was up to the Conjurer to admonish the prince, moreover, had this law not existed, Nellare had invented this torture.

Following a strange ethic, the two women agreed. The coronation of Atlantea had been a triumph; a thousand times reflected by the mental images, in an orb of glory, on the steps of the Temple, on her chariot, ascending to the altar, the Conjurer appeared to her people. The sailors of the ships massed along the continent saluted her, and the laborers prostrated themselves in the fields. Twelve princesses of royal blood wore her train and, when the time came to gird the narrow temples with the headband of selenite with a thousand antennae, the queen offered the symbolic jewels, on her knees.

Locked in his palace of opals, all the blinds of ivory drawn, Hellemar had to follow in spirit the ascension of the Unique Virgin, the Most Pure, the Untouchable – whose very wake and shadow killed.

He was called before her on an indecisive day, when a yellow shadow invaded the grounds of the Temple; for some time, Atlantis had known these stormy evenings, these livid dawns, harbingers of disaster. Somewhere, far away on a vast continent that as yet had no name, huge masses of ice were melting down the slopes, sulphureous volcanoes were piercing the snowfields but no one knew about it and life continued on the Island. Through the vast mural bay window one could see the Valley ringed in shadow, and on the blue lawns, enormous ocelli peacocks circled and wailed.

On her white coral throne, Atlantea appeared, sheathed entirely in gold, gemmed with emeralds; a gold-smithed mask beneath the sixfold tiara of the Conjurers, and two enormous stones, of a liquid green, encrusted at eye level, gave her the air of a terrible idol. Before facing her, Hellemar felt weary: how to resist this weight of sacred principles, traditions, majesty and threats? But they were face to face and his antennae caught a wave of turmoil: he was not only in the presence of a statue – the little girl from the beach, glittering with foam and stars, the snake charmer was there. He saw her again as he had placed her on his chariot, before the people, a white face with loose hair and laughing... The sea conches sang and the Conjurer raised a hand studded with diamonds. It was not she who spoke, but her spokesman, the Priest-King. He accused Hellemar of ruining the Divine Island, by refusing his sister's throne and bed. The sacred blood of the Atlanteans was in danger, the kingdom demanded a progeny of the race...

"The queen's bed?" said Hellemar with deliberate harshness. "It is open to all comers. Nellare could have had sons as numerous as the stars."

"There is the quadruple crown..."

"Listen," said the prince annoyed, "you all know like me that we are living through the end of the world. And especially you, Atlantea! You who announced it from the top of these towers! Too many offenses have rocked the foundations of this island, countless deaths, odious challenges. What is the use of ensuring permanence of a finite race? Leave us alone – we have so little time left!"

A shudder ran through the crowd: sacrilegious words had been spoken. The people already knew that the hecatombs of Nellare had delivered masses of energy, and the worrying phenomena which were devastating the globe were linked to it. But the worst was the ultimate challenge that they hardly dared to whisper: the astrologers having claimed that the second moon announced disasters, the queen had sworn to destroy it.

Everywhere, on the promontories and the hills, towers were erected and oxen drawn on the heights were pieces of strange machines which the Atlantean race had created in the time of its greatness. They had been forgotten for centuries in the underground passages, scholars were looking for their use. Atlantis declared war on the stars in the sky... She proposed to launch (without knowing it) trains of ions, to make them deviate from their orbit.

Hellemar added, in a voice he did not recognize himself:

"If only my sister Nellare had been the one in whose arms every man would wish to die... if she were the Unique and the Chosen! But you know she's not. And I'm neither a king nor a monster – just a man. Let me go alone towards my end."

This refusal was followed by a delirium, a hot madness. Nellare offered sacrifices to the blood gods. For Earth already had its divinities who ousted Atlantean abstract figures and the queen believed in their support in the titanic struggle she was undertaking. These gods advanced in the night, they buried themselves among the reeds of the rivers, their muzzles and their tentacles came out of dead waters and underground caves. Since a certain night, rays as big as iron bars had sprung from the towers on the rocks, the doomed star seemed to lean a blue face towards Earth. Cyclones devastated the shores and vast tidal waves swept the plateaus until then preserved. Was it the Blue Moon that lifted those waters? The navigators were deported to the outer darkness where the anthropoids and giant beasts roamed.

To conciliate the new gods, the queen threw into the ocean caves virgins and youths by the dozens; when the wave was red, the sacrifice was accepted and the people rejoiced and struck cymbals. Meat and poppy wine were then distributed to him, and senseless orgies defiled the shores.

In the midst of a drunken and mad crowd, Nellare prophesied: "When I shall have destroyed in the Heavens this face of a corpse," she said, "this girl will lose her astral double, her strength, she will be no more than a shadow of the Conjurer. She will die and we will survive."

Displaced by the increasing underwater earthquakes, baited no doubt by these feasts of flesh, abyssal monsters appeared along the shores: never had they seen octopuses of such magnitude. The coastal populations were fleeing and the royal guard had to drive back the ichthyophages who climbed to the safety of the cities.

On the eve of the annual festivals, Atlantea pronounced one of her terrible prophecies where it was a question of Earth shaking on its bases and of the star which falls, like a cracked disc...

Hellemar drove in the Queen's tank battles. A slight intoxication, like a sparkling wine, went up his muscles and his broad wings flapped above the fish-eaters and terrified simians. Indifferent to parties, he mighty. When the heads flew under the large scimitars or the ancient weapons sent jets of flame, the queen and her brother exchanged long glances, similar to embraces. But having returned from this exhilaration, they no longer saw each other. The prince knew he was doomed and cared neither for the day nor for the hour. His status as a liege of the Conjurer still preserved him, but until when?

An interior fire wore out the great winged statue; he sought oblivion amid perils and wild games, and royal purveyors filled his gardens with captive virgins and amorous slaves. A tide of groans and prayers made his palace formidable to the living.

The queen took her usual companions to her vivariums and her basins. The most hideous beasts lived in these smooth stone undergrounds, glaucous jellyfish which filled a swimming pool, blind lampreys and pythons. Her ships brought her barbarian continents, captured in traps, saurians and giant felines. Leaning over her caverns, greedily inhaled the stench of musk and rot. She threw live slaves into it.

She had invented sensory mixtures that drive men crazy, hence her name Dispenser of Perfumes. In an unpredictable future, in thick carnal darkness, humanity sought her face, without knowing her name. She would be Circe, Echidna, Melusine – the monster with hers of a woman and the claws of a flying dragon.

Leaning on Hellemar's arm, she said: "If I gave you to my sweet little octopuses..."

"So do it. You will have the Island and its Conjurer against you."

"What do you care? You would be dead and devoured. No incantation can reunite the scattered shreds of your flesh..."

"What a charming conversation! I repeat: do it. I will be dead. You will suffer."

"No," she said, "and then you're too sure of yourself. Your precious Atlantea would allow you to be tortured, she has other occupations: my squadrons are in port, she received Neor with great pomp. He attended the prayers and the consecrations. Do you know that she allows herself to be combed in public, because her hair proves, it seems, her extra-terrestrial origin? It's very beautiful and falls to her knees, so that a man is obliged to support this blue bleach. I bet that today this man is Neor..."

These games annoyed the prince. He constantly had under his closed eyelids this forbidden image: the Conjurer Atlantea. The only woman on Earth who was inaccessible to him and of whom, thanks to Nellare, he knew nothing. The only one whose desire burned him like a straight flame in his flesh.

When the blue moon sank very low on the horizon and its surface showed black streaks, Nellare, panting, dug her nails into her flesh, scrutinized her dull eyes:

"I believe," she said with a cooing throat, "that I am almost as happy to see you attached to this useless brazier as if I had you in my arms..."

But she couldn't kill him.

A night came which was not a real night: the Second Moon, irresistibly drawn into the field of magnetic force created over the Island, blocked a third of the horizon. Immense waters rose. A whole part of the cliffs crumbled into the abysses of the ocean and the people went mad. The riverside villas were looted and burned, they indulged in the worst excesses and, on the road, Hellemar's chariot trampled on the corpses of women and children. He had been awakened by a faithful slave, a foster father who was sorry to see him languish. This Timaeus was urging him to leave the unsafe suburban gardens; the queen, he said, had already retired to her palace in the metropolis.

"And Atlantea?" asked the prince, whom nothing else touched.

"Oh... the Conjurer? Nothing threatens her. She went down to the afflicted villages."

Hellemar was on his feet immediately and, a few moments later, he hurried on his quadriga.

Atlantea never saw the Happy Valley again: she had found it deserted. She had to stop her horses on the hill – the water was lapping under the azaleas. On the left, the village of Dea was dead, its white quartz houses shimmering at the bottom of a lake. As her coachman was shivering with fear beside her fainting servant, she left them without a word and went down alone towards the Temple.

All along the road, her white chariot had opened up the crowd of blood-drunk brutes, she had to get out to bless the dying and heal the wounds. But here nothing lived any more. The tide was rising irresistibly, she could take off her golden mask, under the friendly stars. She rediscovered her Atlantis, wild and pure, sister of the Oceans. She herself had changed little – grown, yes; her azure hair seemed to drink all the sap from her slender body and her folded wings covered her with a cloak. Since his people could not escape the fury of the waters by flying, they had given up diving through the air. His mysterious face shone like an alabaster night light, and having witnessed so many agonies, his lips were full of blood.

Prince Hellemar found her in that state, in the depths of an indestructible and lucid dream, under the oleanders of the sacred hill. She was standing above the now calm ocean, which had cast a huge octopus at her feet, a bloody gray monster that was still throbbing. Her silhouette was profiled on the hallucinated moon.

"You are alive," he murmured, "if you only knew how I looked for you!" And like any Earthman, feeling his heart burst in his chest, he took her in his arms. He had forgotten that her shadow killed, and he covered with kisses that shining face, those icy lips.

It was his third crime. The one that could not be forgiven.

The infrared cannon had been turned off. Minutes or hours had passed. A stream of voices, of violent thoughts crashed against the walls. Arno Heller sat up and Nan realized that she had slipped on the white bear skin and that, as in the caves on the Island, the wounded man's head had rested on her knees.

"Dirty story," he said. "They'll resort to old Earth tactics, against which I'm helpless. It's one thing to scramble encephalographs and deflect radiant energy, and quite another to deceive the scent of beasts. I've never had luck with animals. Are there dogs on this ship?"

"Wolves," Nan answered, lucid and icy.

"Well, they'll release them. Do you have astral armor here?"

"Yes. Earl's. What are you going to do?"

"I'll probably be forced to leave the barracks. Absolutely. Oh... I have a chance... The hull at this level has emergency exits – I spotted one in your closet – and a thin ledge to allow for repairs."

"But," exclaimed Nan, "it's madness! You want to hold on to this ledge – while the ship builds up its maximum speed! It would be suicide!"

"So," he noted with a thin smile, "is it divine solidarity, or are you interested in my fate?"

"I hate you!" she cried feverishly. "Do you think I didn't sense that you were trying to influence my dreams – or my memory? It was because of you that Nellare hated me. It was for revenge that she bombarded the Second Moon and that our Island perished!"

Suddenly, she realized the grotesqueness of the situation: the rocket was hurtling at a dizzying pace through space, the men were preparing for a merciless struggle – and they were there, the two of them, to settle a quarrel as old as a dead world! They were bleeding and tearing each other apart.

A first howl rose from the depths of the spaceship and Arno shrugged:

"They scented my blood on Cross' armor," he said. "And the smell of a mutant's blood isn't easily forgotten..."

Before he could stop her, Nan grabbed some nail scissors from the dressing table and cut her wrist. Green drops fell on the flooring. "That way," she said, "if the wolves come, I'll say it's because of my blood... It's also mutant blood."

Taking her by the shoulders, Arno Heller plunged, as into an abyss, into the clear eyes that frightened men.

"So you love me," he said. "No matter how hard you struggle, it's not just in Atlantis that you've been – how did you say...? – crazy about me And myself, Nan, me... I only exist because you live! Help now. Do not forget the meaning of your gesture: we exchanged our blood – our Island knew no other marriage..."

The howls rose, Nan knew the pack was unleashed. The young woman closed her eyes and felt, for a moment, the mutant's cold lips on her open wrist. When he disappeared, she did not cry, did not cry, she found herself isolated in a royal solitude; memories of a brilliant and terrible life merged with those of a near childhood... She saw again a City under a globe and a plateau peopled with wolves. A little Nan, in a long nightgown, sat on her bed, her legs bent, and from afar she led their choirs. They obeyed her, they crawled, their hair clipped, in the cold light of the artificial moons.

Stretched like the string of a harp, she succeeds in resuscitating within herself this fearless little girl, close to the wilderness. "Wolves," she cried in her silence, "do you hear me? Do you recognize me? I am your sister among men... I have run with you through dew-soaked thickets and smell the meat of deer. I know the wildest ravines... Like you, I hate the hunter with a large knife, the man who kills not to eat, but to feast on his victory. Wolves, my brothers, answer me!"

A high-pitched, old male trill rose—with such perfection, on the corresponding sound wave, that Nan shuddered.

From that moment, she entered deliberately, as queen and conjurer, into the chorus of beasts which howled on the floors below. She was wind on the steppe, stormy with snow, and wolf among wolves. She sent them away and gave them instructions. She told them: "Don't go any higher, there are pitfalls. This whole path is dead – it is iron and nickel. Go down, there are trapdoors, you would be caught. Let's play. You are no longer prisoners in a metal cage, you are wandering on a plain; on a black sky rises a pink moon – and it's spring... The snow is melting in the thickets full of sap, the earth is breathing hard and beautiful white furry wolves are dancing with you..."

What was happening in the corridors at that hour was indescribable, at least in Major Szubinak's authoritative opinion. From the first waves sent by Nan, the beasts that the bestiaries of the guard held in hand and who cautiously sniffed the walls, shuddered and reared violently. Their fur crackled with sparks, they were seen to stretch out, crawl, turn on the spot, as packs do on a full moon, and then they rushed in a long stride towards the shallows. Their leashes stretched, serving them were dragged away like rags.

"Faster!" Nan sang, invisible and powerful, "faster! So we leap! Thus one avoids the trap where the reversed portcullis offers its quills! The familiar cottage is nearby which smells of hair and dry blood! There, mother wolf will suckle her young, there the tired beast will sleep. Come on, come on, I'll lead you!"

Nan presided over the fantastic ride. The pack, in a mad whirlwind, descended the stairs, the corridors of the third – and the doors slammed as they passed, the people, suddenly awakened, showed a strained face.

"They're mad!" someone shouted, "they launched wolves and now the beasts are escaping!"

In Jonas MacLeod's arms, a serene and curious Lizzy brought her fingers to her mouth and hissed, softly.

"Faster! Faster!" Nan gasped. A barrage formed which the big cats avoided. They brought whips and white-hot bars, but amid the smoke, the smell of health and burnt polish, the horde reached the holds... An unfortunate rumor spread "But these animals are enraged!"

The hallways emptied. From a checkpoint, Earl Stanley noticed that the wolves raised hallucinated pupils as gazing at an invisible star; streams of drool flowed from their muzzles. "Looks like they're talking with someone!" yelled Old Mudds in horror. Lost on the leashes, the servants no longer resisted. The whole clan – the spiky old males preceding the thin young wolves – rushed into the cages.

They ran to the gates and blocked them. The beasts, silent, danced in circles.

When the second, Leeth, who had led the hunting operation, came to report, he was still shaking, and a trickle of blood streaked his chin. The man was however a solid trapper from the North. He murmured: "It has never been seen! They went crazy on the second floor... it sounded like they heard a wolf – in the dark."

"There are no wolves on board," said Commander Szubinak. "Come to your senses, Leeth." He turned to Earl Stanley and saw him standing there, his face bloodless. The Commissioner simply said:

"Let's kill the wolves."

Nan, aroused by fierce excitement, ran to the door of the lab: the howls had died down, she was laughing and dancing. Wolf among wolves... "Arno!" she cried. "God, how stupid men are! You can come back, they're all gone!"

A silence answered her. Standing against the entrance, she scanned the empty, white recess: Arno Heller had disappeared. The white bear skin still kept his imprint and some armor was missing from the hangers, but he was no longer there – he was never against the shiny walls. A throbbing note of music – just one – quivered in the air.

Nan cried.

CHAPTER XI
Mutant versus Mutant

"You drove those beasts mad, didn't you?" Stanley asked harshly. "Oh! No need to deny it: I remember your abilities!"

When Nan didn't answer, he walked over to the bunk, took her by the shoulders and pulled her up like a doll. He met only an onyx face, motionless, and lowered eyelids.

"You see how wrong we are!" replied Earl with bitter irony. "I knew you were an alien, not only of another race, but of another plane... but you seemed human and sincere. I wanted to give you a chance and today I'm biting my fingers! But the fight is on. Don't expect any pity from me, Nan."

She was silent, but he thought he heard, like any man who confronts a mute woman, what he was afraid she would answer: "I didn't ask you anything, did I?" He let her fall back on her bed, where she remained seated, elbows on her knees and chin resting on her fist. Earl scanned the booth, throwing out:

"If you don't know, your brilliant accomplice has already killed five people and Una Vere is no better. I don't know how he does it, but it's a perfect technique. She claims that her brain is being bombarded with electrons!"

"It was me," Nan said briefly. "I couldn't hold her back – she's strong as an ox. Besides, I only did it once, for five seconds!"

"You'll also tell me that you forced Elisa to commit suicide?"

"No," she said fairly. "I just wanted to lock her in a closet and maybe bang her head full of preconceived ideas. I would never have killed her, I hate that. Only, when I came, she had already committed suicide... Oh! She had wanted it for a long time... I guess I gave her the courage to do it, that's all."

"You wanted to silence her, you say? But then, you also knew the radiogram...?"

"Of course," Nan replied wearily, "I read it in Elisa's brain – and so did you, though you deny it. Aren't you some kind of mutant too, Earl? You don't want to admit it, but you have, as in the past, clipped your wings to fit better into the crowd – but you can't help reading minds..."

He looked at her, struck with a kind of secret horror. A whole past full of rapid intuitions, of repressed impulses, rose in him – but he had always controlled this wave before. Yet... wasn't he the youngest – and the most brilliant – of the scholars of the Commission? He had been called a "child prodigy". This very mission was due to his exceptional faculties... The white and shiny cabin circled around him. But no, he was Earl Stanley – a purebred Earthman, and his knowledge was the result of his efforts.

He remembered though...

A festive evening, on Earth.

A free lady, Ella Stanley, wavy and lovely in her ballgown, stood out against a mauve dawn sky. She stood against a wall bay and said to someone invisible, in the shadows:

"This child scares me, Glen. I caught him playing – what do you think? He cut and twisted a strip of paper from which he made a well-formed Moebius strip. And a Klein bottle. And he is only six years-old!"

"Ella, you are making up your mind! This child was simply making cutouts..."

"I would like to be sure, Lord...! Oh... I know that his father's a great scientist and that Earl was born on the sands of Mars, in the midst of the uranium rush – but then..."

"Ella, that old Prokofiev fantasy is now playing... Are you coming to dance?"

He had wanted to be a sailor. It was an outdated career; no one crossed the oceans at water level anymore. His parents, who were well placed for this, enrolled him in the astronautical academy. But he retained a tenderness for the abandoned element. During his holidays, he went offshore on an antique sailboat. The swish of the waves, the kisses of mermaids, the murmurs of tritons, rocked his reverie with music he dared not compose – and he knew, he understood ancient, precious, incredible things, of which he never told anyone – because mutants are secretive.

His studies were easy. It was towards spatial distortion that he was drawn, although at that time – ten years ago – this science was considered utopian. But an instinct from an incredible past told him that countless worlds existed, and that one could – and should – reach them. He was even sure, when he slept deeply, that a dead world corresponded to his inner self...

His career was regular and harmonious. Everything was leveling out before him. He owed it, in part, to his family, and even more to his real worth. But sometimes, he reluctantly felt it, an insinuating charm worked in his presence. He seemed so light, and so seductive! As a teenager, his rust-colored curls and long eyelashes softened women. "Earl would make an excellent spy," his father said laughing, "he always seems so sincere!" He penetrated the minds of people and, imperceptibly, shaped his countenance to please them. Without any intention – out of flexibility, out of kindness. It served him well later...

After solid studies, he made some attempts at topology in which he moderated his boldness, for fear of displeasing his elders. These attempts interested some of the greatest Earth scientists. He hardly expected to be admitted to the illustrious Areopagus, but when he was summoned, he knew it had to be like this.

He found himself surrounded by thin, weary people who had just convinced the solar system of the importance of their work. Their political role didn't interest him at all; they complimented him on his youth, adding that he brought them "a breath of fresh air".

"Something of this galactic universe towards which we tend," had said the President of the Commission. "We are the past. It is you and your ilk, Stanley, who are destined to usher in the Space Age."

Yes – but he had never attempted a criminal trial...

They weren't real thoughts or memories that ran through him, though he saw, at a certain moment, his mother's silver lowlon dress and a garland of ivy in her hair, and he smelled the sea air inflating the sail of his boat. They were suggestions of thoughts, an excitement of his nerves.

By now, Earl had measured Nan's terrifying faculties. He tore himself away from this spatial music and regained consciousness of his true mission. Only police work: follow the trail and discover the one who, through his egotism and his madness, had destroyed Andromeda. Dominating the tumult of his blood, the bite of a feeling which Earth had almost ousted, but which, in space, had resumed its primordial violence, he pronounced:

"This man spent the night here?"

It wasn't even a question; he was sure of it. Nan showed, on the bear's skin, the imprint of the body which was already coming apart.

"Yes," she said. "On the floor. He was seriously injured, you know."

"So you know this Walter Cross..."

"Don't lie!" Nan shouted, rising like a flame. "Don't tell me you think it was that minus! Walter Cross got drunk at the dock, and I'm guessing the feds are dealing with him right now."

"So it would be...?" Stanley asked, paling.

"Oh!" she asked, all her excitement suddenly gone, "can it be that you don't know? Have you been deceived too? But no, that's impossible, you belong to the Distortion Committee – and these are its orders! You must have known for a long time before whom I fled... A successful escape, of course! Yes, the one you have on board is called Arno Heller – and that's whom you must want to kill!"

"Listen, Nan," Earl began.

Her voice a strange sweetness; he had understood that she had been sincere in her fear, loyal in her desire to return to the human mass... But this solicitude came too late; Nan spread her outstretched arms, her lips tender; she stood motionless, as a crucifix against the wall, and spoke, and detaching the words:

"I never wanted to fight you, Earl, but your laws are just too cruel! We didn't ask to be born mutants; nature has endowed us with frightening faculties; it is possible that, in this devastated world, we are the relief of a dying humanity. And you seek to destroy us, because you are afraid...

"You will tell me that Heller is a criminal; yes, but like an earthquake or a cyclone, he's not even responsible for his deeds. Your surgeons tampered with his brain, most of his reflexes were modified... Now, even if he had done even more damage, he has already paid back Earth. All your scientists are now looking at his on-board calculations! The instruments he modified give Earth a thousand years of progress! As for him, rest assured, for I believe you killed him. That's all, Earl. No, I don't need anything. Thank you."

Onboard chronometers marked six o'clock in the morning and it was – which day already? – the fifth day of this insane cruise, but all that was now merely convention. The earthly day no longer existed, nor the hour. At the end of a passageway, a crestfallen-faced man – Jonas MacLeod, the settlers' delegate – was waiting for Commissioner Stanley.

"Well," he said embarrassed, "I know that the command has nothing to do with palavers, but I represent them all, don't I? They are no longer tenable... And, after all, they're Earthlings."

Earl invited the Scotsman into the CO's office, which served as his command post. MacLeod's thick shadow veiled the radiant screen, thankfully off, and the Commissioner presented him with a hard, pale, drawn-featured young face.

"Well?" he asked.

"Well!" said the delegate, hesitating, "to start, all these people have decided to give you credit. Because you seemed to believe what you wanted, and probably also because you were sympathetic to them, Commissioner. Only, this ship is a madhouse. Gossip is rampant – not all of it safe – and the passengers would like to know what's what clearly... They say that a document was destroyed and that people were killed... and last night, this story of rabid wolves..."

Earl stifled a sigh of relief: it was just that! He replied, coldly: "Yes, a document has been destroyed. Its importance being considerable, a radio officer perished while defending it. Three interplanetary guards were killed in the line of duty. In addition, a free woman, an Earth citizen, who witnessed the attack, committed suicide. A female member of the brain-trust: Doctor Borelli."

"Ah!" MacLeod muttered, looking taken aback. "I didn't know it was her... So this document was..."

"We don't know its exact content. And you know that the communications limit with Earth has been exceeded."

"But you have an idea..."

Earl looked up and appraised the man. Yes, he could be trusted, he had the stuff in him and a keen desire to redeem himself. But no – no one could be trusted...

He said, curtly: "This is not about making assumptions."

"So," said MacLeod, "the free lady Borelli has done away with herself. But the others? The guards and the radioman?"

"Oh! They were indeed murdered. It seems that due to a mistake by the emigration services, we embarked an undesirable passenger. Emergency operations and even this release of wolves were aimed at capturing him..."

"Did we get him?"

"Not yet."

There was nothing else to add, and Lizzy's high-pitched voice told Jonas to shut up. For the first time since the little mutant was thinking so heavily about her heart and her brain, he was on the verge of rebelling: he really felt a deep sympathy for the young commissioner.

"Well!" asked Earl, "do you need any further clarification, MacLeod?"

"No," the man muttered, "no..." He was wiping big beads of sweat from his brow, and really felt like a Judas. "Beg your pardon for having importuned you, free citizen."

Earl smiled with his usual charm and it was, in the dark command post, like a light. "It was always understood," he said, "that we would try our best to communicate..."

As he backed towards the door, MacLeod found enough strength within himself to say: "You see, free citizen, there are phantasms in the air..."

Phantasms. The word had been uttered.

Stanley had summoned the members of the Team. The radiant screen sparkled, and, at the sight of it, Karpov whistled and Vere bit his lip. Borelli, pale and with reddened eyelids, seemed absent.

"That's what I feared," said the atomist.

"Yes, isn't it?" said Earl. "The commander and I are of the same opinion: the Andromeda cataclysm continues."

"We are in the presence of a typical case of the reduction of masses on displaced axes," said the physicist. "From there a terrible wear, with regard especially to the humus yields and the soft rocks. No atmosphere is there to protect them..."

"Your findings..."

"It seems that, placed in the 'continuum vortex', the satellite underwent a pressure so willful that its core burst; for a time, attraction held the masses together, but other forces came into play. Andromeda is now split into three pieces of debris that are breaking apart and eroding with frightening rapidity."

"In short," summarized Vere, "it's in the process of disappearing?"

"It's not a very scientific way of putting it, but it is quite accurate. I still cannot explain the gaseous ring which scrambles the proportions because it extends over thousands of kilometers; it must be, as for the ring of Saturn, infinitesimal particles which emerge from the nucleus. I'm afraid, Earl, this world we're going to is a wreck."

"We cannot turn back."

"Oh!" Vere launched, "certainly not! For us it will be a study trip and we will bring back armfuls of invaluable research to Earth. But what about the others? Those who must disembark? Aren't you going to warn them, Stanley? After all, they're Earthlings..."

He was repeating MacLeod's own words, and Earl looked up briskly. So that was it! He wondered where the new attack would come from... For a moment, a terrible force had been scattered in the air and was acting on each brain in a specific way. He analyzed his own state of mind: a flood of insidious worry, a presentiment that swirled around shattered globes, steerage stuffed with human worry. A physical feeling of nausea that tightened his throat and wet his hair with cold sweat. He remembered: The danger – the death – was nausea. Yes, that's how a mutant must have felt the worst thing...

He shook himself: What the Hell! He wasn't a mutant!

He wasn't going to take Nan's insult seriously!

He looked at Vere: the squinting pupils, the dry lips, this one certainly hypnotized. The most sensitive of the team, the chemist presented an ideal target... Weighing his words. Earl asked:

"Are you sure you really weighed your last words, Vere? Do you realize the panic that will invade these people, faced with this eventuality: Andromeda lights up – and the extremities to which the crowd might go in such cases...?"

A silence fell. Vere seemed to analyze himself and answered, startled:

"No, in fact, the idea didn't occur to me. It's reasoning like a schoolboy's. And I don't understand..."

Borelli intervened, his face ravaged:

"All right," he said, "stupid, but human. Let me confess to you, Stanley, that I thought the same thing, in similar terms, which may not be mine... never mind. From the start, I had hesitations about the biological effects of this implantation on a destroyed satellite, but I was blinded by routine. Now I see it clear – we can't risk all these lives, we don't have to... and I..."

He suddenly got up and brandished his thermal gun, because unlike the passengers, the crew members were armed. Quicker than he, because accustomed to such circumstances, Major Szubinak, posted in the rear, struck his wrist with the backhand; the gun fell and there was a violent but brief melee. When the biologist was subdued by Earl and handed over to the rushing guards, the commissioner turned back to the other scientists.

"Well!" he said, unhooking his collar. "I don't blame Borelli; Since his wife's suicide, his morale had been damaged. I'm sorry, Szubinak, but it looks like a great hypnotist was at work," Vere stammered. "But then... how so?"

"It's a pity that Borelli is eliminated," said the atomist. "I would have asked him if, in his opinion, the KZ mutants do not have, in addition to their personal electromagnetism, mental weapons. What do you think, Stanley?"

"I believe," said the latter clearly, "that we have the explanation of Dr. Borelli's suicide. I remember having warned you already that we had to watch our reflexes; I will go further. Let us beware of our innermost thoughts and impulses. Frankly, I do not believe that the hypnotist in question can act on a brain that is still awake. In any case, here is the proof that the being we are hunting is still alive. I wouldn't have believed it..."

"Neither do I," Szubinak said. "We will certainly face other troubles, Commissioner."

"Indeed, it looks like it's not over yet," Karpov said dryly. "Do you hear?"

A dull tide pounded the gangways.

Szubinak had risen at once, he assured his blaster and went towards the door. His face, when he returned, showed no good.

"They're downstairs," he said. "I mean our passengers – at least the third ones – they broke the dams. Do you want to talk to them, Stanley?"

Earl nodded and stalked down the passageway; again, like a mutant, in the presence of real danger, he felt frivolous, irresponsible and terribly efficient. In the steerage of the first ones massed this crowd that Jonas MacLeod had described as untenable, with the faces of she-wolves and flickering eyes.

Earl walked straight at these people and didn't stop until he was faced with fear. Hallucinations, he thought. The hypnotic influx would be intended for them; it was a weak wave which had reached Borelli and Vere. He asked:

"What do you want? I'm here to answer you, but I thought you had a delegate."

They walked on, disconcerted by this direct welcome. A voice said:

"He's a coward, he refused to come with us. He said we're all crazy. But we have the right to know..."

"What?"

"Well... it seems that a contact was established with Andromeda."

"Radar contact, yes. This helps to locate positions, it's a common technique. What else do you want to know?"

The man who had come forward, the spokesman, must have been, on Earth, a plowman or a navy man; he expressed himself with difficulty and followed, obstinately, his slow thread of thought. Ideal ground for a telepath, Earl thought. Once the idea has been planted, he does not even suspect that it corresponds to nothing. He digs it. The panting crowd listened... The man formulated, slowly:

139

"So, here it is... It seems that Andromeda doesn't exist anymore."

"Who said that?" asked Earl.

He scanned the darkened, tense faces. They were so visibly influenced by the same thought that heads all turned with the same enthusiasm. What if he tried to fight with the mutants' own weapons? What if he threw the net of his own suggestions over this bewildered crowd? He tried...

"You make me laugh," he said, stretching his will like a bow. "How could a globe of these dimensions disappear? Ask the chemists, the astrophysicists who are among you: such a hypothesis is unthinkable. Weather variations may have occurred since our departure. If we imagine the worst, we would be off to prospect the satellite aboard the *Daredevil* and in this case ,we would communicate with Earth. Decisions will come from there."

"Do you give us your word, Commissioner Stanley," said a shrill female voice, "that we will not be disembarked against our will?"

Earl recognized a lost Olga Karpov in the crowd. Locks of hair covered her yellow face and eyes were shining; she had returned to her norm, to her nature which she had patiently erased, according to modern requirements; she was again, as she must have been, the revolutionary student, the leader of the crowds, or better still the Scythian amazon galloping ahead of the hordes.

Earl directed his mental power, which was still weak, at her.

"If the orders are contrary, if you are ordered to disembark in a world of madness, will you do it?"

"Personally? Yes. The astronautical personnel do not discuss the orders given. I will try to disembark. The others will follow me – or not."

A silence hovered, as always when the inflexible will of a man, his purity, his diamond hardness impose themselves.

Olga Karpov shouted: "If you disembark, Commissioner, I'll follow you!" A big laugh greeted this conclusion to disperse. The air had cleared.

"I won that first round," Earl thought. "But I don't know what to expect next."

Followed by Szubinak, he visited the engine room. The second, Leeth, reported to them. "No, nothing was wrong. The staff showed all the desirable enthusiasm, the hypertensors worked with particular efficiency. If I could allow myself this little joke," he added "The *Daredevil* rushes towards nowhere. If we carry on like this, we'll be ahead of schedule."

Earl surveyed the smooth, shiny, ideal room, with no dark corners or mystery. Why was his feeling of danger heightened between those sparkling keyboards and those batteries whose exact action he knew? Do we have perfect morale, don't we?

"What I wonder," Earl answered between his teeth. "Szubinak," he added abruptly, "set your receiver to code. Good. You don't feel like we're being listened to? Me, too. Listen, is there no other way out than this main door?"

"Oh!" said the commander, "there are many emergency exits in the hull... We use them in case of fire or repairs. But they overlook the void..." His eyes widened: "Do you believe...? But no, it's impossible, no organic life can fit in that space, in full flight, in a thin ridge of twelve centimeters..."

"So there is a partition?" Earl asked coldly.

"Of course. It borders the first floor and the superstructures. But I repeat – it's physically unthinkable..."

"Yes." said Earl. "There are many unthinkable things that happened during this crossing. An enemy who – physically – cannot exist, whom encephalographs have missed, who braves the energized walls and those blaster... beasts going mad and scientists going off the rails..." He seemed very tired.

"Let's see," resumed Szubinak, "what can we do? Let's imagine that the impossible doesn't exist: the intruder is there, against the hull of the ship, and until the landing we cannot eliminate it. Now it's about our brains; we have to defend ourselves..."

Earl had already pulled himself together. He gave brief orders:

"Block all exits in the simplest way: locks. Useless to use electromagnetics, since the enemy makes use of it. Then... would it be possible to run a caloric current through the hull?"

"I think so," said the commander. "At 420 degrees, it wouldn't affect internal structures. But it mustn't last, otherwise we'd blow."

"When will you be able to act?"

"In an hour."

"It is useless to recommend to you, I think, the greatest secrecy. Even in thought," said Earl. He was pale.

CHAPTER XII
Fire and Ice

That night, an incredible reunion brought together the team remnants around the captain's table in the premier hall. Earl demanded the presence of Nan, who came, wavering, seized with an uncontrollable, familiar horror. The room was almost deserted and the dishes tasteless. Nan swore that, landing anywhere, she would throw away those clumps of orchids that smelled of death: if they ever landed – if there was life.

The passengers eyed three empty seats: that of Una and the Borellis. All moved like puppets; a young statistician fainted, a Martian wept. Olga Karpov, with her air of a romantic revolutionary, smoked carloads of cigarettes, demanded vodka and devoured Stanley with her eyes: one could follow on her the slow work of disintegration due to hypnotism and Karpov did not hesitate to do so. Finally, she called him a "lustful viper" and Vere a "conscious and organized pig", and knocked the ashtray down on the rug. In a gray cloud of smoke, she was horrible.

"There's only one man among you," she declared at the top of her voice, "and that's the superintendent. And to think that his cute wife pushes him away! And he's got it! Earl, I would sleep with you, because everyone is going to die anyway!"

The disorder was at its height; people listened at the neighboring tables. Nan couldn't stand it, she put her fingers on the psychotechnician's thin arm and it was instantaneous: the carbuncle eyes went out, her face turned pale and Olga looked around her bewilderedly.

"I believe," she said, getting up abruptly, "that I was talking nonsense. I beg your pardon..."

"It's nothing, my dear," Karpov said heavily, "you were a little tired. Sit down, we're being watched..."

Olga obeyed, like an automaton. The intelligent, reptilian eyes of the atomist passed from his wife's face to Nan's.

"It seems that free lady Stanley helped you come to your senses... Thank you, free lady."

Vere chuckled:

"What an extraordinary situation!" he exclaimed. "We're all going off the rails, do you realize? We accuse ourselves, in our heart of hearts, of the worst insanity and – why not? – of at least four murders! Because, think about it all the same, dear friends, everyone talks about this 'intelligent energy', this 'faceless being', but I don't think anyone has seen it? We accused Freade, then Cross, finally a mythical entity that would cross walls and floors... Isn't it easier to search among human beings? Here we are six at the table, with the commander, and each of us may have had reasons and certainly has means to stage this macabre comedy!"

"Vere," said Earl Stanley, "you're turning this into a detective novel!"

"I love detective novels," returned the chemist. "The elders. Those of our classical era, where we were looking for something – the assassin – or his weapon – or simply the means to punish him... It was so restful for the brain, next to these hands of arsine, of these galactic monsters, of these worlds which jump in two or three stages! The assassin is therefore among us... I think we can cast Citizen Stanley aside..."

"Because she's a pretty girl," interrupted Olga sourly.

"If you want, yes. But above all because, frail as she is, I don't see her knocking out Freade who weighed eighty kilos!"

"There's also mental suggestion," Karpov hinted.

"Of course. And judo. But reliable witnesses – who have since disappeared – spoke of a fight between the two men. Besides," asked Vere, "I think Nan and you were together at that time, Earl? Wasn't it your wedding night?"

"Hey," said Olga, "I didn't know you were such newlyweds! Funny idea, among other things, when we're going to land in hell... But all this leads me to think that here is another unexpected passenger on board the *Daredevil*! We already had Walter Cross..."

The conversation had passed the limits of tenability and all these allusions, insinuations and threats passed over the head of Nan who rebelled. Earl was silent, maybe he was studying his reflexes. As for her, sailing through these devastated consciences, she approached as on firm ground, on a rick, in the elementary brain of Commander Szubinak, and suddenly she shuddered in understanding what she perceived there: an order was going to be given – a terrible order. The greatest of dangers... Desperately, she tried to gain time and, turning her bewildered face towards the chemist, she softened her virid diamond eyes:

"Oh yes!" she exclaimed, "I love detective games! Let's play – let's all play! Anyone can be guilty! The free citizen Karpov was the close friend of the doctor, she knew her secrets and her poison cabinets – who could handle a syringe of morphine better? Spriegel and the other guards were reportedly slaughtered with blaster or disintegrator – and I believe that no one on board, except the crew and members of the Team, has free disposal of these weapons? How many presumed culprits!" She placed a small caressing hand like steel on Szubinak's elbow: "The commander is the only one who has an alibi, for Spriegel and Elisa, at least – he was piloting, we saw it, Earl and me – but where were all the others?"

"Nan," said Stanley, "this game is infuriating."

But she didn't listen to him, she surrounded the great navigator with lulling musical waves and threw her net of suggestions at Karpov:

"Free citizen, I believe you have all the instruments necessary to smash a micro-steel cage? It is true that you were – I have been told – the first to draw attention to this cage, but it could have been the trick of a clever criminal! I see you killing enough Elisa, first because you don't like women in general, then she bothered you so much, didn't she? As for Citizen Vere, I'm puzzled... I don't see him massacring Freade, no. But I think he's glad to know his wife is locked up..."

"Why then?" asked Szubinak bewildered, and Olga Karpov, coming to her senses, said:

"Because he constantly needed 'one meter eighty of fresh flesh and humo'!"

"Free citizens!" began Earl.

But Vere interrupted in a shrill voice, while a little foam rose to his lips: "She spoke the truth! What she said was true! Why was I pulling myself? On board a spaceship, conventions atone – no tapestries or geraniums on the *Daredevil*! One was a crushing burden on my shoulders, you all know them: mythomaniac, nyphomaniac, hysteric... You would have seen her in action among your militiamen! We had to leave Bridge where I taught – magnificent labs, and I was on the verge of a shocking discovery – because the free lady insisted on tasting all the students! I'm not talking about the teaching staff – the ladies warned me they were going to slash it! She made me grotesque, she..."

"Why did you marry her?" Olga Karpov asked harshly. "Isn't it for those eyelashes and her hips? All men are there: they need, not a companion, but an erotic object. You got it. You got what you deserved!"

"For God!" Vere yelled, "I've been riveted to a wild beast! But when you meet suffragettes of your kind, Citizen Karpov, you even appreciate Una!"

Everyone was screaming at table No. 1 and others; giant shadows gesticulated. It was suddenly noticed that, as if under multiple discharges, the lights went down and came on again alternately.

Earl grabbed a jug and threw it on the ground. Shards rebounded. This will take a break...

"Quiet, everyone!" he ordered in an icy voice. "Don't you realize that you are being suggested by a teleniser, of which these are the last gasps? Evacuate, take care of your wife. It wouldn't be nice if the Team massacred each other in front of the passengers... Nan, go down to your cabin. Come on, Szubinak."

It was like a shower of cold water. Nan stood up staggering, and bitterly regretted having such an adversary. Olga fled and her husband followed her. The commanding officer's tall stature disappeared down a side hallway. Vere was left alone, slumped on the table and his forehead bathed in a puddle of wine that looked like blood.

Nan went down to her cabin. An image imposed itself on her brain. Once, in the courtyard of the convent, on Andromeda, the little girls had caught a rat in a dobby... the beast, enormous, leapt. As the little girls dared not touch it, they straddled the cage on a branch and hung it on a hook, under the arches. Then they lit a bonfire underneath. Fey tongues rose, licking the trap. A terrible yelp was heard and an abominable smell of fried hair and flesh filtered through. The bars of the dobby turned red. Under the influence of the pain, the rat succeeded in freeing its muzzle and its forelegs – which were only wounds – but it remained trapped at the waist, charred alive, and, desperately, its claws scraped the glowing grid.

He agonized like this for an hour. The little girls were there, fascinated with horror, not daring to move or cry out. Finally, the sisters, warned by the peeps and the miasma, came running and they had to look for a militiaman who finished off the sad beast. There were a lot of punishments...

Suddenly Nan understood: an isolated wave, tender and in spite of everything mocking, was saying to her:

"I now understand what that means: to be trapped like a rat..."

For a moment, the image of Earl came into view – the drawn features, an implacable resolve shaping the handsome face. "I will do my duty, nothing but my duty, Nan." He was in pain too. But what were his problems, compared to the frightening torture they were going to inflict on Arno?

Because Arno was still alive. She couldn't doubt it...

Nan was about to rush into her cabin when a hand rested authoritatively on her shoulder. She turned and saw Karpov, whose sharp eyes narrowed; he had abandoned his distinguished nonchalance and taken on an unknown mask: that of a beast on the lookout or a hunter on the trail.

"So," he said, "you too have supernormal faculties. I should have guessed; Earl would never have allowed random boarding. Even less this marriage... Of course, it must be up to you – with these sudden bursts that illuminate you and these zones of silence... you are the perfect subject of study. But now, little girl, the game is too serious, I will not allow you to distort it. Come with me."

Nan looking despairingly into narrow yellowish eyes, felt the defenses of an Asiatic race, ancient and ready to retaliate, and sought to tack:

"I don't understand you," she said. "What do you mean?"

(Oh! Those seconds flowing like gold from an hourglass...!)

"I followed your efforts to subdue Olga," he replied, "then to panic Vere and Szubinak. These aren't feminine or human maneuvers. You may be unaware of your strengths – see, I'll grant you extenuating circumstances – but you're damn dangerous. Come along."

"Where do you want...? Earl told me to go to my cabin."

"Oh! That, no. You would be alone there and God knows what shenanigans a creature of your kind can indulge in!"

"Citizen Karpov," Nan said, "you're crazy, that's all I can say. I want to talk to Earl."

"You can do it by intercom."

"I also have to get my coat – I'm cold."

Her bare shoulders shivered, there was no pretense there. Karpov's pupils narrowed until they looked like two pinpoints:

"Ah! Do you really want to go home? Well, we'll get into it together. Come."

Nan felt the hard, cold touch of a thermal gun in her ribs. Despite the tragedy of the situation, she almost laughed. Here we are in the middle of a detective novel, decidedly... They entered the cabin, the aisle, the coffin. "Come on," ordered Karpov, "do what you have to do: open the doors, empty the cupboards..."

She leaned against the exit partition and raised her terrible icy gaze to him. She didn't have a second to lose.

"You accuse me of being a mutant," she said. "Very well. But in fact, what is a mutant? Passionate lovers of Old Earth, you know that it has embarked on an unlimited path; every day it discovers new spaces to conquer. Also to repopulate. Their conditions are worth nothing to Earthlings... To seize these worlds, we need 'fraternal monsters modelled on the

146

human mold' – and who can adapt to them. Mutants are those monsters. Why do you want them?"

She spoke thus, because, like a tongue of fluid flame, she had penetrated into the cells of his brain, where she discovered an abyss – an excessive ambition, the madness of a dictator, of a conqueror. She had touched the sensitive fiber; Karpov had, under his heavy eyelids, a flash, immediately extinguished...

"Mutants aren't monsters," he replied.

"But then... why destroy them?"

"I could give you 999 reasons, but is it necessary? I could tell you that the worlds in question are neither discovered nor conquered yet... that the KZ began their career with assassination... it doesn't matter. You understand me. You are – really – too dangerous, I don't think you can leave this cabin..."

"Would you kill me?"

"No. I would delete you, as one deletes, on a poorly studied planet, a worrisome specimen. But that means that I can speak to you with complete frankness, and you don't know what good that does! On the ground..."

"There's the Distortion Committee everywhere," Nan said softly.

"Yes. Your Earl is one; I never got to be part of it: Mental deviations, right? I could be a greater scholar, I was suspect... And that brings us to the crux of the matter. Each KZ mutant may well be a Pascal, a Da Vinci or a Napoleon, do you believe that humanity can bear this weight? The average being would be reduced to the level of a brute beast... But we, the beasts, cannot accept it."

"So," Nan said with near dizzy horror, "to maintain your current status, you would level humanity down? You would destroy what is most precious to it...?"

"With pleasure," confirmed Karpov. "He is only part of a flock of Napoleons. If Earth were populated by geniuses, the concept would be irremediably devalued."

This parody of discussion, this panting dialogue took fewer seconds than it would have taken to relate it. The black muzzle of the heat gun fascinated Nan, and Karpov pushed her lightly towards the door of the lab.

"You have one minute to make the gesture that was so important to you," he said, looking at his stopwatch. "After which..."

Nan released into her, like a skein, a long, bruised wave that she had sworn to herself never to use. ("Kill – me – me? Who was made to heal, to appease, to create forms and melodies!")

She asked, lowering her eyelashes:

"So you would have one of those mutants in front of you – a Mozart, a Pascal, as you say – a kind of perfection – it's not about me, of course... and you wouldn't hesitate to destroy it?"

The man chuckled briefly. "We have killed a lot on Earth," he said, "Nobody knows if there wasn't a Mozart in Hiroshima and since... My answer is: yes."

The knife-wave hit Karpov between the two eyes.

Nan didn't even look at him. She ran to the lab and her emotion was such at the sight of the simple lock placed on the wall that her knees bent and she fell. She understood immediately that a huge amount of energy had been launched against the locks and had failed on this primitive barrier: an iron bar. A being was therefore there, alive, against the incandescent wall, struggling in the void...

Nan clung to the bolt, pulled it, hung on it... but the operation had been wrong and the lock had melted under the violence of the shock. Its own electric energy, launched with a disorderly violence, succeeded only in blowing up all the lead on the floor, which it plunged into darkness. Nan stood up, half stunned, pressed her hands together, indistinctly sought a corresponding wave, an answer – and was met with silence.

"If he is dead," she told herself with bitter lucidity, "humanity will have lost a thousand years of progress; it will only have the likes of Karpov and Vere to guide it..."

This last name was a shock to her: she remembered. She rushed to the door of the adjoining cabin, that of Una Vere; this one was only pushed back and opened under the blow. Nan's feverish hands felt the walls and she found a second lock not much less deteriorated than the first. Then, gathering, concentrating all her strength, she succeeded in releasing a prodigious wave, which she directed at this lock, even if it meant drilling it and letting infinity enter. The micro-steel crackled like a torch and Nan passed out from the effort. When she came to, the darkness was complete, the atmosphere of the cabin unbreathable for a normal being, and icy lips devoured her face.

"Don't be afraid, beloved," said Arno.

"I'm not afraid."

"Come on. I need to find an ozonator. Here, we'll die."

"Your spacesuit?"

"I broke it. It was burning. What's the matter, Nan? You're shaking."

148

"It's nothing," she said, her teeth chattering. "It's just that corpse. I think I killed Karpov, you understand. In the next cabin. He knew I was a mutant and he wanted to stop me from opening up to you..."

Arno whistled a little, but his chapped lips didn't lend themselves to this exercise. He went into Nan's cabin and came back with a burden. "He is dead?" asked the young woman, closing her eyes.

"Very dead. Don't beat yourself – it's an embolism. You just rushed things and he didn't suffer."

"Reasonably, we cannot leave him here. I'll throw him into the void..."

"Oh... Arno... he will follow the spaceship!"

"For a while, yes. But we're approaching Andromeda – and the dead don't walk through nowhere, you see..."

Nan wasn't sure she heard that last sentence. She had turned away so as not to see the body thrown.

"I killed!" she said to herself, "I have killed!" And she was so terrified that she would have rushed into the dark if Arno had not held her back. He slammed the hatch and took the young woman back to his chest. She was shivering.

"You're cold, Nan," he said in a neutral voice.

"It's nothing. I've been cold all my life."

"Me too," he said. "It's the fault of our isolation, of our green blood. A mutant recovers its equilibrium only when united to its double. But you'll never be cold again..."

In the icy darkness, Nan felt a body made for her, her exact double who embraced her was the model. She stifled a cry as the heartbreaking chord was perfect.

"You made me a monster," she said. "I hate you."

"If you want. I simply awakened your power in you. You forget so easily, Nan. You even forgot that you love me."

"You're wrong. I saved you simply because I couldn't bear the thought of such a death. But I know you deserved it. What fate do you prepare for men by advancing their clocks into the void? Infinite terror, death..."

"No. The Space Age."

"Let me go. I hate you."

"You want me, Nan, like I want you. Do you have to take your lips, open your arms by force? Violence is a convenient excuse, but unworthy of both of us... Oh! Nan – Nan!"

"Kill me."

"Beloved, for us there is no death."

CHAPTER XIII
Passage to Nowhere

This battle he conducted like the others: like a cruel game. He had abandoned the useless, half-melted spacesuit, tightened the armor clasps and checked his disintegrator, the only weapon he hadn't thrown away like a ballast into nothingness. And then he went out into the first corridor, with his rocking step. The Space Distortion's blaster sparkled at his crest, and his dark hair shone a little too much at his temples—like Atlantean antennae.

He walked deliberately past the interplanetary guard post, who returned the honors. The only precaution, he forbade himself all thought. At the door of engineering, he felt a sharp joy invade him: it was ajar, a ray of light was filtering through.

In the large hall, Leeth's two assistants, busy with speed keyboards, paid him only distracted attention. He knew this room perfectly, having walked through it a hundred times in his mind, despite the spectographers and the control robots, and he walked directly towards the radiant screen. Midnight had just struck and the rocket was getting dangerously close to its goal; the viewscreen was already reflecting the dark face of the little fissured globe, a kind of scarlet star. They could measure the extent of the secondary disaster: Andromeda had erupted almost following the shape of a cross, and if the two eastern debris were gravitating together, the western side had already lost a curved fragment in a lunula.

For what the pilots knew, leaning on the space tensors, any landing on this planet surrounded by a red halo of fusion was impossible ,and the very approach was dangerous for the spacecraft. But that was not watching! The fatigued retinas of the two astronauts gathered, then let out the shadow of an officer in Space Distortion gear that reached the board. The purring of the monatomic monsters acted on the nerves of the two young people, giving them an absurd feeling of security; the rest of the ship could boil like a cauldron; the machines were safe, at least, we knew where we were going with them. They weren't falling apart and betraying. Their masters

The partitions had slid noiselessly behind the newcomer. It seemed to Ensign Ronciere that the mechanical symphony was approaching a sort of perfection, and hardly had the slender fingers brushed the dials when they registered a redoubled energy. It seems, thought Ronciere, that the energy has just been doubled. These people from the Committee, all the same, are aces...

Suddenly he shuddered – a quick, inconceivable, dreadful idea came to him: was not Commissioner Stanley the only representative of the Distortion? Now, it wasn't Commissioner Stanley. The latter was fair-haired, or at least gave the impression of it, while this tall astronaut over there... The ensign looked up and met an ironic gaze. Beside him, slowly, his companion, Lieutenant Garcia, raised his hands under the threat of a disintegrator.

"Hands up, free citizens," said a metallic voice. "I won't hurt you, if you're compliant. Throw away your pocket vibragun, Garcia, and you, your thermal gun, Ronciere. No need to protest, I know you have them on you. Good. Now walk backwards towards the cable room. The door's open. Don't try to trick me; you can get in there at the same time. Listen again, these cables, I don't need them at the moment, but if you damage my equipment, it will cost you dearly."

"Be damned, Cross!" Garcia growled.

"Oh," said the other. "Cross, did you say? You definitely give him too much credit."

Ronciere embarked on a desperate attempt – as he crossed the threshold, he seemed to be kissing in the ropes and sprawled at full length. But the strange aggressor did not flinch; he did not lower the barrel of his weapon, as the ensign had expected, and merely stared at the back of the boy's neck. Ronciere felt like a needle of ice penetrating his brain; he made an immense effort to straighten himself, but his muscles were weary and he remained on the ground bathed in sweat. "That'll teach you to be smart," said his adversary. "Wake up." The other complied, like an automaton. "Walk. Good. You'll have a stiff neck for two days, if all goes well, and Garcia will have to put compresses on you. Who stuck me with such weenies on board!"

Ronciere spoke, feeling with astonishment his rough, raspy tongue like a piece of gutta percha:

"I recognize you," he said. "You are Arno Heller. This is how you forced the KI crew to follow you. But why didn't you tell us..."

"Because you weren't in any condition to listen to me," replied the mutant with a knife-edge smile. "Your comrade is on the promotion board and the removal of Cross would have fixed things. Now you will have time to think..."

The door closed behind the two prisoners. Arno went to the abandoned tensors and did a strange, quick job. Green and purple sparks sprang from under his fingertips. It was in no way reminiscent of the blind trial and error of Andromeda – it was so easy now to vary the gravitations! T

he speedometers blazed, a blinding glow radiated from the dashboard and Heller appreciated the *Daredevil*'s insulators: with such tension his old rocket had already slammed! A glance at the spectrographs showed him the shards of the Astral Belt shooting up like dust from rocks, and the giant face of the satellite rising straight, like a black moon: the edge of its deep precipices glowed red – Andromeda rushed to meet the ship.

The pilot's long fingers caressed the keyboard. He hesitated for a moment, but he was playing well and was repeating to himself the sentence he had dictated to the elementary brains:

"They have the right to choose. They're, all the same, Earthlings."

Arno was determined to offer them this choice.

It was at this moment that a violent slam on the brakes caused the rocket to pitch up. Heller swore: he had forgotten that the *Daredevil* had emergency engines, ready to intervene as soon as an engine got carried away. Someone was taking care of it...I n the passageway, footsteps clacked. He stretched out his mental antennae and spotted a man running up: the second, Leeth.

"They're still petrified in the cockpit," he realized. "That leap I made into space... Szubinak yells and Stanley just goes to the moderator keyboard. But in a few minutes, they'll fix the emergency controls – I have to hurry... Leeth is a good brute..."

He let the man grope at the bulkheads and absorbed the simple waves of an uncomplicated brain: Leeth, an old-school navigator, had acted on reflex: he knew no fear, only enormous helplessness. In fact, he wouldn't take off, since the beginning of the crossing – nothing was normal, too many people were involved in ordering and Szubinak, even with his great bulk, looked like a little boy! The passengers were funny cocoons – and we negotiated with that! We would see, on Andromeda! We would have to change direction, otherwise... And then, there were these females who committed suicide or went mad – they were already mad before embarking – and these radio officers who killed each other!

First of all, if he had cared about him, Leeth would never have accepted on board, as a manager, a greenhorn whom no one knew by sight! And a! Fortunately, this Cross story was closed, finished... As soon as the hull was energized and the corridors scanned with infra, no living cell had been found of the man, it was because there was no longer any of Cross. That, Leeth had no doubt. Physical laws existed. There was only that!

And now these machines which were racing... He promised himself to give Garcia a memorable soap and pushed open a door which slid noiselessly. A calming order reigned in the engine room, the encephalographs cast dim lights. Leeth was a little surprised to see only one officer at the dials – Garcia or Ronciere? The boy had his back to him, he stepped on him and his hoarse voice broke the cottony silence. The pilot slowly turned and looked up at him with a shining silver face and terrible dark eyes.

Beneath that gaze, like an electric shock, Leeth staggered and slid on the floorboards. He was neither dead nor fainted, but paralyzed except for the facial muscles. Only his eyelids could move and he tried to dodge the wave that penetrated his pupils. The man bent over Leeth. This one remained motionless, as in the worst nightmares, where one wants to flee, to shout – and where the members become petrified.

"Don't be afraid," said a harmonious, muffled voice. "You're a good technician and we will need you. What? Are you paralyzed? It will pass, it had to, otherwise you wouldn't have listened to me... Who am I? Arno Heller. Yes, if you will, the 'No. 1 galactic hero', a stupid name. Earlier, in the cockpit, you saw what remains of Andromeda and you know the chances of a landing. The *Daredevil* will jump before reaching the incandescent zone. I intend to prevent this madness. Are you ready to collaborate with me?"

Leeth made an exhausting effort, and only managed to roll his eyeballs negatively.

"I expected it," continued Arno, "you're in the tradition of navigators of all times: the word surrender doesn't exist! But if you only knew how stupid it is in this case! Look, I don't have time to waste – I don't want to wear out the engines in a stupid fight. So I'll put you at the door of the machinery and I'll talk to the passengers.

"Your paralysis will soon be over; then, run to report to the cockpit. I give you three minutes. Tell Stanley I'm on to something – I've tampered with the machines and they're 80% better than their old junk. They just have to listen to my suggestions.

"You may leave, First Lieutenant Leeth."

And Leeth was able to get up, like Lazarus. His muscles were stiff and his arms were hanging down his sides. He couldn't turn around or lift a finger, his legs weighed tons, but he moved his feet – one by one.

He swore to himself: he must have offered an unusual spectacle. A working automaton! The walls opened, then closed behind him. He then recovered the use of his voice and some freedom of movement, knocked angrily on the door of engineering and exhausted his repertoire of insults drawn from the dialects of eight planets. Without answer. But a searing pain twisted his neck...

Suddenly, activated all at the same time, the ringtones of the intercoms were unleashed, white screens lit up at all the intersections and the loudspeakers swelled an unforgettable voice ten times.

"Alert everyone. Alert everyone. THIS IS ARNO HELLER TALKING TO YOU. Passengers and crew of the starship *Daredevil*, you are being deceived. The artificial satellite Andromeda, which you were going to take over, no longer exists; its exploded globe is dissolving into space. To verify, look at any radiant screen. The most voluminous debris of the ancient globe is an aerolite ravaged by radioactivity.

"It is physically impossible to land in this hell, even less to hold onto it. You are going to a certain and inglorious death.

"I know: you were promised that they would 'study the landing conditions' and Earth would decide, in the last resort. But there is nothing to study: one cannot live in the crater of an erupting volcano. Earth does not care about 300 lives when it needs an Andromeda station – or at least its illusion. To give the Sol System the impression that its defenses are intact, Earth will sacrifice you, without hesitation.

"Free citizens of our globe, this is Arno Heller speaking to you. I was born on Andromeda and I saw its end, I give you my word that this world is no more.

"And I ask you this question: Do you want to die like this?

"Let those who have courage answer me."

The intercom voice stopped and a terrible silence lasted for a moment – just one. Then there was a whirlwind of cries, howls, the trampling of a panicked herd. All the doors of the between-decks opened at the same time. Leeth panted through the corridors which were filling with a disorderly crowd; people were running, in a disarray like a termite mound, gutted, kissing each other, cursing an indifferent Earth and showing their fists to what, elsewhere, was the sky...Women and children were sobbing. Seated on the shoulder of a giant, a little squirrel-girl seemed the only serene one; inhumanely, she was slurping and sucking on a peppermint.

Again the disembodied voice spoke, through all the transmitters:

"And now, to the two of us, Commissioner Earl Stanley! You tried to kill me at least three times; I don't blame you; you were doing your job. Because Earth has sent you on my trail, like a hunting dog. Because you've been ordered to lure me onto this spaceship and destroy me – by any means. Because, above all, your Committee feels overwhelmed, useless. This is my doing; its tyranny has no longer any raison d'être, I succeeded in the distortion of hyperspace without your help!

"Free citizens of Earth, this is the first hour of Year One of the Space Age.

"You know that, in the present state of navigation, a rocket in full flight cannot turn back. Two possibilities therefore present themselves to you: a suicide landing on a destroyed satellite or a flight into hyperspace – with me.

"We are two hours by normal flight from Andromeda. I hold the engine room and the speed keyboards obey me. The *Daredevil* being a nesting rocket, I can still eject, on a shipwreck raft, those who want to die in the blaze. I offer others the continuum, all the stars – and the greatest adventure ever. It is not without risk. You have five minutes to decide."

In her cabin, where she remained curled up at the foot of her berth, Nan saw all the chronometer dials ticking, the small hand motionless and the large one moving with jerky leaps. She knew that the whole ship had its eyes similarly attached to this inexorable form of time. And Earl's voice came through the cockpit amplifiers. It was clean and frozen.

"Alert everyone. Free citizens, this is Earl Stanley speaking to you. You heard Arno Heller's rant. He speaks well. But while I have never concealed the vagaries of this trip from you, I passed over an essential point. Simply the fact that the disaster of the Astral Belt is his work. It was while experimenting with distortion that he destroyed Andromeda and the relay stations.

"I don't know if his invention is now perfected, but I can tell you what it consists of: certain non-human faculties allow him to modify the structure of the atom. This spacecraft, with all the organic bodies it contains, would undergo a transformation into waves or vibrations. It's in this form that creates what we call an 'hyper-vortex' that he plans to enter the hyperspatial continuum – and if the experience might be beautiful, it is indeed the most terrible of all time.

"Don't get me wrong: a rocket thus transformed shall cross the void. But in the human sense of the term, it ceases to exist, its passengers included. Beyond this margin of non-being, the atom can be, theoretically, reconstituted in its original structure. We don't really know if it actually works.

"Do you know that the ship in which Arno Heller landed on our globe was only a reconstruction of his original rocket? The original had been reduced to unspeakable chaos. Do you know that not a single one of his companions escaped from his adventure in a normal state? You may have wondered why Earth celebrated only Heller? It's because the others no longer had retained their human form...

"It's therefore to this adventure, from which you have no chance of surviving – at least as you are, men , women and children – that Arno Heller eloquently invites you. You wonder: how did he escape himself? It's because, you see, Arno Heller is not human; he is a frightening product of our time, a monster both organic and electromagnetic: a mutant. He told you that I was in charge of destroying him... There is an interpenetration error: I was simply sent to search Andromeda and the Astral Belt for proof of his crimes. Now, I already have it.

"But any human being, put in the presence of a mutant, must neutralize it or destroy it. Earth recognized the terrible faculties of its species which comes, it seems, to replace ours. Humanity is in danger as long as there are KZ mutants.

"Now you know everything. I add that, if Heller holds engineering, Major Szubinak and I hold the auxiliary engines. We can therefore slow down our ship's momentum. This fight can last. If, by any chance, we manage to land on an asteroid, we will receive help in due course. Of course, as Heller said, the venture is not without risk. But whether we survive or die, we remain human. Whereas we would no longer be so if we leave our continuum."

Earl had spoken almost peacefully and Nan felt he had dealt Arno's followers a terrible blow. He was a man and he addressed himself to men, where humanity crying less for death than for unforeseeable mutations, he still held the sacred terror, the ancient Christian dread, before what no longer has a name in any language.

The big hand of the clock had lazily passed two minutes when they heard the voice of Olga Karpov: "He's alone, after all! How about attacking engineering?" She didn't even realize that the speakers were amplifying her voice...

Arno Heller burst into an Olympian laugh: "Try it," he said. "I tripled the magnetic barriers."

Someone coughed loudly in the crowd and Vere whispered: "I believe... there's something else to do. Heller isn't the only mutant on board, is he?"

"No," Stanley answered after an immeasurable silence.

"It seems to me that these beings had – at least for their equals – feelings which resemble ours. Isn't your wife a mutant, Commissioner Stanley?"

("If he could, he would deny it?" thought Nan. "Of course, it wouldn't change much. Vere' is too well informed. But it would be a consolation to have been loved beyond duty and human horror...")

A calm voice answered: "Yes. Nan is a KZ mutant."

"Did you realize that before you married her?"

"About an hour before. It's also because of this that I had to make sure of her person. It was a somewhat neutralized danger – and I couldn't assume Heller would follow her aboard."

"So," said Vere, "if he followed her, he cares about her..."

(They had moved away from the loudspeaker and Nan saw, across the space, that Vere was licking a thin tongue over his lips.)

"You are odious, Vere," murmured Olga Karpov with disgust. "You're there like a cat playing with a mouse..."

"Now is not the time to be sentimental," snapped the other. "It seems that the only way to subdue Heller would be to hit his sensitivity..."

"Explain yourself, Vere," said Earl.

"What, you don't understand? This being – this mutant – gave himself up because of this woman. On Earth the Committee could do nothing against him..."

Earl shrugged: "He barely knew Nan! You exaggerate. He saw her two or three times on Andromeda, I think, when they were children..."

"She's got a lot of charm," Vere mumbled.

(It was her fate they were debating. It was into her sensitivity and that of Arno that Vere plunged his slimy fingers! Nan was surprised to be calm, almost serene...)

"I understand," said Vere, "that it's painful for you, Commissioner Stanley, to consider your wife a hostage..."

"Nan isn't really my wife," replied the detached voice. "To get her on board, I had to use a sham marriage: two members of the Committee played the role of priest and registrar..."

"Nan isn't really my wife..." Nan slipped to her knees on the floor and heard nothing more. She felt surprisingly efficient and light; she had

nothing left to spare – she owed nothing to Neor and had not betrayed him. The big hand crossed the third minute – never had the seconds been so long and full. Nan delivered a mental wave that joined Arno at work on the machinery and she distinctly caught his silvery laugh. However, something was happening in the cockpit – a shock so violent that she detached herself from Arno's eyelashes and lips, turned back, groped for Earl, then Vere and Olga Karpov, but she only touched void.

The loudspeakers amplified a voice she didn't know, whose enormous satisfaction, thick stupidity, she immediately measured. Leeth spoke:

"Listen, Arno Heller. We have your accomplices. An attempt at treason in the cockpit has been suppressed... We give you a few minutes to think it over, after which you will leave engineering and deliver your weapons to the guards. In case of refusal, Nan Nangis will suffer her fate. It seems mutants are hard to kill: we'll just blast her into space. It's up to you to choose Heller."

The large needle reached a number that had no reality. With inhuman joy, Nan perceived the answer:

"Understood, Leeth. I accept the five-minute truce."

Now the hallway was full of the stomping of interplanetary guards, the clanking of weapons... Did it take so many men to grab an eighteen-year-old mutant? But an intermediate partition slipped – Earl appeared on the threshold, terribly pale and his white outfit smeared. He advanced, one hand at the height of his chest where a star of green blood was spreading. When he was in the middle of the cabin, his knees buckled and Nan barely had time to support his bent head.

"I tried to delay things," he murmured, "but Vere suspected. He killed Szubinak who was trying to cover me in the fight, and Olga shot him at close range. Leeth orders..."

A thin blood he could no longer control – a vegetable sap – was choking him. He said again:

"I loved you so much, Nan..."

She leaned over the lips that life was abandoning and made the caress last until they became cold and a waxy whiteness froze the beautiful, sharp face. Centuries had passed in the opposite direction; Neor had returned from spared continents, not to save her, but to die with her.

But a small hand rested on Nan's shoulder. Lizzy MacLeod was there, with her red hair and her oversized slippers, followed by the giant Jonas. A dozen small silhouettes surrounded them.

"We're coming through the next cabin," Lizzy said. "The little ones, the void sick, finally, all those who love you. Come, it's only time. None of us want to burn on Andromeda, and almost all the children on board are mutants. As for Jonas, he agrees to be changed into a KZ or a frog."

The big needle jumped. The door creaked under the weight of the interplanetary guards: no doubt Leeth intended to take his precautions.

And suddenly time stopped: nothing could equal this stillness, this silence, and the *Daredevil* was no longer a three-dimensional concept – nor anything knowable or predictable.

"I acted a little early," said, very close, a dark vibration called Arno Heller: "Because of you, Nan..."

And the gold and silver radiation wave, in the form of a rocket, leaped into the continuum.

"Take off for Andromeda at 8.17 p.m. Specialists and volunteers are requested to join Pier 12."

The first day of the Space Age was coming to an end.

A young girl had stopped, as if struck by a ball. She remembered that it had to start like this – she had traversed, thanks to her mutant faculties, in a few seconds, a week of the future – and she fainted in the terrestrial twilight – crimson and flame.

The Sprawling City repeated a single name...

Under the arches people passed. A sentence stood out:

"This rocket shouldn't take off. They say there's nothing left of Andromeda..."

Nothing...

Nan was cold. A plexi-display presented her without transition a pale young girl, the pearls of the Milky Way and a silver and rose-colored spaceship. A bright slogan springs up:

VISIT ANDROMEDA – THE SPACE PARADISE

The display in front of which she was to meet Earl...

"But since I know everything in advance," Nan noted, stubbornly, "I won't let myself be taken in! The future will not be... this horror! It's very simple, I saw what awaits the *Daredevil* – I won't go up there. And I will not marry Earl Stanley. What? I didn't really marry him...? Finally, I will not lend myself to this comedy, he will live, I will not meet the Other – and determinism will do what it wants!

"There. Now let's hurry, Nan, my girl. Let's scrap this report and go home where Viola will steal one of these scenes..."

She pulled up her gylon fur over her slender, bruised neck, and plunged into the night. Each step brought her closer to a way out, to another uncertain – indeterminate future. Since she hadn't met Earl, his sea eyes, his smile, nor heard his voice calling out to her, nothing could get her on board the cursed rocket. Since she had moved away in time from the shop window with the slogans...

Suddenly there is a chilling notion: Heisenberg's uncertainty principle plays on a narrow margin between effects and causes; in a future built on the basis of the present, the details may vary, the substance remains. (Had Cleopatra's nose been longer or shorter, that would have changed nothing at the end of the Battle of Actium. Whether the shape of the cross had been Greek or Latin, an immense hope was to be born for Humanity...)

Nevertheless, individualistic, obstinate, Nan struggled, she struggled in the crowd that deported her to the quays. Shadows flowed. A giant passed, holding a red-haired squirrel-child perched on his shoulder. A heavily made-up woman came out of a bar, called: "Walter!" then broke her heel in front of platform 12.

All this didn't belong to the original scheme and yet was part of the same plan.

She managed to reach an unknown street.

All that was left was to turn that corner – and nothing would ever happen.

Flee...

At this moment, a harmonious voice, a somber wave struck Nan full in the face:

"Nan Nangis! Where are you running? I've been looking for you since landing, I planted the officials... You don't recognize me? I'm Arno Heller, from Andromeda..."

The gangway leading aboard the *Daredevil* was still there. Nan turned, reached for it – and ran up in one bound.

Fiction
71
Dans ce numéro:
AN PREMIER, ÈRE SPATIALE
roman inédit de
CHARLES HENNEBERG
et de nombreux autres récits complets.
144 pages — 140 F
(1,40 N. F.)
BELGIQUE ... 20 Frs
SUISSE .... 1 Fr. 75

Cover by Jean-Claude Forest

BELLATRIX GAMMA

"There is no planet to which we cannot fly."
Russian song.

CHAPTER I

Half-way between Neptune and Pluto, the reconnaissance spacecraft *RZ-2* raised concerns among its crew.

This consisted of a commander, Jerome Tycho, two line pilots, Walter Angell and Francis Verne, and a mechanic, Bill Ready. A system of accumulation compensated for the lack of space onboard: Francis was a flight engineer, and Ready, a medical student, performed the duties of a nurse. Excellent team, if it weren't for Verne's do-it-yourself mania and the fact that, on the verge of retirement, Tycho was going through a period of depression. At his age – thirty-eight – interplanetary navigation was wearing out this man.

The spaceship was a good little jerk, flexible and resistant, where comfort gave way to speed. With Angell at the helm, he set some impressive records.

That day, the *RZ-2* was moving under the control of a robot and following established coordinates, when Ready noticed a mess. He examined the dials, read the numbers and moaned in horror. A second later, an alarm signal woke Walter in his hammock. The pilot, without opening his eyes, threw out a beautiful uncertain hand, groped and took the audiophone:

"Peace, doctor!" he said. "I just took my shift. Paragraph 300018 of the Interplanetary Code: Every astronaut must have a 'margin of sleep corresponding to his attributions.' Talk to the commander."

"Walter," replied a pleading voice, "you know how he takes it! Come on, please. There's something wrong with the engines."

"Jokes! It looks at you or it looks at Verne."

"It even looks too much," replied the audiophone with dignity. "He would be delighted to go to the hypersphere. Not me. I'm engaged, you know. To an Epsilon poultry farmer."

"You shouldn't have. When one has the honor of belonging to the flying corps, one does not bother so little. But, in fact, what does that give your history of engines?"

"So we accelerated in a crazy way..."

"So much the better, the ride will be shorter."

"I am sure," the audiophone finished, "that we have crossed the limits of the solar system. What? It's impossible. Come check it out. And I have no idea where we are going at this speed."

A second after this bewildering declaration, Walter Angell, first pilot, a tall boy who had the head of his namesake, with heavy blond curls, rushed to the engine. A glance at the dials was enough for him to gauge the disaster. He locked up the gears, and a terrible jolt threw the rest of the crew out of their hammocks. Verne was the first to run; Ready, propelled to the ceiling, wiping off drops of sweat.

He turned to the engineer: "What did you do to the graviplan?" Angell let loose.

Verne was confused: "Me? Nothing."

"Nothing!" cried the first pilot, and his black eyes flashed. A perfect choice of curse words in use on six planets barely relieved him, and he went on: "I repeat my question: what have you done to our machines?"

"I already told you, I didn't touch anything."

"And that?"

Angell's hand indicating a dial of additional gears, adapted with makeshift means to a delicate organ. The incandescence index was leveling off and, in the soundproof cabin, a humming almost drowned out their voices.

"Oh...!" said Verne, who was a sensitive boy. But who could... His emotion was so strong that he sat down. The young people, who were not yet seventy-five, looked at each other. Ready, who had lifted himself from the ceiling, slumped limply at the feet of his comrades. Silence reigned.

The wall of the machinery slid open, and they heard Tycho's thick voice:

"What's going on? Can't we sleep here anymore? Who's the fool who makes the apparatus perform carp jumps?"

"The fool is me," Angell replied coldly. "And we are simply asking the name of the unknown genius who stuck to the machines a tinkering of Verne, a small invention still developed and which he showed us yesterday at the table?"

"The machines don't work?" asked the commander, peremptorily.

"Yes. They even work damn well. So much so that we have largely crossed the boundaries of the solar system and that we are still accelerating, God knows where!"

"It's not possible," said Tycho.

"See for yourself."

Whatever the officer's unwillingness, he must have realized. His face, already bilious, turns green.

He turned to Francis: "You are very inventive," he said. "Your discoveries hang out in all corners of the cabin. That ridiculous dial is one, isn't it?"

The boy looked up at his superior with very beautiful violet eyes which expressed distress:

"But, Commander, I wasn't the one who plugged this thing in! My invention was not complete, I said. I was groping... I don't even know the principle of this acceleration!"

"I would love to know," Angell dropped, "what moron took Verne's tinkering seriously."

The commander bit his lip: Angell had guessed! And no way to make him swallow his insolence!

"The moron," he said, "is me."

"Sorry, Commander. I couldn't believe..."

"Yes, perfectly. I am weary of the questionable jokes of my crew. You, the new generation full of theories, you treat an old jalopy like mine a little high. Verne was delighted with his application of relativity principle to navigation. I tried to prove it."

"Okay, Commander," Francis stammered, "but my invention wasn't ready for practical experiment..."

"It's enough. Can you explain to us now the meaning of this devilry?"

Verne thought about it, brushing aside the rusty strands that slid down his eyebrows.

"I suppose," he said, "that we are drawn into contracted space-time..."

"Always speak," Angell said. "You interest me."

Verne became animated:

"I am not claiming that a small improvement breaks the time dimension. This break exists, it was a question of reaching it. Einstein, Lobachevsky, and all the old religions have the notion of coexistence of the past, present and future. The twentieth century advanced that of the contraction of time. Take a doll, spin it around, to a certain degree its stripes merge to the point of forming a rainbow. Well, that's it... Let's say that my accelerator has succeeded, plugged into the jib, in making it reach, during an infinitesimal fraction of a second, this threshold. The rest is accomplished by virtue of the energy acquired. And...There you go! We are currently doing the biggest experiment since the fission of the atom!"

"You complicate things as you wish!" Ready moaned.

"He means," translated Angell, "that we have crossed the time barrier. We will be able to return to Earth in two centuries without having aged a day. This had been a common guess since Einstein, but no one so far had gone to verify it."

"During any hierarchical sense," Ready spreads swear words specific to cosmonauts: "By Space! By the rings of Saturn! A thousand atoms! In two hundred years, the name of the Epsilon poultry farmer will be dead!"

"You can always marry her great-great-granddaughter," Angell said. "On condition, of course, that she forgot you, I mean your fiancée, and that she married a poultry farmer."

"All this," said the commander heavily, "does not tell me that you do not pay my head. What are your proofs, apart from those dial signs?"

Angell looked at him a little high. He couldn't help but realized that now was not the time. The shiny walls of the cabin reflected them mercilessly: Tycho, brown and stocky, turned them round; Ready's tousled mop; the imperious profile of the first pilot and, against the background of the control keyboards, the slim figure of Verne which was a symbol.

Angell mentally recapitulated the general outlines of the situation: yes, Francis was right, they were part of a disproportionate experience. Thrown out of time, their rocket rushed towards the unknown. They had stockpiles of concentrates, sufficient for a ten-year trip, apparatus to create oxygen in good condition, a nice little spacecraft with resistance calculated for the solar system. They had spacesuits resistant to atmospheres from Mars to Pluto. But the abyss where they plunged was not dependent on any atmosphere and the journey could last an eternity.

Musician, Walter Angell thought he heard the first bars of *Hymn to the Stars*, accompanying the quotation of the names of the glorious astronauts who soar eternally, among comets and meteors, in their sparkling steel coffins. His meditation was interrupted by the shrill yelp of Tycho, who leaped at Verne with all signs of insane anger and sent him rolling against the dashboard.

He cried: "If something happens to us, it's your fault... mop! It's you and your damned fiddling..."

A little blood gushed from Verne's split temple, and the sensitive Ready, already in bad shape since the last shock, turned away, plagued at the symptoms of a violent illness.

Angell intervened and separated the combatants; according to an earlier description from Verne: "He dragged them by the hair in opposite directions."

From that brief brawl that eased the nerves, they all retained a humiliating impression. Tycho wiped his left cheekbone which had made contact with Angell's fist, briefly apologized, and instructed the young people to establish the new coordinates; then he withdrew followed by Ready who claimed that nothing would prevent him from taking his course in medicine by hypnotism: in fact, he was preparing to spend his doctorate on Earth, hence his affectionate nickname of "doctor". But Earth was far away...

As soon as they were left alone, Walter turned to his friend, disaster:

"And now to the two of us!" he said. "I don't mean to excuse Tycho that his inferiority complex is out of order. But since here we're in the same mess, I would like to know a little what goes around in the brain of a genius. What was your idea when you were making that damn accelerator?"

"Oh! I had just made a working hypothesis," Verne whispered. "Do you remember what they said at school about these force fields?"

"I see," Angell said. And he recapitulated: "There are, notoriously, five force fields: the electric field, the magnetic field, the gravity field, the cosmic repulsion which makes galaxies repel each other, and the mesonic field which maintains the particles of the atomic nucleus. We used and abused the first two in the twentieth century; the graviplan allowed us to manufacture gravity and anti-gravity, relegating planes and jet rockets to the museum. Have you discovered, by any chance, the use of cosmic repulsion?"

"That sounds like it..." Verne looked downcast.

Angell hissed: "Good! The damage is done. Or good. Or whatever – depending on the situation. I guess if we had any chance of getting back to Earth, we would be erected statues. But let's not count on it. Now that we're engaged in this funny field, the main thing is to get out of it."

"Maybe by rallying the mesonic field..."

"Can you do that?"

"How do you want me to know? In any discovery, I suppose, there is an element of chance. Obviously, I worked a little in the field of cosmic energy, while the meson... Oh! And then, what's the point? I could only do one experiment. Let's try..."

"No," Angell said firmly. "It's better to stay where we are. I don't see how the situation could get worse, but I guess it's possible. Let me think. A force field crosses all obstacles. However, as long as we remained within the limits of the solar system, the cosmic repulsion was not too much felt: it was counterbalanced by energetic influences, less strong, but closer. The same should happen if we interfere with another strong cohesive system."

"Unless, by accumulated acceleration, we pass through it before we feel any influence."

"And that's likely, isn't it?"

"Yes."

"Devil!" Angell said. "Devil! Something must be done all the same, old man. Or would you not want to live? To return to Earth?"

Verne looked at him through his scattered rusty curls:

"You ask the two questions... Yes, I want to live and come back. No, I don't want to return at all..."

"Would you like it, there, between us?"

The first pilot looked at his space mate, and for a moment his will strained more than a flexed bow. Earth... what was it, in short, for each of them? First there was the dictionary definition: planet inhabited by man. The third planet in the solar system. A variable temperature globe, a little flattened at the poles and whose axis is askew.

There were tons of the same ilk. It was above all memory of some very green valley or of a noisy, teeming alley – a woman's smile – a May verve. And then human fraternity, brand new and not exempt from blemishes, a few great poets and musicians, the flags, the body of Interplanetary Navigation. All these values singularly lost weight and heat in a different space-time.

"I don't know," Verne said, as if trying his voice and looking for a right tone, "if you'll understand me. I believe that our two formations were parallel, but not similar. You told me that you belong to the rare – and privileged – nucleus of conditions that their mothers, in all conscience, entrusted to the State before their very birth."

"I don't take it upon myself to judge such civic heroism. At a certain moment, the urgency arose, because Earth was suffocating and it was necessary to conquer space. We demanded a race of heroes..."

"There was rubbish," Angell said briefly. "Keep on going."

"There was never any question," Verne resumed, "that I was a hero. On an Earth, in the grip of intensive specialization, children are born catalogued: astronauts, footballers or grocers. My parents, a little older, didn't take any prenatal tests, and because they perished in a rocket accident, it was too late to put me in a definite category. I became an engineer, but I could just as easily have become a poet. Or something else. You know that such indecision in trends is recorded in our individual files. We believe at first that it's nothing, but one fine day, we realize that we're dragging a sort of condemnation after ourselves..."

"No," Angell didn't know.

"What if there was only that," Verne continued. "I knew well that tests and series – A – X or Z – are not everything and that I have something there (he touched his forehead marked with a purple and green bump). But voila, I aimed too high. I met a young girl... Oh! It was all silly! *The Princess and the Astronautic Mechanic* kind of tale. She sent me out for a walk elegantly, of course. The day before our departure."

"I see", said Angell. (Verne belonged – decidedly – to the species of the vanquished.)

"I wanted to die," said the boy with violet eyes. "I also wanted to do something huge."

"Well, you can be happy: you did. Now, leave your personal problems there, and tell me if we have any chance of getting out of this freakish adventure?"

Francis lowered his long eyelids:

"I only see one thing," he said. "The solar system, isn't it, is a peanut, compared to Sirius or Rigel. There are giant suns in our galaxy. If you think you can stay the course on one of these stars whose attraction exceeds anything we can imagine, I will do my best to slow down. I say: my possibility."

"Let's try, old man, let's try. Because, as far as I know, we might as well fall into one of those suns..."

Ready, in the meantime, had given Tycho a sedative injection and rekindling his hypnotism. But the Earth course of general pathology was also losing importance. He therefore sought to occupy his hands, if not his brain, and composed a meal for celibates.

It seemed like centuries had passed since the second a lack of gravity had stuck him to the ceiling – to what held its place in the cabin. He made the necessary gestures: take out the plates and bowls in the shape of retorts, pass vitamins under the hydrator, uncap the concentrates.

It all tasted, in fact, tasteless, Ready thought, watching out for alluring labels: Earth beef, Mars canals apples...He chased away a nostalgic memory: the poultry farmer, her farm in Wisconsin... eating chicken. The poultry farmer had well-placed curves. (All of this now mattered as much as the strawless bricks, kneaded by the Hebrews in the Egyptian desert.)

If we come back in a thousand or two thousand years...

They couldn't dive into space-time indefinitely! They would end up landing on some planet. It could be uninhabitable, or populated with giant saurians, or planted with ferns. Everything would have to start over! Ready had read Nietzsche – his insatiable curiosity accommodated everything. Suddenly a dazzling idea pierced him: they were four men on this jerk!

He was so stunned that, Tycho grumbling in his sleep, he went to give him an extra shot so he could think about it. Regardless of how he turned the problem around, it remained hopeless: no women! Here it is... There was a question, some twenty years ago, of providing all spacecraft at least with an observer or a mechanic, but this gave rise to countless disputes: everyone wanted to marry her on landing! And without a woman, no future. No reproduction possible. An all-female crew could have multiplied by parthenogenesis, although, Ready estimated, the system lacked variety. Men were singularly at a disadvantage in such a case! On the other hand, if one landed on an inhabited globe of another galaxy, there was a one in a billion chance of encountering anthropomorphs – and again...

So was his thoughts, when Verne and Angell came in, asserting, and pounced on the vitamins.

"Well," Ready asked in a muffled voice, "do we have any chance of doing this? And how?"

"Oh!" said Walter, "that... We were only discussing. Yes, hope so. No, I'm not sure. To be honest, this moron really made the second great discovery since that of the A-bomb: he introduced us into the force field of cosmic repulsion. We are heading into the hypersphere. It is useful to stick to the periscope: it is a deluge of flames that we cross. This is all relative, of course."

"Finally, you have an idea. Where are we going?"

"That, old man..."

The first pilot shrugged his shoulders.

"Do you think calculation is easy? Assuming that we were heading for Pluto, without deviating, that the space-time contraction hasn't thrown us into any parallel universe and that no force field causes us to deviate;

in short, based on a hundred free guesses, we are heading in the rough direction of Orion."

"Orion..." saw Francis. "*The pearl torso of the giant Orion, beasts of beasts, lover of Aurora...* Don't question me, Ready, it's from a 20th century Russian poem you can't know, because you don't know the language."

"Interplanetary is enough for me," Ready replied, pinchingly. "Explain yourself. There are catalog numbers, to be precise."

"Here," said Angell graciously, drawing on the tablecloth a vague trapeze, surmounted by a triangle. "It sits on the edge of the galaxy we call the Milky Way. The star which forms the upper left angle of the trapeze is a few million times larger than our tiny sun, it is called Betelgeuse and, according to your favorite catalog, its order number is the first celestial body of the above constellation. Aim: Orion Alpha. Rigel is Orion Beta and there are a few negligible units around, where the entire solar system would enter: Bellatrix and also Alnilam, Orion Epsilon, to please you.

"At the rate these two idiots have set us, we'll barely be able to get on the trapeze, and I'll be damned if Rigel or Betelgeuse don't exert a direct attraction on us..."

"So what?"

"So, one of two things will happen: either we fall directly into one of these giant suns and dissolve into the infinitesimal debris that we are, or, at the moment of falling, we're caught in the gravitational zone of some planet orbiting around it. Everything depends on the speed obtained by limiting the cosmic repulsion generated by the gravity of Rigel. As you can see, this is a problem."

"But according to you?"

"Listen, Ready, if you will, I take the atlas and I prick at random with a pin. There; we fall in the immediate vicinity of Bellatrix. Is that enough for you? Give me more carrot juice."

Thus began the enormous adventure which took for cosmic history the name of the *Bellatrix Experiment*.

CHAPTER II

Francis (in his microfilm notebook):

The flight into nothingness... This fall into the void, it was horrible. (He recovered and crossed out the last word.) No, not that horrible. Precisely that one cannot, without intermittence, be based on a single idea. The prolonged physical state creates habituation, and repetition of gestures a drowsiness.

You first had to get used to relative time. What exactly is relative time? It is soon said: And time did not exist any more. The expression is grandiose but absurd. By entering the fourth dimension, we add it to the others, we do not erase it. To conceive of the notion of continuous space-time, I had to, while hiding from Angell, fix the periscope on the void. Experience that seasoned astronauts avoid.

Well, as far as I know, there is no such thing as black and emptiness. The speed of our course, confusing future and past, we moved in the heart of an incredible sun. The radiant screen formed a rose of flames that I stared at, hallucinating, drunk with horror. Red, blue, green – it intensified, scaled the face, the molten novae and white dwarfs created a blaze. Wasn't this furnace going to melt like wax the micro-steel plates of my device?

Another unpleasant observation: the screen was streaked with lines, like the watermark of a paper. Maintained, transparent lines that I would have qualified as obscure if they had not been placed in the heart of an illumination. I understood that they were meteors, however exceptional in these parts: the relative weather condensed them in a motionless rain. My head was spinning and I turned off the periscope screen. And insoluble questions obsessed me: did these aerolites have to go out of their way, to let us pass? Or did they cross us with a rapidity which suppressed all perception...?

Space! I say, it is with such ideas that one becomes bald! Let's sleep. But, to sleep... that is to say to spend in the unconsciousness of the centuries... I remembered the charming fable of Sleeping Beauty: it was therefore right to say that every tale concealed a very simple truth? I imagined myself. by some elementary physics sleight of hand, the king's daughter transported to the fourth dimension; she remained young and beautiful, for her the sleep had lasted an hour or a day, and the forest had grown in a minute, the cedars and thuja were hundred years-old and the guardian dragons had proliferated... I confided this impression to Angell who raised his eyebrows with a brush:

'You always need princesses!' he said. 'It's morbid.'

'...Scary,' Bill thought to himself.

Of course, they don't realize, these action specialists! Francis alone perhaps dreams that he has become a star. In fact, we have become, that's the word. A comet, to be exact, and desperately aspiring to the end of a comet that reaches some solar system or disintegrates. Worlds will be born and others will die, as we tirelessly continue our course in the sidereal abyss.

If my hypno-device isn't lying, this time-erasing is a decoy. I happened to read classics which told how, by some evil subterfuge, men who had experienced the reckless wish: 'Minute, stop!' relived one and the same day interminably. (I have always been curious about these unusual experiences. Have I read any microbooks without any feature in my lessons!) These condemned... to eternity, got up every day at the same time, they consulted with a vague unpleasant surprise their calendar, heard their wife invite them to the same orange juice, they expressed the same timorous considerations about the weather, and the day then unfolded, at an always identical rhythm, which generated a nameless horror ending. For other, older writers, it was metaphysical hell. Would we be in Hell...?

But no, no, I better take a sedative. We don't repeat the same gestures, do we? The fight in front of the dial has not been reissued. On the first day (what I insist on calling this: the first lap of my stopwatch), I slightly cut the plastic of the table with my penknife, taking care not to repeat the gesture the next day: the flap door therefore a single superficial notch, which neither hollowed out nor multiplied. The cause is judged: we live in indefinite, but differentiated fractions of time.

But back to the biological point of view. Although admirably preserved (like pickles in a jar) our tissues nonetheless live for tens of years per hour if not per minute. How do they react? Tycho has a blurred complexion, but with the binge he took yesterday... no, a hundred years ago... (I will not get out of it: such an experiment deserved to be followed by a great biologist, not by a cabin) Francis still looks like a surprised teenager, and Walter is an angry archangel. Myself, I haven't changed much, my movements are smooth, my fabrics in good condition – and I have... how many already? Four hundred or five hundred years?

But then, the wear and tear of bodies would be a relative notion? And old age, a simple disease of autosuggestion?

If I get back to Earth, what a revolution in biology!
By Einstein! Will Earth even exist then...?

Tycho:

It's incredible! These idiots take the adventure lightly! I who triggered it – voluntarily – I tremble. Because there, my heart – let's not cheat: I triggered it. This miserable little vermin Verne would never have dared...

Let's calm down. Quiet. Quiet.

I couldn't bear the thought this time definitely of coming back to Earth. What do I have in common with Earth? The others were pampered children of fate: Angell, selected from birth to be a hero, Verne who grew up between powerfully rich and aged parents, in cotton wool, Ready who lives and exalts for the happiness of worms. earthen! I was picked up in the creek of a camp on Mars, my resistance excited the experts and they decided they had a dream astronaut there. Ah – yes! I hated the sickening profession; just thinking of launching myself into absolute emptiness, I was in a cold sweat. It is probably this, this instinctive repulsion in my flesh which made me who I am: a good average pilot, a little too prudent who never knew how to distinguish himself or to undertake anything.

I would have been good, three hundred years ago, when it was simply a question of lying down, in the prenatal position, in a container. Physical resistance prevailed and we did not have to take initiatives. Today... well, I drove tubs from Mars to the Moon. I haven't had a single shipwreck. There is nothing to brag about. And every time I gave the signal to take off, I had a lump in my throat, my mouth filled with bitter saliva and my clothes soaked. I have been sailing for twenty years: it has been twenty years of fear.

And all of a sudden, it had to be let go, all of a sudden life was over. The medical officer of the center, one of these over-grown kids from the new training, gave me the pill: I had deserved the Earth, my body could still last a long time, but for what was to entrust me with other cargo ships and precious human lives, I had to mourn them. And anyway, the grateful motherland would not forget me... They were going to retribute my services. I know what talking means: a shabby retreat and a square in the ground – at the South Pole or in Tafilalt.

So I recognized (I who have been dreaming of so much to this day, at this approximate release), the same ball that was suffocating me and the same russet sweat...I understood that these people were killing me. Not physically, okay (although there's a lot to be said about that too, and a laid-

174

off astronaut rarely crosses his fortieth year), but by removing me from the roles they took away my sole justification for my job. life...Useless life, completely devoted to this inhuman struggle with myself. I never had a thought for the future! I had lived twenty years in the skin of a condemned man! Of course, I am not married, I have no family. What girl would have accepted... And then, I did not have time. In the ports of Mars and Venus, there were pretty humanoids, especially stupid enough not to be surprised that a man was crying in their arms. At the artificial relays, there were dark bars, whose robots had recorded all the "good stories" of the solar system, where alcohol, Martian or Venusian narcotics made you forget, and or, if you were lucky, you met once every two or three years an old comrade who was scared like you, and at each stopover, crowds of young people who gazed at you with admiration. I was a hero to them. An astronaut from epic times! And I ended up believing it. (The people in the medical department also took this illusion away from me.)

So you understand. I couldn't hold out on this last raid on Pluto. Everything, rather than dying in a dark corner, between the dog's kennel and the Viseo booth, from which no call will ever come. Rather than reliving every night – every night – the horror of departures, the incessant expectation of a meteor, a comet, some kind of cosmic radiation that would disintegrate my cabin and throw me into the thunder of God. Rather than waking up in my bed, covered in cold sweat, suffocating and knowing that these tortures are unnecessary. I know some that led to the shed, and others that Neptune and Mercury spared, and who, bourgeois, hanged themselves in their kitchen. I was on the right road, I knew it.

So, this DIY of Verne and his ramblings... This sort of plastic box, which creaked under my hand and which seemed harmless... I couldn't stand it. I remember I drank a stiff glass of alcohol. No, I was not drunk, I was laughing. I said to myself: To us! Comrades, keep the little house, a plot and a shed; keep everything! At that moment, I swear, I only thought of dying.

But we still live.

Angell:
Three quarters in a row is a bit too much. But who can you trust? Francis scribbles verses. Tycho is drunk. Ready is doing tests on himself: blood, temperature, pulse, and other things I prefer to ignore. He confesses to me that he has a horrible stink of wear and tear. Am I scared? We hear each other, there are revealing physical sensations: inappetence, says

Ready, tingling in the extremities, twisted stomach. I don't feel any of that, just a pleasant void. That must be it, conditioning.

He had put the sunrises at a standstill, hoping that sooner or later a slight pull would occur. So he supported her with all the energy of the jerk! Too bad for those who would be thrown out of their hammocks! He adjusted the periscope screen which reflected – any swarm of stars passing by – a strip of total darkness. It was, probably, what was called an "intercalary space"; the upper course of navigation presented astonishing spectrographs, and Angell remembered: "Anything is possible in an intercalary space (like that of Vega): diamond globes and protein ghosts. But – with a margin of possibility of a millionth, it is admitted that nothing is truly real there."

It was this quote that saved him.

His visual nerves were in a throbbing pain and on the radiant screen appeared the image of a young girl combing her blond hair.

He couldn't believe his eyes. But no, it was not a phosphorescence. Neither an asteroid nor a comet. A human form in absolute vacuum? He was going crazy. A halo of black light surrounded it and, sitting on a black quartz rock, she was for a moment, for the pilot lost in the star chasm – the Primavera of Botticelli and the Venus de Milo, all the wives, sisters and maidens of Earth. He closed his eyes.

It was only a brief moment of darkness that he caught the mad pulsations of his blood. Against his cheek, the screen to which he was pressed was a vision in humanoid form, at the level of Rigel, said the voice of common sense, it is a hallucination or a trap. When he raised his eyelashes, the picture had varied. Imperceptibly at first. She was bathing half-length in a liquid cloud. Scales glistened at the level of fresh knees. An arabesque of actins, or glaucous molds plastered over the screen. The shell-shaped mouth was crimson.

Angell had regained consciousness. He raised his frozen hands to his forehead. "I guess," he thought, "that's what fear is."

"Oh!" Francis Verne's voice said behind his shoulders. The first pilot saw his companion who was propelling himself through the cabin like an automaton, his face was pale and his eyes glazed. Angell grabbed him by the shoulders, he struggled.

"Close your eyes!" ordered the elder. "Close them, I tell you!"

"But, Walter..."

"What you see is an optical illusion. This girl doesn't exist. We are inventing it every moment."

"She's beautiful..."

"Yes. At certain times. At others, her skin is green and her feet are webbed. Whoever created this hallucination knew little about Earth's fauna. Think of something else, let's see. Of our return. To the Princess. Are you getting better?"

Verne had stepped back, his eyelids lowered. A tic twitched his charming face. A moment later he said:

"Thank you friend. Without you..."

Angell threw up her shoulders. "With or without me, you couldn't have done anything at all. We are not a pleasure cruising yacht. Open the airlock? It only works on landing. This too, our galactic friend didn't know."

Finally, Verne whispered, staring at the now blocked screen, what did you think it was? The pilot did not have time to answer: Ready emerged from his cabin with the vague gestures of a swimmer; he carried a glass plate in front of him and smiled a blissful smile. "Guys," he began, "I'm going to show us a marvel." But his older comrade realizing that this smooth blade was a screen, dealt a backhand blow to his wrists. The plate escaped and was shattered into pieces.

"Guys," Bill stammered in a dull voice, "what's the matter with you...?"

"Can you no longer distinguish a bacillus from a visual hallucination?"

As a man of science (or at least he believed himself to be such), Ready reacted immediately:

"Lord," he said, "so that's it! I also said to myself that she was too beautiful, even in a reduced model, on a spacecraft, a siren!"

"A siren?" said Verne, "still hallucinating, I saw a young girl floating on the water like a garland of lilies... an Ophelia. So it was a hypnotic vision, specific to each? Should we suppose that a humanoid enemy bores us with images?"

"In the absolute void, between Rigel and Betelgeuse? No, I don't think so. Let's see, what exactly are you feeling?" Francis tried to analyze his feelings, while Ready confirmed:

"It was both vague and terribly real," he said. "The image was fascinating and at the same time inspired repulsion. As if, with all my exaggerated senses, I wanted, I yearned for something forbidden, for a seduction beyond the unhealthy. She promised – oh, a whole world! And there was this nameless horror..."

"Was the girl you saw dead?"

"Yes," Angell resumed. (He had felt this at a sharper, sharper stage, and his mouth was bitter.) "We both received the image, the symbol of organic peril. The being who communicated it to us was explained in its own way, but Ready, who's read a lot, will tell you that our brains are complicated boxes full of images..."

"Space!" exclaimed the medical student, "I forgot. Psychology section: our dreams are made of ancestral symbols and memories. Any good woman will tell you that dirty water and folded clothes do not bode well, and this simply because since time immemorial men have washed corpses and wrapped them in a shroud..."

"So if someone tried to give you a call, a seductive idea... would you see a woman?"

"I'm normal," said Ready. "The answer is yes."

"What if there was an idea of danger involved?"

"I would probably see a siren," Verne acquiesced. "Do you believe that 'the enemy outside' is trying to hallucinate us? Did he hope that, like the sailors of Ulysses, we would follow her into the void?"

"No," said Angell, "no... I'm not going that far. I don't even think this spectrum was created for our use. We are light centuries away from any planet. What we have just encountered is undoubtedly a mental trap or barrier; it is both terrible and reassuring."

"Why?"

"Because, in all probability, we're heading towards a world ruled by a powerful civilization. So think about erecting, on the fringes of a system, a hypnotic wall that reacts to spacecraft! Even Earth isn't capable of it."

"It promises!" Bill said. "What if these beings were malicious?"

"Anything is better than falling into a sun;" Verne nodded.

"In any case," said the first pilot, "now that you're calm, I put the screen in focus. And if you happen to see Cinderella or Snow White being persecuted, don't be in haste to come to their aid."

Tycho was suddenly awakened in his bunk by a break in his balance. Dull as his senses were, constantly doped with alcohol and Venusian shra-oui, he recognized among all the kinesthetic sensation resulting from an adjustment of artificial gravitation. Something was happening aboard the doomed vessel, and he – master after God – knew nothing about it! But already, above the hammock, a smooth wall lit up, like the radiant screen, it reflected a red and black threat, in the shape of a shark with glowing fins. Tycho didn't even wonder how he came to see, through the plates, the form of danger that had haunted him for twenty years. He was bounding out of the hammock, screaming:

"A spaceship, name of names! A spaceship coming our way!"

He emerged at the command post: yes, the periscope screen was blazing, and these three idiots who made up his crew were silent! He wanted to reach for the dashboard, but his slow, uncanny movements pushed him in the opposite direction. No doubt, inside the ship something was also going wrong! So that was the end of all problems. Tycho cursed his subordinates, but his tongue obeyed him badly; drops of sweat froze on his yellow forehead.

"A spaceship," said Angell, whose voice sounded far away. "So is that what you saw?"

"But in God's name...! Can't you see I'm paralyzed and we're going to have a collision? Do something! Brake!"

"We're braking hard, Commander. Besides, this wouldn't be obvious: we're at the intersection of two force fields." And addressing the others, he added: "Tie yourselves to the seats, by Einstein! I think we're there..."

Angell's voice was drowned out by a hum that the soundproof walls couldn't contain. Space radars reacted with disorder and violence. The entire screen reflected an abysmal white dawn. Tycho cried out: it wasn't a starship, but a giant star filling the viewscreen. It was... he understood why generations of men had seen hell in the form of a flaming chasm. Its spectrum and luminosity revealed it very close: distant a few light years! And they were rushing, they were going to get lost in the fiery core!

Tycho placed both hands on his eyelids, and his knuckles turned white. "In a minute," he said to himself; and he waited, panting, for an end-of-the-world crash, explosion and conflagration. But in a minute, nothing happened.

Except that, when he opened his eyes again, the cabin was full (at least he had the imperious impression of it) of black, stocky bodies stuck on the ground, ostensibly fossils. Preceded by a flint clattering on the metal, they crawled and twisted, limbs wide open and conical heads, a faded scarlet.

They all had, however, the commander thought, a vaguely human form. Long whitish filaments of cephalocereus senilis simulated hair. One of those swarming monsters rose up and, with unspeakable horror, Tycho saw that it had an embryonic face: knots of scintillating veins marked the jawbones and nose and, in the midst of a vast frontal collapse, a dull, glassy Cyclops pupil revealed this unknown appalling planetary life.

Tycho froze. The monster communicated its images to him. He saw openings and underground passages, passages hewn in the rock, bottomless potholes from which these phantoms rose. He made contact, originally, he who did not know the past of Earth, with the frightening genesis of other worlds forever dead and frozen. He crawled with these mineral specters, suffocated in the darkness, felt himself crushed under tons of granite. He moaned, screamed, lost all human appearance within himself. He was finally able to put a name on these fears: Silicones... But no! They were chemical compounds, he told himself. Yet a very ancient Earth author (Isaac Asimov) spoke of a mineral species, semi-extinct, that astronauts found on one of the satellites of Jupiter... an intelligent life based on silica... siliceous beings, but yes, that was it! The thing explained their appearance. Now it was a question of making his way through this exit in this black and red magma, of opening a route, an exit from the caves...He jumped back, his hand groped behind him and, with a sigh of relief, he found in the rack a short and powerful nuclear weapon: a disintegrator.

A clear silhouette stood between him and the mineral herd.

"Attention, commander!" said Walter Angell's peaceful voice. "Paragraph XX0079 of the Code: *'An atomic weapon must only be used in a sealed cabin at the last extremity: invasion or crew revolt.'*"

"I believe," Tycho sneered, "that I am in front of the two! Let me pass or I'll shoot up the heap! These damned fossils..."

"Commander," cried Verne, "there isn't a single mineral in front of us."

Silence fell. Tycho stared, red-eyed, the gleaming cabin, desperately empty. Not a shadow! Not the trace of siliceous scales! Not a squeak. "You won't make me believe I've gone mad..." he started, and his hand tightened on his gun. He felt he couldn't take a rest from Angell anymore, no more an explanation from Verne – their tone of superiority exasperated him. Fortunately, it was Bill Ready who intervened:

"We've been at this point for a while, Commander. You've seen silicious beings, to my great regret, I admit, that I have especially noticed, under the microscope, a naked woman, with a fish tail. Someone is having fun hypnotizing us."

"Yes," Tycho said, after some thought. He spoke slowly; oddly, the awareness eliminating the hypnotic action, delivered him from secondary phantasies: drugs, alcohol. He was becoming himself again: an average, cautious, bitter astronaut. And, after all, he had no reason to hate his crew so much! He sat down heavily and put his disintegrator on his lap. "You, Verne," he began, "who are the scholar of the barracks, could you explain to me what's going on? Or you, Ready?"

"I don't think that falls in the medical field, Commander," Bill apologized, running his tongue over the dry lips. "That's to say, the consequences are of the order, of course. It seems to be happening in the mental realm. Verne will explain to you better than I..."

"Well, Verne?"

"Yes, Commander. It seems that for a moment we're going at a slower speed. Angell and I have calculated that to some degree cosmic repulsion gives way to astral or planetary attraction. The fact would have happened."

"Did you take the co-ordinates?"

"Yes. This star where we're going is located in the constellation of Orion. Bellatrix... her name is Bellatrix."

"Planets?"

"Eleven or twelve. It's towards the third that we're headed. Bellatrix Gamma, according to our service catalogues."

"And you've the impression that's where this hash of images is coming from?"

"It seems like we've hit a mental barrier," said Ready. "Some very ancient civilizations have developed this mode of self-defense."

"Where do you take," Tycho stated heavily, "that Bellatrix Gamma is the seat of such a civilization? Third planet in its system, it mustn't be significantly older than our old Earth. However, despite all our great brains, we haven't been sending damn video walls into the stratosphere!"

"Reasoning that would be unassailable," Angell blurted out, "if we didn't emerge from the contracted time."

"Pleasure?" Tycho snapped back. "Please explain to a simple line astronaut..."

"I am also one and I am proud of it."

Tycho was boiling. He made an effort to contain himself: "Expose your idea."

"Well, I'm just noticing: we have changed dimension..."

"Then we returned to our own. So what?"

"It would be too simple. And wishful. But not in the least proves. The broken equilibrium could be re-established in a different way."

"What does that mean, in clear terms?"

"That we are on the threshold of a real universe – as real as the one we left on Earth. But it is not at all sure that it is the same. Here, the laws of physics may be different, and Bellatrix Gamma may have left its central nucleus a few million years before Earth."

Tycho scratched the back of his neck:

"Well, you might be right. In this deluge of bad luck, nothing is impossible."

"This is not a *sine qua non*," Angel hastened to rectify. "Civilizations do not have an identical approach; Earth has undergone many convulsions; let's admit that Bellatrix Gamma could, on the other hand, develop harmoniously..."

"Do you suppose we are dealing with an intelligence superior to our own?"

"Infinitely more cultured, at least in a certain sense. But let us not be too modest and do not try to create, without proof, an adversary that is too powerful. Ready, do you have any idea of the weak points of a telepathy-based culture?"

"Well," said Bill, "that makes it a whole lot easier, doesn't it? I think that in this case the technical civilization loses a lot of interest. Archaeologists have established a theory of cycles: each civilization experiences an apogee which is followed by a decline. I'll give you an example, if you don't mind? The Quaternary Middle Ages on our Earth were an essentially magical time, then our culture branched off. I believe that Earth was insufficiently populated and that a scourge like the Hundred Years War succeeded in blocking progress. From the – it's the law of the pendulum, oscillating between two extremes – our enthusiasm for the exact sciences.

"But suppose things had taken a different course: the Hundred Years War did not take place, a Doctor Faustus actually discovered the Elixir of Youth, an alchemist – Theophrastus von Hohenheim, known as Paracelsus – transmuted metals and creates androids in jars. They were very close to success, you know!"

Ready confessed, blushing. "I took it all out of curiosity. Their therapy wasn't absurd and their empiricism only bothered with symbols for fear of betrayal."

"Well, we might not have spacecraft that make their own fissile material, but we would travel between dimensions. We would not destroy a belt of artificial satellites, but a mental barrier that defended us from the universe. They probably do, on Bellatrix Gamma. I don't know if I am explaining myself well."

"Admirably," Angell replied. "Bill, I didn't know you had this talent as a historian."

But Tycho asked: "Why the naked women and silicones?"

"We don't know," said Verne, "if it's one and the same message. Let us not forget the spaceship that you saw, my commander, and the flaming star which impressed us all. All of these visions have dominant symbolism, even the mermaid..." (he shuddered.)

"Danger?"

"Yes. Someone wanted to frighten us, to make us deviate from our path. It would be self-defense. These beings may be very happy and fear any change. We Earthmen have based our system on transcendence and overcoming: going forward, discovering, clearing worlds. Imagine a culture based on immanence and stability..."

"If I understand you correctly," said Tycho, dryly, "facing the male principle it would be a female civilization..." He had spit out the word like a blood clot, and Angell had the impression of a black halo around his hardened features. He took it for another manifestation of panic and said:

"We must all the same try to hang this planet: it's our only luck."

"Who told you," asked Jerome Tycho, "2nd Class Astronaut B, that we aren't going to try to conquer it?"

CHAPTER III

The formidable "bang" with which *RZ-2* plunged into the layer of an atmosphere, snatched Angell from the gear levers where he braced himself. Bellatrix Gamma's attraction didn't need to be seconded. The crew was thrown in all directions, but at the last fraction of a minute, just before passing out, the first pilot again felt incomplete and stuck at half time. the imperceptible shock which announced what he called "the passage between dimensions". Coming to himself, Walter tried to handle the periscope which did not move, then the access hatch whose plates were welded. So many revealing signs: they had been in Hell.

As much of him, his companions slowly regained their senses: tied to his seat, Verne got away with bruises. The commander was lying, a little red foam at the corners of his lips. Ready, reminded of his duty, went on all fours towards the injured man.

"Activate emergency screen," Tycho hissed. As the side wall lit up, he questioned:

"Landed?"

"Yes," Angell replied.

"Type 8?" (Habitable planet).

"It seems to me."

"You're not sure?"

"No."

Tycho swore, spat his teeth. Without saying a word, Angell walked over to his leader and lifted him up like a child.

"See for yourself."

The entire surface of the viewscreen was blocked by a strangely fuzzy reddish magma: several semi-opaque sprays superimposed on one another. The matter had the tone and consistency of clay, but it seemed to float and maybe it was alive...? For a second, the navigators were seized with terror, thinking of worlds populated by atomic mists, of living swamps, of sands endowed with intelligent cruelty. But the next minute, masses and values stabilized. As in the puerile subconscious, where the things which are and those which could be confused.

"Looks like," Tycho squeaked, "we sank into a slush..."

"Wait, I'll adjust the viewscreen horizontally," Walter suggested.

First he got a purple glow that flickered. Then the four Earthmen suppressed a cry.

The screen reflected a shadow theater, where nothing seemed real. ("Was it," Verne wondered, "an instability of light, a mechanical imperfection or the violence of colors which struck the retina?") A gigantic sun, very distant or half extinguished, dominated the black and ruby rocks, with sharp edges, the material of which shattered the lights. Encrusted on a violet sky, these cliffs received a dull water that seemed heavy. Framing this Dantesque vision, a maze of silvery vegetation, charcoal trunks formed a landscape that could be traced back to the Eocene age. Huge corollas of nympheas and water lilies bloomed. The landscape superimposed hues of nacarat on crimson. The air seemed dense and alive.

However, Angell thought, something was wrong. This ocher-pink sun and the degree of erosion of the hills. These trees, these various species, alongside horsetails and ferns of the Carboniferous. In the Edenic landscape, something sounded indescribably wrong...

"In any case, it's a living world," resumed the first pilot. "Commander, if you're still willing to conquer it, we'd do well to proceed with tests."

"Overwhelming," Verne noted. "We keep studying this world 'to the length of the gaff.'" Although he had broken ratings – or because he was deprived of alcohol – Tycho intended to assume his responsibilities. "Therefore, we know that Bellatrix Gamma (that's it) is a bit larger than Earth (a few miles in diameter), with a higher tilt axis. And everything is in proportion: the mountains which enclose the immense range where we landed are Himalayas, the smallest fern exceeds a baobab. Air and water (we've taken samples) have a disturbing density, a smell of musk and crushed plants. A vibration agitates and displaces the lines of a landscape that one would think stable (it reminds a little of the thrill of hot air and the game of reverberations, in the desert). Yet our robots, after having overcome a (slight) resistance, move with ease. We plugged the audio phone into the excavator which opens the way into the crater where the device sank: the ground gives way with a sucking noise, like peat in a swamp, the machine makes a small leap of dimension, then everything is normalized and the editor turns round. A giant job is done in twenty minutes.

"And this is not, by far, the only contradiction. Our tests show that Bellatrix Gamma was ravaged by a terrible nuclear explosion some thousand years ago. Our Geiger computers haven't detected any dangerous radioactivity. At least not here. But traces of the cataclysm can be seen everywhere: soil samples have delivered stabilized plutonium; the rocks by the lake (Tycho can't believe it) are agglomerates of rubies and sapphires. I dare not tie up, beyond the ashy plateau, the chain of sparkling mountains – pure carbon, it would have become diamond.

"It seems that an unprecedented disaster has befallen this globe. And then centuries have passed. The atmospheric layer reformed, the geology stabilized with light crests of gems and their sharp ganese peaks. But it was already an old planet, stuffed with seeds and spores: one day, life was reborn. What a life? What strange mutations have developed in this paradoxical world? We don't know yet. And deep down, I'm afraid to know."

As a conscious and organized conqueror, Tycho sent out radio calls to the four winds. He received no response.

"No trace of intelligent life. But with each of our attempts to communicate with the outside, we feel the same soft resistance, a kinesthetic sensation, a disruption of balance – incomplete."

Bill stood behind him reading his notes. He said: "It reminds me of the doseras. Finally, the sundews."

"Yes?"

"Carnivorous flowers. We mustn't believe that light corollas are wide open offering themselves to the passage of everything coming. There's always the elastic opposition of a petal. The insect, fascinated by the pseudo-dewdrop, is all the greedier. It overcomes the resistance. And it dies."

Angell intervened, laughing dryly:

"These are not things to say. When Tycho's sure that the air isn't stuffed with eberthella typhi and that this lake – or this inlet – isn't a breeding ground for microbes, Verne and I will scout... like insects."

"I ask the question that torments me..."

"Bill, if our tests are right, one thing escapes me. It seems that at some point this planet was completely devastated. Life would have resumed from spores. But here are various species and everything also promises the survival of animal species. How do you explain it?"

"Damn!" Bill replied. "You have a mania for locating troubling problems. It's simply the story of moths. You know, when after you've spread your house with DDT and still find a moth in your best suit? We have to believe that destruction is never total."

They had buckled their suits, Tycho had insisted on it, although the air of Bellatrix Gamma had turned out close to Earth's atmosphere, with only a little too much oxygen. The dawn of the third day was breaking.

They already knew that a day on Bellatrix Gamma lasted eighteen hours, that dawn and dusk were very long, and a faint orange light did not go out until after midnight. Then, the three moons which were to raise formidable tides, stood upright over the Diamond Mountain. For they were also beginning, as befits conquerors, to give names to the sites: the lake was Ruby, the plateau, drowned in immense cuts of alabaster with a penetrating scent, was called the Forest of Nympheas. Beyond stretched the Plain of Ashes. It was agreed that Verne and Angell wouldn't go far, that they would go around the forest and fly over the plain in a helicopter. They had to communicate with the spacecraft every quarter of an hour. They carried hand disintegrators.

The first step on an unknown planet is something intoxicating. Accustomed to the fanciful stops in the solar system, the two young people were eager to set foot on unexplored ground. They already knew it was firm, but elastic, and Ready, who accompanied them to the cutaway, saw them without concern first sinking slightly, then performing a recovery, in the pearly mist of the morning. He waved his hand and the pilots signed back to him. On the ridge above the crater, their silhouettes seemed strangely small and vulnerable; for a moment he felt horribly helpless.

"Looks like they left me centuries ago," he analyzed. "And how far away like Earth – in time and space... Lord!"

When he took his binoculars, they were gone. Bill tried to remember exactly the last words of his crewmates, their youthful voices and their laughter – and couldn't. He returned to the cabin where there was only Tycho, furious at being injured, and who was storming. "Then? They left? What are the personal observations of the illustrious medic?" he cried. "What is there to say?"

"Nothing," Ready replied. "They disappeared a bit quickly, that's all..."

The two astronauts had climbed the hill which dominated the spaceship and which hid it from their sight. The filters of their suits began to give them, gradually, a glimpse of the atmosphere of Bellatrix Gamma, its touch like that of warm water, its taste of fruit and musk. A few moments later, they could raise their visors.

The enormous sun was emerging from the lake, in its orange glory. It darted its rays. And it was an indescribable impression, for in the pearly, iridescent mist, the whole landscape tilted slightly. Verne let out a cry.

There was a moment this landscape was empty. The red cliff, encircling the crater, descended limply towards the lake. Now that height towered over a city. The astronauts had never seen it on their screens and yet it was there, beautiful, with the inclined and shining planes of its buildings, its arenas and its streets, its octagonal or conical towers and the zodiacal wheels of its crossroads.

It had been built of almost translucent and yet impenetrable materials, like certain pale and smoky gems, and a harmonious civilization had presided over its geometry.

The center of this city was a palace or a temple with unforeseeable angles. Verne understood that each spiral of its stairs and each cornice must have a symbolic value; it emanated from it a sensation, already known, of dread and gloomy and gilded, in the course of certain symphonies...The walls of a malachite green or a deep jade became iridescent in the heart of a strange hanging garden where the Earthmen recognized oddly blooming aquatic plants: colonies of madrepores and corals, mauve and pearly actinias, kelp, milfoils and elodea, similar to mimosas, pondweeds with translucent leaves, purple gorgonians and indigo wrack. A white bloom, where Bill had recognized, with astonishment, corals of female vallisneria and imbricated esperiopsis sponges, nested on crumbling battlements: flora of the marshes bordered with fauna of the oceans. Giant diatoms and moreens, the color of old ivory, covered the enclosures. Was it an underwater city that rose up in the crimson dawn...? Angell and Verne watched, fascinated. The youngest of the astronauts raised their hands to their camera and the reverse shock erased the dazzling picture.

Verne passed this uncertain hand over his eyelids: "A mirage!" he said.

"Quick, the helicopter!" Angell commanded.

The dismountable apparatus sprang up, in a spin. They flew over the site of a triumphal arch, a pink colonnade...

There was nothing under the cliff. Nothing, except a grove of poplars – ash and grayness, except a pool covered with duckweed and sagittaria, degenerated products of the force seen. The Crimson Forest was starting its curtains of lianas; python-shaped roots lifted humus. At a certain point, they spotted an indistinct ruin, a crumbling white jade wall...

Verne suddenly felt cold.

"Would we have dreamed?" he said hesitantly. "Is this world populated only with shadows and mirages? This fabulous civilization would only be a reflection hovering on a dead globe. What do you think, Angell?"

"I don't think so," replied the other worriedly. "What attacked us in the void, looked terribly alive..."

Leaving the motionless forest, the helicopter veered towards the Plain of Ashes. A wise name: the immense gray expanse, spangled, covered with light graves, deserved it. Cut by faults and ravines, it was flush at the foot of the mountains (was this the real site of a destroyed city?). An almost palpable feeling of desolation emanated from this no man's land: no life seemed possible or desirable. And yet...

Verne put a hand on Angel's shoulder: something yellow-brown was moving under the glittering rocks. An animal. A gecko of the lygodactyl genus, it seemed, perhaps a salamander – but enormous – a saurian of three elbows, emerged from a chasm of crystal. It had retractable claws and strange ruby eyes, singularly shining. It crawled on its stomach, moved forward, then backward... the stealthy pace suggested a sense of danger, a tactic, in any case, a reasonable behavior. Angell glanced at Verne, and their helicopter dived. But they didn't have time to photograph this second vision, a waterspout of transparent wings, hairy legs appeared above the gecko, and the silence was no more.

The buzzing, screeching thing that had befallen the lizard was – they saw it with some horror – a monstrous mutant, a hippobosca, a blood-sucking "spider fly". Brown and red, flattened, leathery, half insect and half vampire, it clung to the scales – and it was a fight to the death. The gecko clawed, it took terrible blows with its caudal appendage, but it was out of breath under the attack and at times threw back its swollen throat, which throbbed. The hippobosc's sucking trunk, greedy as a sucker, found a hold; the neck of the lizard, under the fine white scales, swelled to rupture...the two astronauts, fascinated, saw a red mouth open which must have spit flames, but from which escaped an almost human cry. The trunk hungrily sucked in life, and the topaz patches tarnished.

None of the combatants inspired the Earthmen with any particular sympathy, but the attitude of the defeated, anthropomorphic salamander, its slender paws clawing the ground, and the horror that one feels at the sight of a vampire at its work, had because of the moderation of Angell who grabbed his disintegrator. Verne grabbed his friend's wrist. Too late! The thermal jet had sprung out. The prothorax pulverized, the insect heaved itself again with a dry jerk, among whirlwinds of ash – and it dragged its prey.

Then something happened that Bill called "extremely curious". Verne's enlarged pupils recorded this: the moment before, the fight had a three-elbow headed saurian and a dry fly the size of a pterodactyl, clawing and rolling, into the heart of the Gray Plain. A moment later, the same plain was bare. The debris of the fly still dotted the ridges of the rock, tracks of the lizard on the ground were clear. But the gecko and the hippobosca were gone.

Angell and Verne looked at each other. The disintegrator was still smoking, and the helicopter skimmed the sand. At the same moment a sharp noise, a rattle of rattle, rose. The two Earthmen lowered their eyes: emerging half-length from a fault in the rock, a singular being – glaucous and endowed with webbed extremities – raised a conjuring paw, launched an ironic laugh and faded away, like the fly and the gecko.

Delicately placing his camera on a purple glade:

"We would have said," Angell observed, "that this toad forbade us to go any further. If this is the higher species of Bellatrix Gamma, it is our luck! Unless he shares royalty the with flies and geckos..."

"You shouldn't have shot," Verne said moderately. "Paragraph XXX056 of the Code: '*All unknown life on an explored planet is sacred, for anything can involve a minimum of intelligence.*'"

"Lord! You won't tell me that this fly had morals? And then, if I hadn't fired first, you would have discharged your disintegrator. And as your hand was shaking, you killed the two beasts!"

"Do you believe? The caiman was very pretty... There is, on Titan, a race evolved from lizards..."

"Yes. Yes. What I find most curious is their disappearance!"

"Wasn't it?" Verne murmured. "It was as if they'd been erased... as if they'd never existed. Did they really exist?"

"In any case, the debris on the bushes exists. Verne! You're not listening to me. What are you thinking about?"

Francis turned his beautiful amethyst eyes towards his companion, veiled by a vision:

"This city of crystal's also disappeared..." he said.

Now cautious, having left their helicopter in the clearing, they decided to join the spacecraft on foot. They alerted Ready on board. The forest opened before them, mysterious with its ash and red foliage, of pink or brown velvet umbels, giant cryptogams. It seemed alive and singularly populated. Pale shadows followed them, then faded, wavy antennae fluttered among the reeds, a winged fan Verne. At the same time, the sharp senses of a young engineer felt a kind of impulse, an insistent wave that could be a thought or a silent cry. Someone would like to communicate with them. The unknown creature also used symbols. Verne thought he heard: "Danger." And then: "Me and you..." It was painful and slow like the advance of an underground spring, wavering like a melody in the winds.

Guided by an obscure sense, Francis broke a reed, drilled holes, transformed the hollow stem into a syrinx. Angell watched him do it. It was an unexpected and incomplete success, like everything else. From the first note (Verne improvised a variation on a Schumann lullaby) the branches of certain poplars quivered, strange figures – white birds, little simians with silver coats – fell into the shadows, an influx of light thought brushing the two Earthmen. Then suddenly, from the very heart of the forest, rose a crystalline melody, cold and brief like a cry of despair. "Go away, strangers!" it said. "An appalling danger awaits you. Dark and underground forces, slow like black waters, enveloping like weeds, heavy like rocks, carnal and merciless forces make Gamma a cursed world. Nothing can be saved. Go quickly!"

The song broke off on a high note. And there was silence. The white shadows were fading. The beautiful planet suddenly seemed crowded. It was an empty and closed trap.

The Earthmen quickened their pace. The red ridge of the crater which imprisoned the spacecraft appeared very close, clear against a golden sky. Seized with anguish, Verne was the first to run. Angell looked around for the ultrasonic excavator they had set up, but only encountered a clayey, undeveloped slope. Ready must have brought in the robots...Verne was already on the embankment, he turned to his comrade his face pale and frozen and shouted something, but his voice did not stop.

"We should have foreseen it..." Angell thought.

Francis was running down the slope. He was panting a little. He said: "The spaceship has also disappeared."

It was the worst thing that could happen to them. How could *RZ-2* have taken off without them? Tycho lay motionless, and Bill was a good fellow, a decent astronaut who never let go of his teammates. Besides, barely a quarter of an hour ago, they had communicated: the spaceship was here and everything seemed to be in order. However, the fact was there:

the two navigators were standing on the embankment, and at their feet an empty funnel was hollowed out which did not keep any imprint.

A precarious situation, if there was one. An hour ago their adventure was one of all astronauts landing on an unknown globe: they had shelter and even a faint hope of returning to the home planet. Now they were being thrown destitute into an alien universe.

The *RZ-2* was gone with their robots, their air tanks and their provisions. And what was worse, their self-confidence. They had two weapons left, the contents of their individual packages – that is, a few bandages, a little water, a little alcohol, a sachet of concentrates and vitamins; they also had their armor left which would last as long as they could.

Verne looked away from the bursting crater. He had a vague impression 'that it might not be', that it would be enough to lower the eyelids, then to look ahead to find the shape of the "big silver fish" lying in the clay, to hear again the excavator's hum and the joyful voice of Bill.

But nothing had changed when he turned around: they were very much alone on the Evil Planet.

"Well," said Angell at last, "I guess it's Act II of the adventure. Verne, there's no point in wringing your hands."

The young man turned a convulsed face to his comrade:

"How can you talk like that, when Bill and Tycho... So you have no heart? I guess that's your conditioning... We still lost our comrades!"

"For me, they're the ones who lost us. They're better off than us, and Bill is a reasonable boy. Tycho, he is immobilized, has something bad luck is good. In any case, it's useless to stay here: the *RZ-2* won't come out of the ground to please us. Are we going back down? I have an idea that the city should now be in its place."

He was not wrong. When they came up the hill, the Magic City stretched out before them, with its barbaric jewel grace, and incense rose from its gardens.

Verne thought it was going to fade like a dream when he set foot on its onyx pavements: it didn't happen. For a moment again the orange sun created this instability of shapes and colors which disoriented him, for a moment Bellatrix Gamma was double or triple, full of fearful signs and faceless perils, all the more appalling than the human imagination could not predict anything. Then everything became real again. The astronauts' footsteps echoed on slabs of jasper and jade. The buildings which they passed sprang up, constructed of eternal and precious materials, with infinite art. These walls didn't have the smooth, dull appearance of objects created by non-human hands. Their builders seemed to know all the techniques.

And yet this city was empty.

Deserted were the squares with their open gates of warm pink alabaster. Monumental bare staircases. Uninhabited houses...Verne stopped. Suddenly, the same deep, concrete sensation imprinted on his flesh – a rupture of balance – aroused before him, at a square, a fragment of a deep Neozoic forest, a fern, a grey poplar which seemed to hover above the ground. A glittering wall seemed to dissolve into blocks and collapsed on a moss-eaten pavement...

"I'm dreaming!" cried Francis.

And Walter:

"No. It seems that several landscapes coexist on the same location. The adventure goes on."

"You mean?"

"We believed ourselves saved, to have found the attraction of a planet, we escaped thus to the fourth dimension."

It was, of course, an idea of earthlings, ignorant of other worlds and their laws. "It looks like we've fallen between Charybdis and Scylla – for whatever reason, Bellatrix Gamma suffers the fate of *RZ-2*. We live in time dimensions. In the place where we are, there is at the same time an ancient and sublime city, which is the summit of art, the Pleistocene forest which preceded it and the ruins after the cataclysm which destroyed it. In all this..." He hesitated, his conditioning told him to save Verne, but the boy spontaneously finished:

"The most terrible thing is to ignore the mechanism of our movements, isn't it?"

Their attention was caught by a mental wave, almost palpable. A stealthy, benevolent, weak creature was dying of fear and calling. She will suggest to them the idea of a melody and a hollow reed flute: it was she, of course, who had spoken to them in the forest. Verne impulsively jumped into the direction of the call coming from, and Angell followed him, his hand on his atomic weapon. They crossed several places and courses – deserted. Yet Verne was overcome by the concrete sensation of a huge crowd circulating around them, he seized the shadows and the sparkles; a stale smell of swamp suffocated him under a vault, he felt the damp contact of scales on his cheek. The anguished creature preceded him, she seemed to flee into lower levels, and from window to window, she called them by syrinx trills.

Suddenly, they came out before the central building of the Megalopolis, temple or palace, carved in jade and crystal. Its starred planes hurt the retina. Eyes half-closed, stumbling, Verne passed the doors of an unknown metal – selenium or orichalcum – which opened silently, then fell behind him like the flagstones of a grave. Angell, on the lookout, followed his friend.

It was in the Ivory Gallery that they met her and she was an indescribable and lovely being, just human enough to reassure them, belonging by other characteristics – a white, smooth plumage, and a silver egret – to the bird kingdom. Her intelligence having been able to match human thought waves, she was able (Verne understood immediately that she was a female) to transmit to them more precise and differentiated notions.

"My name is Ary," she told them. "I belong to the people of the Free Air. You too, don't you? I want to help. But I have so little time – and so much to tell you! Come, you will see for yourself. Follow me..."

She took Verne's hand in her delicate little talon and led him, half running, half fluttering. As in nightmares, they followed the twists and turns of corridors, climbed gently sloping stairs, built for non-human beings, crossed rows of circular halls.

They finally came to a large temple hall seemingly cut from a colossal diamond core. Among garlands of seaweed and barnacles, dancing lights lit up, and the walls were carved with moonfish, octopuses blooming like stars, and starfish. Without windows, the room was filled with a glaucous, opaque phosphorescence, that which must radiate in submarine abysses. Even before having crossed the threshold, Angell realized that an unspeakable, intangible dread inhabited this place, but he could not let go of Verne who surrendered to this magic. So he followed him, but like a hunter; in the face of danger, he became again what he would never have ceased to be: the astronaut conditioned to explore, conquer and die, the great solitary space adventurer.

At the four corners of the room, four statues stood.

The closest, roughly cut, in black basalt, represented one of those beings they had called 'Silicones'. Stunted, his talons clenched on a heap of glittering metal, he was the miser or the slave. But slave to who...? The second statue modelled in snowy alabaster, resembled the species of Ary, although undoubtedly this effigy was more animal. On the third plinth stood the man-fish. Not a Lovecraftian monster... From the most impressive of images emanated a horror mixed with charm. Where did the beast end? Where did the human being begin...? The metallized jade material, the cylindrical shape, betrayed a supple grace, a kind of decadence in beauty...Yes, it was a human form, lovely, glimpsed and deformed by abysses. A very handsome god, fiercely stylized. Nacreous scales sheathed a perfect body, large fins evoked wings...

The fourth – oh, the fourth statue, Angell silently knew what element it would be! This elongated and frail form was a flame in the wind! Among long braids, or rays, of supple gold filaments, the white onyx silhouette soared towards the light. But the astronaut recoiled before the face of the mysterious goddess: a small triangular figure, with raised eyebrows, eyes of sandy gold. One foot trod the spine of a saurian. The expression of the features was appallingly barbaric and cruel.

Angell understood: these were the four species – better still – the four kingdoms that divided Bellatrix Gamma.

He turned to the bird-girl. But the gentle semi-human face froze, the feathery talon clung desperately to Verne's hand. Ary was trying in vain to unleash an intelligible mind wave – and she was shaking. No separate notion reached the Earthmen. Then, with a terrible effort, she managed to untangle her fingers and, with a stumbling flight, came crashing under the fourth pedestal. There was a hieroglyphic inscription there. Ary's regret swept it aside, when she slipped to the ground, her head hanging down, as if an invisible hand had crushed her vertebrae.

Verne had followed her. He saw the white plumage tarnish; a little red foam beaded at the corner of the vast open eyes which guessed glassy. A long shiver stirred the indescribable and delicious body, and Francis received the dead bird-girl in his arms.

"Dead for trying to help us!" he cried. "Oh! Angell, I swear, if I ever got hold of the one who killed that charming being, they would pay dearly!"

An incredible silence reigned in the room. The faces of the statues seemed to sneer. Walter feverishly noted the hieroglyphs. There were three lines in all, but his hand grew heavier at the end and a thick darkness fell over the two astronauts.

Bill had just changed Tycho's bandage. At nightfall, the triple moon flooded the Diamond Mountain with whiteness.

"Aren't they back yet?" the wounded asked.

"No, commander."

"I shouldn't have allowed them to scout!" growled the officer. "Verne is too emotional."

"Angell is a perfect astronaut."

"Angell is an adventurer!" interrupted Tycho, dryly. "One of those guys who dream of conquering a sun for their own sake, and marrying a star princess! This is called hero conditioning. By crushing the kid's mind, we end up creating monsters. I'm sure he deliberately kept our radars away..."

"They communicated with us."

"How many times?"

"Twice. The first communication in the morning ensured that all was well. They had met a city mirage, a native species of lizard, and pulverized a hippo...well, a big beast. Later, they announced that they had landed, in the helicopter, at the edge of the woods and that they were joining the spacecraft. 500 meters from here, they were 500 meters..."

"And then?"

"And then nothing."

"Nothing...!" Tycho grumbled. "You can see that wooden edge on-screen – and we haven't changed places, have we? They should've been here hours ago!"

"Yes."

"I told you, this is a dangerous move from Angell. He must have moved away into the forest. Oh! We'll talk about it again!"

This peremptory statement made Ready smile. Bitterly. Bellatrix Gamma's atmosphere was straining his nerves. It seemed to him now that centuries had passed since the departure of Angell and Verne: their very features faded in his memory. The morning events were lost in prehistory. And Earth... did it even still exist? It was such a pretty planet indeed. He had heard of it... once.

But on the communal table, an astronaut's glove modeled by the powerful and slender hand of a comrade made him operate an abrupt recovery in the present. He ran to the airlock and opened it, he anxiously inspected a lunar landscape, with pale phantoms of mimosas and vast cups of nympheas full of perfumes. The triple moon (wasn't this an ancient myth that spoke of Artemis-Hecate-Selene, 'the triple goddess with the brazen forehead'?) wove evil magic; the surface of the lake, icy silver, was so quivering, so insidiously close that the spaceship was reflected in it and Ready had the stars under his feet...

Surprised, he could not suppress a cry: they had been avidly calculating the tides, but no one expected this silent advance of the lake! The crater was half full and water was licking halfway. It kept going up. Bill ran to wake Tycho who groaned.

"Commander," he cried, "the water is coming!"

"The what? Name of names! Close the airlock! Who then encumbered me with a congenital moron of this kind!"

The student left without arguing. But closing the airlock turned out to be impossible; the joints were blocked. Terrified, Bill felt a dry dust come loose under his fingers, patches of eroded, rusted metal – as if the mighty machine had crumbled for centuries under the sun and the waters. Bill ran back through the cabin, the hull inside looked the same incredibly dilapidated. The implacable enemy, the time they had defeated, returned to the charge: at the command post, Ready stumbled in the robots in crumbs and the shattered dials... He wondered, with horror, how in the midst of this decrepitude he and Tycho were still alive!

"Commander," he said as if to report, "I don't know what's happening to us. The airlock's blocked. Water rises everywhere, and – Heaven forgive me! – *RZ-2* is only a thousand-year-old carcass..."

"What nonsense," Tycho began, but he stopped dead; Ready's hands, lifting him, left streaks of rust on the bandages. On the ceiling, the neon lights flickered, then died, and the hiss of air pierced the shipwreck, escaping from demolished tanks and the slow, deep shudder of the rising tide. Tycho stiffened and clenched his fists.

"Go away, Bill," he said in a changed metallic voice. "I can't...It's my spaceship."

"But, Commander."

"Leave, it's an order."

"He's lost his mind," Bill thought. "It's equal, he has allure! But I can't give up on a wounded person either. The Hippocratic Oath – and all that...We seem to be playing Crow!" He looked around for a blunt object that hadn't been totally gnawed and worn down, with which he could knock out Jerome Tycho, and drag him from the doomed apparatus. But he did not have time to practice this means of anesthesia, for a creaking screeched through the hull and the ship was shaken by rhythmic blows.

They were steps. Very heavy footsteps.

The cabin door hung on its rusty hinges.

They were there. The Silicones.

Their very appearance was less terrifying than the appalling slowness of their movements. They moved like a wall towards Tycho's hammock and tore him from his blankets. They grabbed Bill, glued against a wall.

Oh! They didn't seek to do harm, they were neutral and frightfully cold. A musty smell enveloped them. They arose from the shadows of darkness; mineral corpses, they left their graves – for what sinister tasks? Bill's heightened sensitivity seized some mental images that accompanied them: chasms, black void, absolute void. Desolate asteroids, or their like, subsisted on carbonic rock. Incandescent core of the planets where these demons worked (he understood now, why humans placed their hell under the earth). And a total absence of selectivity, of any feeling. Perception itself, in the sense that man understands it, must have been lacking.

Anyway, they let Tycho fight, scream, cut his wrists with his teeth, then vanish. They might as well have taken a dead man. Ready let himself go between the rough tentacles and followed his commander. He had the incoherent impression of living a dark and ancient terrestrial tale.

CHAPTER IV

Verne was pulled out of the darkness by an insistent call. Not his name, strictly speaking, but three-note music that twirled and penetrated his brain. He would never have believed that a simple melody could be both an exasperation and a torture. But it was. And while he remained devastated, plunged into this black liquid, in a well of shadow, an unconscious part of himself struggled and darted before the intangible voice.

He obeyed and stood up, stumbling. Around him the night was opaque, the air humid and heavy. Without knowing exactly, he understood that it was an underground gallery uniting the phantom city with the lake. The ground plunged, gently sloping. Verne took a few steps – his limbs were stiff, but no one had thought of binding him. And yet he knew he was doomed, without remission. For a crime? No, a worse fault. Or an intention...

It just didn't make sense. Groping, he found an automatic weapon under his armpit. The heat gun in hand, he gathered courage and called out to Angell, in a low voice. No one answered him. But the melody returned, insistent, shrill, like a white-hot soul. It was a very soft female voice.

"Ary!" he whispered. But no, Ary was dead and he barely remembered his features. The music, in revenge, created in him a feeling of lucid intimacy – as if someone had known him better than himself.

Verne shrugged – such a being did not exist; he was reserved and secret, he had never laid bare his soul in front of his comrades, he dreaded their carelessness, childish games and the clear laughter of great astronauts. Not even Angell...

Suddenly he started.

"Aurea!"

He had recognized the voice.

A little Martian prostitute, a port girl. He couldn't even remember her face (all these cheap girls looked alike). Only that her coral red skin was dry and smelled of sagebrush and her long, straight hair enveloped them both. That was what she needed that night: to be buried in the darkness of the Magna Mater, to cease to exist. He had literally picked her up on the scarlet pavement of the camp and nothing predisposed her to the heavenly hells that a creature from another planet could open. And the red on his forehead, he remembered: he had told her about Aelis. Of that white and

black orchid, for which he had longed to live and die. He had sullied Aelis'
name... (was that the inexpiable fault? No. No.)

"Aelis."

The melody had changed. He saw again, with incisive gentleness, his
last night on Earth. A crimson sea, a white yacht, a siren's white swimsuit.
He could smell algae and citrons on her face and that fine breeze from the
sea. They had swim and swim. Now, lying on a rock, Aelis offered him
her full mouth.

"Aelis, I'm leaving for Pluto."

"Dear, come back for my wedding."

"You can't marry Kairn. He's old."

"He's strong. And hormonal injections aren't for dogs."

"You don't like him."

She raised herself on one elbow, gazed at Verne's upside down face,
let out a golden trill...

"If you weren't," she said, "parodying the classics, one of those 'god-
damn astronauts', I'd marry you. But a husband who travels through eternity! Very little for me. I don't have the fabric of this lady who continually
undoes her tapestry. Penelope, isn't it? Farewell, sidereal hero."

"Farewell."

This is how a world is swallowed up, a star falls.

And there was Aelis here.

She called him. This music which he had taken for the voice of Ary,
then of Aurea, it was his. How could he have been wrong? In the deep
darkness, she spoke very closely, she begged and whispered, she promised
so many delicacies! A fiery ecstasy he had never expected. And also something beyond all fear and humiliation. He was on the edge of an abyss
where monsters were swarming, from which long white flames rose up.
And nothing could stop him from rolling in it, because deep down inside
he wanted to.

Verne groped about. Under his hand, the texture of the walls, the invisible glyphs, came to life, tied to the musical motif, participated in all
the magic of the planet. He had the intuition of a secret, refined and barbaric civilization which interested the touch, the tactile sensations dominated, they were prolonged in all of the Earthman's nervous system and
awakened in its fibers an exquisite and horrible tremor. Now, oh! Now he
wanted to stop.

In the background of the hypnosis, a conscious thought burst forth:
"And if this was punishment? What if death took on that face and that

voice on this dark and magnificent planet? A Space Trap... We compared it to a plant – which one already? Ah, the sundew – the Cape sundew – what a mockery!" The sight of insects struggling in the warm, living cone, the pit suited to them, filled him with horror.

Too late: he couldn't go back. Music, glyphs, perfumes, Bellatrix Gamma had captured all of his senses. Fire roses bloomed on his retina, the air tasted and smelled of myrrh and spikenard. The very shadow, warm and quivering, became a caress. Verne moved on, he had forgotten Earth and the spaceship, everything, even the names of his comrades. He was...but yes, happy. As if the disoriented human being, thrown to the cold stars, finally found, in this deep matrix, its place, both immanence and rest.

The corridor led to a huge cave, white and black. Stalagmites and stalactites, it hollowed out in the heart of a single diamond, a monstrous gem. A white crystal sand bounded a black water. On a giant altar quivered a high colorless flame. At its base, a chasm opened.

Verne felt more than he knew: the call was coming from there. Something nameless, shapeless, unimaginable, was lurking in that darkness. Something gelatinous, primordial, from before ages and beings, even older than dread and chaos. It was this which possessed Gamma, which attracted and captured the wandering ships in the infinite, which populated the dungeons with phantasies and precursor to ecstasy.

...This unspeakable force that he had sworn to destroy, in a moment of aberration or recklessness...

Now it was in him, it was him. It slowed down or precipitated for pleasure the rhythm of his blood, and worse, it crept into the depths of his soul, to taste, with monstrous delicacy, the memories; it increased tenfold, breaking his veins, its anxieties and his joys. For a moment angry, he wanted to struggle with that appalling softness which rose in him to the jerky rhythm of a tide, which stiffened his muscles and bent his body like Ary's, but it was beyond human strength.

Overwhelmed with horror, carried away by a scarlet flood, Verne knew, physically, that his being was dissolving in nothingness.

"Take a seat", suggested a moderate wave. "I know that humans on Earth have made these rules of civility. Let me watch you. Oh! It's not worth the trouble to tighten your hand on this... weapon: you will have neither the time nor possibility to shoot." A silence. Then: "Yes, I believe you are perfect for my purposes."

"You don't know," said Walter Angell.

"No. But I am reading your brain. Does it not surprise you to hear me? You are teaching me Terrestrial language."

They were face to face, in the green shadow of the temple. The being, half-stretched out on his smaragdite throne, exceeded human stature. He was beautiful to make people shudder. His folded fins were shaped like wings, his scaled breastplate glittered, and his hands were reminiscent of swans and lilies. Under the tiara of luminescent opals, it was the Angel of the Abyss, Lucifer, inaccessible to any order of human emotions.

To shorten the preambles, he introduced himself:

"I am Aes. I guess in your language it means a king. But the word is not exact, not implying continuity. There is always an Aes and, although appearances vary, probably always the same."

"A god of Gamma?"

"What is a god?" the Being asked, haughtily. "The principle in you is vague – and we are real. The soul itself lives in the midst of its people and I am not its male mirror, as the Present are its parts. We own this planet."

It was all too complicated for Angell. He said coldly:

"Me, I am just an ordinary earthling, of the human species. But we respect two or three principles there, one of which is freedom of the browser. Stranded on your globe, we probably owe you a toll. It is a given. But before committing to pay, I want to know the fate of my comrades."

"In what you have just formulated," continued the aquatic after a silence, "there are concrete data and things that I do not understand. We respect rules, all laws. You will explain yours to us. That said, you will inquire about the fate of the living entities who accompanied you on your ether raft. You certainly have rights over these beings, rights which do not concern me. I answer: two creatures remained on board. I moved them in time, because I wanted to bring you here and my people could not contact you. The creatures you call Ready and Tycho were later kidnapped by the... Silicones, because their ship was in a bend of time when the tides will invade that part of the planet. With a little care, or could find them."

"Who are the Silicones?" Angell asked. (The fact that *RZ-2* had been snatched up by another dimension, confirmed his intuitions. Since, on Gamma, cities could appear and disappear like mirages, why not a simple spacecraft?)

"These," patiently explained Aes, "are part of my people, underground. They work in the depths, to extract and shape the things that we will need. Yes, they do just that. They are there, always. I read in your brain a term: slaves. But they are not that. Neither do robots, although they look like them. How the Silicones were made – and the people too – I will explain it to you later, if... if you accept the mission that I want to entrust to you. Yes, mission is the word I was looking for."

"So Tycho and Ready are with the Silicones," said Angell. (He imagined Tycho's head!) "But Verne?"

Was this an illusion? A livid shadow passed over the dazzling face.

"Does this one belong to you?" asked a precise, almost mathematical wave. Modelling himself on the mentality of the extraterrestrial, the pilot repeats clearly:

"So much so that you could not imagine."

"To kill or to use him?"

"What?"

"I don't know if we fully understand," resumed Aes. "Mentalities and intelligences are diverse. Our people have not communicated with other universes for a very long time. In the past, yes, we visited them, not on ether rafts, but in a more subtle way. I even believe that we once established regular relations with your little globe, but this is lost in the mists of time... The dawn of time; what a deep and just term! I took it from your brain, thank you.

"Let us return to the notions which are, respectively, foreign to us. The intelligences have different levels. (I am not talking here about the shade of the dermis or the shape of the mandibles.) Let me explain: even at the lower stage, in a tribe which aspires only to nourish itself and to perpetuate itself, there are... masters, and also what you call 'slaves' and who for us are 'objects'. Take my case: my people are an integral part of the mother soul. Me too. But as a differentiated entity, I am its master. Together we reign over the waters and the depths."

"And on the surface of Gamma?" Angell asked, abruptly.

Conditioning or whatever, he didn't like that word 'master'. Not when it applied to living property, anyway. He had hit the nail on the head, for an icy flame flickered, then was extinguished in the fish-king's murky irises. For a moment, in his perfect numbness, Aes crystallized all the threats, all the long-winded anguish of Gamma and much more... In the background of the appalling and lovely statue, Angell felt, obscurely, rise up immemorial perspectives, develop the genesis, weld and die the philosophies and religions of planets unknown to Earth. He knew that Aes of Gamma was one of these legends and civilizations. When? And under what mask had his fellows visited, even though he was old, the memories of the prince went back beyond his creation...

The storm of the centuries subsided, as the waves died down.

A stiff, thinking thought, like a metal, formulated:

"On the surface of Gamma roam bestial tribes. They have their masters and their destiny. We will talk about this later. Now... am I wrong? it seems to me that you belong, on Earth, to our species. Is it correct?"

Angell skewed:

"I never thought about it," he said. "I was good at my job. On my spacecraft, I was first pilot. But Earth has a lot of spaceships."

"That's what I thought I understood," Aes said with satisfaction. "Being a master cannot be recognized by the number... of slaves, but by the hold we have over them."

"And your slaves are...? The Silicones, right?"

"Yes, as well as some barely more evolved species."

"The people of the Free Air?"

"That's what they call themselves," replied the prince with detachment. "Yes, some of these tribes belonged to us, as well as the hippoboscs and the amphibians. (I see that you have encountered samples of them.) Some are used for our work, others for our games.

Every object has a special destination for us: the utility or the excitement of our nerves. This clarified point, I come back to my question: is it to kill it or to use him that you have acquired this... Verne?"

"To use him," Angell said, coldly.

"I feared him," Aes said, simplistically. Angell felt his heart sink. The shadow which passed over the hard and perfect face was this time deeper and slower; the astronaut could be mistaken, but what he thought he understood of the fate reserved for Verne struck him with subtle horror. He stiffened so as not to betray his dismay, and a cold sweat wet his temples.

Aes got up with a sinuous wave movement: "Verne will be returned to you," he said. "If you accept my mission."

"I accept," said Walter Angell. "Speak."

The city of Silicones stretching beneath the lake was, in Bill Ready's opinion, a particularly successful nightmare. Lying on his back, in the narrow corridor of which he occupied a corner, the student did a little mental work which was hygienic and necessary for him. Here, he said to himself:

"I am on Earth, in front of the counter of a small bar. The Venusian bartender (they're the best) has a head of zinnia in bloom. The beer is cold and I ordered platypus sausage. The great luxury, what! The guy I tell my stories to is a stocky little guy who's only ever been on a moon cruise, and he listens to me, like I'm the good Lord... I start by describing the city to him: to me the bright colors! 'Imagine, I told him, a termite mound under the ground. These beings drill both clay and granite. They don't have to be cool: their average size is a meter thirty...I have met smaller ones, but practically not larger ones. With that, I don't know how they do it, but they all look crumbling. Maybe it's skinny or clumped up the grime, because I guess they never wash – at least not on purpose. Not that they hate water: I saw them cross the lake, without wiping off the water that dripped off the bituminous crust of their faces, or whatever takes their place, because, to be precise – hands on. There are also those long white filaments running down their necks and breasts like the dwarves in Snow White, only more horrible, if you see that.

"To have this for company, day and night..."

Bill mechanically extended his hand as if to pick up the beer mug, shrugged his shoulders and continued:

"So I say that for the first few days (I guess those were days, I couldn't verify) the Commander and I only saw Silicones. Space! I still wonder why they took us away! The captain was taking it very badly. These zebras first put us in a gallery as wide as a station platform and where it was fifty degrees of heat. They were working downstairs, I saw through a small skylight. Well, that was a hell of a hoot! From what I understood Bellatrix Gamma has an incandescent core twice the size of Earth, and that explains its tropical temperature, with a sun so far away. So I saw...the exits of a furnace! I saw my siliceous fellows wrestling hand to hand with rocks which were less tough than them and piling up on rolling docks blocks of pure carbon, as big as that, and masses of rubies, sapphires and emeralds – enough to drive all the misers in the galaxy crazy! They would haul it all over the surface, like simple quarry workers, and up there big chitin-barded beetles, halias and clavicorns carried the freight to the cities under construction.

"Because it is constantly building on this planet, I mean on all levels. And there were also the questions of town planning, in all these cities. Remember that we have only one Rome and one Paris on Earth. And again we put them under a globe. They, the Silicones, had as many as there were plans in the system. They were great builders.

"It doesn't mean anything. Seeing these metals which melted and flowed in grinding stone vats, these mountains of gems, these uranium cargoes, I felt a little cold in the back. You see, those Silicones, they never came to the surface. Except on exceptional occasions... So, these cities of sapphires and these palaces of emeralds, they had never seen them! A damn job, what?

"But do not believe that they were unhappy. They felt nothing, voila. Except a few, very rare...

"I was just lucky enough to come across a phenomenon. As the captain was infected and I couldn't carry him out of that heated bench cellar on my own, I hung up a dead old, little pyramid-shaped that brought rough diamond into a wheelbarrow and puddled it all. his stuff down. Believe it or not, but he showed it to the mood. He was swinging his short arms – real beaters – and making a sound of his mouth. I explained to him about the commander. I don't know if he understood, but he left immediately, leaving his cart. I was beginning to despair when he returned.

"He had with him a kind of little creature – half ape, half bird, very friendly. She had a beautiful turquoise blue plumage and a pretty golden-brown head that hesitated between a young girl and a marmoset. A real godsend, in our situation! She spoke in a flute voice, and the funniest thing is that I understood her and the Silicones too... She crouched down next to poor Tycho and blew him with her wing."

" 'Sick?' she said.

" 'Yes,' I replied.

" 'Broken something?'

" 'A little.'

"And I lifted the bandage on his sides, which bandage was the color of charcoal. She ran over the inflamed dermis her delicate little claw – and, God forgive me – the commander whispered:

" 'Thank you, Katie! You realize!'

"He took this bird in the miss for a good friend! I did not deceive him. She hovered around the Silicone that was shaking its red hood a bit and then it did help charge the commander.

"We took him up, to a cooler gallery, where there is even a window with a view of the lake. And the little one came and brought me some herbs to cure him. Arnica and febrifuges: she had some notions of medicine.

"So I tried to chat with her a bit, following the classic methods: I took a diamond that was dragging and I traced the sun, the planets and all the stuff on the basalt. I pointed to the third one and said, 'Earth'. Then I indicated myself and said: 'Earthman'. She began to cackle and she made an incredible tangle next to her with her left paw, then she pricked her right paw right in the middle, and here she was yelping: 'Nest!' And in the direction of herself: 'Bird!'

"I have lost all hope of being heard.

"She didn't give her address, or what...?

"With the Silicone, it was a whole different story. I was not caught observing them. When we look for a long time, we end up distinguishing them from each other by cracks, by imperceptible signs. And then, we realize that they are not that many, although the galleries are swarming with them. And that they are always the same: they do not sleep. How? Perfectly! They spin in circles, then they'll recharge somewhere, with static energy.

"I saw that like an open door or they rushed in – there was a white flame, dazzling and almost blinded me. It burned silently. But the first time, I did not distinguish anything at all, I was immediately thrown to the ground by a discharge and the Silicones would have passed over me, without Sais. She grabbed me by the feet and dragged me downstairs. I know, I forgot to tell you, she's the bird.

"So, let's recap: Silicones don't come out, don't wash, don't sleep, don't eat. (It disgusts the robots, what!) They must reproduce by parthenogenesis and fission, because I have never seen a nursery of Silicones. However, they die; rarely, I agree. That is, they begin to erode, then to cover themselves with deeper and deeper cracks, until pieces come off and they fall, literally, to crumbs. So the deceased's companions tip him over with their shovels into a very red crater. I thought they did not resent anything to that and I was very happy.

"But isn't it that I notice in my personal Silicone, the one whose cart I had jostled, a crack, just at the base of the skull. And it was deep. It must have disturbed something, he could not find his balance and it made him look bleak. One day, as I was passing, I saw him come out of the Static Energy gallery, he rolled from right to left in a disordered way: probable that now the discharges did not succeed him. I thought: Watch out for the crematorium! And all of a sudden, here he is bending down and thrusting himself, with full tentacles, crumbled rock into his fracture. You see, he was trying to plug it up, the poor old thing! It hurt me.

"When I left the *RZ-2*, I don't know why, I took, in addition to the concentrates and vitamins, my mechanic's bag. There was an autogenous welding machine, for robots. The case, even my body, was preserved from wear. So, I thought about it: in short Silicones, except that they consume static energy instead of fuel, are robots and should be treated as such. They consist of a siliceous magma with metallic veins. It could weld together, right? In short, I proposed my services to the Silicone. He didn't understand anything, and Savior was out. Tired of war, I gave him a little blow on the head with a hammer. It completely stunned him; I recommend this anesthesia procedure.

"When he had regained his senses, I had just stuffed his fracture with small chips of gold lying around the foundry, and I'd soldered. Good God! It was a spectacle to see! My Silicone getting up, rushing towards the Energy room, coming out like as if drunk! My word, he was dancing! He was circling his legs. And the others, in line, too.

"As a result, they got into the habit, as soon as they had a problem, of bringing their patients to me. This is how I did illegal medicine. I became very popular. These Silicones, they had, among other things, a small crystalline eruption that had to be pierced, and from which carbon dioxide came out. It bothered them. I came to the end of it, with a diamond punch, then I applied molten silver to them.

"The commander had started to get up and he was dragging himself around, covering the Silicones with curses. Of course, he wanted to get away from it all. But the basement windows were at the level of the lake and there were minerals at all the doors. Until the moment where...

"This is where I come to the most unpleasant experience. One night I was sleeping. Well, I guess it was one night, Tycho and I had screwed up our stopwatches. In short, I was awakened by an order. Inaudible, but dry as a whip. I was a little scared, it was at the beginning of our captivity, before these welding stories, and I still didn't trust silicones. So I got up stumbling, I was groggy. The order was like a thread of fire hanging from my brain and it led me straight down the halls. I threaded galleries never seen. The doors opened on my passage. Silently. I counted more than eight. Quartz first and sliding. Then in orichalcum, then in gold. The last one was of an unknown blue metal.

"As I went along, I felt it was worth nothing to me. But I couldn't stop. How to explain? Things on Gamma are different from simple Earth experiences. But here's a comparison: imagine you had to parachute, into absolute vacuum. Your stomach is smeared, an icy sweat down your spine, you know perfectly well that it will not help, but you have to jump. And right now, someone is inserting a scented candy in your mouth, of a disgusting sweetness. That was enough, but multiply by x.

"Finally I walked and walked. I didn't think of Tycho, whom I left behind, nor even of Earth. A strange notion of duty to accomplish sustained my energy. I think that the stretcher bearers who go to look for a wounded man under Martian napalm have feared it: we know that neither the wounded nor anybody will be better, but there is discipline and the oath. And then I moved forward, the more the sensation of the foul sweetness became intolerable. It looked like we were entering a digestive tract where someone was blowing a beat, full. Oh! I can't explain myself. But just thinking about it makes me nauseous.

"Space, no! I didn't meet anyone all along the corridors. Just, at a bend, something, snapping – a piece of stuff gnawing away. You know those lowlon aprons that you still see in small provincial towns, at counters...? No, I'm not sure it was an apron. On Gamma...?"

(What Bill does not admit to himself, like a good little boy from a Puritan family, is that the red apron, worn by a beautiful barmaid from Venus, symbolizes for him sin. A barmaid with whom he was in love between thirteen and seventeen. She ended badly: under the dazzling of a drug. Sin and death can fit in a shred of red fabric.)

He continued, leaning towards the unknown listener:

"I didn't even notice that the path had changed: I walked along sculpted galleries or greenhouses. Haunting music filled the vaults. Me, I only like brass and clean air. Incense and Polovtsian Dances, it drives me crazy.

"Finally, I ended up with a room – or rather a cave the dimensions of a cosmodrome. Here, it was a dazzling day, columns and giant pendants threw a thousand fires of diamonds – white, blue and pink. Under the stalactites there were at least three hundred black jade thrones. (No, I didn't count – the perspective was too fantastic and followed an inhuman geometry.) I thought I saw statues of lazulite on these plinths at first, but this illusion was brief. With a feeling of horror, mingled with nausea, I understood: the blue matter that I had taken for lapis lazuli was skin, the skin of a corpse! All around the room, draped in scales and crystallized algae, three hundred monsters neither dead nor alive were smiling. And their disgusting smile – eyelids half closed – was that of satiety.

"Oh! I wanted to run away! I don't hide it. Only it was impossible. And, strangely enough, in this terror which had reached its final limits, I conceived, outside this motionless and frozen conclave, another, infernal danger which did not concern me.

"It was he who distilled the horrible sweetness, thick and bland. It is he who... No, it was not a question, however dreadful that it was, of satisfying these dead standing. A vampire, after all, has a name, a form, we can fight against him; he belongs to a definite plane.

"There was, in the influx that I received, a satisfaction beyond all pain and all physical pleasure: intense, dark and voluptuous...

"But that did not concern me.

"I was thrown into the middle of the room. There was (I remember vaguely, because from that moment on, all my sensations are as if obliterated: or wanted me to forget) a sort of altar sum of a white flame. Maybe it was the Energy that fed the Silicones. I do not know. Here she was formidable and naked. There was also a bizarre design on the altar. But no door downstairs. In any case, I haven't seen any. I was told later of a door that opened onto a well, of an abyss where things were swarming so hideous and so blasphemous that the human mind cannot bear the idea...

"On the ground, at the foot of the altar, there were scattered heaps of very soft feathers and blue and white fur. Forests of birds, like Sais, empty, flat remains, like the skins abandoned by snakes. And under the threshold, I bumped into Verne, my comrade Verne.

"At first I thought he was dead and I fell on my knees close to him. I took his hand; it was warm and full, thank God! without resemblance to one of those completely empty bodies of which someone (I dared not think who – for what abominable purpose) had drunk the essence. But in his colorless face, his eyes were glassy: eyes of someone who has descended into horror deeper than is ever allowed in a human being.

"I think I tried to understand the situation all the same. To analyze. Someone was there who fed on... let's say life force. Probably those blue corpses that looked like frogs and fish. It was a species that I had not yet encountered and which had formed this particular cemetery. But there was something else more powerful and more demanding too, a supernormal entity that turned torture into ecstasy. And that was the worst: because you could never be released. I could not specify my fear, I was sick with disgust. Then these waves of fear and of a more than filthy delight became less frequent and I was able to reason: after all, I had only been sent to rescue Verne from this impasse. But him...? How long had he been trapped? What had he suffered...?

"I helped him up. Slow, inconceivably slow and heavier than the Silicones, he took a few steps, leaning on my shoulder, then straightened up and walked like an automaton, deprived of memory and of will. By a spiraling path, I brought him back to the lower galleries. Sais fled before our sight."

CHAPTER V

"My people are very old," said Aes of Bellatrix Gamma.

He received Angell like an equal.

In the octagonal room, iridescent like an enormous pearl, its throne-bed dominated a platform of pink coral. (And everything, thought the astronaut, recalled those childhood tales where the adventure takes place under the waters, at the palace of the Ocean King, in the Cave of the Undines. Everything, except that the city had emerged, this time for good.) Between the nacreous pillars quivered silver strings, and these Aeolian harps imitated the music of the sea. Long purple and golden seaweed, ulvae and giant chlorella, floated behind the crystal walls. The turquoise and pink colored birds brought aquatic dishes, new varieties of caviar, sea urchins and crustaceans, and poured into the firm containers of lilies and ammonites, strange acid elixirs or honey.

"You can eat and drink without fear," Aes said, "this diet is designed to save oxygen and phosphorus."

"But yourself?"

"I will share this meal...h ow do you say on Earth? To honor my host. And leaving a simple question: Of course, we are sustaining ourselves, we have a digestive system." His mouth parted and showed white, sharp teeth, a little small perhaps. He continued, searching for his words, of which he asked for an exquisite propriety: "It seems that we need you less than this mode of combustion. I always speak of my people, the other species of Gamma have retained a little more repugnant uses. We, our metabolism is twofold."

"All of this is the result of various mutations that have taken place over ages of night." He repeated, with visible delight, the word which enchanted him: "Night... This word for us has a serious and deep meaning..."

His murky eyes closed, and Angell thought him at rest and blind; his face was frighteningly beautiful.

Their interview had lasted for half an hour, and the astronaut was struck by the ease with which Aes grasped human notions. He was still drawing words from the Earthman's brain, but his own thought was emerging, astounding in logic and precision. (Angell tried to hide his apprehension before this formidable mental machine.)

He himself gave a glimpse of the world of Bellatrix Gamma with complacency, at once barbaric and refined, exquisite and cruel like his symbols, frozen, so to speak, in the heart of a radiant dead civilization. No emotional nuance, except in the area of appetites. ("And if there's a moral," observed Walter, "it would make Earthly philosophers crazy.") Paradoxically, the arts played a magical and preponderant role, the intelligences of Gamma had discovered unknown correspondences on Earth, between music and mathematics, scales, colors and lines in their interaction on the nerves...

As if to confirm this idea, the strings of the harps shivered, a crystalline and pure melody prelude: the murmur of springs, their pearls scattered on the columbines. Aes said:

"I want to inform you, because for the Water People your mission, its success or its failure will be of capital importance. You will be my messenger."

"But why an Earthman?"

"Precisely, let me explain. Listen."

(Was it the music of the harps or the voice of the speaking prince? Harmonious and raspy, like the thrill of the waves...)

"My people are very old, I told you. Maybe predating this planet. I do not know how and from what plane Gamma detached itself from her original nucleus, but on all the globes, the only traces of passage are ours.

"Besides, we know little about Bellatrix Gamma herself. The law of radioactive transformation, so telling for other universes, only gives fragmentary information here. A relatively recent cataclysm (half a million years at most) has turned all the data upside down. We can only assume that at that time the civilization of this planet had reached a level equal, if not higher, than that where your Earth is today. Yes, I read your mind, thank you. Then a catastrophe occurred. It was appalling and followed by a resurrection. Oh, but only after a long interval! We can state here a cyclical hypothesis which is at the base of all theogonies: the planets and their gods are born, develop and die, only to resurrect again. But that would take us too far."

"Is that your philosophy?" Angell asked.

The brushed eyebrows rose:

"We have precise knowledge. The cosmos is established between two poles: conception and death. Perhaps it is only one same transcendent notion, It is in the middle that immanence and stability are found: Life.

"After the initial cataclysm, our planet found itself in these conditions unsuitable for organic life. Most of the devastated globes set off again in the white. But Bellatrix Gamma had been too civilized, its culture too high, too permanent, and its intelligent species had considered such an eventuality. They had taken, before the apocalypse, their survival precautions. My people were already one of these species. We had made sure of impenetrable shelters.

"Ultimately, they were not so, since the largest located under the Equatorial Ocean, collapsed, burying its occupants, and in the others, there were mutations…"

Aes was silent for a long time. He had forgotten to lower his eyelids. There was in his eyes the reflection of an immemorial dread, as old as the cosmos. And this revealed to Angell much more than the words. He remembered: There was always an Aes and maybe the same… This one had certainly seen… How did he survive?

As if to answer this question, the Prince of the Waters continued:

"You already know that we are called Aquatics. Did I tell you that most of our shelters were in submarine chasms? The Ancients had discovered that the water of Gamma offered some resistance to atomic discharge and that it modified the effects of radioactivity. For a long time we have been practicing living underwater. We smoked a handful of preserves. And centuries passed."

"Something escapes me," Angell intervened. "As far as I can tell, your species has the ability to move in at least four dimensions. It seems to me that you could have avoided the exact moment of the cataclysm."

"This faculty came to us at that very instant," Aes replied sharply. "Nuclear fission shattered the dimensional framework."

"Was your race the only intelligent species saved?"

"No."

"The Silicones?"

"Yes, I am thinking of the Silicones too. But it was already, it seemed at the time, a very old and degenerate race. Their regression continued. They do not seem to originate from Gamma either; perhaps they came from a system similar to yours, aboard an exploding asteroid."

"Have you made an alliance?"

"They are not annoying."

"Are there other species as well?"

Aes lowered his long eyelashes like those of an Earthly maiden.

"You have seen some of them. These creatures that you have called birdies and who give themselves to the people of the Free Air... They are only a degenerate branch of our species. Let us call them, for convenience, the 'Pselles' named after a scientist from Earth who mentioned them in his works, a certain Michael Psellus..."

He waited a second, listening for the pilot's reactions. But Angell, conditioned as a space adventurer, had never read the Cabala, nor the *Commentaries* of Psellus[1], nor the *Dictionnaire Infernal* of De Plancy[2] (moreover these books no longer existed on Earth, except in leaded pyramids, for the use of generations to come). Reassured on this point, the prince continued:

"I will not hide from you that we attach great importance to names. There is also a term heavy with meaning, ancient and magnificent, to designate the people of the Waters, but you may know that these words have a weight and a magical character, so we refrained from pronouncing them."

"So the Air people, the Pselles, are a decadent branch, for having exposed themselves too early to radioactivity."

"They are lovely," said Angell, smiling.

"Above all, they are disorderly and incapable of any progress. But they do reproduce. Like animals. Silicones are dependent on a certain parthenogenesis. Do you have something to ask me about this?"

"I would like to know," said the Earthman, "if the Winged Pselles were already so messy before the cataclysm and what cause prevented them from taking full advantage of the shelters?"

"First of all," resumed Aes, "the individuals of this race are not all winged and, on the other hand, the Aquatics, of which I am, have, as you

---

[1] Michael Psellos or Psellus was a Byzantine Greek monk, savant, writer, philosopher, imperial courtier, historian and music theorist born in 1017 or 1018, and believed to have died in 1078, although it has also been maintained that he remained alive until 1096. He served as a high ranking courtier and advisor to several Byzantine emperors and was instrumental in the re-positioning of power of those emperors. Psellus made lasting contributions to Byzantine culture by advocating for the revival of Byzantine classical studies, which would later influence the Italian Renaissance, as well as by interpreting Homeric literature and Platonic philosophy as precursors and integral components of Christian doctrine.

[2] Jacques Albin Simon Collin de Plancy (28 January 1793 – 1881) was a French occultist, demonologist and writer.

see, 'vestigial wings' most often filled as fins, these appendages have evolved, that's all. Many Air Pselles have ape-like appearances.

"Yes, I believe that at the time of the cataclysm, they constituted an independent class, noisy and which proclaimed itself progressive. They caused disturbances in the shelters and were evicted a little early. Fortunately for them, the group consisted of mostly females, because, as you know, radioactivity has sterilizing effects on the male."

"It was the Aquatics who drove the Air People back?"

"Yes."

Angell didn't tell him that he considered this to be a great cruelty: it was an affective notion, therefore meaningless to the person he was talking to. From his point of view, the Air Pselles, useless, had to give way, in the shelters, to the most precious elements. Earth once knew this term: useless mouths.

(The Air People, their grace, their free courage, Ary's stoic sacrifice and the softness of her feathers, their kinship, offered in a smile, and until death...)

Decidedly, apart from their culture and Aes' high intelligence, the Earthman didn't like the Aquatics.

"You have been in the Temple," continued the prince. "You have seen the four effigies symbolizing the races of Bellatrix Gamma. Before I tell you about the fourth – or what replaced it, I will try to make you hear what we stand for: the juice and marrow of our culture.

"We too have experienced mutations. We once looked a lot like humans on Earth, and our travelers were able to blend in with your crowd to study it. We are now more substantial and less differentiated. Certain animal functions fail us and we have developed others. I repeat, however: we are the oldest species, in its entirety. Our experience is immense. We know that to be born or to conceive, to die and to disintegrate is to mutate, to overcome, therefore – to lose. Once this insane passion has already brought this world to ruin. We don't want a second cataclysm. We are the guardians of acquired values. For us, transcendence is evil."

"Do you believe in a creative principle?" Angell asked. "In the 'Prime Mover', in Energy in Action? Finally, do you have a god?"

"We believe in Life. For us, to conserve is to create. Let me explain: your mind, while we were talking about the Air Pselles, used a term, immediately repressed, which indicated hostility towards us: cruelty. I do not blame you any more than a chemical reaction. We have eliminated the useless and dangerous Pselles, not without giving them chances of survival. Conservation, and immanence, requires, of course, sacrifices. But what about the alternate pangs of death and creation?"

"It defends itself," Angell agreed.

"Does it? I recognized in you a rectitude of judgment which allows me to tell you the integral truth. For I'm going to entrust the fate of my people to you, you see. You will represent me. You will kind of be... myself."

It was scary to imagine, although in his capacity as an ordinary Earthman Walter Angell must have been flattered. But Aes of Gamma continued, with muffled elation:

"It is for this purpose that I have chosen you. Understand me. Our power, in principle, is unlimited. We are the only species on this globe to fully develop our mental faculties. We are evolving in at least five dimensions. But, practically, an Aes is prisoner in his lakeside city...

"Here we come to the vital point of our civilization and our incredible survival. Earlier, you were wondering my age: I could not calculate it, even approximately. Gamma has been reviewing and correcting Earth's biological data for a long time. For us, organic death is only a shutdown, true annihilation occurs with molecular disaggregation, that is to say with a new creative process. We have succeeded in slowing down organic wear and tear to a degree that you cannot imagine.

"Indeed, Silicones live four, five hundred years, simply because their matter is almost unstoppable and they recharge their static energy. We have therefore established that life has two conditions: the maintenance of matter and the contribution of energy. Of course, we are not siliceous robots, and the panacea that our bodies claim is different. But we have discovered this elixir and its source..."

"In short, you've been able to delay organic death," Angell said.

"We did better," Aes said. (A dull, cold flame rose in patches of a dark scarlet on his cheekbones.) "Five hundred, six hundred years pass like a day, and the humanoid organism does not have the resistance of silicas. It always requires more additional energy, until the moment when, through irreparable damage or wear, organs shut down on their own. So, to put them back into operation, if only on the backburner, they no longer need... fuel, but a discharge..."

"And you get this discharge for your living dead?"

These words, to pronounce them, Angell mastered a nausea. But they had already gone too far, he had to know everything. And he managed to keep (at least he hoped) a serene face.

216

Aes nodded: "Oh!" he said, and his voice sounded to the Earthman singularly human, "we hesitated a lot before resolving ourselves to this conquest, to this victory over the respected, established order... But you know that nature is ambivalent. From the moment we succeeded in prolonging life beyond known limits, and our species risked becoming too numerous, the law of compensation acted: our reproductive capacity fell, then fell... I dare not say to zero. Currently, almost the entire population of the cities is male or asexual. However the species needs renewal and it is the bitter fact.

"We have observed that the same burst which rinses our dead, sometimes ignites the flame of life in an original matter. There must be exceptional circumstances.

"This matter, this plasma, this entity which transforms energy in action, resides in the depths of Gamma. Here in this city. Let's say it is a goddess of which an Aes is the guardian. Have I been clear enough?"

"As much as the subject would allow," Angell replied. "Let's say you're attached to your post, whether it's an altar or a spaceship."

"Yes."

"And this spaceship or this temple are threats, Am I right?"

A faint gleam that must have been a smile lit up the features which were perfection itself:

"How do you say on Earth? What a pleasure to converse with an intelligent man!"

The nacarat and turquoise Pselles had followed the service of giant sturgeons, with hard-boiled eggs and milt, by the cauldron of eels and pyramids of green and red fruits with exotic melon flesh. A melody of shells mingled with the Colian harps. On the lake where purple reflections ran, rose the triple moons.

Now, through a kind of symbiosis established by his partner, Angell captured the mental images that weren't intended for him. The danger must have been terrible and recur regularly. A high, upright, frozen flame burned in total darkness: anguish or desire? The whole set up in the memory of the Earthman an old fresco, seen in the ruins of a devastated continent: a black icy ocean, a dull red horizon, and on a charred rock, a great green and black silhouette, wings folded, forehead in his hand. The catalogue legend said *Satan contemplating the Apocalypse*.

The great Aquatic looked like this Satan.

"The fourth statue..." he said.

"It is very beautiful."

"It represents a people who are less so. Let us go back again to the great cataclysm. We will see that all the species known as intelligent did not seek refuge in shelters. In any community there are weak beings, or criminals – or simply reckless. These exposed themselves to disaster in its plenitude. Almost all have perished; a handful, hidden in the caverns and crevices of the ground, undergo the strangest mutations: scales, deviations of vertebrae, loss of vertical station, what else do I know? Cerebrally, it was much worse. Truly, it would have been better for Gamma – and for these beings, too – to let them die out as a race."

"Because they did not leave...?"

"No. I think... rare individuals escaped the law of mutations. Their number and their characteristics? We ignore them. This species has no history. For a long time, the refugees locked in their shelters believed that there was no substitute for the surface. Then huge insects appeared, the larvae of which had undergone metamorphosis underground. Then amphibians came out of the fresh, infected waters. One day we found a mush of flesh on the shores of this lake. It was one of ours – lacerated, crushed. A flint weapon beside it bore the imprint of a prehensile hand."

"Didn't you think a new humanity was born on the face of Gamma?"

"Yes. It is always possible. I could not tell you how many centuries the radioactive period lasted, then decontamination of the soil. A new species could have evolved from tarsiers or saurians. We don't know anything. And even if space travelers, less fortunate than you, had fallen in these charred plains, we would yet not know.

"Only this: today this brutal force which procreates like a killer, has proliferated. It has its leaders and helots and calls itself the Ertosi or Pi-Rhé race. Do not look... these are old earthly names that Earth itself has forgotten. These people have neither temples, nor cities, nor traditions, they go like the wind on the plains of Gamma, their polarization is opposed to ours, they worship Death and the Resurrection and propose to destroy us."

"Do they have any chance?" Angell asked.

Aes smiled thinly:

"Another earthly notion that I am learning: sportsmanship. I will be frank: yes, they have a chance. Not because they outnumber us: with Silicones (the bird-people will always be neutral and fluctuating), we represent, all the same, a sufficient mass. But they are animated with a ferocious hatred and only one point of our civilization is vulnerable... terribly so.

"Now, if you want, we shall go from theory to practice. You cannot, of course, feel great enthusiasm for the cause of a people you know only from yesterday. But I do know that Earthmen are sensitive to emotional movements and like to see things with their own eyes. Come. I will show you our opponents."

The three crescents were standing very high over the plateau. The sky had lost its coral luminosity.

The tower of malachite dominated the city. From its platform. Betelgeuse and Rigel were two crystal lamps and Al-Nilam sparkled with a double Sirius twinkle: green and blue. Aes took the astronaut by the hand and led him to a selenium railing. Angell shivered at the cold slimy touch.

"Look," Aes said. "Yes, in the direction of the Ash Plain. I am helping you. Follow my thought. What do you see?"

And Angell saw:

The immense gray plain stretched out in the glow of a brazier lit by titans. Gigantic Carboniferous ferns set the sky ablaze. And there was nothing, among Precambrian rocks, in the middle of a ferocious desert, under a dreary, empty and leaden sky (when Earth dies, her sky will be like this) than an indistinct melee of a red and black body and a powerfully toothed scaly form.

It was a vision from before the ages and yet the Earthman recognized the plain he had visited this morning. Next to the ceratosaurus, the zygodactyl gecko was a lizard.

Broken and covered in viscous blood, the brute succumbed to the assaults of another monstrous beast, all claws out and red mane blowing in the wind. This one leaps on the spine of the saurian.

"A simian creature... But was it really a simian?" thought Angell in horror. "This caricature of human behavior, this terrible embryo of a face..." He did not finish. The apocalyptic rider on the spine of the ceratosaurus, raised a flint ax and struck. The beast descended, with an excruciating howl. Black blood spurted out. The victor received it in his open hands. And while he gorged himself with it, the head of the saurian, half off, slipped on the sand: the flattened skull and the bloody globes thrown back, it too clearly belonged to the human species.

"The Pi-Rhé race and its helots," said the voice of Aes lost in the distance. "But look still..."

This time, the landscape had hardly changed, it was the same plain, hand in this corner, it was undoubtedly fought a furious battle, for mounds of dust marked the shapes of the corpses. The pale moon stood very high

– the third moon. A jackal or a wolf throws a heart-breaking trill. In the foreground, as on the edge of a parascopic screen, lay an indistinct silhouette; the breeze lifted and caressed with pressing a woman's long black hair.

There was hardly any flesh on the elegant bones.

On the neighboring hillock, a naked half-ape, its red lanugo sticking with blood, scratched with its nails a skull, the marrow of which it sucked.

"Look, look again!"

Beyond the ashy plain, the dark abysses opened, they disgorged an avalanche, a living tornado...

They walked along, their vertebrae bent to the ground, their bodies covered with a rough fleece, their muscles huge, their muffles flat and drooling, and the most horrible of them was that just human appearance. They went crushing, trampling, igniting tall ferns behind them, dragging after them herds of saurians and giant insects, the corpses of which filled the swollen rivers. They were going, seized with blind fury, destroying everything in their path. When the three moons joined as a high tide, they seemed to remember a forgotten world, a lost humanity, and suffered terribly. They threw themselves into the sand and rolled around. Some crouched down, entwining their knees with their ape-like arms and rocking tirelessly back and forth. Others shouted in guttural voices the names of missing creatures. But despite their despair and their savage strength, all avoided the heart of the plain and the direction of the lake.

"You saw," Aes said. "These are our enemies. This is where our succession is on Gamma."

"What should I do?" Angell asked.

The prince looked at him for a long time.

"First," he said, "here is what we will do for you. We will let you communicate with your friends... with one of your friends who will give you the news of the others. I suggest the little medicine man, he is the most reasonable. Whoever looks older does not have a strong enough nervous system, and your chosen mate is... ill.

"Then your companion will be free to return to the spacecraft in its current condition. They can leave immediately or wait for you. We are not rushing anyone. Whoever intends to settle on Gamma will receive hospitality from the people of the Waters. He will be one of us, he will be us. But am I being made clear? Was this what you wanted?"

"My turn," Angell asked, "what do you want me to do?"

"Not much," said the prince. "I'm sorry... you provoked me... but no, the notion would be untranslatable. Let us say I wanted to keep you here. But state affairs take precedence. I am sending an ambassador to the Fire Beings' camp. (That's the name the Pi-Rhé call themselves.) You will give their leader a message from me. A message of peace."

"Of peace?"

"Yes. They can cross the plain. Laknea, our city, is an open city. I am waiting for them."

CHAPTER VI

"The four cabbalistic elements!" Bill burst out. "Gnomes, Sylphs, Undines and Salamanders! It all looks like grandmothers' fairy tales!"

"However, did men believe they existed?"

"For centuries, old man! And what men! The great Rabbis and Psellus, Paracelsus[3] and old Michael of Balwearie[4]..."

"I always believed that there wasn't a single legend or fantasy or nightmare of the human brain that didn't come true in some corner of the cosmos," Angell said. "We had to fall on it... Help me strap this breastplate."

"Thin defrocked ambassador!"

Standing out of the dungeons, the little Irishman gazed at the crystal and jade rooms, the soft seat beds, among Aeolian harps, with his mouth open, and squinted at the birds on duty. He hissed in admiration at the iridescent armor, felt the sapphire cloak and stood in front of a mirror, capped with the star helmet, like a triton.

"Old man," he concludes, "you're good for the Crazy Continuum!"

Angell tried to laugh:

"Don't you want me to face a fierce Ertosian under the wreckage of my spacesuit? What would we look like?"

"What if it was a beautiful Ertosian?"

"It would be too much to ask. Don't forget that the fourth element's represented by an 'urodele batrachian'. Joking aside. How is the old *RZ-2* doing?"

"Like a pure wonder! It's to believe that I have never seen it fall to pieces. Of course, Tycho claims I had a hallucination. It's like the siren... And by the way, old man, I'm astonished that with all these extravagant natives, we haven't met any such siren yet!"

---

[3] Paracelsus (c.1493 – 1541), born Theophrastus von Hohenheim, was a physician, alchemist, lay theologian, and philosopher of the German Renaissance. He was a pioneer in several aspects of the medical revolution of the times, emphasizing the value of observation in combination with received wisdom. He also had a substantial influence as a prophet or diviner, his *Prognostications* being studied by Rosicrucians in the 17th century.

[4] Michael "the Wizard" Scott of Balwearie (1175-c1232) was a Scottish alchemist, astrologer, mathematician, and scholar.

"It seems that the Aquatics are male and reproduce by exogenesis. Don't ask me what it is, I noted that term in their king's brain."

"It's true that you now hang out with kings! It's the height! Well, exogenesis, my little father, knows me, we've worked hard on Earth to deliver mothers from their worries and young generations from the weaning complex! But say so, say so..."

"What?"

"I haven't seen any genetic labs on Gamma. Do they exist?"

"I don't think so," said Angell. "Let's return to these nursery tales. There are some very frightening ones, aren't there?"

Bill darkened: "Yes. They are usually fantastic, crazy stories that we try to take lightly. In the 'tween-decks of space vessels, as in the past on the prows of caravels, we tell, in a low voice, fabulous or blasphemous adventures, which we try to forget at stopovers. Because we don't want to flinch and it's impossible to live with an open abyss at our feet."

"With the idea that water, earth and fire could be other things than simple elements? And that the world an orchard or man can touch everything, pick everything...?"

"Yes. And also that intelligences more subtle and crueler than ours, can have closer relations with the cosmos. But they can, Bill, can't they? Water for example. This is the primordial element..."

A cold wave reached the little Irishman. He looked around him: nothing had changed in the seductive decor, a blue glow bathed the sections of berries similar to digitalis, the thalli of kelp, the arabesques of red asterias and barnacles which embraced the phosphorous columns. A source complained in his basin. The silence of the palace was deep. And suddenly Ready understood: it was Angell who was bombarding him desperately with mental waves, who was trying to tell him, to warn him...

"Water," he repeated, a little lost. "Yes. We've always believed that life began at the bottom of the sea. Moneres, lumps of albuminoid substance, without nucleus, whose appearance was an 'autogeny' were sought in the oceans. Huxley made a fool of himself by leaning over a jelly he dubbed Bathybius Haeckeli, after a colleague's name. It was only a precipitate of lime sulphate due to alcohol..."

"But there can be something more than that?"

"Yes. Oh, yes!"

"So tell me those nanny tales, Bill. Those in any case that are current today."

There, he had finally understood how serious it was! He was strange, but in keeping with the character of his people, Angell thought, as the voice of the little 'medicine man', stained with his own, took on a contradictory accent: these ancestors had been the last Earthlings to suspect the horror of darkness, hear the step of 'strangers moving in the dark'. Face almost livid, Ready began, breaking out the words:

"Well, these are still stories of life... different from ours. The stories of planets and solar systems that have disappeared, we don't know why, sometimes those of crimes and invasions, and traps established in time and space. Ghosts of the void have replaced the evil genies, and the beautiful princesses live on globes of great danger, or inevitably fall for brilliant astronauts."

"Like us."

"Like us. I'm starting to believe," Bill said ruefully, "that most of these anecdotes are true. And this is hardly reassuring. Because, basically, the main character of these stories is the monster. Usually these are huge cores of elements, deaf and blind, evil powers that project their tentacles into the continuum. These beings seize the globes and crush them, they replace civilizations with jungle, they are nourished by life and are propagated by death."

"Imagine an animate – living acid that dissolves everything. No. Imagine a globe in the grip of a gelatinous mass which burns and devours. A cosmic jellyfish. The day it decides to leave its estate, everything is eaten away, minerals and metals..."

"I do not see," said Angell, coldly, "how a world so owned can delude itself?"

"In other stories," Ready resumed, panting slowly – and drops of sweat shone on his upper lip – because he had finally understood the game played by Angell: he could not speak without betraying himself. But his comrade leafing through the museum of horrors, a nod would suffice...

"In other accounts which seem to extend the tradition of the old cabbalists, these forces have other games. Imagine the monster on an inhabited globe. It would take hold of brains and bodies and shape them, use them at its mercy. What, that is not enough for you as a fear...? This world, the Flying Dutchman of Space, would then be the worst of traps...it would attract ether vessels to itself, like a magnet. Imagine a spacecraft captured with its living charge... The Force-Being would seize men, it might even, later, like from a keyboard. It could penetrate them, drink their life, it shed their sensibility, like from a keyboard. It could even later use them as weapons or spies on their own globe..."

"I'm not going that far," Angell said. The tone was dry.

Had the sign been given? And when? Ready resisted, his gaze still obscured by the horrid and fascinating image of a colorless mass that crushed a world and dissolved them.

"Everyone must return to their planet. The swifter the better."

Angell had stood up. Under an arch, against the background of the immense low and bloody sun, which plunged into the waters, he shone with the radiance of a wicked angel. A last king lit his breastplate and the triton of his helmet. Seized by the reminiscences: Such, thought Bill, on the sacred Way, the triumphant ones marched to meet another star, a meeting of glory and death... But he was ashamed of the romantic image.

"Yes," continued the pilot, "I've been assured that you could take off without waiting for me."

"But, Walter..."

"There's no 'but'. Tell Tycho."

It was when he left the palace that Ready noticed: he hadn't been able to give Angell news of Verne.

On the deserted plain, in the high wind of the equinox, Aes presented to Walter Angell his traveling companions. The coral tanks were dragged along by giant white Halias. Riders mounted screeching, golden brown clavicorns, trained for galloping and wrestling. An Aquatic, his forehead encircled by an opal tiara, greeted them from his turtle-shell seat. This one was closer to a fish than to a man, the scales rose to his eyebrows and his dull and glassy globes protruded under the transparent lids. Beneath his vast purple robe, Angell caught sight of the tips of a three-lobed tail.

Aes leaned down and brushed his lips against the monster's forehead, motionless and silent:

"Here is Pi-Joh," he said, as if he were granting a higher title of nobility. "He is one of our elders. He has the rank of ambassador, but he no longer speaks. You will replace this deficiency."

He turned to a soft blue shape that was lying under the seat prepared for Angell:

"And here is Sais," he said. "She is Ary's sister, she also loves Earthlings. The ease, for the languages, of the bird-people, is proverbial, Sais will serve as your interpreter. But do not trust her too much: she's just an irresponsible object."

There was something threatening about those words – advice or mockery? The prince of Gamma was suddenly on familiar terms with him, but perhaps it was a custom, in front of his subjects.

"I would like to tell you again..." The prince had already seized, with his fine and powerful hand, the reins of the white Halias which reared up. "It doesn't matter whether Sovereign Ertosi accepts or rejects my peace offer. I make this attempt by acquiring consciousness. The main thing is that the message be delivered to him, in person. You will see this creature..."

"I understood well."

"After..." Aes' voice suddenly became very soft, like a murmur of waves or a shiver of a lake, and his murky eyes, full of mysterious gleams, plunged into those of the Earthman. "Then you will come back. I want it. I wish your prompt return."

Strange, Angell believed it. Not to this friendship. He knew his mission was a trap. However, his disintegrator in hand, he regained his confidence. When the purple waterspouts of the plateau had concealed from him the glittering escort of Aes and the tall hieratic figure with the folded fin wings, he felt almost free. He was going to live his destiny.

But imperious, by waves, the earthly voices called him Tycho, Ready and Verne had re-entered the *RZ-2*, they were free and the spaceship, already, waited. Using a secret code, Angell said:

"Go without me!"

"Not for three weeks," Tycho's angry voice replied. "Paragraph XXX017. *'You do not abandon a member of the crew on a mission.'* You deserve, of course, to be cowardly! Prospect a ghost town! These silly initiatives! Land in this bloody place! Only, at the end of my career, I don't want to go before the Interplanetary Council! My retirement screwed up! You would like it, damned adventurer! We'll see..."

Strange also how little this anger mattered to Angell. And how much were earthly preoccupations, normal!

Of the four comrades of the *RZ-2*, despite appearances (he was twenty-seven, Ready twenty-four and Verne twenty-three), Walter Angell was the one who had lived the least. He was not a violent obsessive, as Tycho, centered on a single terror, neither a researcher like Bill, nor – like Verne – a sentimentalist. An old adage said: "Astronauts leave for life with their eyes in the stars." The commander was, in short, right in his estimates: Angell was the Adventurer, in the sense of (rare) dreams, because he had a peaceful sleep, he was rushing towards the impossible and the unknown.

Other than that, his existence was exemplary simplicity. He had no family and considered all pilots to be friends. He pushed back love with a gladiator's shoulder: "Make yourself small. Before you, there is Space, a beautiful and ferocious world, danger and comrades. If you want to be considered, be a miracle or not be."

The journey across the Ash Plain was monotonous. Angell discovered that the Barbarians (as he called the Ertosians) were going around and hiding like a nomadic horde that they were. Vast blackened places, bones and embers, betrayed their passage, then suddenly, all traces disappear. A great silence crushed the steppe. The Earthman questioned Pi-Joh, but the latter, motionless and frozen at his side, looked like some ancient statue.

So he turned to Sais. Under a turquoise plumage which lit up towards her elegant head, and blossomed into a silvery train, she was at the same time more human and wilder than Ary, coquettish like a young girl in a ball gown. He said for a long moment to convey to her, as he had learned from Aes, soothing images. She crouched down at his feet and rested her smooth head on the disintegrator case. When she spoke, it was not the flutis of the bird-people, but correct language, albeit a little panting from the Earthman:

"I like this weapon," she said. "I'm glad you have this gun. Ready thought about his often, he regretted not having it anymore."

"Have you met my comrades?"

"Yes, often. I brought them good herbs."

And in a pearly laugh that scattered her green-brown egret:

"Ready is funny, isn't he? Carrot hair and beak in the air! Always snooping around and looking for something. He speaks to me first, how do you say? As a little cat or dog – a dog! Like a beast! But if I were a beast, they wouldn't have sent me to you!"

"But did you have a friendship with him?"

She reflects, then:

"I understand. Friendship is your Earthman's secret. We love our people, not individuals. Or else we want, that's something else, isn't it? Yes, Bill was like one of the bird people to me. But for the other Earthman, the odds broken. He is a barbarian."

"And Francis?"

The Pselle shivered and her egret seemed dull:

"Sometimes he seemed very gentle to me and then suddenly I felt an evil shadow in him. The same as in the lower corridors. He was in great pain. No, I cannot say anything..."

It was cloudy and worrying, Angell wished he had seen Verne again. But his conditioning made him appreciate the present minute, the race which was becoming vertiginous, the arabesque of large Halias which flew away without touching the ground, the whirlwind of Pselles with out-stretched wings. He drank the desert air like a potion and felt young, ready for any exploits and relieved of worries.

Night fell without their meeting a single nomad.

"From that minute on," Angell thought, "it was the real adventure, the one we dream of. From those sparkling days nothing fades. This vague-ness which haunted us for so long on Gamma, this shift in contours and sensations gave way to an extreme sharpness; the world would recover the colors and the stable seasons. As we sank into a distant violet, on a steppe whose coral and gray ochre plants were those of Earth, my sensations be-came more acute, my vision more direct. I recognized the absinthe, the mugwort, the tall wild oats, where our Halias and our Clavicorns plunged like in a wave; each breath of air concealed an icy taste of mint.

During the first three days the Diamond Range appeared on the hori-zon like a dazzling mirage, a planted and translucent surface, out of the real world. At night, they camped, usually on the edge of a crevasse. Fol-lowing an ancient process, the Pselles descended before all the Scarabs, and the latter immediately hastened to dig the ground and to roll up the blocks of clay, to form an enclosure. Then they would lie down all through, and they would graze. Wings folded, heads hidden in their pretty plumage or under a shorter coat, of a delightful white, the Air folk rested behind this double rampart, also forming a square...

Pi-Joh, Angell and Sais met inside the improvised fortress. The Aquatic stretched out even on the ground, in a sort of sleeping bag, a case of scales, a side of which he folded over his forehead. No one saw him undo his micaceous breastplate, or put down his diadem, and one might have believed that this sparkling apparatus was part of his body. Angell found, from the first stop, in his delete tank, a layer of eiderdown and a plastic shelter. He slipped in, but he didn't pull the selenium zipper that sealed his tent; he had thus, all night long, on his forehead, the cold sparkle of Rigel and Betelgeuse. The fourth night, their reflection on the rocks was dazzling.

The next day the caravan reached the foot of the Diamond Range. Suddenly (was it the equinoctial head or an incidence of the deviation of the axis of Gamma?) A shroud of ice fell. The Earthman understood the need for scale armor and tents stuffed with down. The Scarabs shed a layer of chitin overnight which weighed them down. Pi-Joh only moved in his nacreous case: he was being carried by the guards, like a cocoon. Alone, fearless and restless, the Pselles trembled under their plumage swelling with the wind. Angell gave his coat of seaweed and sapphires to Sais, who, quietly curled up in his chariot, took on the air of a well-bred young girl.

Night returned, icy, on a first buttress. It was a strange feeling to stop between two abysses: a crystal ground from which the wind swept the dust, a star-studded sky reflected there. Not having been able to dig the pure carbon, to raise their low wall, the large Insects lay down heavily even on the transparent rock. Their chitin patches rattled softly. Shortly after midnight, a flake of silky feathers, thin, slender limbs and a hot head landed on the Earthman's feet: the bird-people generally have a high temperature.

Angell reached out and recognized Sais's egret. She was shivering. No cloudy thought reached the nautical, to him it was only a graceful semi-animal creature, something like a small cat or a familiar pug. He pulled her onto his shoulder and covered her with a side of his tent. Sais modulated a flutis or he distinguished the name of Verne. Then they both fell into a dreamless sleep.

Remembering, therefore, how short the memory of the bird-people is, the following days, he asked her questions. And first:

"What do you know about the Ertosi people?"

She shivered as always, when someone asked her the direct question, then raised her beautiful agate eyes to the Earthman:

"I...," she began. "I have heard a thousand contradictory stories, so that it gets mixed up a bit... Nobody knows their number, because they come and go with the wind, but it is always increasing, because here they are sharing Gamma with the Aquatics. It is a people of warriors, they worship Fire and Iron. The Aquatics have told us that they feed on the blood of their enemies, but I believe they consume the flesh of any prey. When they set off, they rustle up everything in their path. I think... they say," she corrected with an unexpected rigor which proved her good faith, "that they burn their sick and wounded with their own hands. They do not eat anything that has not been killed during the day, and only wear the skins of animals slaughtered in season. And even, before cutting clothes, they walk on it – and also on the ground, before setting up their shelters – sort of little clicking boxes."

She was speaking, and through the images of her thought, Angell recognized the harsh customs of a people who had suffered from radioactivity. Earthmen, on a devastated planet, would not have acted with less cruelty.

"I have been told," continued Sais, "that in a fabulous past. The Ertosians committed a... how do you say? A sin, that is to say, an inexpiable crime. Then the chastisement arrived, which reached us all and they were left in the outer darkness. They suffered a lot and even when the sun came out they were sick for generations. But then a Liberator came. Maybe it was an inhabitant of another world, yours, who knows? Since you come from a distant star too. This Being had a white face..."

"And the Ertosians?"

"Oh! They are rather black or red... The Being wielded storm and lightning. It is he who united the wandering tribes and gave them laws. It is since then that they have been able to face the Aquatics, and the war has lasted for centuries and centuries, some lurking in the folds of the ground or under the water and the other sweeping the plains, like downpours of fire."

"We, the people of the Air, we suffer from each other. The Ertosi slaughter us as prey, to devour us, although their laws forbid them to eat their likes, but who would recognize an Air Pselle for their like? And the Aquatics capture us in snares and reed traps, they lock us up for a long time in their dungeons, until we are half mad with hunger and stink, and then they throw us onto the mountain peaks, the one against the other, the feathered Pselles against those with fur, so that we fight before them until death..."

"And you let yourself be?" exclaimed Angell.

Sais inclined her charming head with its golden reflections on its flexible collar.

"What would you do in our place? We are excitable and fragile, our heart beats too quickly, hunger and dread follow behind us. We also know that at the end of the game we will be given seeds and fruits to feast on, and some will have nests and, perhaps, a brood. So we throw ourselves into battle like bundles of crazy feathers. We have, moreover, in freedom, dances and rites that evoke war. But that only evoke, we do not kill anyone. These are parades, you understand."

"Yes, sport, we know that, nothing less disposes of the killing." Angell sought to comfort her, he had a deep pity for these people of Air, emotional and unconscious, torn between two dark powers.

"What about the Silicones?" he asked, to change the subject.

"Oh! Them!" Sais said contemptuously, and Angell understood that the Air people were also capable of contempt, "they weren't really people. They understand and feel nothing, until you hit them with a hammer!"

"I would have thought, though," Angell argued, "that you sometimes have to make an alliance with the Silicones."

Sais's plumage ignited slightly:

"It happens," she said. "When we were abandoned for dead, in ranges. Or when the Silicones found a brood. These beings have no sensitivity, only reflexes: they do not like something to be lost needlessly. But the fate of these adoptees is not better: I speak of it knowingly. I had... a Silicone foster father, me."

She did not want to say more and the astronaut returned to the Ertosians who interested him.

"What do they look like? I only saw them in the distance."

"Well," Sais modulated, "there are three kinds. Those who have suffered most mutations (that's the word, isn't it?) are horrible. We have lizards. The Aquatics divide them into Progressive or Reactive Mutants. Oh! It is very obscure! They are, in any case, descendants of a minority who would have remained all the time in the outer darkness. Yes, even during the great cataclysm...I do not know why."

"I saw a yellow-brown gecko and then a ceratosaurus," said Angell, "would they be Mutants?"

"I think yes."

"What about the other categories?"

"Well, there are the Primates or the Defectors. The exposure to radioactivity of their genes was shorter, either because their ancestors did not leave the shelters until after the explosion, or because these beings belong to a new species. They would look more like you," she added, examining the Earthman. "But they are less beautiful. They also resemble the furry Pselles, only their fleece is fawn or black. Unlike Mutants, they stand. They are smarter and meaner too. Once they caught me. Life! Life-Mother! I thought they were going to pluck me."

"And the third category?"

"Oh! These we don't know. None of my people have seen them. They descend, it seems, from the Being of lightning and light. There is still one at the head of the Ertosi, but a Pi-Rhé prisoner dies, rather than talking about it. All Aquatics know this through Aes. They have entered 'the darkness of fire'."

"An Aes would therefore leave the City of Waters...?"

Sais shivered:

"No. An Aes does not need to move away to see without being seen. He is one with Life-Mother."

CHAPTER VII

Angell was beginning to wonder if the nomads that Aes had given him a glimpse of, and that Sais was familiar with, weren't a myth or a mirage. Apart from the location of the extinguished pyres, no trace confirmed that the Fire People existed. The caravan had made its way for two days now, among the whiteness, silence and glow of the Diamond Mountains. On the slippery slopes, a few black or purple pines were clinging to the collected humus. Angell searched in vain for words to describe the track and the landscape: reflections of silver, iridescence, sky and ground of white onyx, ice, crystal... World of pure carbon, that was still the most accurate definition.

As they climbed the cold became bitter. By day, a crimson sun would reverberate in the smooth foothills and the air was filled with red vibrations. The nights were long, terribly bright; a dawn of fire was still blazing in the iridescent walls, and already the three moons were multiplying in the abysses. A star lit up at each peak. Halfway up the slope, the snow fell. It was impalpable and drier than on Earth; the astronaut had the impression that its consistency was not the same. Finally, Sais, who fluttered, worried, on a crystalline path, showed her companion a claw print:

"A Fire lizard has passed through here..."

Angell studied the inhuman trace. So far, God knows why, despite Aes' best efforts, he had felt closer to the Fire People than to the Aquatics. This animal imprint disconcerted him. But Sais raised further the hollow left by a high and light arch.

"There was a Primate with him. We are a Defector."

"Why by a Lightning Ertosi?"

Sais shrugged her shoulders:

"I know what you are thinking: the Lightning Beings may be your race. But nobody saw them, how do you want me to recognize their mark? And I doubt they will walk among their warriors. That said, there are centuries that we have not heard of a landing and if their dynasty exists, their descendants have mingled with the Mutants."

It made sense. There was nothing to discuss about it. But Angell asked:

"Do you know the inscription of the Temple?"

There was probably only one 'Inscription', because the golden-brown plumage fades. The brave little creature threw her head back and quoted:

When the lightning falls again, there will be alliance between the sky, air and fire and on the earth the days will become empty. ENVH."

"Our mothers make us repeat this, until we break our heads," said Sais. "I learned it from Ary. But Ary is dead."

Angell wavered as he received Planck's formula in a bird's flute. The quanta... Yes, that was an explanation: this world in the grip of a sixth force field and which awaited its liberation... Again, a myth opened up, to betray a spark of truth.

On the evening of that day, they were attacked by the Ertosi warriors.

The tornado arose from the cracks in the ground. They were really red and black Hominids, hairy and hard mounted on saurians. They employed elemental and brutal flamethrowers, propellants lined with embers and skins, from which an explosive liquid spurted out. (Probably a methane condensate, the Earthman noted.)

It was a rush, an avalanche. The flaming projectiles bounced off the quartz, blazed on the ledge above the chasm, the geckos whirled around and the enraged horsemen raised soot-smeared masks from their flowing crimson hair. Angell counted a number of assailants.

Immediately, the Air Pselles troop disbanded. Only one was hit and its plumage sizzled in a blaze. The others let go of their clavicorns and rose, in a low and level flight. The Ertosi let out insulting cries and ferocious laughter. Weighted down by their harness, the beetles slid down the slope. Pi-Joh falling from the chariot, mingled with the snowstorm. And Angell was left alone, shining figure in his chariot, with his rearing Halias and the blue bird, huddled at his feet.

"Tell them I'm coming as a friend," enjoined the Earthman to Sais. "I carry a message intended for their sovereign. A message of peace."

The girl modulated a cry and a series of chirps that were greeted by the hoots.

"They don't believe you," Sais translated. "They say no good can come from the swamps. Flee, oh! Flee, Lord, or you are lost! The Ertosi are very cruel and they burn everything!"

"Here," Angell said with a thin smile, "so they're incombustible around here? Tell them I'm ready to give them a lesson in politeness."

The bird had not finished translating that the flying dragons were launching themselves. Angell, calm, aimed and fired his disintegrator...

Sais, who had closed her eyes so as not to see death coming, reopened her transparent eyelids with a sigh and looked in front of her: the slope was clear. A large black mark marked the spot where the first wave had massed. Lower down, on the ledge, the fugitives were rushing down. A black giant, covered in scales, manhandled his gecko which he could not restrain. He stood up on the spine of the saurian and uttered cries that Sais translated with lightness, taken up again by the confidence that the bird-people had in the Terrestrials:

"He curses you by Iron and by Fire! He only saw a flash – and he wonders where his people have gone. But if you're a god, which he fears, you should know they don't have a king."

"No king? So an Aes, a chief, some manitou, a high priest? Someone who cries higher than the others, ask them..."

The fugitives disappeared in the setting red, like a vague tug. Sais turned her golden head towards Angell:

"They say they have Bellatrix..."

It was not an answer! All the people of Gamma undivided shared in the terrible bloody star. "What the hell!" exclaimed the Earthman, "the sun is shining for everyone! I also have Bellatrix!" But there was no longer a Barbarian in sight: they had eclipsed as they had come, as an element. A great silence fell over the abysses and peaks. A few embers still screeched on the snow: the Pselles of the escort and their scarabs were only a memory. Angell swore dreadfully: here he was launched on a mad planet in search of a king who did not exist! Aes, if he could get hold of him, would have had a bad quarter of an hour.

But something creaked under his feet: emerged from a crack filled with frozen moss. Po-Joh manifested himself. Angell jumped out of the chariot, leaned towards him. Sais was coming in plane flight. She read what the cripple had written on the snow:

"*Go straight ahead. HER NAME IS BELLATRIX.*"

But things had started at the beginning of the previous solar cycle.

The Ertosi people who, like all barbarian peoples, respected their own laws, all the more irrefragable as they were vital, waged war on the Aquatics. The beginnings of this affair were lost in the mists of ages and, like all oppressed ancestors alike, the Ertosians had short memories.

Therefore, they had forgotten whether they were fighting, because in an indefinite time, beings stronger than them had condemned them to die, among the hell suns and radioactive clouds, or so simply they claimed part of the land.

Besides, these ancient stories of outcasts, shelters and cataclysm were of no interest to a people who live from day to day, for hunters who throw prey killed from the hurdy-gurdy to the four winds. But there was the law – and resale insults. Each people has, for its neighbors, a base of stinging insults but this time, all things considered, the Aquatics had gone a little further as regards the Ertosians: they had suppressed their god.

Here are the facts in their historical simplicity: at the beginning of this solar cycle (which lasted five years), the chief of the people of Ertosi, a direct descendant of the Being of Lightning, had received messengers from the reigning Aes. Messengers of peace, of course. He was, in the opinion of his subjects, a very wise being, but old, and who did not like war at all. He imagined that one could, since the people of Waters were becoming less and less numerous and that oppressed species proliferated, share equitably, among all, the surface and the resources of Gamma – because the Lightning Being of the Ertosi (at least by his ancestors) came from afar and he had his personal views on racial equality. In any case, he agreed to meet the Aes reigning over a neutral territory which was dominated by the plain between the Lake and Diamond Mountains. Although the Aes invited him to this meeting 'with his people', he came alone and we never saw him again.

Since then, every Ertosian endowed with articulate language (because the geckos only mooed or chirped) swore to avenge his god-king. They would have invaded Laknea, but an Air Pselle whom they incidentally killed had brought them a supreme message, something like a testament from the Lightning Being, which expressly forbade them two things: One, to engage in fratricidal struggles; two, to attack their enemies from the front, until they have a leader.

The barbarians, sorrowful, burned the forests around Laknea and they even bent on the grass which grew back. They killed the simians that ventured into the mountains and smashed the stray Silicones with diamond hammers. This way of acting bothered Aquatics a lot, because Silicones were irreplaceable and the forest took centuries to grow back. But what exasperated the Barbarians was the impossible they found themselves in performing the funeral rites demanded by the majesty of a god. Since time immemorial, when all remains were dangerously radioactive, the Ertosians burned their dead. The smoke rising to the sky symbolized the delivered souls. A fortiori, a Being of Lightning, come from the stars, should he return, he deserved, moreover, an honorable pyre of ferns or branches sprinkled with aromatics, and the presence of a people weeping with all their souls around him. But the last Star Man of Gamma not having received this final homage, his uneasy soul was to wander on the shores of the Lake, and the Fire warriors were ulcerated.

This war of attrition continued with various alternatives. On advice of their priests who were also bonesetters (because the Lightning Man had decided that he would have no priests) they stole from the ruins of an abandoned Aquatic city a coffin of opalescent stone that they assumed had come, like their god, from space. On the walls flew flaming birds, flying fish and even, in vast plumes, the smoke which had followed 'the sun of death'. The barbarians threw the ashes contained in this sarcophagus into the swollen river thus destroying the last vestige of the Before-Night Beings, and they hoisted this empty ark on their shoulders, which thus set out in search of its dead.

Over the next few years, the Ertosians destroyed many of these abandoned cities and set out to surround Laknea with a circle of scorched earth and braising pits. The Aquatics who ventured against the backwaters of the Diamond Mountains were mercilessly destroyed. But Laknea, the treacherous city of corals, spices and light, still existed, and the priests despaired of being able to hold back the nomadic hordes indefinitely. Sometimes whole tribes rose up and disappeared on the horizon clouded with ashes; they were always the wildest, the most warlike clans, and those with a majority of very righteous men. Their more naked names never returned.

No one seemed to notice. The Pi-Rhé people were always numerous like the sand of the seas. The moonstone arch, under the bloody Bellatrix sun, continued to trace concentric circles around the doomed city. The warriors, as they walked, sang dark prophecies and everyone waited.

The day came when the bird-people spread great news in the air. The horde had bypassed the Diamond Mountains and, like a swollen torrent, they invaded a narrow valley. In deposit of equinoctial storms, the air here was mild and the sun's rays, reverberating, took on an emerald hue. The second cycle since the god's disappearance was ending. The cries of the bird people told the wandering Simians, Silicones and even Aquatics that the Ertosians were about to induct a new leader. And this one was a survivor of the Star race.

The camp was established on a soft height. After the purple and white, violent and unusual landscapes of Gamma, a messenger of Lightning would have liked the smaragdin reflections of this valley and this twilight glow. The lunar coffin was placed in the middle of the camp. A priest who had the rank of a poet sang, touching the strings of a rustic harp, the merciful, wise and peacemaker Beings of Light who came from the chasm of stars to the aid of the oppressed, heal their wounds and give them victories. These beings have lightning weapons, they appear – and everything flees. They recognize the good seed of the tares, and under their feet, the branch blooms again, the bee makes its honey...a glance of the Star Being is enough for the daughters of Fire to give birth to beautiful sons, and strong like him. Since the time these formulas, the same for all solar myths, had lost their weight, but the people listened to them with pleasure. The stars were a bit far away and no one knew if other messengers would come. The mysterious yoke of the Water People weighed heavily on the planet. But the Holders of the Fire knew that the fateful moment had come: they would march forward. They would go beyond the evil circle. It didn't matter what awaited them.

It was in this frame of mind that the horde (who had, for a day, drunk the juice of certain plants and the fermented juice of fruits, prayed before the ark, shouted and repeated oaths) found themselves. the fugitives from the ledge, haves, black, panting, arrived, without unsealing their saurians, and threw themselves, facing the ground, at the feet of the priests. Naturally, they were telling incredible, unbelievable things: Lightning and Grace had changed sides, a Star Being had made an alliance with the Aquatics, he wielded lightning, he had destroyed their companions. They had seen it, with their own eyes. No, of course, they hadn't raised their spears against the deity – it was inconceivable. And yet... The Pi-Rhé priests looked at each other in agony: for so long they had sung the praises of the Thunderers, that they ended up believing it... However, the panics did not lie: they held out their hands that the fire of the sky had blackened, one of them, tearing his tunic, showed, drawn on his skin, an aquatic embroidery, in colored thread. The disorder was at its height, because the people recognized the Old Curse...

The one who denied himself the most was the yellow and black giant who had repelled the stranger's advances. He swore that this one had uttered threats against their Being. "And yet," he said, "he did not know her name!"

"I hope," said the aedis gravely, "that you did not reveal the sacred name...?"

238

The giant was about to swear, when a muffled rumor invaded the valley, the prostrate fugitives groaned and the last rays of the star Bellatrix, green by reverberation, struck the immense prism of the mountains. At the entrance to the range appeared a chariot carried by Halias and a slender iridescent figure, preceded by a colorless flame.

The rest was indescribable: Primates, Geckos and Mutants mixed in a red cataract. At the top of the hill, before the moonstone coffin, the Sages fell face down to the earth: they had some privileges to preserve. The buffalo hide tents collapsed, disgorging a flood of children and primate women wielding arms. And quite below, in the hollow of the valley, geckos, whose muzzles emitted a muffled mooing, and reactive mutants sing the sacred song that they only sing once in a lifetime, when they face victory or death:

We are men as they are! Our members and our hearts are equal, We suffer and die like them..."

"Space!" Angell said. "Where have I heard this song before?"

Sais did not know what to answer. Hovering over the chariot like a blue flame, she was having an exhilarating moment.

On the hill, everything was fleeing. A priest adorned with clavicorn antennae bowed down to the Earthman

"Take me to Bellatrix," said Angell.

She was laying on a pile of heaped saddles, covered with snow leopard skins. The remains of an aquatic warrior – breastplate of translucent scales and chainmail of orichalcum – molded her slender body. On her forehead was a thin band of sapphires. Each fabulous gem was engraved with a letter of the ancient prophecy.

In the green and mauve twilight of the Secret Valley, she had the face of an earthly maiden, a tender, pouting mouth, and long grey, shifting eyes.

She looked like the effigy of the Temple.

When, chasing before him the black and red wave of her guards and her priests, Walter Angell entered her tent, as large as a palace, it did not rise only on her bed. Her hand played casually with a sharp blade. Their eyes met and Angell lowered his disintegrator.

She said:

"Greeting to the messenger from the stars!"

He expected anything and everything. Like a vortex of fire. An extralarge Silicone. A scarlet monstrosity. But not that white girl with her long golden hair. She pushed it aside impatiently, leaned on her furs and asked:

"What are you looking for? Are you from Sol III? Come closer."

She spoke, with a close accent, an old Earth language. But generations of Lightning Beings having succeeded one another on Gamma, she united a finality to the androgynous grace of the people of the Airs. Angell stepped forward, embarrassed by the long cloak of seaweed and the aquatic diadem. As in a more stable world, he entered the frozen light of her eyes.

"You are very handsome," she said. "I have never seen anything on Gamma that comes so close to perfection. Our legends say... But we'll talk about it later. You bear the signs of the Water People who are our enemy."

"I come as a messenger of peace."

"Do you believe that?" she said. "The last message of peace, from Laknea, caused the loss of the king, my ancestor. Is it the same Aes who addressed this for me? He was saying that they are immortal. The one who killed our leader was beautiful too, albeit green. I would like to strangle him with my hands."

They were white and tapered. Angell looked at them, smirked. She was indignant:

"Do you think I couldn't?"

"Yes," he said. "You can do anything. But take this message."

He never thought it would be so easy! Po-Joh had handed him a rolled-up parchment, sealed, which he nonchalantly protected.

The Sages seized it immediately, to submit it to the rites of purification (another ancestral measure against radioactivity). The Warrior Maid shrugged her shoulders.

"I don't understand," she said. "So Aes is afraid of us? And he sends you, you, who are neither of his race nor of this planet...? Yet Aquatics believe that there is something stable and immanent in this varying cosmos, and that their empire is based on eternity. But we who pass with the wind and fire, destroying the form so that it is reborn, we know: life and death are the same two poles of evolution. The Water People are right to fear us: we are their antithesis."

"There is no immanence, but a closed circuit. Like the stars, atoms follow their orbit. Aes knows that, that's why he's sending you here. But you don't know. And you are one of us!"

"Are you sure?" asked the Earthman.

She turned away to answer:

"Choose."

While on the hill the pyres of aromatics were consumed among opalescent columns of smoke, while the geckos were rolling in the heat of the braziers and the primates were singing their dull laments, Angell and Bellatrix exchanged the words which make no sense. only for lovers. He didn't ask her if her ancestors came from the little blue and green planet she called Sol III, she didn't ask him about the purpose of his journey.

"Let me look at you," said Angell, stretched out at the foot of the throne and her face raised, as if towards dawn. "Imagine, I looked for you from star to star, I told myself that since the universe was so beautiful, you must exist. But let me see your features. I don't know you yet. What a mask delighted a young girl's face! Who could believe that these pink lights and these petals hide an inflexible spirit and a thirst for revenge and exploits? Our passions shape us and I would hate for you to change.

"Let's imagine that Bellatrix Gamma does not exist. Yes, you are the Queen of Fire and I am only a traveler, captive of the Aquatics and their messenger. But should we lose this moment of fragile perfection? We met in spite of the chasms of darkness and the light-centuries that separate our planets. The beings or the continuum will take us back soon enough, but when I am dead we are thrown back into space-time, I would like you to remember this unique moment, when our souls were in tune, like the currents and the stars..."

"I would like to know you better," said the young girl, stubbornly. "How do you expect me to accept a separation, without hope of finding you again? You are an ally of the people of the Waters, and what else...?"

"If so, would you hate me?"

Under the sparkling azure that the Ertosians had surely not woven, her shoulders shivered:

"How could I, since you look so much like me? I have been looking all my life for a face to mirror myself in. My loved ones are no more and I cannot find any traits in my people. They think I'm their goddess, but I'm not, I'm sure. Oh! Tell me that I am a being like all the others! It is an afflicting thing, the solitude of the gods..."

"You will never be alone, since I am here. And my planet is populated by billions of people who look like us. That doesn't stop you from being the only one. I would never have dared to talk to you like this on Earth, but we're so isolated on Gamma, and this minute is short! Tell me, could you love?"

She opened wide her gray eyes:

"That means?"

"Is your heart becoming like mine too big for your chest? Would you like this moment to last forever? Would you bear to see me dead?"

"Oh, no!" she cried, leaping wildly from her throne. She dug her pink claws into the astronaut's breastplate. "I prefer to die with you, before you! Oh! Earthman, messenger, I don't know what's happening to us. There were many nights when alone, in the midst of my people, I dreamed of meeting my double, my brother, but I did not know that would tear my heart to put it in your hands. Is that called loving?"

"Yes I think. Because I too."

"Oh!" she said, "I am happy! We feel the same, we are the only being. My name is Bellatrix. And you?"

"Angell."

CHAPTER VIII

Standing on the hill reflecting the green ray – incomparable – Angell watched.

The Horde, at his feet, rustled like the forest or the sea.

No doubt it resembled other nomadic peoples. He couldn't know. Product of a millennial injustice, it was rough and bestial, knew no other pastime than hunting and war, admitting no property. Each clan had its customs, based on the simplest imperatives, so a primate woman, strong and well separated, was the equal of the hunter and brought her prey to the campfire like him, and the camps and the children belonged to the maternal clan. "As many solar revolutions as the ancients had filled their fill." But this equality went even further: having reached the end of a race, Primates and Geckos lay pell-mell on the ground and with the same movement tore apart – claws and teeth – their game, and the little Hominids hardened in their games with the young salamanders.

All this did not at all resemble the images of Aes: it lacked a note of decline, a mire, an air of abandonment and despair, as the Prince of Gamma had shown Angell only relegates.

Here, the beings were healthy, with the grace of young beasts. Angell was struck by this observation: apart from the priestly caste, no one seemed to have passed thirty years. Of course, savages have a habitude for living quickly; no doubt, in the extreme cold, isolated on their crystal trays, they froze and suffered from starvation. But this simplistic explanation does not satisfy the astronaut, like all the earthly solutions, brought to the enigmas of Gamma, it included a threatening corrective: neither hunger nor war regularly mow down, every twenty years, an entire generation.

He thought that the state of the Horde depended a great deal on this: the experiences, if any, had not had time to grow, nor the knowledge to transmit. Someone had given these people the firebrand propellant and had learned how to collect the methane that erupted. But they walked still, thousands of years after the Cataclysm, naked under animal skins and, as if peaceful knowledge had been useless to them, they ignored the cog-wheel and the halter.

Yet the fire seemed familiar to them and they drew from its simple use, their reason for living. Seeing the tiny children, with a movement of their fingers, ignite sagebrush stems or cause sparks to spring from the rock, the Earthman understood that Aes did not overestimate his enemies: rather than beings of flesh and blood, they were batteries of energy.

The witness's impressions were contradictory. Sometimes, in the mysteriously purple evenings, while around great burning trunks, primates with flamboyant lanugo modulated their wide melodies, Angell came to think that these people had behind them a past of long wisdom. But a giant horn beetle, hollowed out, sounded the kill, and red whirlwinds shot up, packs of beaters, little blue jackals or empusa larvae, found themselves on a large grass-eating animal or a feline, the embers set the slopes on fire of crystal and, under the calm stars, the Ertosians were transformed into brutes of the first ages.

Anyway, he never saw them knock out a 'brother-gecko'. Nor desecrate a fresh grave. And it seemed that lately the priests had gotten the Horde to make their fires away from the copses, on bare ground or on rock.

Based on the figures he had, Angell tried to calculate the age of this people of Primates. The results were disappointing! In eight thousand years, Earthly humanity had progressed, it seemed, from shepherd-kings to Roman jurists. Then, two thousand years opened the interplanetary era. According to the most modest calculations, the people of Fire, more savage than the nomads of Canaan, were fifty thousand years-old!

"Or I could..." said the Earthman. But to the problem of her people, Bellatrix herself gave no answer. At the call of the parish priests, she too jumped on the back of her favorite saurian, flame-red, whom she treated less like an animal than a playmate. She flew over chasms, challenged her subjects with shrill laughter, and during those fantastic rides where she seemed to barely see him, Angell followed her, as if drawn by a magnet, totally absorbed in his presence, and wondered bitterly what he was doing.

Was it the day after his arrival or another day...? (They rolled like a river.) The Ertosi priests came to Bellatrix's tent. To receive them, the Earthman dropped a propellant whose simple principle and grace he was studying.

"They say," threw Bellatrix, "that if you have a wife and a home on your own, you must report it. Fire does not accept sharing, it burns everything."

"I have nothing to forget," answered Angell. "And you burned it all down, no need to talk about it."

The nuptial blessing was very simple. The vegetable resins and sea amber were consumed, the bread baked under the ashes was broken and the brides divided, salt was offered on the blade of a sword. Then the priests gave the Earthman a new name – a secret name. It was like being new was born on Gamma. "You are ours and you are us," sang the syrinxes. "You are the spirit and we are the flame... Everyone is free."

Oh! He loved Bellatrix. Their union was complete. Under the triple moon of Gamma, in the diamond caverns, they knew nights of acute perfection, minutes that Angell had vainly sought of old in the cold starlight. But all this adventure seemed to him a crystal dream that an imprudent word or gesture could shatter, so he held back all thought, all useless questions. Landing on a mind-blowing planet, being received, accepted by a legendary people, becoming the lover of a barbarian queen – beautiful, secretive, passionate – what astronaut hasn't desired such a fate?

Sometimes he thought that of all the mirages in Gamma this was the most beautiful. Also the most dangerous. But it was probably only a mirage.

Bellatrix gave him a ring engraved with her name, and the horde accepted the astronaut wholeheartedly. They offered him what they had best: their jousts and their games. The young Primates with muscles on their lips a modulated language, some were experienced in uttering earthly words. Strange: they always chose abstract terms: energy, action, matter. The Geckos rolled at his feet, perfecting their wrestling holds. All admire his weapons, but without astonishment.

"Looks like they know about the Disintegrator," Angell told Bellatrix. She laughs, showing her beautiful teeth:

"I think so! All my ancestors held the lightning!" Then she frowns: "Above all, they know the horror of disappearing... Oh! My people! One day we are armed, young and strong, we ride a Hermoine or a Flying Dragon, we know neither masters, nor enemies... And then, the thing happens..."

"You mean death?"

"Or disappearance. It's not the same thing, not always? I still prefer death to combat, red and frank, a clean break to an obliteration. I prefer death: I want to believe that the blood shed fertilizes the soil, that the grain germinates and that the souls, with the smoke, fly away towards the stars. But..."

"Is it something else?"

She clutched her temples with both hands and the sharp nails marked her smooth skin. In her grey eyes – icy lakes – danced ghosts of sand and gold. She said:

"I do not know yet. And then, it does not concern you! Singular conversation, when one loves one another!"

"When we love each other," Angell smiles, "does that therefore involve forbidden subjects?"

"No. Yes. You come from so far... From my planet, I would like to give you only what dazzles and charms: the brilliance of the Diamond Mountains, the ardor of our hunts, the taste of fruit and honey. What do you care about our darkest secrets?"

"I would like to share them with you," he said gravely.

She seemed to weaken, laughing through the tears and twisting her white, ray-like fingers.

"I don't know if that's a good thing," she said, a little bewildered. "It all pays off, right? We are happy. Of course, it will have to be paid for one day."

"You see, the destiny of my people is strange. We almost never know our ancestors. Formerly, each spring, the Ertosians went away, leaving their children at the station of the temple, the children only. With us, women go to battle with their husbands or their lovers. The priests remained in the valley, you saw them, they are our only old men. I was raised in the temple, like the others. When I was fifteen, I was given a secret message. No, I can't tell you again. I don't understand... Since then, I've been thinking, studying myself, looking for connections... oh! I am getting a terrible education! I am learning to be queen. But when everything – the origin of evil and how it comes..."

"Well?"

"I will fight!"

It was not ridiculous at all! She held arms like a trained warrior, and behind her massed a terrible horde! And yet, Angell shuddered. He asked:

"Will you know soon?"

"At the Solstice. At the Feast of Swords."

However, at the dawn of certain purple nights when the horde howled and raved around its fires:

"Why do you stay with these people who don't look like you?" he asked again. "You are neither of their blood nor of their species. Leave them. We will find our place under the stars."

She shook her head:

"Do we abandon children or the blind? And then, this planet is so beautiful! We gave it a name in the Ertosi language: Sundew. It is like a shining drop, like a tear falling from heaven, she reflects and irises all the lights, but what it promises is death. To everyone: to the Being of Lightning who sails among meteors, to the fearless warrior on the backbone of the dragon, to the child who has just become a master and will never see his mother... to the beasts and birds from Gamma..."

"THE SUNDEW...," repeated Angell. "This name... who said this name?"

"Imagine", Bellatrix went on ardently, "that black abyss which is infinity, those dazzling suns, those spiraling stars – and among them, in one corner of the sky – the darkest – a crystal trap. A diamond globe that sparkles, trembles and reflects... oh! Whatever you want: your dreams and your desires. Even those, especially those that you have always hidden from yourself as from others. It frightens you and calls you. But you are a man and you are coming. And from that moment you are lost."

"Do you know all this? Bellatrix? Where did you learn it?"

"We are taught things at the temple... an oral tradition. But I think I always knew. Do you understand now why I cannot abandon my Barbarians? More than did my father who preceded his clan on the Plain of Ashes – and never returned. On my ancestor who was leaving for Laknea. The Ertosians are... the only certainty on Gamma. They are tough, but not mean. The gestures they make are their words: there is nothing beyond. Evil does not come from them."

"Bellatrix," he said, heaving himself on the snow leopards' fur. "I forwarded this message to you. My only excuse is that I was an ignorant Earthling. I was walking in darkness... If you love me, promise me one thing, just one..."

"Speak."

"This Plain of Ash, or the Lake... never go down there. Stay away from Laknea, Stay away."

She looked at him for a long time, she seemed surprised: she was riding among the stars, he was bringing her back to earth. She thought that was probably the task for men. Yes, before being the lover of the Queen of Fire, he was the messenger of Aes... But she answered him sincerely:

"War is a matter for the whole people. It is they who will decide whether we must return, whether we must carry words of peace or iron and flame, in Laknea. Every year, on this date, we meet. At the Sword Festival, arms are blessed and our sages read the stars. Then the assembly of the people decides. The only thing I can promise you, An-n-gel, (she dragged out the consonants, deliciously), is that I will never wage a useless war. Whether it's delivering captives or avenging offences – then, yes, I am

247

Bellatrix!" She was referring to an ancient earthly meaning of her name: "she who makes war." But not for fun or to see blood flow...

In the days that followed (it was then that he went up the hill), it seemed to him that the horde swelled beyond measure. Every morning, infiltrating through the faults in the rocks, new torrents of lizards, new red horsemen clad in scales or thick fleece, descended the slopes, horns and trunks tore through the thick fog and the horizon was scarlet. But when he came down to their tent, Bellatrix played with the emeralds and sapphires on her necklaces. She offered him her lips, and Gamma, its unleashed Elements and the cosmos itself lost value.

(...They did not ask themselves, like the lovers of Earth: "Will you always love me?" Angell already knew that it was possible to relive and eternalize their love seemed to him sacrilege. Every minute was precious. And nights and days passed.)

One evening they were still hunting. They had wandered away from the camp, having tracked as far as the Gray Lands one of those snow cats whose silver coat the Ertosi prized: a tiger-lion. It was an insidious and cruel beast which, even when gorged with blood, slaughtered the herds. Shooting him down was a feat.

Bellatrix had chased the enemy to exhaustion and riddled them with spears against a wall of ice. But when she turned to cry victory to her subjects, she saw no one on the snowy slopes; Angell alone followed, his disintegrator in his hand. She danced with joy in her saddle and, jumping on the crystal ledge, held out her arms to him. Their two bodies intertwined. Down on the plain, ashen waterspouts passed, and for an infinitesimal fraction of time, Angell thought he saw a ruby glow rising from the Lake.

Had Bellatrix grasped that red menace? She tore herself from his arms. An icy blast passed.

"Let's go," said the queen. "It is a cursed place. You sense evil forces there. The power and desire of Aes..."

That night, Bellatrix slept in his arms, among the gleam of her flowing hair, with that childish smile he knew on the threshold. She found a haven of safety and rest in the arms of this stranger. Angell eagerly savored the last moments of total happiness, but fallible and threatening. Later he needed these memories.

A side of the tent lifted. He saw a smooth blue shadow slipping through it, and perceived a flutis:

"Danger! Oh! Danger for your people, Earthman!"

Sais. It was centuries, it seemed to him, since he had heard that faint song, nor seen Sais again. Neither Pi-Joh. If they were in danger...He felt responsible in a sharp, awful way. And Verne? And Tycho? Catastrophic images of spacecraft, attack, flames, flashed in his eyes. He was immediately on his feet and put down with infinite delicacy, the gilded head of Bellatrix on the cushions; she threw her golden arms in front of her, blindly, and murmured:

"Angel..."

"I'm here," he replied. But he was already walking away. Sais crept towards the exit of the tent. On the glazed hillside, in his somewhat tarnished astronaut cuirass, Verne was waiting for him...

"They attacked the *RZ-2*," he said briefly. "Tycho wanted to leave without you. So I tweaked the engine a bit and took off in a helicopter. Come, we just have time to join, Aes is furious with you."

One asks stupid questions in serious circumstances. Angell couldn't help asking:

"How did you get to the chopper? Did you get it in?"

"Oh!" said the other, "I had allies. Bill, you understand... he's very popular, he's set up a little clinic for Silicones, he gets a hundred a day. He resounds their quartz and puts splints on the Birds. But even with the defections on this side, we can no longer hold on..."

The icy wind whipped their faces. Angell looked at Verne: how could he have come this far? In his waxy pallor with violent dark circles, his eyes were unrecognizable! That Verne shouldn't have spoken of the *RZ-2*, nor of the engines, nor of anything that evoked their life...before Bellatrix Gamma and its ordeals! But he would not have been surprised to hear him pronounce in a neutral tone, even: "The night of the ages..." or again: "this people is very ancient..." Suddenly, Walter Angell felt: it was not the high winds that froze his heart and his hands, but the fact that Francis Verne, landing without warning in the valley of the Diamond Mountains, looked terribly like the Aes of Gamma!

He pushed that idea away.

"We must take Pi-Joh with us," he said.

"Do you believe?" Verne asked. "Come see what happened to him."

He took him to the chopper, half buried in snow. There was something that looked like a mound, and Angell quickly recognized what little remained of the Aquatic: a sheath of scales and a light skeleton.

"I believe," said Verne coldly, "that he had worn himself down to dust. Otherwise, Aes wouldn't have sent him here on a mission. We were all in control from the start: Tycho, Ready and me. You, of course, can stay here..."

He went no further, but the accusation was clear. Angell clenched his fists and teeth.

"Contact Tycho by airwaves," he said.

"Useless. The *RZ-2* no longer responds."

A silence fell. Then Angell:

"Good. So we take off."

"To join the spacecraft?"

"But yes."

Every word was a drop of blood. Walter Angell saw again Bellatrix, asleep on his shoulder, her smile, the richness of her white-gold hair. She loved him, she trusted him. For a moment Angell the Adventurer felt bound by dark forces to the Fire People, Gamma, the Blood Sun, and the Young Queen who bore the same name. But he pulled himself together. Bellatrix reigned over Gamma, in the constellation of Orion. But the simple astronauts, Tycho, Verne and Ready were his earthly comrades. His choice was made, though his heart failed. Looking around him for a token to give, he found only the steel bracelet that was worn around the pilots' wrists at the time of their oath and which accompanied them – to death. There was his grave order number and their motto: Eternal. Angell took off the bracelet and handed it to Sais:

"Put it on her pillow," he said. "I will not be able."

When she came back, they took off.

CHAPTER IX

The return trip was brief. Verne flew very high above the camp of the nomads. Overcome by fatigue, Angell closed his eyes and plunged into black void, where a haunting image shone. The Crimson Forest was bathed in shadow. Angell, waking up, noticed that the Silicones were making a lot of noise.

"Tycho must have repelled the assault," Verne argued. "Now they're hiding. They hope to wear us out, don't they, Sais?"

The Bird lowered her head. Angell felt a convulsive shiver run through the elegant body. He had the impression that the Air Pselle was desperately trying to communicate with him and dared not; this mute terror was more significant than the screams. They flew over the crater where the *RZ-2* was tilting. The access lock closed, the crater empty, nothing testified to the fight. Francis circled above the forest.

"We land?" Angell asked.

"No," said the other, "not yet. This silence, this immobility seem suspicious to me, I left RZ in the middle of a battle. I'm looking for a place where the helicopter will be safe."

It was a normal precaution. Why did Angell feel that incisive chill in his chest? A void that was widening... His hand, which instinctively sought the disintegrator at his side, did not find it. Who had taken it: Verne or Sais? And why? He couldn't believe that Verne... The craft began a spiraling descent over the forest.

"I spotted a clearing," Verne said in a singularly muffled voice. "A perfect way, for those who desire...your speedy return..."

It was – more or less – the very sentence on which Aes of Gamma had left him. Thoughts raced through Angell's mind with frightening rapidity. If, by some inexplicable aberration, Verne betrayed, nothing was lost: the young man overestimated his physical means: whether it was free-style wrestling or judo, Angell would easily be right. But Verne was armed. In addition to the disintegrator, he also had a heat gun, an inconspicuous weapon, very handy. It was a question of paralyzing it before... At the moment when the helicopter touched the ground, the first pilot jumped on Verne.

The struggle was singularly brief. At the first touch of a skin that seemed to Angell singularly cold and viscous, the young engineer's body

251

sank like an empty envelope, slipped between the hands of the opponent who was watching, frozen with horror. In fact, it was an empty envelope. It had Verne's features, his slender waist, his curly hair, but to the touch the rough skin floated like a garment that was too loose and already melting. Beneath the half-closed eyelids, a cold, glaucous glow betrayed the strange life that had slipped into this Verne-like bag, which made him move, talk and act. Angell felt like he was about to vomit and violently pushed back the form which rolled under the ferns and remained prostrate there. But you shouldn't give in to the horror, there was something else to do.

Pushing Sais away, distraught, the pilot returned to the living corpse and searched his suit. It was indeed Verne's armor and he found, under the armpit, the formidable little weapon, a jewel. Under his hands, with frightful rapidity, the body, which had just been animated, was liquefying.

Thermic gun in hand, Angell felt himself on firmer ground. He checked the weapon – it was real and heavy in his hand with a charge of several months, unfired. Beneath the ferns, what had been Verne was no more than a blackish mass, among the viscosities of which the spatial armor shone faintly. Angell shoved Sais with icy fury: "Did you know it wasn't Verne?"

She tilted her head. So this pollution was real! However, he did not have the heart to mistreat the fragile creature...

"Did you know who it was?"

He only got a gasping flutis. Besides, did he need to know? An extension, a tentacle of the dark power that dominated the planet, had animated a martyred body – and he had let himself be caught in this trap, like a novice! For a moment Angell swayed: he thought he saw a greenish flame escaping from the rotting mass, then darting under the trees, with the agility of a reptile.

"Come on," Angell said with cold rigor. "We will try to reach the spacecraft."

When they were close, after an interminable path in a quivering, silent forest, they understood that the worst had happened. The rims of the crater were lined with siliceous debris and chitin patches. Here and there unrecognizable heaps, charred, indicated that the fight had been hard and that the crew of the *RZ-2* had sold their skin dearly. Someone had fired his disintegrator on the Beetles and the Silicones until it went out, but the fight had been unequal and the access hatch was gaping. Why had they opened it? Angell wondered in horror. Had an appearance of himself presented itself, imploring, calling his comrades? Or had the terror that had been Verne, that had inhabited Verne's body, betrayed those too...?

A terrible acrid and insipid odor exhaled from the hull at the same time, Angell had to hold his breath to enter. He lit his torch, and with a single glance he saw the disaster. Nothing had been spared: the oxygen tanks burst, the on-board instruments reduced to debris, the RZ-2 was now only an empty shell, the corpse, too, of a beautiful spaceship.

And the crew had disappeared.

Angell lowered his head. He had suffered terribly when he left the Fire Camp, but his face remained calm. Faced with the hideous form that had been his best friend, he hadn't let out a cry. But now, at the sight of the irreparable destruction of his ship, he felt a burning sensation in his eyelids.

A stain of blood was spreading at the floor of the cabin where they had laughed so often or hardly at the calculations. He touched it with his finger: it was cold, half coagulated. Human blood...Who died here? Tycho or Ready? He would never know...

Suddenly an association of ideas formed in him: Death. To be opened only after my death... Each of the astronauts kept a secret notebook which, in the event of an emergency, was to supplement or replace the logbook. These rolls of microfilm, with their seals, lay in the commander's safe. And that commander's safe. And this practical safe, right in the hull of the vessel, had been the only piece of furniture to go unnoticed by the vandals. Angell's icy hands held the spring: thank Heaven the rolls were there. He hid them under his breastplate and descended slowly, stumbling against the dark heaps.

Sais limped along. Arriving at the edge of the crater, he stopped. Where to go? The RZ-2's hull was radioactive, and for nothing in the world would he have gone down to the woods where a terrible green flame roamed.

There remained the City.

He smiled mirthlessly. It was quite in Angell's way – to seek shelter "in the lion's den". Something told him that the notebooks of his companions would explain many obscure points to him. Perhaps he would find a weapon there, for him or for Bellatrix...But the white and gold image of a charming young woman who resembled her Earth sisters and reigned on the borders of Gamma, paled in this darkness. Did she even exist, this Bellatrix, tender and wild? He was no longer sure. An insurmountable anguish invaded him. He descended the cliff.

By incredible luck, the city was there, dazzling in the gray dawn. Sais tried to pull him away, shouting weakly, but he tore himself from the frail talons and walked ahead of him, like a blind man.

He must have gotten lost in the maze of streets, because instead of coming out in front of the Crystal Temple, he ended up in a small octagonal square, with pink walls. A fountain rustled under a rock of madrepores. Angell bent down to drink and saw in the basin a haggard face and gloved hands with dry blood. Mechanically, he cooled his burning forehead. Sais arrived at his steps and challenged him with a sorry flutis. She pointed out to him, at the foot of a wall, a ventilator and he understood that the wave of Sais, her tender anxiety, had led him to the hidden nest of the Winged Pselles.

It was urgent to leaf through the microfilms. With the silence of the small square and the cool touch of the water, Angell's bewilderment dissipated, he once again became the dangerous hunter, the solitary astronaut.

He patted Sais' bristling plumage and followed her into the cellars. There was a small room there, with an wicker-lined floor and a nest-shaped bunk, where he let himself go with a sigh of relief. In one corner was heaped a little pyramid of fruit, red ears, similar to corn, and a spring was dripping into a marble hollow: he realized that these were the provisions of the two sisters. Seeing Sais reveal her secrets and poor riches to him in this way made his heart sink. But he had no more time to waste, and, using a binocular attached to the rollers, he began to develop the first microfilm. It was Bill's diary.

The first two rolls included a succinct account of the *RZ-2*'s journey, up to the accelerator crash. At the beginning of the third, Angell found a kind of report that the astronauts had signed, on reentering the *RZ-2*: the ship seemed to be in perfect condition (this document appeared on a loose sheet). Immediately afterwards came the facts recorded as events unfolded, when, having returned to the spacecraft, the student thought he was in relative safety:

"Meet Angell. Obviously, I was prevented from telling him everything. Physically hindered. However... my impression is that he understood certain things before me. Ultimately, this story is as much about astrophysics as it is about biology, don't Walter forget to be silly. In case we do not see each other again and for his information, I record my observations here.

"Let's start with the beginning. I took notes:

"At the Verne relief on the threshold of the Cave of the Living Dead. A state of extreme weakness, obvious amnesia, very weak pulse, temperature below normal: 28 and even 25 degrees. Constricted pupils, extreme flexibility of the body, with stiff movements. I applied the treatment for asphyxiation. Sais does not want to approach Verne, for whom she feels a visible repugnance. I feel extremely tired from the care given to my comrade. Drowsiness, heavy eyelids. Sleep.

"Tycho wakes up screaming: he had a nightmare. Verne is motionless, cataleptic stiffness, imperceptible pulse. I wonder if he's not dead, when Sais brings the Silicone back; he rolls a covered bowl in his cart. Sais shows me by signs: I must make Verne drink. I dip my finger and get a weak electric shock. I'm dripping: it's blood! My friends explain to me, as they can; this could save Verne. Let's try, since I don't have anything else handy. As he cannot swallow, the muscles of his throat being paralyzed, I introduce a hollow tube into his mouth and pour the liquid drop by drop. A noticeable improvement occurs, the pulse quickens, temperature 28 degrees, then 35 degrees. The body regains its flexibility and, remarkably, the stains, the purple or blue streaks which covered it disappear, but the patient is still unconscious. I wonder the cause of these marks which I fear to take for blood infiltration in the thickness of the tissues: they indicate a constant pressure exerted on the body.

"Back to Tycho. He sits on his mattress, his eyes bulging, and claims that Verne tried to strangle him. As I explained to him the state of our comrade, he blames Sais – "this damned female." (It's fortunate that the natives don't care much about the commander's assessments.) My legs falter but I can see the blood from the bowl, well, it's the blood of the mammal; I suspect the Silicones accidentally crushed some Simian.

"In the morning, Verne sleeps. Tycho tells me about his nightmare; he felt a presence, a weight of granite on his chest, something was suffocating him, but it wasn't unpleasant either. Above some well-felt insults.

"The Silicone brings a change of blood – this time from a bird. How worried I am that they have something like a blood bank, for emergency aid to the wounded. What wounds? It seems to me that there are games where accidents are frequent.

"Verne is better. If only I could take a blood test from him!

"Evening falls. We recognize the evening, because the vents which open on the surface of the lake no longer allow their glaucous light to pass through. Sais and the Silicone come to get me, they understood that I wanted to know the source of the blood. As I am very tired, the Silicone

255

takes me to the extreme galleries, north of the lake. From the curved corridor that we follow, we find ourselves here on a height, pierced with skylights, where the diffuse luminosity of the setting sun penetrates. It resembles, my faith, bathtubs of ancient theatres.

"The Silicone allows me to sit on what serves as its shoulders and I see: below, there's a circus as big as that of Gavarnie – all the capitals on Earth can line up! The floor is in pink or white marble, with sloping channels. All around, the amphitheater of rocks has windows and, no doubt, balconies identical to ours. While I study all this, a band of Silicones arrives, they must have filled themselves with static energy, because they frolic and disperse at the openings, with an infernal noise. I ask my guide if there are other paid seats at the theatre, he doesn't understand. Sais has disappeared. From an upper gallery comes like a wave, a suffocating smell, it smells of seaweed, musk – the tide!

"I'm starting to get used to the misinterpretations of my friends, but this time, the limit is exceeded: funny people who promise to take you to the labs and take you to the benches of a circus! Unless the Silicone figured out that I'm running out of distractions!

"Thin entertainment, between us! Here is a door opening in the red rock opposite. Screams, squawks – out comes a surging wave of small white simians and birds with clipped wings and dull plumage. They rush before them, as if they were pursued by the devil – and it is the devil himself who springs, in the end, from the hole. First, I don't understand what it's about: the world is moving. A bundle of thick cables unfurls, an infinity of greenish and gray diamonds move around to make you feel sick: it's a python. The biggest I have ever seen. This endless and moving body smells of mud and swamp, it could, it seems, go around Gamma and as it moves, I understand what gave the idea to the inhabitants of this planet, that they could change size. This body overwhelms a small and flat head, split across its entire width; the scales are lighter, almost white at the approximate location of the neck which swells...which swells already...A hissing that freezes the spine – and I too vacillate, I cling to the shoulders of my Silicone : I understand the desperate flight of little simians!

"They can go no further – in front a trapdoor opens. The first fugitive falls into it with a hideous yelp – for the whole trapdoor is filled with the gaping red muzzle of a huge saurian.

"A snap of jaws. The body with the soft white fur is cut in two and disappears. A spurt of hot blood splashes the flagstones, it falls back into the channels, whose destination I also understand – and the little victims flow back, they settle into a compact square that quivers and undulates – facing the snake, back to the giant saurian.

.".Like those slender bird heads, those reversed faces of simians are human!

"Two legs bristling with sharp scales, armed with claws are thrown out of the trapdoor. At the same time, the python advances with a sinuous movement and launches its enormous weight on the nearest victim who bends and falls. Two fountains of blood, two crackles of broken bones – a long, terrible cry of anguish. The channels fill with red liquid. Blood banks! Here are the blood banks!

"Here, the microfilmed graffiti became barely legible. But on the evening of the same day, Ready went back to his notes in a precise, medical tone.

"Tycho refuses to stay with Verne, for whom he feels a strange mistrust. The Silicone is sulking: I didn't appreciate his favorite distraction. However, it extends well with Sais? I try to reason with myself: Earth also has these anomalies: we love our dogs, but we sometimes send them to the pound. Vivisection exists...no, it doesn't (the birds of Gamma are obviously human). But we have wars! The 20th century had concentration camps! Maybe the Silicone doesn't understand that these pretty beings are suffering...?

"Night is falling. (we scrupulously observe the circle of the hours). Tycho sleeps. And now Verne is delirious. He is lying motionless, the muscles of his face are frozen, but his open mouth exhales a monologue...no, a whispered dialogue, for there are two of them, although I am not stretching out the Other (Split personality? Possibly, we know it on Earth...)

"The first sentence is a gasping cry:

" 'Angell? No. No... NO! I don't want to! You will not force me!'

"Terrified, I listen, since it is about Angell...

"Verne continues, in that same dull, dead voice:

" 'Yes, I recognize you. You are the Force. You hold me, you are in me, I know it. This feeling of anguish that twists the nerves, this absolute helplessness and this almost filthy sweetness are the signs of your presence. I have experienced them near the threshold, in the grotto of gifts to since... Oh! I still struggled! But there was a moment when through some crack in my consciousness (because I was expecting and hoping for something else, I believe) a torrent of strange sensations came over me – it was both dread and delight, gave a tragic meaning to the term 'possession'. I became the plaything of cosmic powers. The world was colored with dazzling or muffled vibrations and each note of music was a color that reached his nervous keyboard to draw from it agonizing resonances. And as life withdrew from me, I struggled in this agony, annihilated, defiled to the very depths of my being and there was such joy in sinking! Then there was only darkness, the thick satisfaction of the Other, his joy – and a kind of spasm that was to be my death.

" 'But I am not dead. There was a moment when the vibrations stopped: I should have ceased to be. How is it that, in this physical nothingness, unable to govern my body, I am still here? That a remnant of will and conscience survive? It's worse than being walled up alive! It's... No, I tell us, it's enough that I'm in this hell. Nobody else...'

"And then this heart-rending cry:

" 'Aessa! You are Aessa!'

"I remembered the name.

"The next day I was given to hear its male version.

"Verne had fallen back into his cataleptic rigidity; if it were true that two consciousnesses fought in his body, one of them had just paralyzed the other. I did not see Sais or my Silicone again. On the other hand, a troop of his more restless colleagues, probably younger, came to fetch us, took touching care of our equipment, polished our breastplates and led us by a magnificent gently sloping path, just in front of the crater where was, sparkling like a new part, the *RZ-2*. They even went so far as to transport Verne on a stretcher!

"I was so convinced that we had lost our old clunker forever, that seeing it like new on the track made me cry! Tycho, of course, overwhelmed me with insults: one would have said that he had not even seen the *RZ-2* demolished! We feverishly checked the machines, everything was in perfect order, it seemed enough to press a start button to take off for other skies. But one member of the crew was missing: Angell.

"Tycho roared: he knew what he was saying! These conditions were the plague of an expedition! He would make Walter think of the Interplanetary Council! Having regained the hair of the beast, our commander bullied the Silicones and judged the events a little high: everything had happened according to his forecasts, the authorities of Gamma (there must have been authorities!) had realized that it was better not to joke with the Humans of Earth... there existed a Solar Federation, by Jove! We were under its protection, and those damn siliceous beasts were not going to dictate the law to us!

"It was there of its vaticinations, when the signal of the audiophone started. A metallic voice echoed in the hull of the *RZ-2*:

" 'Earth humans on this raft, Aes of Gamma speaks to you. He tells you: You landed on this planet without our authorization and in spite of our sensory barriers. We are willing to admit that you were forced to do so. Our world is neither wild nor hostile, it is OTHER. And it intends to stay that way.'

"Tycho sneered, I've rarely found him so stupid.

"The voice resumed:

" 'We do not need your culture or your presence. But we mean you no harm. Some wrongs have been caused to you by our passive defense, we have tried to repair them. Now you are back on board your ship and free to leave: you owe it to one of your comrades...'

"This is how we learned that Angell, to save us, had accepted a mission.

"The voice hadn't finished as Tycho exploded:

" 'Accept an enemy mission! Making a commitment, without the authorization of his commanding officer! This pilot's liable for court martial!'

" 'You have already said it,' I interrupted, for I was tired of this comedy. 'And you also know that the good disposition of this Aes (whether he is prince or principal), depends on the success of this mission. Listen, Commander, we've put ourselves in a case of major force, there's nothing to do but wait for Angell's return...'

" 'And to prepare triumphal arches for him, I think not! Free we came to this damn globe, and free we'll leave! I put out a call, and if that damn fool doesn't come back, we'll take off on the hour!'

"I sat down on the ground near Verne's stretcher and crossed my arms.

" 'Take off, if you like,' I tell him. 'You have a plaster cast and your right arm hangs down. Verne's unconscious and I'm not a pilot. After all, nothing worse can happen to us, with a spacecraft that breaks down intermittently, and piping still flanked by an accelerator whose exact operation no one knows. In addition, I refer to the paragraph of the Interplanetary Code thus formulated: *The penalty of retaliation will be applied to the crew master who has abandoned an astronaut with a regular body in full vacuum.*

" 'A thousand million galaxies!' Tycho swore. Then, having reflected and swallowed his saliva, this amiable man added: 'And the worst thing, dirty little carabineer, abominable Earth fly, is that you're right!'

"The next day, Angell advised us to leave without him.

"Tycho swore at him, but stayed."

The next roll was impressed by Jerome Tycho.

Towards the middle of the film, the thick and confused graphics that reflected the character underwent a singular metamorphosis: it was as if the faults of the subject were aggravated and defined, the features became more irregular, the signs overlapped – a psychiatrist saw in it a pathological sign.

Angell read:

"Space and double-space! A thousand million times... I'll be able to record the real truth. This is all against the rules. Let it be known: this raid was marked from one end to the other by insub... insubordination – and I know about it! There was talk. Where is this Angell? I will not bear...

"It is inadmissible that we're being rolled by stones and ostriches. I have not seen any other form of so-called intelligent life, and I still believe there is none. I draw the attention of the Solar Council to the fact that this planet, rich in space crystals and fissile materials, of a tolerable although trying climate, is practically depopulated. An ideal colonization site... We could give it my name: Tychia or Jeromie: the commander of the vessel who discovers a globe in space is considered as its inventor, except in exceptional circumstances.

"And there are no such coincidences. The low level of civilization of the natives... practices of magic and sorcery... my crew has shown itself to be below everything! It should be admitted, in high places, that muscles and theories are nothing compared to an interplanetary experience..."

Then a date. That of the day Angell left on a mission.

"Inconceivable insolence! Speak in this tone to citizens of the solar system. Aes... who's this Aes? We're summoning Ready to contact this Angell's... Who orders here, I ask you!"

Here, the graphics began to change. It was as if someone had held – and embarrassed – the writer's hand. The expression remained vulgar, but beneficiated from an unexpected force and a furious slyness.

"Angell has the nerve to advise us to leave immediately. Leaving without expecting him? Damn! There is certainly a ruse there. We would come up against the barriers and even, if we ever touched Earth, Ready and Verne would have a good time accusing me...

"Fortunately, I feel better, I feel a singular sensation of fullness and balance, my ideas are admirably clear. I will foil this plot. Ready left with his stupid way of healing Silicones. In the absence of this pretentious carbine, I'll take some measures. Regrettable, but necessary, of course. The spacecraft must be cleaned. Verne is still comatose, but I'm watching him. He's dangerous, because he's holding Angell's hand. But he took it. These nightmares that wake me up every night... I'm sick of it! No one will take away from me the idea that Verne carries a contagion, a virus. Paragraph XXXX3820: '*Any contagious principle on board a spacecraft on a mission must be eliminated as a matter of urgency.*' I know my Code.

"I stole some of that laughing gas from Ready that he carries around in his satchel. I suppose on Earth they are used to put down particularly expensive dogs."

A long, disorganized paragraph broke through the film, then the notes resumed with a new cohesion and logic:

"No need to bother me. My right arm hangs down, I can't handle the hypodermic syringe. And yet it must. The feeling of satisfaction that lives in me, since I decided to kill Verne, to extinguish this tenacious flame which is a Verne and which seems to me from now on an obstacle to my plans, this feeling grows from hour to hour. Ideas for expedients come to me (would I be, in my own way, a genius?) Everything becomes easier, if I were one of those little snobs from the Interplanetary School, I would say – but yes – that the world has a bright red color and a resonance of brass...One of the incredible birds of Ready rode around the *RZ-2*. I saw – with my own eyes saw – such an ostrich helping Bill with injections. I'll try to bait this one with some food.

"I have to kill Verne. I don't quite remember why, but it has to be. It will be objected that an astronaut's life is precious. We must act quickly, before the rifle returns."

Here, the confession became delirious:

"That damned stilt-walker has just fled. I tried to appease it, pure loss. In looks like it's scared of me. From something inside of me. Could a bird know...? I shot it. (I thought he was going to yell at Bill... but that's nonsense.) I fired up my close-range blaster and was sure I'd hit him, when suddenly he made a little leap of fire side and hop! No more bird than on my hand. It's infuriating, Bill claims these beasts have intelligence, where do you see intelligence in that...

"Verne is agitated. He repeatedly said the word 'drink' and 'one drinks me', which makes no sense. I don't know why I always feel better about myself. It's all the stranger that I experience an indefinable sensation: it seems to me that people and things, Verne, the moving shadows and I are all bathed in the same lukewarm and slightly viscous liquid, where our movements and even our thoughts reverberate on the airwaves. All of this is, of course, nonsense, but Bill told me about these symbiotic experiences...

"Night falls, when I hear: plop, plop, plop. I leaned over the access hatch. That's it: it's Ready's personal Silicone, I recognize it by its molten gold scar (the medico is very proud of this weld). It walks with a frightened air in the crater, dragging the suction cups of its base which serve as its feet. No doubt he is looking for Bill. The idea occurs to me that I could use Silicone to handle this sacred syringe. I wave to it, then I hail it. I don't know what kind of delicacy the human voice produces in these monsters, but this one began to scoot. There, I think I allowed myself a good joke (Ready claims that minerals are practically immortal); I had the blaster on hand and this scar shone in the moonlight. I fumbled around a bit – my left hand's still clumsy – and then I pulled.

"It's special what happens to me when I shoot. Here, because on Earth I didn't notice anything, I had other concerns. It seems to me that here all the physical perceptions are sharpened, My cracked sides make me suffer a martyrdom. On the other hand, when I do an authoritarian jest or I perform a violent act, it provokes a kind of voluptuousness. Well, it's almost as good as love."

"(...Love. I have in my mouth a bland sensation, a taste of blood. That girl on Titan we chased one night long...when it was my turn, she was still hot. Death? No, I don't believe... Love. Death. That's all there is.)

"A dry explosion: I surely touched the Silicone. It was dark, I couldn't see anything. I was shaking – not with fear, but with excitement. To check, I tumbled into the crater – but yes, of course – the monster had burst into pieces. This obstructed the path dug by the excavator. A faint phosphorescence hovered above that I drank... yes, I drank, with delight. And then, without knowing why, I rolled the excavator without the span."

Above, some hasty, confused notes:

"Ready came back. Scratch at the access lock. Surely didn't notice anything: these young people, hardly observant. Silence. Silence. I must hurry. This influx of strength... my right arm is still immobile, but I can move my fingers. I have to finish with Verne quickly, then I'll go to bed,

I'll look like I'm sleeping and the medicaster didn't notice... that I'm not quite me."

Hands freezing, Angell picked up the last microfilm reel. He recognized Ready's clean, crisp graphics and almost sighed in relief. But from the first lines, the tone darkened.

"Tycho is mad," wrote the little mechanic. "I suppose he had an evil nature, held in check by discipline; under too strong emotions, this sheath cracked. I had in my kit a compound of nitrogen which we call the last chance serum, an invaluable product for an astronaut alone or wounded on a desert asteroid or in the sands of Mars, a marvelous means of euthanasia which we swear never to use only as a last resort. I would never have noticed its disappearance if chance had not led me, on the set, to a mortally wounded bird, the poor beast (should I say beast? Its human head, its claws searching the ground...) was in terrible pain, I wanted to inject her with morphine, I rummaged through my kit and took out the last chance bottle of serum: empty! Seized by a premonition, I ravished running towards the spacecraft.

"The airlock was closed, I had to use my torch to weld the Silicones, to force the lock. Back in the cabin, I found Tycho leaning over Verne's bunk. He was fighting with a hypodermic syringe; the bottle was broken, the serum was leaking. I jumped on our leader and we rolled on the ground. Tycho was dreadful to see, his eyes bulging and his lips foaming; I'm shorter than him, I had to hit with all my might. Fortunately, he is still feeling his injury. Dropping his needle, he flopped against a wall.

" 'Be cursed!' he belched, wiping his bloody mouth. And then: 'I'll move you to the Interplanetary Council;'

" 'Agreed,' I said. 'And Angell, if he ever comes back, because he volunteered to save us. And Verne, if you haven't murdered him.'

" 'No, no!' he whispered. 'I failed the injection. Oh! Bill, it was like poking dead flesh! Nothing is left. He was... like a piece of ice.'

"(I was cold too. Very cold. One of the first tests to recognize organic death indicates: the tissues of a corpse do not retain an injected liquid).

" 'Shut up!' I said authoritatively. 'He was alive when I left. He was better. He even spoke...'

" 'Don't you understand,' moaned Tycho, 'that it wasn't Verne? This thing that drank his life, it settled in him and it watches us all. He infuriated her, because he was still struggling because he was fighting – beyond death! So it looks for other prey – it spreads through the air... I'm telling you, Ready, we'll all perish, if we keep this corpse alive!'

"However, it was no longer a living dead. If Verne had preserved the slightest spark of life, with a drop of the 'last chance serum', his account was good. Besides, at this hour, I vouch for it, he was no more. The 'rigor-mortis' does not deceive and molecular disintegration was already doing its work. Our comrade's wide-open eyes reflected unspeakable horror. I swear I got them shut. I also pulled, piously, on his forehead, the closure of the sleeping bag. Quite a few of ours have no other shroud, spears in space.

"I crushed with my heel the debris of the 'happy death' bottle. Night had fallen, and the robots had to go inside. I went out. Tycho followed me, like a child. He was visibly afraid to be left alone with Verne – and what could I tell him? I hated him.

" 'I didn't kill him,' he repeated. 'Oh! Bill! I don't know what was inside me!'

"It was while moving the excavator that I discovered flint shards and the large black mark left by the use of a molecular weapon. My hands froze and I dared not look at Tycho.

"We were still on the ridge when the access hatch opened slowly, and we saw this inconceivable, unspeakable thing: Verne appeared in front of us.

"He moved with the stiffness of a mechanism and, in his pale face, his eyes, which I had closed, cast a glassy gleam. He had put on his astronaut armor and, under his armpit, the holster of a thermal weapon shone. With each step, his boots made the dull sound of a very heavy robot moving in jerks. This automaton step led him to the exit of the crater.

"I shouted: 'Verne!'

"He didn't turn around. I'm sure he didn't hear me. Could he hear, in the human, earthly sense of the word...? On the embankment, among other machines, the Silicones had placed our helicopter. We saw Verne board without hesitation – and take off. The machine was heading towards the City."

A long interval followed. It was obvious that, for days, deprived of Verne, deprived of the Silicone and Sais, Ready had lost his taste for his notes. Then his graphics resumed:

"This morning, I saw a Mineral lapping, with precautions, around the crater. I thought it was my old Red Hood and I called him. He didn't turn around and disappeared behind the embankment. When I got back into the spaceship, Tycho was there, his blaster in his hand. I should've snatched it from him, but I was so tired! Nothing that happened to us mattered to me. I walked past him saying:

" 'Does it take you back, the urge to kill?'

"Tycho showed his wolf teeth. For a few days he had been doing quite well and had gotten rid of the casts. He asked:

" 'Why do you say that?'

" 'Because you have already used nuclear weapons, and it is expressly prohibited out of regular combat.'

" 'How do you know there was no combat?'

" 'Listen, I say, don't take me for a fool. I can say 'yes, my commander', or 'no, my commander', it doesn't change anything. I know you well enough. At the bottom of the bay there is a charred imprint and a piece of flint. I hope that the other Silicones will not have noticed this.'

" 'And if they noticed it, what do you want me to do?'

" 'Dear and revered Commander,' I exploded, 'there is no need to leave school to know that the less a people has evolved, the less its internal cohesion is strong. A nation is made up of differentiated individuals, but a clan is one body. The primitive species which survive are those which have never allowed one of their own to be sacrificed without avenging it, nor lost without having tried to recover it. Now, what could be more primitive and older than a Silicone?'

" 'You told me they hardly noticed the death of their comrades? Except to cremate them – and again...'

" 'Yes, because this death was in one sense, natural. We, too, bury our dead from old age or illness, but we destroy microbes and gas the murderers.'

"Tycho grimaced a smile:

" 'You'd make an excellent lawyer, Ready. I defend myself alone. Your Silicones, like everyone else, do not support thermal discharges well. Entrenched in the spaceship, with our provisions and our disintegrators, this time we'll not be surprised.'

" 'No,' I said. 'But you forget there is a force that can open the *RZ-2*. Or make us quit. Or I don't know what.'

" 'Yes, when I'm hurt. You forget that I don't have the nerves of the net. I won't open the airlock, even if the cabin seems to be blown up. Even if the water – or the fire – passed through the plates. And even in case Verne – or Angell – or Satan calls us for help, all night long.'

" 'I admire you,' I said, 'but I reserve my opinion. When I see this...'

"I was unfortunately right. There's little time left for me to record the facts which were unfolding at a dizzying pace. The *RZ-2* was no longer – white-hot plates and devices in disarray – just a well-conditioned hell.

"Because they were there, them, the Silicones. And it's time to tell me again (a confidence that Sais slipped into me): they don't understand anything and don't feel anything.

"In complete darkness they invaded the crater *en masse*, and they were accompanied, the periscope showed us, as far as the eye could see a black and brown swarm: the giant beetles moped to the assault in the smell of chitin. We anticipated, against the soundproof walls, the muffled shock of mineral bodies and the rustle of antennae seeking a hold. It was a rush, a hurricane.

"Tycho riddled the air with disorderly S.O.S.s addressed to every-one—to Angell, to Verne, and even to the mysterious Aes, they never re-plied. In intervals, he cursed Walter who had, he said, failed his mission, otherwise we wouldn't be at the mercy of the Silicones. I begged him in vain to interrupt this comedy, humiliating for all of us.

"And suddenly he recovered. It won't have been that bad, our last moments. Me, I still hoped that we were attacked by sensory evils; I sat, motionless, in a corner and I avoided moving, because I felt – I knew – that in the dimensional storm, the slightest movement could bring down a world...

"That's when they brought in the Geckos.

"Prisoners. Skies that they nourish in their undergrounds, with phos-phorus. I thought fire-breathing dragons were legendary. It is not so, it seems. Now the *RZ-2* is a furnace. The micro-steel plates are smoking, and we've spent all our Earth water supplies on them. I... Tycho's very good, true astronaut, it seems that the madness that inhabited him has withdrawn from him. He overhauled our weapons: we still have about ten discharges. It's impossible to bear this infernal heat any longer. Under my hands, the film rolls ignite. Presently, our disintegrators in hand, we'll open the air-lock – and this will be our last fight.

"Long live Earth!

"I'm going to put my notes back in the safe that's still intact. I regret having crushed the bottle of 'happy death.'"

The report ended there.

What followed, Angell never knew if it had been dream or reality. He must have fallen asleep, overcome by fatigue. The face in the microfilm, perhaps he had seen a particularly lucid dream. But he had also been able, falling into an interplane, to be transported to the hall of Aeolian harps, where Aes, motionless and perfect, awaited him on his throne. A green light that was neither day nor night bathed things. In the distance, the innumerable complaints of the lake could be heard.

Angell walked straight up to the tall emerald and black figure with folded wings.

"You made fun of me!" he shouted. "You knew no one wanted to attack Laknea. My mission was useless. The nomads are not those fierce ghosts you showed me, they are simple beings who want to live on the face of this planet. Queen Bellatrix doesn't want war..."

A silence.

A cold breath.

A jet of water cried in a basin of coral.

A frozen voice asked:

"Who is Queen Bellatrix?"

"When you sent me to the Fire People," said Angell, "you knew they had an Earthling at their head. It's because of this that you chose me. You wanted to draw this horde and this naive queen into your nets... And I served you, I who loved her!"

A laugh, weak and cold as at the shiver of water, responds:

"I do not know what fire phantom or what female lizard has charmed your nights. Your earthly aberrations are not our forte."

"Well," said Angell. "I've completed your mission. What have you done with my comrades?"

"According to our conventions, I left these entities free in their spacecraft," said Aes sharply. "These beings have killed each other. Do you want to know the details? The one you called 'your commander' injected your second in command with a dose of nitrogen-based poison: the man died instantly. After which, seized with furious madness, the fanatic fired at our wings, Pselles and Silicones, and he ended up turning his weapon against himself. We had to send minerals to capture it. The fight was murky. I do not know the fate of the last Earthman..."

"This is how you present it!"

"This is how things happened. Unfortunately, your spacecraft has been destroyed."

"Not to the degree you'd hoped," Angell said. "Not to the point of destroying the testimonies of your victims. Bill Ready recorded the events and I have the notes on this tragedy at hand. My comrades are dead, as Earthmen. But you will answer for this crime before the cosmos!"

267

He had his hand on the disintegrator. He walked on the throne. A harmonious voice, singularly sweet, stopped him:

"Is it a characteristic of Earthmen to be mad?" he asked. "Can we not speak as intelligent beings according to our kind, Angell? Don't think you're scaring me, while you're threatening me, I'm a hundred leagues from here: we easily delegate our shadows. Your comrades were only sad brutes, but you... you awakened something in me that I had never known before, an attraction made up of curiosity, of similarity almost. No, it's not what you on Earth call 'friendship' – that lame feeling... it's deeper. I found in you the features of a complete being – of my negative double. It's quite simple: if I had desired a being or a thing, I would believe I possessed it through you."

"But you wouldn't have it!" threw Angell. "I'm more than sick of your symbiosis games! Don't try to create this troubled, hundred-dimensional climate in which you indulge, you Aquatics. You are you, and I am me. And the best proof is that I'm going to kill you. Like a dog. I apologize to the beasts!"

He was facing the green and black throne. He raised and fired his weapon. In the smaragdite stream, the ideal form seemed to split and for the infinitesimal fraction of an instant, he saw in place of Aes a slender shape, a dazzling whiteness... He had taken me no less. Thermal blaster flashes. When the cloud dissipated a large black trace marked the marble strewn with debris

From far away, the caressing voice spoke:

"Poor panicked Earthman, this is not how we are killed! You have, of course, a formidable weapon, but you do not know how to handle it. We are soul, energy and matter – double or triple – and you cannot knock everywhere.

"But I am overwhelmed, I am overjoyed: by your behavior, you have just revealed to me the master qualities that I covet. One day will come, my thirst will be quenched at this source. Your comrades really disillusioned me, they were weak or not very generous. With you, I will drink from the very cup of Sol III..."

The voice died away, it had been the music itself. Angell passed a wandering hand over his eyelids: strangely this tone, this sound had just evoked before him the camp of the Barbarians, the high flames in the green evenings, the smell of honey and bitter herbs...

And Bellatrix.

Bellatrix...

This name was a powerful help to him. Without knowing how, a moment later, he found himself in the underground, on the little pink square; he was almost sure he was dreaming, but his hand was still tensing on the hot butt of his weapon.

An uncertain light filtered through the skylight.

Angell very gently woke Sais who was sleeping on the mats, curled up in her plumage. He took the silver crested head, so human, by the temples and looked into the wide-open golden eyes.

"Listen, Sais," he said, "I'm going to ask you some very simple questions. But your answers depend on my life and the future of Gamma."

"Your life!" Sais fluted. She was shaking. If his girlfriend had been a human woman, Angell would have understood long ago that she was in love with him and jealous, to death. But she was only a winged Pselle, and he questioned her as such:

"Aes doesn't exist, does it?"

"Yes. Yes, there is. When I lean over the lake, I see him there."

"It's just a reflection. He has no distinct life."

"If a boat can break it. You can love him or hate him."

"And Aessa?"

"Energy is double: positive and negative, male and female. Aessa exists, as much as Aes."

"Are they brother and sister?"

"They are... dual. I do not know any more. They are what they are. Oh! Do not ask me anything more! Oh! I am scared!"

"Well," said Angell. "I guess we're being listened to. Let's talk about something else. Can Silicones project sensory images?"

The Air Pselles' extraordinary contempt for Silicones restored Sais' confidence.

"Of course not! They can hit, break, destroy. Even the Air People are only able to excite – a little – their brains."

"So, if you heard that the Silicones walk preceded by images, would that mean that a Force opens the way for them?"

"Yes."

"And the Geckos? Is there an alliance between Silicones and Geckos?"

Sais looked at him, as if he had said something enormously stupid:

"What do you mean? They never meet. No Silicone has ventured into the Diamond Mountains. And no one from the Fire People has ever come to the shores of the Lake."

"Nobody, really? How do you explain this?"

"I do not know," said Sais, after a silence. "There is something stopping them on their way. They are furious, they rise like a wave, they invade the plain and then..."

"Yes?"

"They never arrive."

Angell felt a cold sweat at his temples...

"But they leave anyway," he said.

"Oh! Yes, we captured their Lightning Man! But since time; they have a short memory, you know, they start to forget. There is no danger there." Obviously, Sais no longer understood Angell's thoughts very well, she looked him in the eye, with a humility, an adoration; and suddenly she cried: "Yes, but today there is you!"

"You mean that..."

"Oh! Yes. They recognized you! Do you believe that they would have accepted you in their camp, if you had not carried the signs? You had the dazzling weapon and the crown, clothes of a prince and the hair of honey! And their queen loves you! Do you know what they called you? Rigel, because they believe that the stars are male and female and that Rigel is husband of Bellatrix, like Al-Nilam that of Betelgeuse. Oh! I now understand why Aes sent you to the Diamond Mountains!

"You're very smart, you know. It wasn't so long ago that I figured it out myself. I thought I was fulfilling a mission to serve a peace project, in reality I was myself a bait and a hook. That a fish had this idea, that shouldn't surprise us, shouldn't it?"

Angell's voice was so bitter that Sais hid her head in her blue plumage, but he pulled himself together and continued:

"Well," he said. "Let's admit that it wasn't the Fire Barbarians who wanted to attack the very wise and very human species of the Waters, but that the Masters of the Lake were trying to catch the savages in their traps. But this enormous human and animal mass, these Geckos, these Primates, these Defectors whose number they've never been able to know, they crushed Laknea just by walking! How do they plan to kill them?"

"Kill them?" wondered Sais. "Who ever said...? They lure them into the area of the Waters to use them, that's all."

She repeated the very words of Aes, bringing to this enormity the good faith of a quiet bird who no longer realizes, among the frightful dangers that mark out her life, what is – or is not – monstrous. She explained:

"The Fire People possess, in quantity, one thing that the Aquatics covet. And they have the means to strip them completely. After which... well, I suppose the Ertosi are no longer to be feared. Not at all."

"What is it about?" asked the Earthman, short.

"But... of Life!" Sais answered.

He bumped into that wall again: foreign conceptions! Ideas from another planet! They didn't want to kill the Barbarians, but simply take their lives. His head was spinning, he punched the plaster.

"Why do you stop?" said Sais. "You know this wealth, since you possess it. Everything is double, like lightning that burst in the clouds. One holds positive energy, the others are negative. Do you know that the Aquatics, for wanting to keep life too long in their hands, no longer have enough to feed it? Their Presents, their Silicones, all of that would disintegrate if they were not nourished with vital energy. It has different shapes, of course. For Silicones, it's easy: gamma rays are enough for them. But there is the soul itself..."

"Tell me about it."

"But I do not know anything!" Sais groaned. Her elegant skeleton haloed in azure braced itself anxiously. "And if I had known, I would have forgotten everything! We winged Pselles, we are only allowed to live because we have neither memory nor will. Thereby..."

"Yes," replied Angell, cursing a necessary cruelty, "you are only beasts, you do not know how to desire or love. You were just a little spy among a thousand, who was sent to distract me and dig into my brain and who, today, brought me back for the torture... How could I believe different!"

"Me!"

Sais, angered, threw herself against the man's chest. Her egret passed through red, orange and violet flames, and her whole slender being quivered. As he pushed her away, without harshness, she straightened up and sang – and he recognized the short, desperate melody that once haunted the woods by the Lake:

"Me! Me, Earthman! So you believed that Ary – that I... that we were just that! Oh! You are breaking my heart! Oh! I love you so much! Because my body blooms into feathers and I fly, do you think Bellatrix of the Primates is the only human female in this universe? But we, Winged Pselles, the Sylphs, are the oldest and purest race! Ary and I came from the oldest royal nest! I accepted all the humiliations and all the terrors, to follow you,

I even betrayed my people that misfortunes will now overwhelm; and all this why? Because I love you! I love you!"

"You say it," Angell said, reluctantly. "You were dear to me, Sais, and Ary too. I wouldn't have left you on the road injured, nor on the edge of a trap, without warning you. This is how you act towards me. You have a secret that could save me. And you keep it."

"What do you want to know?"

"Life Mother, what is it?"

The vast golden pupils closed, and Sais slid down at his feet.

"Put your hand on my heart, under the feathers," she whispered. "Hear how it beats: it's for you, Oh! I know what you're thinking! 'It's a pretty animal creature!' But I will prove to you that I know how to love. Listen: the life-mother, is there... the plasma. It is the prime cell that they recreated in the abyss of the seas, from a virus. That which absorbs, nourishes, reproduces. But I think they have gone too far – they can't do anything halfway – they have given it a diabolical intelligence; or, perhaps, being the work of their hands and the counterfeit of a higher work, it had to possess it. I do not know.

"It lives in the Temple. There is a chasm under the altar. It is there. It is a huge protoplasmic mass whose nucleus projects sensory images and Aes. The Aquatics maintain it, like an oil lamp, with multiple animal lives. Our people serve almost exclusively for this purpose. But to operate what they call a discharge, animate corpses or generate new life, it reclaims the strength and warmth of human beings. Young and violent beings, like Barbarians. Or you Earthmen. I think it likes it better. It eats better.

"So it takes on exceptional strength. It brings its victims to the peak of their cerebral, emotional and physical faculties, to their greatest intensity – hate or love. It presents them with various faces, it becomes wave, perfume and music. I have been told that this game amused it prodigiously."

"So," Angell muttered between his teeth, "it would promise an Earth crew possible return to Earth? Tycho had a rush of Silicones? And maybe to me Bellatrix...?"

"Maybe," Sais whispered. "Then it drinks from this cup. The living being, its principle, will join it and merge into it, it seizes its forces and its memories. Then it lets the dead body fall, empty..."

"Well, I have told you everything I know, A-n-gell. And now, me too, they will make me die..."

She sagged at his feet, like a light fleece of feathers.

CHAPTER X

Bill Ready wanted to straighten up and banged his neck against the rock. He was enclosed, inserted in a rock gangue. The darkness around him was opaque and almost tangible. He tried to convince himself that it was his first night in captivity, that he had just been transported under the lake and that all those dreadful adventures: Verne, the attack of the beetles, Tycho firing until he stopped to have only one white blaze discharge from the nuclear weapon, and this body pulverizes, disappearing in a flash, while widening on the ground a large pool of blood... blood... blood... that all that, after all, was only a nightmare from which he was waking up.

"I'm sleeping," he thought. "When I open my eyes, there will be a red skylight up there. I will hear Tycho swear. The Silicones will pass with their carts. Since in this world things may not have been, why shouldn't it be the first night?"

But a touch of blood-sticky feathers and a faint rattle rising from the depths taught him that not everyone could juggle dimensions. Obviously, the jail was full to bursting. The company of Sais and the Silicones having considerably developed his telepathic faculties, Bill tried to orient himself. Slow, heavy thoughts trailed at the bottom of the well. Were there only Birds and Simians? As he mentally concentrated on an image of escapism, of open air, a wave of good company, of a moderate expression reached him:

"There's no way out of here," assured the stranger. "Except for a hatch that opens onto the arena. It is through this that we'll leave, alas! As soon as possible, I hope."

Multiple and variable voices moaned.

"Who are you to speak an Earth language?" asked Bill, dumbfounded. Unexpected and shocking in this low pit bottom that smelled of blood, animal sweat and filth, sounded a light laugh:

"I'm what's called a Regressive Mutant – and that's not your planet's dialect, is it? Your brain just sent me the image of a green ball spinning around a tiny sun..."

"What's a Regressive Mutant?" Bill asked.

"Oh! I suppose a character who returns to the beasts."

"It doesn't look like it. You're telepathic."

"I'm a Blue Mutant. An Aquatic gone wrong," the wave explained kindly. "Don't move like a top, I'm under your feet."

"How did you come to be here? I beg your pardon if I trample on you."

"It's nothing. Actually, you're right, I shouldn't be here. Neither should you. They pile up here the wild Air Pselles, Birds and Simians captured in the woods, sometimes even Primates. But never an Aquatic or a Voyager. We have failed badly, you and I. May I know what are you being blamed for?"

"I really don't know," Bill replied frankly. "We were shipwrecked on Gamma and there was even talk, at a certain point, of letting us go again. And then, the Silicones invaded our spaceship and my commander fired on them..."

"Where is he?"

"He had time to commit suicide."

"I see," said the other after reflection. "One of you must have learned things that are not good to know."

"I would like someone to tell me what!" Bill exclaimed. "Don't you find it vexing to be at the bottom of a pit, because of discoveries that you don't know? And you, why are you here?"

A silence. Then a little sigh, a flutis.

"There you go," said the stranger, "Milly answered you. Milly is a white Simian who lost her coat by mutation. Progressive mutant and regressive mutant, our paths have met. I am here because of her and she because of me. It's silly, right?"

"It's nice," said Ready. "But that doesn't advance us. Do you think we'll be made to fight saurians or pythons?"

"Or seahorses – or lampreys. The games vary, but the outcome does not," said the mutant philosophically. "I've been there for three days, the bottom rows are gone. Tomorrow or tonight, it will be our turn."

"But," exclaimed the Irishman, "since you're a fish-man, I apologize, I meant an Aquatic, you must have their faculties! They do things over time..."

"Life-Mother! What are you asking me? I suppose on Earth there are people who sculpt, or paint, or compose music, and others don't? Some of us can turn the fourth dimension around like a glove; only a few and it is an upper caste. They have their secrets. It is probably that you walked in their flowerbeds?"

"Do you know Aes?" Ready asked.

Another silence, followed by sniffles, told the earthling that Simians sometimes cried. Then, below, a mineral crunch announced that a wall had slipped somewhere and a large scaly body fell. A terrible howl arose, revealing such physical anguish that Bill closed his eyes and cowered in the dark. Milly was sobbing.

"It wasn't our turn yet," announced the faint voice. "There, there, don't cry like that, Milly..." And, changing wave: "It seems that 'they' threw a big lizard on their head... they 'sometimes' get angry these last days. Now it's our turn, comrade. There are three rows left in front of me. If I go out before you, take care of Milly."

"But anyway," cried the little Irishman fiercely, "we're not going to leave to death like that, without trying something? We're not a flock of sheep!"

"I've never met a sheep," mused the Aquatic, "but I don't see what we could do?" Variable voices were complaining. He continued: "The pits are a little wider at the bottom, here we're crammed together at twenty; in front of us, the sliding wall reveals a gully where three wouldn't enter abreast. The only exit leads to the arena and you immediately have a bat or a good-sized saurian on your neck..."

"But where do the prisoners come from?"

"Like you, from above. I don't think you can go back up, the walls are smooth and you probably have a dozen newcomers on your head. Am I right?"

"Yes."

"So do like us. Let's wait our turn."

The hoarse sigh of a hairy simian mingles with the moans of more frail shadows. An exhausted body sagged against Bill's side. A panicked bird cackled. Then there was silence again, opaque despair, the expectation of death.

"I believe," the Mutant announced after listening, "that the last game is over, nothing more is being extended. We still have one night ahead of us. Do you feel uncomfortable?"

"I remember," said Bill, "I studied in time, among many other useless things, the songs of primitive peoples – on Earth, of course. These people only knew a few notes that they varied and stretched to infinity: this gave bizarre effects, quite nauseous, and – I realize now – a certain realism. *'Oh! night – and you, one night, and you, one more night!'* they sang. Believe me if you want, it doesn't make me want to laugh."

"Me neither," the Mutant conceded, "especially since it reminds me of the upper caste hymns. In short, the cosmos is a small thing! The last time I heard these laments, we were lying in a boat, Milly and I, the water smelled of honey among the water lilies, they didn't have time to wither on the lake and we..."

A sharp screech interrupted him. The voices choked in their throats. The end, Bill thought, this was the end... They waited for what was to come – a fall, a cry. But nothing came. And, leaning over the shoulder of a hairy Pselle, Ready saw a faint light at the end of a corridor and he heard a familiar plop plop plop.

A Silicone was coming, with a cart.

He rolled, with the indifference and insensitivity of Silicones, compressing roughly the living mass in front of him, and only stopped at the level of the earthling. No words were exchanged, since Silicones are silent just as well, and Bill dropped into the cart. But his hand gripped a soft fur and he whispered to the Mutant:

"Lie down."

They weren't only three to imitate piled up corpses. When the Silicone backed up, he must have found his truck a little heavy. But he showed nothing of it, and Bill was able to console himself for the ingratitude of the evolved beings, by noticing on the two faces of the mineral pyramid flows of molten silver with which he cauterized the itching of his friends.

The Silicone demoted, with its same obtuse air, as if it had absolutely no idea that it was walking backwards, the doors slid open and a few seconds later, the cart and its load found themselves in the white arena, under the icy glitter of Rigel.

Bill raised himself slightly and looked between two Bird's wings: a purple and orange evening was falling. A crowd of Minerals, harnessed to their carts, crisscrossed the white marble floor, carrying away debris and corpses or collecting small kegs of blood. Others opened floodgates and ran large rakes and esperiopsis sponges over the flagstones, and all this work of clearing and cleaning had the most bourgeois air.

Those who carried the corpses passed in front of a turnstile where a larger Silicone sprinkled the carts with a jet of quicklime. Bill's heart sank, but the decidedly distracted silver controller poured his jet aside, scorching only a few feathers. The Itchy Silicone sank with his peculiar grace, in a three-meter-wide trench that was lost in the night. "He's going to the dump," Bill thought. "They're going to throw us into some hole. It's all a nightmare..." Another glance over the fake corpses revealed to him that the wheelbarrow was rolling over a precipice.

The triple moon rose. She bathed in her whiteness little Milly, soft as flower petals, and sparkled on the short red fleece of her neck. Milly hugged a slender blue youthful body.

The wheelbarrow passed a second turnstile, unattended, and suddenly rolled over stony ground. The fake corpses, half a dozen in number, ended up on the ground. There was a big black half-ape, who turned out to be not an Air Pselle, but a Primate, two bewildered Birds, the Aquatic, his friend and Bill. The helpful Silicone had dumped them all into a small ravine, and with an inexpressive screeching he stalked away, waddling with his own grace.

"He said," the Aquatic translated as he stood up, "that he hated things getting lost – unnecessarily."

The survivors had no weapons and very few clothes. Hunger twisted their stomachs, and thirst corroded their throats. They held council in the hollow of the rock. Above them bats hovered on their membranous wings, the sentinels of Laknea calling out to each other in the dark. With their usual inconsistency, the Birds decided to return to the forest: they had already forgotten why and how they had been imprisoned and they hoped that no one would remember. The Primate growled, sniffed the air, then, rolling his bloody eyes, he pointed out to the vast steppe. He avoided the Aquatic's gaze and addressed Ready. The fish-man explained:

"He invites you to join his people, that is to say the Ertosi. They are wild, smell bad, eat pell-mell game, simians and birds, but they have some reverence for travelers."

"Will you come with me?" Bill asked.

"Why not?" said the Aquatic. "Milly without coat is not very well seen by her people, and I...don't talk about it. But you know, the road will be hard."

"Never mind," said Bill. "I don't think it could be worse than the well where..." He didn't finish, he thought of Tycho and Verne. He tried to reassure himself, telling himself that he might meet Angell at the end of his mission. In any case, he could not stay in this ravine. He gallantly offered his arm to Milly, and the little group, which included an Earthman, a humanoid ape, a progressive simian and a Mutant, looking like a handsome newt, set off across the desert of ashes, towards the unknown.

What that trip was, Bill wouldn't tell in any bar in any world. They walked. The flints hurt their bleeding feet, and Milly dressed their wounds with plants she knew. They burned in the merciless sun by day and shivered in the bitter cold at night. They drank water from small brackish ponds and ate roots. Having captured a child grasshopper one meter long, they ate its haunches grilled over a fire of thorns and were cruelly ill, because this bland flesh was inedible.

Bill suffered perhaps more than anyone else, for the Primate was constantly buoyed by the hope of seeing his loved ones again and sniffed the air wildly. Milly and her Aquatic, at each stop, looked for a hollow in the sand, a bush, and they fell into each other's arms. They were so ingenuously in love that one could not talk reason to them; and that was obviously the only regressive symptom in Ao (this was more or less the fish-man's name). Milly, wrapped in a reed loincloth, was fresh as a cucumber.

But Ready, within days, was slimmed down and black, his plastic jumpsuit was falling apart and his abrasions were festering. He tried not to think of his missing companions, of the spacecraft, of Earth, but came back to them constantly, sadly. There were days when the meagre attentions of his new comrades got on his nerves. They were very nice, okay! But Harr, the Primate, under his lanugo, walked bent to the ground, he swung his long arms and spoke in grunts! Milly looked like a pussycat that would be naked and the man-fish, well! It was among these monsters that he was going to live henceforth, without hope of return!

They walked like this for a time he refused to appreciate and finally reached the foot of the mountains where an Ertosian patrol fell back on them. Without the presence of Harr, the Primate, they were lost. But, having made acquaintance, Ready was received with touching regard. As he could no longer stand on his swollen and bleeding feet, they made him a litter with branches on which he allowed himself to hoist Milly.

But it was his last conscious act, after which fatigue and fever took over and he was delirious for days.

He only regained his senses when, gently inclined on the shoulders of four Barbarians, his stretcher began to scale the first pass of the Diamond Mountains. The viscous heat of the lake and the dryness of the plain afterword were only a bad memory. Here, under an almost mauve sky, the freshness of the peaks, the fluid smell of mugwort and honey, the shade of tall resin-coated pines, the rhythm and noise of the marching patrol, powerfully reminded a little Irishman an Earth he had never known well, a planet of dawn spoken of in poems and songs. Buried in the furs his rescuers had thrown over him, he wept, mostly in spite, at the thought that

Verne, Tycho, and, probably, Angell, would never see this Earth again, and then he felt sorry for himself.

But at the first stop, Milly and an adolescent primate came to bring him a jug of lygodactyl milk which advantageously replaced cows, and the simian Pselle declared to him that the Barbarians were charming people, that it was wrong to fear them and that if they burned everything and anything on their way, it was laughing at a religion and not natural wickedness. The Aquatic had taught his companion to form rather complex mental images and she did not hesitate to do so.

"You see," she said, sitting on the edge of Bill's litter, and swinging her pretty legs, "fire to them is like air to us, or water to the Aquatics. It's their life. Finally, I understand myself. They venerate the embers and an old sword hidden under a tent which is their temple. A light that kills springs from it, so it is placed under the surveillance of the priests, before being handed over to the queen..."

"A queen!" Ready came alive, for the first time in many days. "A primate or a simian?"

"Neither," said Milly disdainfully, considering the smooth skin of her own hands. "First, she has no fleece. She has just a tail of red hair, but the rest of her skin is whiter than mine. It was the warriors who told me, and they saw her. She is... how do you say? Beautiful as the day star, so her name is Bellatrix."

"This star towards which we were going..." muttered the superstitious Irishman.

From then on, he never stopped until the patrol reached the camp. And he didn't stink any more, not at all. Since these people had a queen they could talk to, Angell had certainly contacted her, and he trusted Angell. On the sixth or perhaps the seventh day of the journey, a dull noise filled the mountains – the rolling of wheeled carts, the cracking of great pine trunks in the braziers, the bellowing of Saurians and the vast, slow melipe of Primates. The porters quickened their pace, and Ready, seated on the litter, encouraged them with cries. It was a bizarre sight to see this little man, red and sallow, whose hair and beard had grown out of proportion and surrounded his sharp features with a halo, restless and hopping above the placid giants.

When they crossed the pass, Ready saw that they weren't the only arrivals. All the parades disgorged rows of carts stretched with skins, riders appeared on flying lizards, war chariots to which someone had recently adapted the cogwheel projected showers of sparks and quartz debris. They

279

were all descending towards the Secret Valley. Pinned down in the crowd, the patrol had to stop and, despite Bill's impatience, the Barbarians acted calmly, according to their Barbarian code, they jumped down from their onagers and their buffalo and joined the other clans to light their pyre.

A thousand fires were bursting on the distant peaks. Reflected by the crystal slopes, their pink flame created new dawns. Between the unharnessed carts, the geckos rolled on the ground, the tamed wolves gnawed the bones, the female primates suckled their young, and the great nomads, stretched out, their arms behind their necks, in attitude of stone recumbents, played syrinx where their sad and slow songs sang, like the ebb of the ocean, sometimes swirling and ferocious like the wind in the steppe.

Suddenly, the rumor spread that a "lightning man" was haunting the camp. His presence was immediately considered a good omen, some priests came to observe him from afar and Ertosi warriors brought him the best pieces of grilled meat. This diversion was fortunate, for Harr had plunged and disappeared into his native element and Milly, with the versatility of Pselles, chattered among a herd of barbarous girls; Ao and Ready found themselves a bit left out.

Bill feared at first that the Ertosians were hostile to his companion, but the nomads seemed benevolent and even friendly! He discovered the reasons for their attitude by leaning down to drink from a copper vessel. Reflected by the dark water, he saw before him neither an Aquatic nor an Earthling: he himself had made himself a tunic of cheetah skin and braided his hair in the shape of a red tail; his broken chest armor revealed red hair to the delight of the primates. In addition – a sign of solar favor – freckles dotted his face. To imitate them the priests smeared themselves with dung. The effect wasn't so beautiful.

Ao had kept his loincloth of scales, but the cold was sharp, he threw on his shoulders a snow leopard fur. Under the action of the sun and the wind his skin was tanned, his muscles had hardened and he looked like a handsome, wild youth. However, he had confessed to Ready his age: three hundred years.

Squatting near the fire, he kept on his knees a harpoon with the tip of stabilized plutonium, a terrible weapon whose attack was not forgiving. Bill reproached him for this:

"Why do you need this dangerous thing? We're among our friends!"

"Of course!" The Aquatic shrugged. "Well-armed friends, judging by their methane bags and fire engines. One of these days, they will rise, and we will be obliged to participate in their antics: nothing is as demanding as the friendship of a Primate."

Softened by the gentle warmth of the hearth, Ready asked:

"Do you think they will fight? And with who?"

"These are," replied Ao, "two questions not to be confused. Do you hear their songs? They say the Pi-Rhe people go with the fire and the wind. It's in the nature of people who walk to come up against some wall. Judging by your school memories, Earth history is littered with such examples. You have your Fire People..."

"We had Goths and Huns," Ready conceded, "of whom Herodotus said, it seems to me, 'those barbarians who are good in slavery and bad in freedom'. Unless it was Julius Cesar, the other colonialist. But the free Ertosians seem very sympathetic to me. Also, remember that the Huns lived some two thousand years ago!"

"Your evolution," replied Ao, "was more harmonious, but why speak of such ancient peoples? Haven't you come up against more recently, after the breathing barrier and the sound barrier, that of time? There's nothing to be ashamed of, these facts confirm the vitality and genius of your race."

"I think," he resumed, "that if the inhabitants of Gamma, instead of bombarding their own planet first, and then sinking into singular practices, had directed their attention towards infinity like you, we would not be here, warming ourselves with a meager fire, wondering what new apocalypse is going to fall on our heads. But these are just pure speculations."

"Your second question requires less philosophical development. Against whom will these sympathetic Barbarians fight? Of course, not against the Winged Pselles; and the Silicones, if they know how to take them, will follow them, carts and all. There is on the face of Gamma, only one powerful empire, dark, elusive, full of treasures and founded on laws against nature – that is to say in diametrical opposition to the Fire Peoples."

"Rest assured that we will fight against Aes..."

"And you don't mind?" Ready approached. "After all, it's your king and your country."

"Did I tell you that I will fight against Laknea? Of course, in a calamity such as war, and civil war, the Water People will suffer. But they may be saved. The survivors will no longer look at the light with dead pupils...In any case, for the good of worlds without number, the empire of Aes must cease to exist. It's a monstrous anomaly in space and time and I don't want my children growing up in its shadow."

"Because," he added, with a little fearful pride, "you must have noticed that Milly is pregnant? Yes, my little old man. It seems that, having left the empire, the Aquatics once again become 'men like the others'. It is also possible that I died earlier, to have entered death-conception cycle. But whatever? It will be a small blue Pselle or white Fishman. When our races mingle, bringing into this fusion their essential qualities – the Aquatics their science and the Barbarians their virility – the world will be ours!"

"You mean Gamma," Bill corrected, "because, otherwise, you still hit a few barriers! In any case, my friend, I congratulate you."

"It's that you become a Barbarian, to live near these fires," Ao noted philosophically. "Yes, you are right, everything needs a brake."

And he went to find Milly, whom the female primates taught to milk aphids.

Night had fallen in the meantime. Around pyres, blooming in scarlet roses, the warriors rejoiced like children, they jumped, howled and deserved their nickname of 'fire demons'. Curled up in his furs, Bill thought that the fourth element had both metaphysical and carnal value for the nomads, it defended the Horde against a hostile world; during long cold seasons, it was warmth and joy, it made meats tasty and awakened a sweet joy on the surface. But it was also the supreme purifier and the memory of an abominable disaster.

Fire was birth and death, the beginning and end of the cycle, the atomic cataclysm and the bright sun of Bellatrix...

It was on this consoling idea that Bill Ready fell asleep.

"What did I tell you yesterday?" Ao asked with a look of grim triumph. "There is a festival in the village: it is the Benediction of the Swords. Put on your cheetah, a cock of the rock feather behind the ear wouldn't be out of place. Hurry up, we are invited to the ceremony."

The Earthman was still weak, and Ao carried him, like a child, up a hill. Sitting on the moss, Bill saw: the nomads had grouped themselves with their tents and their carts in a huge circle, with a pagoda-like building as their center. Large sections of orphraze fabric, probably removed in the aquatic cities, and white furs formed the enclosure. An altar of a block of smaragdite, erected in front, supported a kind of sparkling tank – the ancient coffin work.

Ready noticed that around him, the Barbarians had made themselves beautiful, braiding their hair with sheep fat and the extract of aromatic herbs, showing off rare furs and loincloths of iridescent scales. Some had planted on their foreheads clavicorn horns or a bronze helmet, the sum of a gecko's head. Women wore headdresses of feathers and cut-crystal amulets, and Bill trembled for the sensitivity of his aquatic friend (assuming he had any): the most becoming tunic was cut from a translucent undercut reminiscent of Laknea. Primates and Progressive Mutants were often beautiful, in their robust form, free stature and harmonious gestures. Ready admired the fruitfulness of the Horde: there were more children than adults and some were charming.

But at the bottom of the slopes, in the heart of the Secret Valley, swarmed beastly masks, trunks covered with rough horns, beating caudal appendages to slice a man lengthwise, opening muzzles that could have spat flames.

Ready shuddered.

Eighteen giants who represented according to Ao the eighteen barbarian tribes (unless these were 'the houses' where the sun of Gamma dwelt) ascended to the altar and bent their knees. They were young. (Bill thought he hadn't seen any underage yet.) Their loose hair fluttered in the wind, as did the manes of their helmets. There were seven black with fleece and skin, seven tawny, with pale eyes, four finally, affected by some crossing with the Aquatics, wore hair like seaweed – smooth and green. All of them with the same gesture turned towards the tent and drawing their naked swords, rested the point on the ground.

"It means," Ao whispered, "that this 'peaceful' people (he had read the term in Bill's brain) will defend with the sword what they conquered with the sword."

"On Earth, very good people have already proclaimed it," said Ready. "On Earth a thousand years ago."

And then he no longer listened: he was all about the show. Below, the people modulated their high plaint. A side of the tent was lifted, and priests appeared. These, Bill thought, were all alike with sixfold tiaras, their bodies adorned with amulets and their ritual gestures: a Celt or a German from Earth would have recognized them. They are a Scythian. (But Ready knew little of the Scythians who, under the leadership of a wild and beautiful maiden, six hundred years before the so-called Christian era, invaded the ancient world.) He simply realized, with a shudder, this truth: on all the globes of the universe, the behavior of humanoids is similar, hence this slow, wavering and full of pitfalls, which resembles the Stations of the Cross. Man falls, gets up and falls again... It doesn't matter, if he fulfils his destiny.

Suddenly he heard a cry. The procession was coming in front of him! the sages advanced slowly, carrying on a litter of purple corollas, an oblong object, wrapped in a faded fabric, but still scintillating. From the shape, it was a sword...The Sword. And when they placed it on its moonstone base and stepped back, with the signs of the greatest respect, Bill could not doubt: the magic weapon was nothing more than a mere Earth blaster!

The choirs, however, told the legend: the Lightning Man came from the skies to save his people and roamed the air on board a silver bird, the wise laws he had promulgated, the prohibitions which had saved the species. The voices of men and women alternated, then they united in a brilliant hymn, they glorified the divine descent, the Daughter of the Stars, the Avenger, the Warrior Queen, Bellatrix, the face of the sun given to the people of Fire.

Ao's hand had tightened on Ready's shoulder and one last time he translated, with his moderate triumph:

"They say... the stars have spoken. And that there will be war."

Three times the hollow horns pronounced the name. And the royal tent opened again. Prostrate with the others, facing the earth, the incorrigible Irishman risked a glance towards the heavens.

He saw, on a brazen shield carried by the warriors with green hair, a slender figure entirely sheathed in gold leaf. A mask of the same material was crowned with a tiara of emeralds. This inhuman face united the characteristics of the four races of Gamma, it was enigmatic and terrible like the planet itself. Necklaces and chains of diamonds, huge space crystals streamed on the breastplate, iridescent, sparkled, so that under the rays of the sun reflected a thousand times, this idol was only a gem, only a drop of solar dew, than a star.

The Sages brought the magic weapon to She who was worthy to carry it. And, raising the Earth blaster with both hands, Bellatrix blesses her people.

An immense cheer lifted the camp, whipped the crystal mountains, filled the vast coffers of the chests and the deep defiles. The Queen pointed the sacred weapon in front of her. Her voice sounded clear:

"We are men as they are! Onto the People of the Waters! Up to the soul-mother!"

CHAPTER XI

Bill took a hit when she refused to receive him. But after all, she was queen, and he, an unfortunate mechanic. However, he was selling Earth... The thing seemed to him a bad omen. But, bearers of refusal, the priests were no less burdened with good words and gifts, among other things, the queen offered her guest a small tent made of tanned skins, stretched over the wicker bungs, and a sleeping bag, stuffed with down, a marvel. It was, in any case, an invitation to stay, and the Fire Peoples performed a dance around the igloo.

The Horde showed a singular ease in assimilating the most diverse elements: Earthlings or Lizards, winged Pselles, simian Pselles and even Fish-men. (Like the flame, thought Ready, always like the flame that does not reason...) For his knowledge of the terrain Ao received the title of Royal Guide.

The two friends rarely saw each other. The days flowed like a torrent, and Ao was the first to stop counting them. He would travel on the back of a gecko or a flying beetle to some distant plateau where new tribes joined him; he then happened to walk for a long time, at the head of the riders, with his slippery Aquatic gait; bronze, his blue hair flowing in the wind, nothing distinguished him from the young Primates any more, except his stature and this elegant bearing which they sought to imitate.

Ao walked, and the human river flowed down the slopes. The reed flutes, bagpipes and terrible little tambourines made of tortoiseshell resounded in the distance, the geckos raised clouds of dust and whirlwinds of sparks; the Barbarians dreamed of the long paths in the steppe where corymb mingles with absinthe, where the flowering hawthorns spread its fine scent, of the hunts and pursuits of fearful or ferocious game; all their simple riches poured into the guide's brain: tactile, precise sensations, sounds, colors and perfumes – the vision of the pyres at evening, and the wide chants of the clan, the smell of smoke and skewered meats, or pearls a unique rose drop of fresh blood, the taste of wild honey on the girls' chapped lips... Ao, who readily called Milly "my reward and my despair" or even "jungle of my tenderness", envied the Barbarians for being so fully and so violently happy.

It was then that the thing happened, as he had just led the vanguard to the Plain of Ashes.

Evening was falling, mauve and orange, with the softness of ripe fruit. Where the quartz rocks limited the grey sands, the guide had to stop on a last cliff – and it was sudden. He felt an icy chill in his chest and in the air, a known, familiar, forgotten threat... His handsome face convulsed, raising his hand he was going to scream... Suddenly he understood, the gesture and the cry were useless: the Horde walks like fire and wind, it is its reason for living, and it trusts in its gods.

How to tell them: "Stop! Retrace your steps! This milestone passed, you fall into the power of a terrible force! This flat plain as far as the eye can see and this firm ground is a trap. Behind these thickets there is nothing. It's the end of the world, at least for you..." A leaden shroud fell on Ao's bare shoulders; it seemed to him that someone was laughing at him in the darkness: the word for "end of the world" does not exist in the Ertosi language.

They passed in front of him, all of them.

("I couldn't have held them back," he thought later, flabbergasted. "Even if I had rolled under the claws of the Geckos: they would've quietly passed over me, they're used to it. Besides, how could they have could believe? There was neither swamp nor fault in front of us. The bare plain extended, just veiled at times by fine ashy waterspouts. We could see the red glow of the lake on the horizon...")

They passed, the chiefs waving to him, the women perched on the carts uttering shrill laughter and the younger ones kissing, because they thought Ao was handsome. The whole vanguard engulfed itself on the Plain of Ashes, with its pennants made of animal skins and its crests of saurians, dancing and preceded by these little syrinxes which always seemed to complain and accuse Heaven of a supreme injustice, quite simply because they do not have the holes drilled regularly. The tall Aquatic stood on the rock, horrified, frozen like a lifeless body, and he raised his hand too. Suddenly...

(A hundred years later, he would relive this moment, this agony...)

There was nothing in front of him. Neither geckos, nor carts, nor Barbarians. A horizon the color of blood. The bare plain. Brushwood. Cloudbursts of dust that the vanguard had raised. And in the air still quivered an echo of the little flute.

It seemed to Ao that this trill was going off – and there it was, a huge burst of laughter. If a cosmic amoeboid could laugh... yes, a gigantic radiolarian organism, covering a planet and devouring it, it would be so. Pursued by this laughter, Ao ran away.

He returned to camp after dark and lay down by Bill Ready's fire. Milly, on a nearby peak, was chatting with the girls. The Horde was still as vast as the ocean and no one asked anything of the guide, no one inquired about the fate of the vanguard... Bill, who was cooking chestnuts under the embers, handed him a handful – the soft-fleshed fruits burned the lips. The hour was sweet. The ocher glow hovered in the air.

"Is this a sign?" Ao asked weakly, accepting the chestnuts. "We are talking about an earthly secret which would be the friendship. Do you accept me as a friend tonight, Re-a-ddy?"

"Tonight and every night," replied the Irishman, magnanimously. "We are friends among... people of goodwill, and we all are here. Even the lizards who are such good boys!"

The Aquatic looked up:

"It's very serious, what you just said there," he nodded. "Since a law of your blood has become mine, I will entrust you with an important and terrible thing: they disappear, R-e-a-ddy. And they will all disappear."

"Who's that?" Bill asked cheerfully.

"The Barbarians. I think I always knew that. Symbiosis is such an ancient and powerful state among our people that each Aquatic carries within them the germ of knowledge. Of course, supporters of the lower castes like mine – I was a hunter... who still hunts in Laknea? – we make people forget. The reminiscences are put on the account of the legends of the Lake which circulate: there are so many! But today I saw..."

"What?" Bill yelled. "You drive me crazy with your circumlocutions!"

So, Ao tells him everything. And all of a sudden: the Horde flowing in its savage majesty, the ash tray suddenly empty – and the laughter.

In silence fell. A brand was consumed in the ashes.

"Eh?" Ready exclaimed. "But where have they gone? What does this mean?"

"Simply that the legends are not wrong. As soon as a Barbarian sets foot on the Plain of Ashes, he disappears. Inexplicably. He vanishes, with his engine, his chariot, his women and his herd of aphids. And he never comes back."

"He cannot," said Bill.

"Of course, it is known. Why do you think they've been going around in circles for centuries? Without approaching the lake, they who fear nothing? Only this time we will attack anyway!"

"Because the Stars said...?"

"No," said the Aquatic, "because Bellatrix loved an Earthman. He was...abducted. History repeats itself and this is how the Empire of the Waters survives. The Force (I know not any other name) does not act outside of a certain area. It will attract them and destroy them. All."

"Let's see," said Bill, "let's see. I believe that a certain resentment leads us astray..."

"You mean I hate Aquatics? But no. I am of Water, these people are my blood and my flesh. They would kill me if I were caught, but then I am angry with them. I...the notion escapes me..."

"You are a deserter, by force of circumstance. But not a traitor. It's good."

"It was fine so far. But now, Re-a-ddy, now I must defend ourselves! This incredible thing happens to me and changes everything: Milly is going to have a little one." He closed his eyes and his face, lit up from below by the glow of the brazier, suddenly became very handsome and very serious. "A child of mine!" screamed his thoughts. "A child who will perhaps be white and perhaps blue, smooth or covered with scales or fur – but who will carry within them my species – and this spark of life which is me! This means that we are deceived, odiously, and that, having left the life-soul area, our people can survive and reproduce themselves! We are neither demons nor a chosen race – we are simply the misguided!"

"Because of that child and Milly, I have to do something, you taught me that. Or at least I'm talking to someone."

"Talk," said Bill.

"The Empire of the Waters subsists through death. At each moment of its existence, life-mother kills."

"Who?"

"Pselles or captured beasts. Large insects too. The Barbarians, when they venture into its area. The space travelers, when their raft washes up on the shores of the lake. Today, it seeks to destroy the People of Fire."

"It's impossible," said Bill. "Think about the time we lived on Lake Ruby, we only saw isolated individuals and again... And then where do you want them to put this mass of animals and people, whether they want to trap them or can it be canned? The swamps are not large enough. Lake? it would fill up and poison. Besides, how do you get them into the lake? By hypnotism? I doubt that sensory images have a hold on geckos..."

"How did they do with the Silicones?"

"Because Silicones too..."

"Oh! It was a special case, of which the lake dwellers are not a little proud. They came from a distant planet – they were minerals. Landing here, they were panicked by the natural wealth of Gamma: all these mountains of gems and mines of fissile materials! They formed colonization projects. It was easy to isolate them, to prevent them from communicating with their Galaxy, to drive them back underground, finally..."

"And then?"

"You did see. We did not exterminate them, because their envelope is almost indestructible and neither do we, we do not like something to be lost, something that can be useful to us...It was enough to remove this little spark of life from them and of spirituality, which feeds the soul-mother and which it communicates to its people. Oh! The Silicones only gave it a small dose of food, but they were very useful afterwards. We have employed them for menial tasks."

"And the Air Pselles?" asked Ready, aghast

"These are from Gamma. Note that this is also a particularly tough species, since they survived."

"And the Travelers?"

"First of all, it was pure and simple accidents. In the torrent of centuries, many strangers tried to seize this globe. It was such bait a rich and sparsely populated planet! Many came, no one left."

"No one?" repeated the shivering little mechanic.

"Oh! Some succeeded in fleeing among the Barbarians. It was backing up to better jump. I suppose," Ao continued as if descending slowly into the darkness of an ancestral memory, "that at first the Water People were simply struggling to save Gamma, but one day, having noticed how these interplanetary invasions served it, it perfected its techniques. Hence the sensory barriers. You ran into it, didn't you? They operate a certain selection. There are precious qualities and substances. The cowardly or unexcitable beings, those who lacked energy did not interest the Prime Cell. But, beyond the barriers, all foreigners were welcome."

"Because you're vampires!" Bill exclaimed heavily. "I thought so, come on!"

"Vampires?" Ao wondered. He was so far removed, so obviously integrated into the unity of his people, that he hesitated on the edge of this foreign definition and seemed shocked. Then a pale smile appeared on the blue lips. "I am," he resumed. "It's a metaphor. What do you want us to do with the blood? It is a protein combination easy to reconstitute, and besides there are arenas... Silicones are satisfied with it. What concerns us is a psychic matter. Life Mother feeds on the vital forces of beings and so far we have believed that it alone could serve as a transformer..."

"That is to say, it digests living creatures for you and that..." Bill gasped in disgust. Ao shrugged wearily:

"It's much more complicated as a case of symbiosis, but you still get the idea. However, time is pressing on us and I must tell you many other things before dawn, because I suppose that tomorrow it will be my turn to descend into the plain... How ironic! Our significant conventions are always colloquies of condemned."

"You were talking about canning: it exists and the Air Pselles case illustrates this technique brilliantly. As these pretty, versatile and messy creatures breed a lot, they are a choice livestock. So we have not completely emptied them of their psychic energy; for a people to proliferate, it must be left with its illusions. The Pselles believe themselves to be free – and far above Insects and Minerals. And since they forget very quickly, it is easy, between two harvests, to maintain them in this state of blissful assurance and almost drunkenness. Do you have something to say?"

"Nothing. Except that you are odious!"

"Oh!" said Ao ironically, "always this earthly injustice! Or is it willful blindness? Have you not had on Earth (I read in your brain) during the existence of your tiny planet, feudal or capitalist societies, theocracies or people's republics which have fed on the blood and brains of their herds? And who have kept their livestock more or less shiny, more or less fed? Those who have not skimped on bread or games have even left a solid reputation for philanthropy...

"Agree that the Gamma system has the advantage of being less hypocritical. Our wars (if one may so call the operations which bring nutritive cells within reach of life-mother), our barriers, our traps are exemplary in that they require neither flags nor slogans. The only weakness of the Force Being consists in this: it does not strike very far. But when an organism delivers its substance to the life mother, it is an individual affair between It and them."

"This digression leads nowhere!" said Ready, wiping the sweat that was rolling down his face. "Don't be so absurdly doctoral, Ao! You have changed sides and you admit to yourself that your state has tricked you! What do you think they intend to do with our Barbarians?"

"I repeat, each case is strictly individual. The most violent beings will probably be used to create the dumps. In Laknea, modestly (because Water Pselles are modest), it is claimed that it is a question of reviving the almost disintegrated dead. But it also plays an essential role in the perpetuation of the species. We no longer reproduce – or very little! So these energy discharges, the Prime Cell transmutes them, say, into an equivalent of gametes or zygotes. It makes chosen beings there. They were born, of course. There is nothing monstrous in this, if you consider that it is a universal law: the ovum captures the sperm, the drone bee falls eviscerated, at the end of the nuptial flight, etc."

"The great mass remains. It simply constitutes the provisions. These people are transported in small packets, if I may say so, in some fold of time, in the Tertiary period, for example, on the shores of this same lake. Their vital energy will be used gradually. They will be a little slower, a little less manly, subjected to lower temperatures and they will eventually waste away, isn't that the common fate of the weak? Earth, too, has experienced the disappearance of certain species. You and me, dear Bill..."

"Shut up!" growled the Irishman. "It's not my own fate that worries me!"

"Yes," said Ao, "that was to be expected. You Earthlings are terribly romantic. Well I think (he avoided Ready's gaze, lowered his eyelids and looked – only – horribly, like a fish)... You don't have to worry about her...about Bellatrix. Her end will be... very sweet. You know that the soul mother is both male and female, Aes and Aessa..."

The Aquatic pulled away, and Bill stood by his half-extinguished fire, feeling like a nauseating chasm opened beneath his feet. His prostration was such that he could hardly find the strength to crawl on his stomach in his little tent. Laying down, he swore horribly.

But in positive spirit of Earthmen, despite the fascination of horror, was looking for a way out. The resignation of the Pselles and the Silicones, the kind of bitter triumph that overwhelmed Ao was not his doing. His first idea was: "We must warn the queen! As usual, he even decided on the terms of an interview laced with metaphors such as 'Rose of Gamma' and 'Daughter of the Crystal Hills'". But he realized right away that Bellatrix wouldn't even listen to him: he was just a miserable stranger "with suspicious words", she had her guard, her advice, and then did she even extend the interplanetary?

As for acting through the intermediary of the Barbarians, he knew them well enough to hope for nothing. These advantageous brutes would not admit that they could be defeated! If he spoke to them of the power of the Lacustrines, they would take him for a spy and break his bones, that's all.

He was there in his gloomy meditations and he opened his igloo to breathe a little and contemplate the huge stars in the black-violet sky. The pearls of Orion's Belt all seemed near and terrible, the red Betelgeuse and the icy Rigel dazzling. Ready missed the familiar, unglamourous skies of his home planet.

A hand brushed his forehead. He flinched and stifled a cry. He had at his bedside a scintillating spectre with the features of Walter Angell.

The phantom put a finger to his lips: it was time. Around them breathed, groaned, delirious in thick nightmares, the huge sleeping camp, and the braziers crackled under the ashes. Beneath the side chariot, Milly muttered indistinct and tender things in Ao's arms, and on the spaced peaks the sentries modulated their call:

"We are men as they are!"

Walter sneaked into the student's shelter.

"Here," he said, "touch the hand: I am neither a sensory image nor a living dead."

"How did you come?"

"I found Verne's helicopter in the forest. A bit messy, but it still works. Look, Bill, this is terribly urgent."

"And Verne, where is he?"

Angell's eyes grew hard:

"You couldn't kill him," Bill murmured, panting. "He... he was already dead when he left the *RZ-2*. That's why he was able to get up and walk. It seems obscure to you, but I understand myself. You see, Verne was admirable: as long as he had a spark of life left, he fought against this horror that possessed him, he struggled, he refused to harm you. But then they made Tycho kill him and they disposed of his body, as they saw fit."

"I want to believe you," said Angell. "God knows if I suffered at the memory of that odious end! I would like to think that Verne ended up as he lived, to be free from it, that he wasn't imprisoned in this mannequin or in the heap of viscosities, in the stifling undergrowth where a green flame wanders. I would like to be certain that a principle in us escapes vileness, torture! But we don't know... Oh! Bill, I've never hated our narrow specializations so much! To be ready for a fight, armed and not knowing how to act, is there anything more pitiful? We miss the times. Of all of us you have always had the most open and curious mind. Maybe you could help me..."

"In whatever you want!" said Ready. "Anywhere I can! Speak."

"I'm the one who has to strike," resumed Angell, "and I don't know my adversary. I tried once, without success. Bill, is it possible that the monstrous entity that rules Gamma is truly invulnerable? I mean, that it escapes the material world?"

"I don't think so," said the student after reflection. "You see, this world is as real as Earth. I have been taught – I know – that its masters play with time, that they succeed in transporting masses of men and animals across centuries... But they cannot strike beyond certain limits of space, of a certain plateau... I am tempted to believe that there are space-time knots around the lake caused by nuclear fission. Is this within the realm of possibility?"

"Yes."

"Beyond the Plain of Ashes the people of Laknea are content to send pictures..."

"I know," said Angell. "Aes can see the barbarian camp. And even show it, exiled in the tertiary, because it was indeed the relegated, dying Horde that he showed me! But to contact the living people, he needs messengers."

"A limitation of this kind is no accident," Ready continued. "Let us put forward a working hypothesis: it is a matter of a material fact which supposes a localization: the Being would occupy a point in space."

"So... oh! Angell, while I was imprisoned in the pits, an Aquatic said to me, 'You have caught secrets that are not good to know.' This explained, for him, my different fate from that of Verne and Tycho. Me, I simply believed that I had been confused with the crowd of Pselles I was an unimportant character, is not it? But that wasn't it! On the contrary, I was the dangerous enemy, not to be put in contact with the Thing! Do you think me crazy?"

"No."

"So listen to me! I continue my demonstration. What more did I have, me, a modest mechanic, than Tycho, a brilliant fighter with irregular reflexes, or Verne, sensitive and physicist? I understand now, since they read our brains: it was knowledge acquired outside my strict conditioning!"

"That is to say?"

"I learned, for my pleasure, a lot of things. Medicine led me to biology, to chemistry; therapy with elements of parapsychology. I am the only one of you for whom science does everything, without watertight partitions between... let's put psychic and experimental magic. I was already beginning to understand that in the case of Gamma, it was – all reservations made about the esoteric conception of this universe..."

"If a protoplasmic nucleus," Angell interrupted. "You don't teach me anything. Don't complicate things. What do you know about the origins of life?"

"You ask me for a world!" And the little Irishman spread his arms, as if to embrace the universe. "Shall I tell you about the works of Olga Lepeshinskaya [5] and G. Bochian[6]? Or those of Friedrich-Freksa and Schramm[7]? From Brown-Séquard[8], from Serge Voronoff[9] or from Constantin Levatidi[10]? Or even evoke studies on ultra-viruses, from the same century and..."

"We don't have the time!"

"I know! So don't ask me the question in a way that makes it insoluble! I'm going to tell you what I absolutely don't know about the drawing: almost everything. We don't know how it happens. Here I quote a 20th century biologist, a precursor: 'Living matter appears in the form of a periodic system. This organization of permanent structures, starting from simple elements – atoms, ions, molecules – could only be done through

[5] Olga Borisovna Lepeshinskaya (August 18, 1871 – October 2, 1963) was a Russian revolutionary and Soviet pseudoscientist, who advanced her career as a biologist in the USSR Academy of Medical Sciences through fraudulent claims and personal ties with Vladimir Lenin, Joseph Stalin, Trofim Lysenko and Alexander Oparin. She rejected genetics and was an advocate of spontaneous generation of life from inanimate matter.

[6] Another Russian scientist from the lysenkoist period of the 1950s who also claimed that spontaneous generation of life from inanimate matter was possible.

[7] Hans Florian Friedrich-Freksa (February 23, 1906 – October 2, 1973), German biologist, biochemist and virologist. Gerhard Schramm (June 27, 1910 – February 3, 1969), German virus researcher, pioneer of virology and one of the fundamental researchers in the field of genetics.

[8] Charles-Édouard Brown-Séquard (8 April 1817 – 2 April 1894), Mauritian physiologist and neurologist who, in 1850, became the first to describe what is now called Brown-Séquard syndrome.

[9] Serge Abrahamovitch Voronoff (July 10, 1866 – September 3, 1951), French surgeon of Russian origin who gained fame in the 1920s and 1930s for his practice of xenotransplantation of monkey testicle tissues onto the testicles of men, purportedly as an anti-aging therapy. Ultimately almost all his works were later proven false.

[10] Constantin Levaditi (1 August 1874 – 5 September 1953), Romanian physician and microbiologist, a major figure in virology and immunology, especially in the study of poliomyelitis and syphilis.

the intermediary of a special organizing field, which draws its strength from the ambient radiant energy.' The ancestor that I quote to you proposes several names to define the phenomenon; it appeared to him as a periodic electrokinetic field, alternately organizing and dispersing – or molecular capacitor... what, you don't want to hear any further?"

"What I want to know," the pilot said firmly, "is if it's something that can be destroyed – and how."

"Oh that!" Ready muttered, descending from the heights of pure science. "You have a way of phrasing things! Let's see, this phenomenon is an indivisible grain of life, it's quantum life, the quantum being any indivisible unit...But are they carbohydrates or amino acids...?"

"Planck's quantum theory has something to do with it?"

"I think so! The notion extends to energy as well as to matter..."

"So? Your last definition? I warn you that I will endure only one."

"Let's see," said Ready, a little bewildered, "let's see... It would be 'the smallest free space, in which would unfold, autonomously, the phenomena of life, at the primitive and fundamental stage...'"

There's nothing metaphysical about it, I hope?"

"Oh no! Do you see anything that can help you in all this?"

"A world, as you say. My second question now. Remember the Cave of the Living Dead. Revisit your path, step by step. As if you were there. You experienced fear, nausea. How did the sensations present themselves?"

"I see," Bill said, concentrating. "Oh! It's hard what you're asking me! It wasn't a flat, even horror. There were moments when I could reflect and others which abolished all thought. It was like... dripping. Yes, quanta. Oh! Angell! Would it only exist at times?"

"The whole question is to know," replied the pilot. "Let's sum up: Gamma would be the prey (because the Aquatics exaggerate their power) of a molecular life, existing only intermittently. It is at infinitesimal fractions of time when it is that the entity would be material and that one could strike it."

A thin smile appeared on the starry arch of his lips. Bill thought: This is how the Angel of Death introduces himself! And suddenly he shudders:

"Space!" he cried. "I forgot to tell you! Tomorrow the Horde will cross the Plain of Ashes!"

"I knew it," said Angell. "That's why I came. Now, Ready, the hard part... can you lead me to Bellatrix?"

"To the queen!" cried the Irishman. "You're crazy! I never spoke to her. And if you think her tent isn't guarded... You're going to stir up the camp!"

"This is exactly what should be avoided. I could have presented myself in broad daylight and whatever foolishness I have committed, I believe that they would have received me." A kind of convulsion contracted the handsome face of the astronaut, then he shrugged his shoulders: "Because I made a big mistake, you can imagine! I left her to follow Verne and Sais. I thought the *RZ-2* was being attacked..."

"Sais," said Ready, "she's very bad, that. I think she would forgive you easily, if you had only followed an Earth astronaut. But I know... I know women: they're terrible!"

He said these enormities with an inspired air, and Angell didn't even protest. He simply cracked his knuckles.

"As if Sais existed!" he said. "Or any girl in the world! Haven't you seen the queen?"

"Yes. At a party. She wore a tiara and a half-fish, half-gecko mask, with a hint of Pselle and Silicone, and it had been inserted into a metal case. It wasn't very pretty."

"But you're in love with her, it's eye-opening. I'll do what I can for you, though..."

"Come on," Angell said, dragging his lithe long body out of the shelter. "You will show me to her tent and warn her. The rest is up to me."

Ready found her standing before the altar, where the Sword rested in its sheath of old terrestrial silk. He needed all his knowledge "acquired without conditioning" to enter fully into this absurd, pathetic and sacred world, where cassolettes smoked before an empty coffin, and where a statue of gold and emeralds, motionless, symbolized the Gamma revolt.

"Listen," he said, "you can, of course, have me kicked out by your guards. But then you won't know anything – and I guess a queen must be more curious than an ordinary woman. Behold, someone has come from afar to speak to you. This guy has committed an unforgivable blunder, but exceptional blunders must be part of the special fates: witnesses Phaedrus, Romeo... You will tell me that Othello too, but that has nothing to do with it.

"If it was a question of your personal loves. Majesty, I'll leave it up to you alone. But it's about more than monsters and pyramids – it's about the fate of Gamma. At least he told me so and he asks you to receive him. I'm talking about my comrade, Walter Angell."

He admitted that it wasn't very convincing but he had done his best...

The voice came, muffled by the mask, from the other side of the abyss and the light-century. And the response was in line with Bill Ready's worst predictions.

"Who is Walter Angell? I don't know this name."

"That's not the crux of the matter," Bill said, taking a deep breath. "It's someone from my house. Will your Majesty deign to grant him an audience? (he was not unhappy with the sentence.) Or is it impossible?"

"I do not see," said the spectre of gold and emeralds, "what could prevent me from receiving an earthly creature. No, don't go. Guards, bring in the stranger."

And it was worse than anything Bill had imagined. Standing on the brazen shield, with the sages and warriors to her right, painted with ochre and vermillion, and to her left the cassolettes and torches, her favorite saurian, the color of scarlet, lying at her feet, she received Angell, as befits a sovereign of a barbarous world. Her golden mask defended her. He couldn't know...

At the very moment when he crossed the threshold of the sacred tent, the queen saw all that she wanted to see, she drank (like someone who has dragged herself for long days in the desert and finally finds a source) this what she missed: an earthy face, pale, dazzling, the violent dark circles under the too long eyelashes, the narrow and passionate mouth that he loved. And in the depths of her consciousness of being young, of her entire character, savage, enamored of ideals, Bellatrix, Queen of Fire, found enough strength to say: "What does this stranger want from me?"

Angell stopped, as if punched in the face. She had the murderous elegance to address Bill Ready:

"He may not understand. Translate."

"No need," Angell said, "Bellatrix, I agree that you are right and that I deserved this cruel comedy. But calm down. I do not come to ask your forgiveness for an involuntary fault nor to drag myself at your feet. I know that I am unforgivable and I accept the punishment. The only idea that led me to your camp is this: I understood too late that my good faith was played with, I was not an ambassador of peace, but a hook thrown to attract prey.

"It is possible that in interplanetary politics such calculations are commonplace, I did not know. I'm just a simple astronaut. It was the duties of my profession that I obeyed when I left you, and I recognize one coward: I did not dare warn you. But you know why.

"Our past is ours. If I came back here – and believe it cost me – it's because I know you and your people are in danger, Bellatrix. And this danger, I am partly responsible for it. It is said that the Fire People never abandon their own, kidnapped or captured. There was a time when I was accepted among yours. They say you were going to attack Laknea, to save me. Well, I come to reassure you about my fate: I am free, this team is useless. In lures your people into an ambush."

A silence. The crackling of aromatics on the tripods. The drops of myrrh that are slowly falling apart...

"Interpreter," said the queen, "this time it is I who do not understand this man's language. Yes, there is a millennial rivalry between the peoples of Water and Fire. But I do not remember any embassy of peace and any foreigner that we received and accepted among us. If this torments your comrade, reassure him. The People of Fire are marching, because they are marching and the time has come to put an end to compromises. Is that all he had to say to me?"

After a look at Angell, silent, Ready wiped away the sweat on the back of his neck with one hand.

"I believe," he said. "I'm sure, Majesty. I beg your pardon..." It was at this moment that Walter Angell almost acted like an adventurer. He waved aside the tall red and black warriors who stood between him and the throne. He advanced and Bill Ready, a poet at heart, could only admire, among the crimson lights, his face blazing with combat.

"Bellatrix," he said, "I have borne it all: your anger and your contempt. And I will still die for you. Yes, for you alone, for your doomed Horde doesn't matter to me and Gamma is not my land. But this is more than a man can accept. You are ignoring me! So you forgot our nights in this tent – and that you were everything to me? And that you are my wife, according to your laws? Everything forgets our love... oh! Bellatrix!"

His voice failed to crack. The queen raised her hand and her somewhat slow guards move.

"Take this stranger away," she said.

To the great astonishment of Ready, who adored beautiful tragic scenes, unfolding between royal persons in tears, blood and imprecations, with many corpses piled up in the corners, the interview was cut short. Angell left the tent, without another word, and Bill followed him to the helicopter, which was lying on a platform of snow, like an abandoned toy. The little Irishman thought bitterly that galactic destiny is unfair that leaves the fate of worlds in the hands of lovers who are too young. If

Walter Angell, breaking the chain of guards, had taken the queen in his arms, many questions would have been resolved. He was going to tell his friend, but he was already taking off.

CHAPTER XII

Angell had never kept a diary. But returning to the "area of water", as a precaution, he erased even the images embedded in his memory. He saw Gamma as a biological monstrosity, and he discarded a cliché: the octopus watching, from the depths of the continuum, the imprudent travelers. He rejected Aes's axiom "nuclear fission breaks the dimensional frame" and Ready's quantum theory hypothesis applied to the parent cell. Having also cleared his brain, he landed on the edge of the red crater. He was, in fact, no more than a perfect fighting machine.

A thin smile touched his lips: trap, hunt, treasure, the Damned City spread out before him. In a fantastic violet light, every angle stood out with formidable clarity, the opalescent towers sparkled among the gardens of seagrass and madrepores; a living murmur rose from the squares, a perfume of temple and port: seaweed and incense, tide, spices and crushed fruits.

Standing on the cliff, Angell saw what had always been hidden from him, the crowd of Lacustrines. The Water People accepted his challenge.

It was not a comforting sight. The mass was not human, nor could it far from pretending to be animal. It was far from these monsters to the demonic harmony of Aes. Beneath their scintillating copes and their opal headbands, the Aquatics surprised by the strangeness of their pace: in the thick air, they projected themselves forward, then fluctuated, like seaweed or fish. They had a silvery or livid color, sometimes glaucous, flattened skulls and webbed extremities. Some were dragged along in chariots made of a clam valve and harnessed with batrachians or strange amphibious sharks; a dugong or an anthropomorphic manatee held the reins and an escort of lobsters followed them; others travelled on the back of a halias or a hippobosc: all the species enslaved by the Lake.

Angell understood that the very atmosphere of the City was made artificially dense and humid, to allow this life of the abyss. Did the opacity of the air increase the smells tenfold, sharpen the senses? It was, in any case, oppressive. Setting foot on the cobblestones, the Earthman had the impression of advancing against a current of hot water, saturated with aromatics, which left on his lips, a taste of fruit and salt. On the other hand, the wide bulging eyes of the passers-by did not seem to notice him, and they did not hear his footsteps on the amethyst slabs...had he become, for them, a ghost?

But no, this icy indifference was part of their behavior, because a vehicle whose folds concealed a huge pearl, swerved in front of him, and two little Air Pselles hovered in his tracks, like curious children. It was a strange experience, this walk through the city which seemed to say like Bellatrix:

"I ignore this stranger."

Hand clenched on his weapon, head held high, it seemed to the Earthman that he had been walking like this for centuries. That his entire stopover on Gamma could be summed up as follows: "I walked in Laknea." With a cold dread, Angell understood that he really was there in a foot space-time knot. Eternally, eternally – the people rippling in the waves would move between the phosphorescent walls, eternally, among seaweed and the stars, a slender human figure, lost in a hostile universe, would move towards Horror.

That was metaphysical hell.

He had to move on.

Angell figured the best policy (if there was one) would be to stay as icy, as indifferent as the Lakneans. However, arriving on a small pink square that he recognized, he shivered. He had heard a great deal about the cruelty of the Aquatics, but he had only seen it at work on Verne; yet his torture remained mysterious to him.

Here in the middle of a platform with iridescent decorations stood not a cross, but an Egyptian ankh. A group of guards armed with narwhal-tooth spears stood at the four corners of this scaffold, and on a board the little Air Pselles, restless and whispering, spelled out the word: "spy".

On the tau (Angell hardly recognized that bundle of dull, yellowish feathers and that long, blood-coagulated beak) hung nailed Sais, dead.

The Earthman wanted to rush forward, to pull her out of this wood of torture. Only then did he realize that he was attached to the pretty and crazy creature; she was no longer a bird for him, but a human comrade. And here she was, dead. Killed because of him: he could not doubt it. She had warned him: "I told you everything I knew, An-n-gell. And now they will kill me!" This sweet flutis pursued him, like a reproach.

He clenched his fists: "On Earth whoever did that to my dog would pay!" The very words of Verne, in the temples. Verne wanted to avenge Ary. Since then, centuries had passed... Sais was dead and already stiff, wings spread on the ankh. A big black thorn had shortened her agony by penetrating into her heart. Mechanically, Angell turned away and noticed on one of the greenish faces a grimace of satisfaction and something like satiety: the symbiotic entity of Laknea fed on all suffering.

"Hold still. Show nothing. Don't give them that joy."

He walked away, leaving the pink square forever – and Sais. He was beginning to know the laws of this marginal world. It was necessary, above all, not to give up his thoughts.

The door of the Temple was open. In the diamond room, among the mauve gleams and iridescences, were enthroned the Four Effigies. He went straight to the pedestal of the one with the cruel and charming face of Bellatrix (now he knew the artist who had sculpted her – the only Aquatic who had seen her from a distance and who felt for her this cold and heavy feeling, fact of desire and morbid delight that the Water People probably called love).

Angell knew that there was, at the exact spot where Ary had collapsed, a sliding slab, the entrance to the underground, the straightest way to reach the lakeside city. And since there was no other way to reach the Monster, he would take this path.

It was then that he saw her.

She leaned against the pedestal of the fourth Effigy, so that her body blended with the ivory and gold of the ornaments. At first sight, he was not surprised to meet a priestess in the temple. He had forgotten Aes' confidence: "The Aquatics are male or asexual." Besides, was she of the species of the Waters? Yes, by nacreous iridescence and lily whiteness of an oblong pearl. Hair of an almost glaucous gold shimmered, mingled with seaweed and stars.

"Do not look!" whispered the voice of reason. "She doesn't exist. It's only a symbol, an image..." But her long eyelashes rose slowly and Angell stepped straight into a lake of green light, where all hesitations were spared and where all memories were erased.

He was not given time to experience what had been a warning signal for Verne: anguish or nausea. He was there, standing, motionless, as if caught in a trap, and every nerve quivered with a delight beyond all physical joy, with a static and perfect delight.

"Come on," she said. "I will lead you to my home. I have been waiting for you for so long! My thirst is so deep... Earthman, my name is Aessa."

"Wake up," said an imperious voice above the igloo. Ready, furious at being disturbed for the second time in one night, sat up in his sleeping bag, but all swearing died in his dry mouth.

"Do you know how to drive an air raft?" Bellatrix asked.

"A rocket?"

"I don't know what you call it. One of my ancestors left it to the Fire People who never knew how to use it, but as it is a mysterious object, come from the sky, the Sages take great care of it. Come. She's there."

"But where?" Ready asked, stunned.

Bellatrix made an impatient gesture:

"There, under my tent. Or do you want it to be? My people would have burned her if she were somewhere else."

"In that case," Bill said thickly, "it can't be a rocket. The temple is small. It could be a glider or a helicopter. I will see. Let me get dressed, Majesty."

"Put on a skin. You think I don't know how a man is made? We have no time to waste on watchfulness."

The Diamond Mountains reverberated the mysterious stars and Bill Ready, catastrophe, had before him, with her purple cloak and her breast-plate of gems, having removed only her mask, to breathe freely, a tender and wild young queen, secret and passionate, supported by an Earth blaster. She was holding it, he thought, like a staff or a parasol...and was this machine even disarmed? Bill jumped to his feet, losing all shame, and wrapped himself in a fur.

"Come on." Bellatrix repeated.

She led him into the tent, where, indeed, under the shields and tinsel, they discovered one of those tiny two-seaters that astronauts use for exploration flights. A sub-ether chip. A somewhat antediluvian chip, of course, but in working order.

"Can it fly a thousand meters above the ground?" Bellatrix asked, as Ready struggled with the engines.

"That high? I think so, but is it really necessary? The cabin is not air-conditioned, and it is cold."

"Maybe you don't see the need," said the young queen, biting a red lock that was dancing at the end of her nose. "Me, I see. I have no desire to find myself in the Pre-Cambrian. The Prime Cell acts on a certain area."

"How do you know it? It is a revelation."

She raised her delicious nose:

"I believe you are questioning a queen...? No, a little analysis work was enough for me, as it was for you. End of digressions. Do you have an atomic weapon? No? Good, that is to say too bad. I have one. You will drive."

"Where?"

"Where do you think? To Laknea."

"But..."

"There is no 'but'. He's on his way back to the lake, isn't he? And you think I'll let him face Death of a Thousand Faces alone? Him, Angell? You didn't look at me."

She had put in the name of the Earthman such tenderness, such thoughtless passion, that Ready rose up:

"Since you love him so much, why did you let him go in despair? Didn't you see that he was going to commit the worst stupidities?"

"How could he be, logically, desperate," she protested, "since I was in front of him? He should only think of death if I was a ghost or dead!"

"I like 'logically'. You pretended not to recognize him."

"Didn't he act like I didn't exist? If he had admitted to me that his comrades were calling him, I would not have intervened. He treated me like a hollow, empty creature with no sense of duty! Me, a Queen of Fire! I had to pay!"

"You are horribly proud," said Bill. He couldn't take it anymore. He was also bursting. "You deserve to receive the change of your coin, but I believe that it's especially a lack of education. You are a queen, yes. But for him, you were simply the woman he loved. And that's exactly why he didn't dare see you again: he was afraid he wouldn't be able to leave you, I know Angell! You punished him, because he loved you too much!"

He stopped, fearing he had gone too far. In a mask with closed eyelids, blind and pathetic, Bellatrix's mouth was full of blood. But she said nothing, and as the two-seater rolled slowly down the slope, she joined forces with Ready.

They went up. The tiny contraption soared into the air with an angry insect buzz, and Bill could appreciate the unknown fuel the Fire People were using: it doubled the speeds. They flew over the sparkling mountains and the gray plain. Below, the phantom city shone like an amethyst.

"A plan of action now," Bellatrix said. "From what I grasp of mental waves, for once the City of the Lake is placed on our dimensions, he has come there and he is heading towards the Temple. His intention is simple, too simple: he has understood that the Prime Cell is vulnerable between quanta and he intends to destroy it at that moment. For him, for his simple Earthman logic, the operation consists in killing a giant octopus, an octopus – and he believes that, to do well, he must face the monster. He will therefore give himself up to Aes, descend into darkness and...the cosmos alone has idea of what can happen under these conditions!"

"How do you intend to act?" asked Ready, gasping.

"I am not an aquatic scientist, nor a 'time turner,'" Bellatrix declared. "But I hunted the octopus in the ocean sands, and the Carbonic Beast at the South Pole. It did not always happen to me to reach the head on the first blow, especially when the brain is lodged in the abdomen, nor to pierce the heart attached to an appendix, but I am sure of one thing: that we hurt a living tentacle or spiral, one always hits the beast – and after that, it's just a matter of luck, endurance and skill. Bill Ready, I intend to land on the Temple terraces and I will burn everything I find in my path, be it Aes or Aessa, or any other extension of life mother. During this time, I think Angell will manage."

To anyone other than Bellatrix, Queen of Fire, Queen of Free Pselles, Primates, and Geckos, Bill Ready would have said what he thought of such a senseless amalgamation. But he was silent. Without knowing why.

A high-pitched buzz that twists the brain and twists the nerves. A slow, horrible and delicious hesitation, in which one does not know where torture ends and where pleasure begins. A chaos of sounds. Colors and sensations that follow one another with such rapidity that musical agony encroaches on visual joy; terror and delight are resolved in the same spasm.

(In the depths of this abyss, one must keep intact a force of resolution, the outline of an act. Do not forget. Do not give up.)

The mental wave unfolds in scarlet swirls. It sings:

"I am Space and Origin. Earth named me: the Archobius. I am the Prime Cell where life flows and dwells, like the tides of the deep ocean. I am what is."

"Molecular synthesis, I appeared before time and I was reborn in the abyss. This is the secret. I was before this globe, before this constellation and even this galaxy. The beings who seized me in a secondary abyss thought they were seizing kinetic energy: it was I who enslaved them."

(Here floats the sharp, painful thought of another being. Verne, probably, for Angell still has the strength to recognize his sentences. Verne, almost non-existent, dissolved in the darkness and crying out to him: "Remember: each discovery has an element of chance... They created, at the bottom of the sea, two periodic antagonistic fields... the spark that sprang was Life. But a different life, Walter. A creation due to a monstrous intelligence. The devil is the ape of...")

The mental symphony smothered the rest. It continued:

"Like so many other elements, those of Gamma have become my slaves. They tried to capture me: they gave me a form and a point in the universe: their world. Limited creatures, they imposed limits on me: I now move only in time Fixed to this globe, I feed and I dream, and my dreams are the very life of Gamma. I mix species and plans, I arouse spectres. From the azure valley of the swamp, to the beautiful green and black Satan, from the mirage of a city to an army which is dissipating in mirages, here is the framework of my games. But I wake up sometimes. To feed the energy that recreates me, I must grasp and absorb the living sources.

"This universe of minerals and obtuse beasts is starting to run out and I'm looking far, ever further...

"I have the memory and nostalgia of planets that I once visited, all terrible worlds, all magnificent... an outbreak of stars, roses of fire. I thirst for these new forces. Earthman, I recognized in you an energy close to mine so I coveted your spaceship, and I attracted it from the depths of space-time.

"Here you are. You still resist me, it is because you know not the glorious destiny that awaits you and this infinite world of which you are already a part. And this struggle is your torture, but I do not mind prolonging the game. I am tired of absorbing brutes and resigned slaves! What I need is the flame of life that soars, it is your desire for discovery and conquest, it is the door open to the mysterious cosmos.

"Because I will entrust you with my secret, my second secret. I was made to invade the universe and I did once. When the limit will be abolished, between your consciousness and mine, you will commune with the memory of fabulous globes, extinct stars, planets fallen into dust – once fiery and populated. You will be part of life, of all lives. You will experience all the delights and all the cosmic terrors.

"Listen, I will give you the dark life of minerals, asteroids that sail in the black and icy void... And the first shiver of life, waking up on a globe that has ceased to be for millions of years, and the first nuclear explosion, of a sun, at the center of a new constellation. I will give you the slow swarming of worms that feed on an ideal rot – and the tremendous blossoming of a Carboniferous forest – and the glory, and the splendors – and the apocalypse of countless living species.

306

"Because I am all that. And I am something else again.

"I am all these dead, motionless and preset in this cave, corpses in which lives a spark of consciousness, but greedy, but relentless to drink your life that I deliver to them. I am the Sages and the princes of this race, perhaps the oldest in the world, because it was born from the original plasma at the bottom of the seas, and it returns there, in its mutations. They are my servants and my images. Each of these rigid and icy dead lives your existence at this moment and is exalted by your memories.

"Rarely have we been, them and I, to such a party. Because you open the cosmos to which you were predestined. Let us go higher, always higher! Each of your joys, your impulses, your desires and your sorrows are prolonged in me in multiple quiverings. I am finally going to possess this self-transcendence, this transcendence which exalts your globe. I will be...you. Because here is my third and supreme secret: thanks to you I will leave this ghost-planet, I will take on an earthly form and face...perhaps your face. I tried to do it with one of your companions, but this being too weak preferred death to a glorious existence of symbiosis...

"You are strong. Together we will soar towards new flaming suns, towards the burning stars of other skies, and we will conquer them. We will even reach, through space, this tumultuous globe whose name you spell as one cries for help, this Earth whose pulsations agree with the frantic beats of your blood. If it looks like you, Earthling, it is beautiful. I will drink it like I drink you. Come closer.

"One step, one last step. You still steal from me a corner of your soul which seems made of a single impetus towards infinity. Anything. The joy will be greater, when I will have completely invaded you, and the transmutation will take place in a cosmic ecstasy, from which new cells and new universes will be born..."

With a fantastic crash, Bill's two-seater broke wood on a terrace of the Temple. He and Bellatrix jumped out, with no apparent damage. Blaster in hand, the Queen of Fire descended the winding staircase, spiraling among the glare and iridescence. Bill looked around for a weapon, grabbed an orichalcum flare, and followed the princess.

"If anyone had ever told me," he thought, "my medical career would end like a gangster movie! Finally, it's for a good cause. 'For my lady and my honor' – or should I say 'for my queen'?"

These chaotic reflections didn't prevent him from noticing that the galleries and courtyards were deserted, as if their people of ghosts had flowed back to the underground passages.

Bellatrix and Ready stormed into a pearly room from which, amid the garlands of diatoms and the glow of blue beroes, a swirling flight of Air Psellae fled. Bill understood their panic, when a crystal wall reflected in front of him a little red-haired savage, girded in the skin of a cheetah and waving a lighted torch at arm's length. This sight fills a future Doctor Ready with confusion. But he and Bellatrix burst into an amphitheater where cephalopods and pythons were smothering a few simian Pselles, to the rhythm of deliquescent music, and Bill felt like a liberator.

At the end of the room, among a delirium of tetrahedrons and Aeolian harps, on a bed-throne of smaragdite seemed to float a long greenish shape, with the folded wings of a damned angel. When they came to this nightmarish entity, Ready with a single glance, saw all there was to see: a priestly diadem and a seaweed dalmatic, ending in a three-lobed tail, a cuirass iridescent like a sea god and a frighteningly beautiful, motionless, horrible face. He understood at the same time that this ideal form which harmoniously united the two kingdoms did not avoid by itself, that Aes of Gamma was not... But Bellatrix was already marching on the prestigious monster and unleashing her blaster with precision and fury. When the smoke cleared, a black mark marked the location of the throne and there was a mass of black viscosities on the flagstones. Although several hundred years old, the Earth weapon functioned admirably.

Bellatrix was panting a little. She had chosen the right moment: she had pulled between two pulsations of her blood.

"There," she said, "he's dead. He will no longer come and dive into my dreams at night."

"Do you believe?" said Bill. "I think you took out an empty envelope..."

"Is equal. I burned in a tentacle. Come!"

They continued their insane route, threading corridors, stairs. A giant Silicone who seemed to be on guard rushed to meet them, but Bill, with habit of his Mineral operations, struck him with a candlestick blow to the base of the skull. A hippobosc, crouched in a corner, received the burning torch in a faceted eye and flew away, buzzing. More stairs – and clouds of fleeing Pselles...

Suddenly, down there, in a kind of grotto, Ready saw a stream of tongues of flame, white, erect forms: Sirens! Sirens! He howled. He saw a host of slender strokes, each of which symbolized death, watery waves of flowing hair – all female hell. The silver faces, reversed, expressed movement. He was about to rush there, when more disintegrator flashes dissipated the mass, not slimy shapes, just a huge spurt, a black swamp where a light wandered. The tide had receded, like a retreating tentacle. One second, and the galleries were empty.

Bill sat on the floor and wept, and Bellatrix walked past him, with a proud expression of disdain.

The staircase plunged into black abyss, and to take each step was to raise a mountain. But Angell couldn't stop. The insinuating voice punctuated the pulsations of his blood, it echoed in his marrow and stiffened the fibers of his body with repulsion. She came from in arms. So that's where you had to get off. And she would say, she would whisper huge, blasphemous, fantastic things – which had no name in any human language.

He understood how Verne had succumbed. And Tycho. And the others. Angell was so far from the material world that the image of Aessa and her indescribable and charming mermaid body had disappeared. Only the bare Horror and Pleasure remained.

Anyone who had looked from above would have seen an undead, a rigid human statue, sinking jerkily into hell.

Muscles tense, nerves shattered, this human body still lived. Angell, however, had the impression of falling apart, of becoming muffled, his blood mixed with the monster's lymph. Tentacles entwined him. An enormous suction cup sucked in its last revolt. He was one with the Terror.

Suddenly, the pain and revulsion that had crested a wave ebbed away. It was as if a nerve, stretched to the extreme, had been broken. And with it, the feeling of ice, the morbid irony that kept watch in the depths of a pain. A sneering witness defaulted in agony. Inexplicably, Angell saw again the long glaucous eyes and the troubled smile of Aes of Gamma. He understood that he was rid of Aes – yes, for quite a while. And at the same time – that it still existed.

But other fluctuating, moving notes made his being a keyboard of torture. They were like tongues of fire that caressed and burned, and their throbbing heat penetrated deeper than the dermis, to the very depths of his being, like an irremediable defilement. However, he had a respite and he could then see before him the open doors of orichalcum, the white and black cave, and the Areopagus of grimacing dead which awaited him. But he already felt dead, sharing their rot and ice. Nothing mattered to him, not even his name shouted aloft by nearby Bellatrix. Nothing awakened an echo in him.

She who called him from the depths was more powerful and more beautiful than Bellatrix. Beautiful as nothing. Like death.

And the second wave ebbed with its tingling of flames and its more than filthy sweetness. It was clean this time and stiff, like a break. The second tentacle was cut off. The multiple ties that had held him helplessly bound were falling apart.

Beings who fought on his side had won victories, and with blinding certainty he remembered what he had forgotten in the searing depths of pain: he had come here to fight. To defeat. And he could.

A fraction of a second earlier, this claim would have seemed laughable to him. He was caught, carried away by a tidal wave. But now the world was becoming stable again, lines and colors were being recomposed. He was no longer part of an unspeakable, unnamable entity, the lines and colors were being recomposed. He was no longer part of an unspeakable, nameless entity, he was a distant being – Walter Angell, Earthman – he had to fight, even beyond human forces.

The Thing (he could find no other qualification and dreaded any magic term that could evoke it, make it reappear) had withdrawn into its lair, like a wounded beast, and it projected, panicking, then folded back its invisible tentacles. Its humming still promised and threatened, with a kind of rage, but it only reached the superficial wisps of his brain.

Angell had reached the threshold of hell. Slowly, slowly he raised his Earth weapon which, just now, seemed useless to him. The hollow – the cave – the abyss – filled with a mad whirlwind of dread and the last tentacles let go. There was no more Aes or Aessa, just a mass of plasma animated by a diabolical hatred that possessed a globe. With a spasmodic movement, horribly alive like a wounded animal, the colorless flame on the altar throbbed. The quanta... At one point, when it was low, choosing the viscous depth for his target, astronaut Walter Angell pulled the trigger on his disintegrator.

CHAPTER XIII

The power of the explosion was such that the landscape changed face.

It is at the place of the City that the Lake now spread and the former "Area of Waters" turned upside down, gutted, spread out the menacing architecture of its underground passages. Giant ferns had been uprooted and thrown as far as the mountains.

On the lacustrine space swirled panicked Air Pselles, Silicones were moving empty in the craters.

But the great metamorphosis of Bellatrix Gamma lay elsewhere – in a special burst of colors, in a relentless and new stability of lines. The reverberations, the purple phosphorescences, all that prism decomposing the solar rays no longer existed. At the same time, the vagueness and uncertainty of several superimposed landscapes had disappeared. The weather, finally stable, resumed its course, each flower half-opened its corolla without hesitating between the blossoming and death of the petals, the fish which sprang from a source was no longer simultaneously an aquatic germ, a beast and a humanoid prototype, the very star of Gamma was situated at the zenith of its brightness and not at dawn or at the end of its days.

Bellatrix, Queen of Fire sat in the middle of a recent clearing, on a stump. The forest of water lilies surrounded her, and Angell's head rested on her knees. She had lost her tiara and her blaster, but her hair sparkled like honey and liquid gold.

Having slipped from the branches of a willow, where he had been scouting, Bill Ready reported:

"Majesty," he said, "the Fire People – your people – are on the march."

"They finally crossed the Ash Plateau. The explosion shattered the dimensional frame. Space-time nodes no longer exist. Our allies are coming! Victory!"

The young woman decided to give him a distracted look and rolled up a blond curl of Angell's in her index finger.

"How do you feel?" she asked.

"Admirably."

"Majesty," resumed the Irishman, with pomp, "here is your planet saved, delivered, reintegrated into the cosmic order, it will no longer be a space trap nor Drosera of the Infinite! We will get to work. There's a lot to do: drain the swamps, lay out roads, build cities – not necessarily of crystal, but of bricks."

"I think there will soon be a lot of people to house. Air Pselles have two broods of four per year. And I'm not talking about Geckos: for these one would first be content with spacious and airy stables. Silicones will help us in these tasks: there are quite a few..."

"You hear him, Walter," said the queen, touching the Earthman as if she had always done it, "he already wants to make the Silicones work! Soon he will realize that there are too many Birds! You are a dangerous man Bill Ready!"

"We'll get in touch with the federated planets," continued the other. "Their techniques can be profitable for us and we'll make a large trade of uranium and crystals. This globe will be rich and powerful, Majesty!"

"I thought," said Angell, "that you had mostly social projects?"

"Of course. Build dispensaries and colleges. And also childbirth clinics. A few genetic labs would be essential for us to select and protect mutations. Ah! I will miss you! But first of all you will have to work, Majesty, to establish essential laws: I fear that the morality of Air Pselles is too elastic and your Barbarians have no sense of property. We will need doctors, lawyers and school teachers. Some accountants too..."

Angell and Bellatrix exchanged a long, meaningless look to each other.

"It's a lot of worry," said the young queen. "I have before my eyes the policy of my ancestors: live and let live. Look, Bill, how fragile water lilies withstood the explosion better than the foundations of the City! As long as there is free soil, free air or flowers, they will feed on sap, and the bees will make their honey there. Stables for the Geckos, teachers for the little Pselles, and what else? I'm surprised you don't mention concentration camps for aquatic scientists, if there are any left."

"It would be a barbarism worthy of the Middle Ages!" Bill protested. "Besides, these people can be useful to us: under the direction of Ao they will build factories and artificial relays in space. It will probably be necessary to renew the sensory barriers and include something more substantial than the sirens..."

"Don't talk about sirens!" Angell and Bellatrix said with one voice.

"If you want," Bill nodded distractedly. "They were, as far as I remember, pretty inconsequential creatures. But before anything and everything ceases, Majesty, I put Ao and his comrades to work: building a spaceship! And what a hurry!"

"Why?" asked the queen, looking up at him with wide gray eyes where ghosts of sandy gold passed.

"But, princess... high lady... shouldn't we return to Earth?"

"Why?" Angell asked.

And he smiled at Bellatrix.

www.ingramcontent.com/pod-product-compliance
Lightning Source LLC
Chambersburg PA
CBHW030342020726
47493CB00003B/642